A MIDWINTER
MURDER

BOOKS BY VERITY BRIGHT

A MIDWINTER MURDER

VERITY BRIGHT

bookouture

Published by Bookouture in 2024

An imprint of Storyfire Ltd.
Carmelite House
50 Victoria Embankment
London EC4Y 0DZ

www.bookouture.com

The authorised representative in the EEA is Hachette Ireland
8 Castlecourt Centre
Dublin 15 D15 XTP3
Ireland
(email: info@hbgi.ie)

ISBN: 978-1-83525-630-5
eBook ISBN: 978-1-83525-629-9

To Yorkshire – every time we return, we love it that little bit more.

1

_____

'It's only a few miles further now to Auldwyke Hall.' The fair-haired young man grimaced apologetically, his soft-spoken voice incongruous with his vigorous northern accent. 'Give or take a mile, that is.'

'All of which will be equally beautiful, I'm sure,' Lady Eleanor Swift said over-cheerfully, hoping to lessen the poor fellow's nerves.

Sitting opposite her in a smart, if dated, dark-blue worsted suit and stiffly knotted tie, he ran his pale hand through the neat side-parting of his severe haircut. 'If I might say again, I blame myself entirely.' He looked at her penitently, pressing his hands together. 'Especially as I can't explain how the misunderstanding happened. I was so sure you had replied "yes" to his grace's invitation to his annual Christmas shoot. But I confess, on looking again after our telephone call, I could not find your RSVP.'

Knowing that her butler, Clifford, seated in the front passenger seat, would be horrified by such inefficiency, she offered an extra breezy, 'These things occur, Mr Porritt. Who knows who made the error? Don't concern yourself.'

He fidgeted with his owlish spectacles, gazing at her fiery red curls and piercing green eyes while pretending he wasn't. He seemed very young to be secretary to the Duke of Auldwyke. She smiled to herself. He also seemed the conscientious sort to send every spare penny he could home to his mother.

Looking out of the window at the snow-flecked landscape, she felt displaced. She was hundreds of miles away from where she'd planned to be for the festive season. It was only three days until December the twenty-fifth. And this Christmas was to have been the most magical one imaginable; celebrated, for the first time, with her dashingly handsome fiancé at her home, Henley Hall. Not uprooted to the wild Yorkshire Moors as the guest of a duke she'd never met. Nor, in truth, ever heard of until that invitation arrived out of the blue. And if she was going to be totally honest with herself, she and her fiancé both needed uninterrupted time together to discuss their future, including their open-ended engagement. They both wanted to set a firm date for the wedding, but she was acutely aware each time either of them had tried to bring the subject up recently, life seemed to have got in the way.

She sighed. Despite what she had said to Porritt, she was sure she was to blame for the mix up. Which was the only reason she'd finally agreed to come.

She carried on brooding over the matter until the awkward silence in the car brought her back to the present.

Chin up, Ellie! Nothing is going to lessen the magic of this Christmas.

'Watch out, Mr Porritt,' she said with a bright laugh. 'With all this passing Yorkshire landscape so festively dressed in pristine snow, I'm moved to break into a rousing carol. And Gladstone here in my lap will likely join in, if less musically.' She restrained her bulldog's enthusiastic tongue from flailing any closer to Porritt's face.

The earnest young man shook his head. 'No, really, I must apologise again for—'

'Nonsense!' she said firmly. 'Besides, we're all here now. After you finally secured permission from his grace for the ladies of my staff to stay in one of the estate cottages.'

She turned and waved out the rear window at the rather less grand car following them.

Porritt's brow wrinkled as he tugged on his jacket cuffs. 'Yes, yes. All of you are now here. Except your fiancé, Detective Chief Inspector Seldon, that is?'

She had found that part of the invitation reassuring at least. A titled lady and a mere policeman being engaged was far from the done thing in high society. Yet, it seemed the Duke of Auldwyke did not share the common view among the aristocracy that only marriage between two parties of equal social status was acceptable.

'Oh, I thought I'd explained about Hugh the last time we spoke on the telephone?' She heard her butler's quiet admonishing cough from the front seat. 'I mean about Mr Seldon, my fiancé. Poor chap is still manacled to his office desk, I shouldn't wonder. Which is usually buried under his burgeoning case files.'

'Terrible,' Porritt muttered.

'Yes, but he's used to it after his many years on the police force. I'm not sure he even registers he hasn't slept for nights at a time any more. But he will be here first thing in the morning.' Her shoulders rose with glee at the prospect.

'He will?' Porritt seemed placated as he sat back in his seat. 'That's excellent news. I mean, his grace, and myself, of course, are very grateful you will both be in attendance for the main three days from the twenty-third to the twenty-fifth.'

'Wouldn't do to have uneven numbers at the shoot or dinner, I suppose,' she said airily. 'I'll admit, I don't know what to expect. But I was relieved when you explained during our telephone call that the shoot will be a bloodless one.'

'That is correct, Lady Swift. But please don't worry. Everything will become clear when we arrive.'

She gazed again through the window. The narrow snow-dusted lane wound up steeply, leaving the sweeping moors spreading far below, swaddled in a downy quilt of angelic white.

A few moments later and a set of imposing gates greeted them haughtily. As they passed through, her apprehension at being a guest among strangers on a remote moor-side estate rekindled. Her rather bohemian upbringing abroad meant she was woefully deficient in matters of decorum, etiquette and especially small talk.

Never one to cower in the face of challenge, however, she rolled her shoulders back and considered Porritt more intensely as the car trundled along the twisting drive. There had to be some way to get this tightly wound fellow to loosen up to make her stay a little less awkward.

The majestic, rolling snowy lawns on either side leading down to the grand façade of the house caught her eye. Its discordant symphony of asymmetrical towers and turrets doing their best to reduce the austerity of the five storeys of grim grey stone.

'Perhaps we share the same favoured choice, Mr Porritt? A tin bath is best, yes?'

'Tin... bath? Golly, no!' he stuttered. 'I can reassure you that the, er, facilities... that is, everything a lady like yourself could need whilst a guest of his grace will be more than satisfactory. Despite its outward appearance Auldwyke Hall has every modern comfort.'

Eleanor somehow kept a straight face. She'd hoped he'd reveal a more fun side of his character, surely present in a young man in his late twenties? Especially at this, the most joyous time of the year, the run-up to Christmas? However, he had obviously misunderstood her.

'I was talking about sledging preferences,' she said gently, pointing out the window. 'Not bathing ones.'

Hurriedly averting her gaze from his flame-red cheeks, in the front passenger seat she caught her butler's weary headshake at her faux pas. Clifford was a stickler for decorum. She realised he would consider she'd just made a double indecorous blunder. Not only had she inadvertently painted the image of herself splashing naked about her ablutions, but her allusion to playing around in the snow was hardly the done thing. Not for a titled lady!

She smiled at the back of Clifford's bowler-hatted head. Their relationship had come a long way in the few short years since she had inherited him as her butler, along with her late uncle's estate. Far enough for them to hold each other in equally staunch admiration and unspoken affection. Albeit, amid frequently locked horns over their diametrically opposed approaches to life. She was a whirlwind of chaos in his otherwise meticulously ordered existence. And he was the embodiment of rules and restraint that made her fiercely independent spirit chafe. Yet, despite their frequent bouts of teasing and squabbling, neither could imagine life being any other way now.

'What did you say, Clifford?' she called, even though he had said nothing. She needed his flawless mastery of polite conversation to rescue her. As he turned around, his ever-impassive expression disguised the respectful admonishment in his eyes.

'Apologies, my lady. But not a word was uttered from my quarter.' He returned to staring fixedly through the windscreen. She bit back a smile, knowing his deadpan reply was his mischievous way of telling her he'd explain later when they were alone.

Thinking on her seated feet, she gestured at their black-capped and jacketed driver.

'I imagine our chauffeur must have been born and raised in the area? He's managed so well on these snowy roads.'

Porritt's cheeks coloured again. 'Mr Lofthouse is actually the first footman. He doubles as chauffeur when required. I should mention, his grace is a gentleman of... singular and retiring habits. And thus has little use for a full-time chauffeur.'

That explained it, she thought. With its slightly musty interior and sporadic splutters on the steeper hills, the car had the air of having been press-ganged out of retirement.

'Then I shall be sure to thank Mr Lofthouse for his excellent care in navigating these steep, slippery roads the moment we alight.' She frowned. 'Oh, but then who's driving the other car?' She spun around, just in time to see it turn off to the right.

'That's Amos. I mean Mr Bowes, his grace's gardener,' Porritt said in a reticent tone. 'As I explained, at Auldwyke Hall, you might find things a little... different.' He cleared his throat awkwardly. 'And speaking of which, I need to apologise again because I must detail his grace's, er... rules for guests.'

Eleanor opened her mouth in disbelief, but quickly shut it. She nodded genially. 'Indeed, Mr Porritt. Please do.'

After all, Ellie, how could one possibly enjoy Christmas without a raft of rules!

2

In the passenger seat, Clifford's lips quirked. 'Heartening news, Mr Porritt. Her ladyship is a resolute believer in ordinances, directives and edicts of all kinds.'

'As I said, I'm all ears,' Eleanor repeated sweetly, throwing her traitorous butler a deadly glance.

'Thank you.' Porritt raised a finger. 'Number one. No guest must ever go further than the second floor of the house.'

'Ever, ever?' she said, fighting a frown.

Porritt nodded. 'And no guest must ever approach, or speak to his grace if they see him.' He held up another long, pale finger as her jaw fell. 'Ever. Ever. That's rule two.'

'But he's our host!' she couldn't help blurting out.

Porritt swallowed hard. 'Apologies again, Lady Swift. I must also point out that if either of these rules are broken, the offending, er, guest, will be asked to leave. Immediately. There is also a third rule, but,' he hurried on at her incredulous look, 'I don't think I need bother you with that now. More importantly for the moment, his grace insists that all guests take part in all events during their stay. And the pre-competition practice has already started. The other guests have been measured for their guns as his grace does not allow guests to bring their own. So, when we arrive at the Hall, if you would be so kind as to—'

'Wait a moment!' She stared at the young man in horror. 'What competition?'

Porritt paled. 'Didn't I say? Ah! More apologies then. The Christmas shooting competition. It's all in good, er, you know, fun. But please, everything must go according to his grace's wishes. So, if I could trouble you to hurry to your room and change, I will meet you on the west terrace in ten minutes? On returning to the entrance hall, simply take the right-hand passageway marked by the portrait of the fourth Duke of Auldwyke.'

She glanced at her butler to see if he was taking this all in. By the rigid set of his shoulders, he was. As the car rumbled to a stop under the stone portico she relented at the secretary's pleading look.

'Alright, Mr Porritt. Point me in the direction of my room and I'll race up and hurl myself into something suitable.'

'Too kind.' He fumbled for the handle as Lofthouse shot out of the driver's seat and marched around to her. He whipped off his cap, revealing close-cropped black hair framing his boxy face, and opened her door, evidently now back in his first footman role.

As she climbed out, she briefly marvelled at how tall he was. And at how Gothic the façade of Auldwyke Hall was, close-up. Dominating the centre of the dramatic edifice, the impressive arched portico extended the width of the driveway, allowing visitors to alight in relative comfort no matter what the Yorkshire sky rained down on them.

Then she noticed Porritt hopping from one foot to the next. Clifford's brow flinched as she shrugged discreetly to him. Lofthouse having opened the boot, Clifford placed a selection of her trunks, hat boxes and bags on the ground.

'These will need to reach her ladyship's room *before* the

lady herself,' he said firmly to the footman. He turned to her. 'With your permission, I shall seek out the kitchens to have your handwarmers heated, my lady. And then meet you on the west terrace when you feel suitably attired.' He glanced pointedly at the anxiously hovering secretary.

'Thank you, Clifford.' Taking Gladstone's lead, she tried to glide gracefully up the wide steps to the imposing front doors, but reverted to type and hurried up instead. And if this was how her holiday was unfolding, then so be it. She was going to enjoy herself, no matter what her host's idiosyncrasies.

If the interior of Auldwyke Hall was as intricately designed as its exterior, she missed it. A woman much her own age in a crisp maid's uniform hurried her and an exuberant Gladstone across the vast marble entrance hall and up the thickly crimson-carpeted stairs. Eleanor barely had time to admire the enormous Christmas tree towering up beyond the second floor to the forbidden third, before she was being swished past a bewildering number of panelled oak doors. Finally, the maid showed her into a palatial bedroom, dressed in sumptuous cream and peacock-green silk. Obviously, Clifford's polite but firm insistence had prevailed. Somehow, her luggage awaited on the stand. In truth, she was grateful to be rushed. It meant she had no time for nerves over what to wear to meet the other guests. Nor for fussing that her long, slender frame fell short of the feminine curves she admired in other women.

Having gently but firmly declined the maid's offer to assist her dress, she yanked out her green tweed skirt with a pleated front overlay and matching belted jacket, which she teamed with thickly ribbed, fern socks. Adding her favourite wool cape for good measure, she turned to her hat box. Selecting her sage felt one with a stylish brim, she smiled at her housekeeper's thoughtful addition of a sporty feather in the leather band. Then cooed aloud as her hands fell on a darling quilted tweed

coat with a ruff for Gladstone which matched her own
ensemble.

At the sound of a crash, she spun around.

'Gladstone? Where are you? This is no time for making
mischief, old chum.'

She hurried towards the noise of dripping coming from the
bathroom, grimacing in horror at the upturned water pitcher
knocked from the washstand. The one forming a puddle around
her bulldog's ankles as he lapped noisily.

'Finished, you monster?' She laughed as he sploshed over to
her. 'Come on then. Quick. Dry your feet on this towel. It's cold
outside. You might catch a chill, even with this warm jacket.
And then,' she frowned, 'we'll whip out to the west terrace, the
directions for which I'll hopefully remember when we get
downstairs.'

At the bottom of the stairs, the grandfather clock chided her
that she had taken fourteen minutes to get ready, not the ten
prescribed by Porritt. Resisting the urge to poke her tongue out
at it, she spun in a circle in the imposing auditorium-sized hall,
trying to recall his directions. 'You take the right-hand
passageway marked by the portrait of...'

Which duke, Ellie?

She rolled her eyes at her bulldog. 'I didn't realise this was
an art exam as well as a shooting competition.' She chose one at
random and set off at a brisk pace, Gladstone panting alongside.

At the end of the corridor, she stepped out onto a flagstone
terrace. But her ready smile faltered. No other guests were
milling about. No one was being measured for a gun. In fact,
there was no evidence there was to be a shooting competition
there at all.

Because there isn't, Ellie. Wrong terrace.

She cocked her head to listen. Ah! Voices. Beyond that

smart glass-canopied walkway must be the correct terrace. She hurried along the walkway, Gladstone now straining on his lead with excitement. On her left was a collection of low brick storehouses, each sporting a pristinely painted bottle-green door. As she passed the second to last, she noticed it was open. Inside, her eye was drawn to the unexpected sight of crates of glass balls. She marvelled at the amount as Gladstone whined and strained on his lead, keen to explore this new wonderland. She reined him in as gently as possible.

'The duke must really go to town with the Christmas decorations, Gladstone. Despite Porritt's nerves and the duke's oddities, it's obviously going to be a very festive time here.' She frowned for a moment as it registered that none of the glass baubles were painted in the traditional seasonal colours of red or gold. She shrugged, putting it down to another example of the eccentric duke's way of doing things.

Jerked out of her reverie, she was pulled over the threshold of the storeroom by her bulldog.

'No, boy! You'll smash the lot with your ungainly bulk...'

Her mouth fell open as she saw what he had actually been straining to reach. Lying between two rows of crates, sprawled face down on the floor, was the body of a man.

3

Eleanor's breath caught as she dropped to her knees beside the prone figure. Even in the gloomy interior of the store-house there was no mistaking that blue worsted suit and fair hair.

Porritt!

Some kind of accident must have befallen the duke's secretary. But why here? He'd been insistent he'd meet her on the west terrace as soon as possible. So what could have been so important that he'd detoured via what seemed to be the Christmas storeroom?

'Can you hear me, Mr Porritt?' she urged.

His lack of response was disconcerting. Her nurse's training from the war flooded back to take command of her racing thoughts. Shaking an unconscious person was too dangerous unless any chance of spinal damage could be ruled out. And given that the poor fellow was face down, one arm flung out, the other twisted under his body, the cause and extent of his injuries were far from obvious.

She tapped his shoulder gently instead.

'Mr Porritt!' she said louder.

The only response was her own words ringing around the cold brick building.

Her fingers reached to his neck to check his pulse, but stopped. She hadn't noticed that in the car. And she wouldn't have missed it, would she? Not that angry red line above his shirt collar?

Pulse, Ellie!

She applied more finger pressure, but not even a frail beat met her touch. Her hand flew to her mouth.

'Oh, gracious!'

'My lady, what is it?' her butler's concerned voice called from the doorway.

He strode over to her and whipped up the smart tails of his black wool overcoat to sink to his haunches. He scanned her face, then caught sight of the sprawled angular figure beside her.

'We're too late, Clifford,' she muttered sadly. She felt dazed, barely registering Gladstone sliding his head up under her arm with a soft whimper. The young secretary couldn't be dead. She'd been talking with him only minutes before!

Without a word, they both bowed their heads.

'Rest in eternal peace, sir,' Clifford murmured.

Silently offering her own prayer heavenwards, she ran her hand over her bulldog's head. 'It won't help him if we pine, old chum,' she whispered. She looked up at Clifford. 'We'd better go and—'

'Hullo? Porritt?' a terse voice called from outside. 'You in here? 'Cos the guests is all gettin' restless by half.'

The tall form of the first footman dimmed the already shadowy light as he ducked his head to peer in. 'Oh, it's you, Lady Swift and Mr Clifford. 'Scuse me for sayin', but folks are waitin' for you on t' west terrace.'

'Then they shall have to wait a little longer, Mr Lofthouse,' Clifford said. 'Whilst you inform his grace of some tragic news.'

Lofthouse shook his head vehemently. 'His grace won't have none of that. 'Specially at his Christmas shooting party.'

Clifford's lips pursed. 'It has occurred nonetheless.'

'I'm afraid Mr Porritt is dead,' she said gently.

The footman's brow knitted. 'Dead, by crikey! Well, he had no business bein' in here, mind. Maybe—'

'Mr Lofthouse!' Clifford said more firmly. 'Might you be so good as to save your postulations for later?'

Lofthouse stepped forward and drew himself up to his full height, which Eleanor couldn't miss was a good two inches above her butler's six-foot frame. 'I couldn't do that even if I wanted to, Mr Clifford, havin' no idea what it means?'

She held up a placating hand. 'It means please hurry to his grace and tell him the news.'

Lofthouse's mouth turned down. 'Can't, m'lady. Sorry and all, but I've no way of gettin' to him.'

She shared a confused look with Clifford. 'Why? Where is he?'

Lofthouse's expression suggested she must be particularly dull-witted. 'Why, he's in his third-floor apartment. Same as always. But I've no key for t' door at the top of the stairs up there. Only Porritt was allowed that,' he said, with what sounded like a tinge of resentment.

Turning away from Lofthouse, Clifford slid his right hand up inside Porritt's jacket and back out, a key pouch on a plain chain in it. He flipped it open to reveal a black iron key.

She marvelled for the umpteenth time at her butler's sleight of hand. Taking it from him, she straightened up and handed it to the footman who was inspecting the shine on his shoes. His indifference felt callous when he'd just learned his colleague was dead.

'Hopefully, this is the right one,' she said. He swallowed hard as he reached out and took it tentatively. She'd been mistaken, she realised. He wasn't indifferent. And he was obviously also nervous about going up to the duke. Not surprising, given the news he was being asked to relay.

'Perhaps I should be the one to go?' she said.

Lofthouse's jaw fell. 'To his grace? A guest? Never, m'lady!'

'Oh yes,' she said, fighting a frown. 'Never. Ever. I remember. Then please hurry and tell him.'

With a nod, the footman hurried off. She rejoined Clifford who glanced at her and sighed. 'I wish I could persuade you not to confront death at such close hand, my lady. Although, this is hardly the first time. However, I have learned you will always try to aid the living. Or the dying. Or indeed the deceased, no matter what. So I shall endeavour to temper my natural urge to protect you from such.'

She was amazed. As her beloved late uncle's batman for more years than she'd been alive, Clifford had promised in her uncle's last moments to look after her. And had dutifully carried out his vow with iron resolve. It seemed he'd finally accepted, however, that she would not live her life wrapped in cotton wool. And that meant the world to her.

She studied Porritt's body again and then glanced around the room. She grimaced, noticing Clifford was drumming his fingertips together.

'You too then? I didn't want to raise an unnecessary alarm without being sure, but something doesn't feel quite right, does it?'

He nodded sombrely. 'Would I could say otherwise, my lady.'

'There's no sign of a struggle. Not with all these crates of glass baubles still intact. And no blood. But look at his neck. See that mark? So fresh. And thick. Almost like a... a burn.'

'Not good.' He whipped out his pince-nez to peer at it more closely. 'Hmm, not good at all. Regrettably, I must conjecture Mr Porritt's passing was not an accident.'

'I agree. It looks like...'

He nodded grimly. 'Murder!'

4

Eleanor turned back to Porritt's body. 'Well, whoever killed poor Porritt must have struck like lightning. We were both talking with him not that long ago.'

'Indeed. The gentleman was mercilessly dispatched within a precise eighteen-minute window.'

A huff of frustration escaped her. 'Clifford, even with your infuriating determination to live by the dictate of your pocket watch, you cannot possibly know that.'

She stared again at the ugly red mark on the dead man's neck and shivered. The cold was increasing as the daylight waned. Her handwarmers appeared in her eyeline, the heat radiating out too welcome to resist.

'Thank you, Clifford. And alright, dash it! I'd love to hear how you know the timing so precisely,' she said contritely.

He half bowed. 'Mr Porritt gave the command to hasten upstairs and change at twenty past three. After exactly fifteen minutes, I set out knowing how easily one particular member of the Swift household becomes distracted...'

She pointed at her bulldog. 'Gladstone?'

His lips quirked fleetingly. 'No. *You*, my lady.' His attempt at levity was intended to ease her upset for Porritt, she knew. 'My quest concluded at twenty minutes to four, when I found you here. By which time, you had unfortunately already ascertained that Mr Porritt was dead. Which, given your medical training—'

'Would have taken me about two minutes to confirm. So you're right, it was close enough to eighteen minutes since we left Porritt and I found him dead.' She looked at the deceased secretary, and then Clifford. He nodded.

'I think the best course of action is to let the police examine the body further.'

Lofthouse appeared in the doorway.

'I'm back, m'lady.'

'Surely you haven't seen his grace and returned already?' She noted he was alone. It seemed even the sudden death of his secretary wasn't enough for the duke to leave his ivory tower.

Lofthouse frowned. 'His grace is a gentleman of few words. I gave him news about yon Porritt there and he told me to secure the storehouse and gather staff in the kitchen and guests into t' drawin' room. Last two which I've done. He said everythin's to continue exactly as planned and, so as not to inconvenience his guests, not to telephone the police until after dinner has been served.'

Eleanor was staggered. 'Even though Mr Porritt has been... Has died?'

Clifford's raised eyebrow showed he was equally taken aback.

Lofthouse nodded firmly. 'Things run as they do at Auldwyke Hall no matter what. His grace insists on it. And it'd take a braver man than I've ever set eyes on to question his wishes!'

'Or to get an audience with him,' she muttered. Then she realised she shouldn't be surprised by the duke's reaction to a dead body in his storehouse. He was obviously a law unto himself. And being a duke, the highest rank of nobility in the land, to all intents and purposes, he was above it as well.

She was about to mention her belief that the duke's secretary may have been murdered, but hesitated. She'd only just arrived and until the police confirmed her, and Clifford's, suspicions they were only that. Suspicions. And the duke wouldn't take kindly to her 'interfering', she was sure. She needed to speak to Hugh, but he wouldn't be here until tomorrow. So, the next best course of action, she told herself, was to wait until the police had examined the body too. She took a deep breath.

'But who will take Mr Porritt's place?' she said calmly.

Lofthouse tapped his chest. 'Me. Stands to reason. But don't you fret. All you guests'll be set righter than fence posts, m'lady, with me filling in.'

'A well-deserved honour, Mr Lofthouse, no doubt,' Clifford said smoothly. 'But a doubly industrious time surely lies ahead for you?'

'Gracious, you can't do both jobs.' Eleanor hesitated, even though she knew what Clifford was hinting at. This was supposed to be at least a partial holiday for him, too.

He nodded imperceptibly, clearly having read her mind. She sighed.

'Lofthouse. I shall lend you Clifford here. He can assist you where necessary.'

He eyed her with a glimmer of scepticism. 'Most kind, I'm sure, m'lady.'

After Lofthouse had secured the storehouse and left, Clifford turned to her.

'My lady, I believe you acted prudently. Well done. Might I be so bold as to suggest you visit the ladies and inform them of events before dressing for dinner? Hearing it from the horse's mouth is preferable to hearing it from the gossip's tail. The old gamekeeper's cottage where they are housed is but five hundred yards beyond the fork in the driveway, I understand.'

She nodded. 'Alright. If only to save you from haranguing me ad nauseum that shock is not to be trifled with.'

'As if,' he said innocently.

Leaving Clifford to join Lofthouse, she crunched along a path lined with trimmed shrubs topped with high bonnets of festive white. The snow had started to fall in earnest, deadening the sound of everything except the crunch of her footsteps. To make progress easier, she tried to walk in footsteps someone must have helpfully just made, as the snow hadn't yet covered them. But she soon had to abandon them, as they veered off the path.

Joining the driveway, she slipped and slid up to the fork, Gladstone frolicking in front of her. Turning off, she was soon standing at a narrow swing gate, beyond which a dove-grey stone cottage, cosseted in snowflake-speckled ivy, beckoned her. As she approached, the smell of wood smoke overlain with aromas of cinnamon and sausage meat wafted to her nostrils.

Up close, the old gamekeeper's cottage, with its quaint lean, and dormer windows in the thatched roof, looked like an iced Christmas gingerbread house. The simple but lovingly woven wreath of greenery, dried quince slices and ribbons on the door, left no doubt she was in the correct place. Only her ever-clumsy maid, Polly, could have hung it upside down!

Before she could lift her hand to knock, the door flew open.

'What a treat to see you, m'lady!' Mrs Butters, her housekeeper, flapped her inside with the beaming smile of a doting aunt. As Eleanor's bulldog climbed up her housekeeper's legs in excitement, she patted his head and chuckled. 'And Master Gladstone, too, of course.'

Eleanor stepped into the diminutive quarry-tiled hall.

'He looks very dapper in his beautiful new coat. Which I detect your expert sewing hand in, thank you.'

''Twas a pleasure, m'lady. But 'pologies here for the mess,'

Mrs Butters flustered, looking suddenly horrified at the piles of half-unpacked cases, boxes and baskets scattered around.

A scurry of eager footsteps heralded her cook, Mrs Trotman, and the two maids, Lizzie and Polly, who squeezed into a line beside Mrs Butters and curtseyed awkwardly amid the unpacking.

'Hello, ladies. Ah, and Tomkins!' Eleanor said, delighting in her ginger tomcat's enthusiastic welcome. 'Forgive Gladstone and me not calling ahead.'

'Fancy the mistress thinking she need do such a thing!' her housekeeper tutted, helping Eleanor out of her cloak.

Mrs Trotman looked hopeful. 'Perhaps, 'twas the smell of my cooking, m'lady, as had you skippin' up the front step?'

Eleanor laughed. 'Since Clifford isn't here to chide that titled ladies must never skip, I confess, yes, it was mostly that which had me throwing decorum to the wind.'

Mrs Butters cocked her head, scanning Eleanor's face. 'I don't s'pose Mr Clifford'll be joining us in a minute?'

Mrs Trotman nudged her friend. 'I'll bet he's giving the staff over there what-for at things not being up to his exacting standards for her ladyship!'

'Actually, the poor chap just temporarily became one of the staff,' Eleanor said. 'There's been a rather unseasonable development, you see.'

Mrs Butters clucked like a mother hen. 'How 'bout telling us while warming up by the range, m'lady? With a slice of Trotters' cake and a tot of fortification?'

Mrs Trotman's eyes widened. 'Fortification? Already? Oh lawks!'

In a flurry of flapping aprons and cooed concerns, Eleanor found herself at a scrubbed wooden table next to the toasty lit range. A hot toddy, releasing whispers of brandy and ginger, together with a slice of delectable, warmed plum cake, was set before her. Tomkins curled around her neck, purring softly and rubbing noses with her, as Gladstone settled into her lap, laying his head up her chest adoringly.

'Best get it out and over with, m'lady.' Mrs Trotman poured two small measures of toddy for the maids and topped them up with ginger tea. 'Long as you and Mr Clifford are alright, can't be too terrible.'

'And Master Gladstone.' Polly clapped her hand over her mouth at speaking up in front of the mistress.

'It's alright, Polly,' Eleanor said. 'You are all on holiday, so the rules are relaxed. Only please don't be upset by what I have to tell you.'

'Promise, m'lady,' the four of them chorused.

'Well...' Eleanor faltered, wishing Clifford was there with his infallible knack of knowing just what to say. 'It's Mr Porritt. The duke's secretary who met us all at the railway station? Unfortunately, the poor fellow is... no longer with us.'

'Dead! Poor man,' Mrs Trotman said with feeling. She pulled Lizzie closer into her side, Mrs Butters doing the same with Polly. 'Mind, the gentleman seemed a right bucket of nerves. Was it his heart as gave out, m'lady?'

'We don't know what it was yet. That will be for the police to work out.'

'Police, m'lady? Beg pardon for askin',' Lizzie said with her soft Scottish burr, 'but is there a worry, then? 'Bout how he died?'

Eleanor nodded. 'There might be.'

Mrs Trotman shook her head. 'I bet his dukeness is all of a dither.'

Eleanor savoured another sip of her toddy. 'I don't know. I haven't met him yet. But I'm getting the impression that very little rattles him. Speaking of which, his grace has insisted the Christmas festivities continue exactly as planned. Which absolutely applies to you, ladies.'

'Well, you know us, only ever doin' as we're told,' Mrs Trotman said with a chuckle.

She laughed. 'As Clifford would say, that's the spirit!'

''Tis a shame though, m'lady.' Mrs Butters cut her another generous slice of deliciously moist cake. 'What with Chief Inspector Seldon coming up 'specially tomorrow, only to arrive in the middle of a police investigation. It'll be as if he never escaped his desk!'

Eleanor choked on her drink. 'No, no. Hugh won't have anything to do with it. He wasn't even here when it happened. And the local police chaps will be here later this evening.' Despite this, she sighed inwardly.

So, Ellie, your first ever romantic Christmas with your fiancé will be spent at a murder scene!

5

The two figures in the bedroom mirror blinked at each other.

'I know, Gladstone, old chum!' Eleanor leaned forward to peer at her reflection. It was inconceivable anyone shimmering in such an exquisite fern silk evening gown could have been crouched over a dead body in a freezing storehouse only a short while ago. Her fingers traced the beaded bodice down to the velvet waist-sash tied above the cascade of luxurious folds, which flattered her slender frame perfectly. The swish of the hem against her satin-heeled ankles felt sensuously soft, the dainty wrist cufflets fastened with emerald-studded clasps adding extra sophistication to the gown's glamour. It was just one of the latest designs she'd treated herself to in readiness for the romantic Christmas originally planned with her fiancé. She wanted to surprise him. And convince herself that she might actually have the makings of a sophisticated lady in her somewhere.

She smiled, thinking back to Clifford's barely disguised eagerness in organising several shopping forays up to London's most notable fashion houses. And now, with her matching beaded wrap and rose-pearl necklace, she felt stylish, confident and feminine. Gladstone, smartly attired in his festive green and red bow tie, sat at her feet and woofed. She laughed, burying the wistful wish that her fiancé could be there tonight.

'I hear you,' she said fondly. 'You'll be my chaperone in Hugh's absence, old boy. And I'll take dinner with the duke's other guests as an opportunity to practise being ladylike.'

And more importantly, her investigation notebook on the walnut tallboy reminded her, an opportunity for observing potential murder suspects...

Out on the second-floor landing, her eager bulldog poked his nose through the banisters to sniff the gossamer-winged angel. Unusually, it adorned the middle of the Christmas tree, which soared on up, undecorated, to the closed-off third floor. Peering down to the tree's base two floors below, she felt a wash of child-like joy at the glittering ivory baubles cascading down the branches, accompanied by tiny silver lanterns, each one home to a flickering candle. The enchanting effect made her think of a celestial waterfall of light and hope trickling from the heavens down to earth.

Further cheered by the uplifting scent of fresh pine needles, she descended the double-width carved staircase to the ground floor, where Clifford was rubbing his eyes in mischievous disbe-lief at her transformation. She waved a teasing hand in reply over his uncharacteristic white bow tie, striped pewter and black waistcoat, and box-cut bottle-green tailcoat with lavish brass buttons.

'I say, dashed noble of Clifford to have taken a part in this evening's after-dinner pantomime for us all,' she said to her bulldog.

Clifford arched a questioning brow.

'It is the fairy tale of *Cinderella* that has Buttons the pageboy in it, isn't it?' she asked impishly.

He half bowed. 'Touché, my lady. Thankfully, however, his grace's plans tonight do not include acting out such an indignity. The Auldwyke livery I am wearing naturally features the family monogram, since it is the traditional uniform of the house for footmen when serving at formal dinners.'

She leaned in to inspect the jacket button he indicated, marvelling at the detail of the stag's horns interwoven in the elaborately scrolling letter 'A'.

'Well, dash it, Clifford, if this dinner's the sort of formal affair spelt with a hideously large capital "F", I shall need your assistance. To be precise, your infuriating but indispensable knack of pointing out potential faux pas to me before I make a spectacle of myself.'

'Alas, my lady, I shall be too engaged with serving duties.'

She folded her arms. 'What's this new strategy of yours? Leaving me to flounder in social situations, you terror? It started with Porritt on the car journey here.'

He gave her that look she always dreaded. The one that said he was right, and quietly she knew it. 'Merely a respectful attempt, my lady, to hasten you up the steep learning curve of high society etiquette by removing the crutch of a piggyback.'

She pointed at his uniform. 'Just as well. A piggyback from you in that jacket would be like riding a circus pony!'

He rolled his eyes good-naturedly. 'Finished?'

She laughed. 'Not a chance. But lead on so I can think up plenty more to rag you with while devouring whatever is on tonight's menu. While keeping an ear open, of course.' She glanced around. 'Have you learned anything new from Lofthouse or the other staff?'

He shook his head. 'Regrettably not in the manner you mean, my lady. However, I have learned the guests have all but finished their pre-dinner drinks in the Burgundy Room, since the dinner gong is but four minutes from sounding. Hence, Mr Lofthouse is waiting impatiently to announce you. This way.'

While trying to restrain Gladstone's exuberance at the word 'dinner', she followed her butler as he glided along the maze of oak-lined passageways adorned with gold-framed landscapes and marble-pedestalled objets d'art. The flickering wall lights cradled in deer antlers, however, merely cast eerie shadows rather than brightened their route. Eventually, he stopped at a deeply panelled door, tutting as she tugged on his sleeve.

'What are the other guests like, Clifford?' She groaned as he mimed buttoning his lips. 'Oh, come on! Forearming your mistress is still allowed, isn't it?'

'Of course, my lady.' He lowered his voice. 'However, colouring the impartiality of your observations about his grace's other guests may be unwise as whoever is charged with handling Mr Porritt's death may well be reliant on them.'

She sighed. 'Good point.' She rolled her shoulders back and flapped for him to open the door.

Her name not being announced felt immaterial compared to the hush her arrival was met with. Clifford's brow flinched in apology for Lofthouse's unexpected absence as he hastily stepped forward.

'Ladies and gentlemen, Lady Swift of Henley Hall.'

From one corner of the room, a tall hunting hound glowered at her bulldog, a low growl emanating from the depths of its belly. Gladstone cowered, but as the hound stayed where it was, she ignored it.

'Good evening, everyone,' she said brightly. 'I finally made it. Last one gets the bill though, they say!' Despite the continued silence that met her words, she resolutely approached the nearest guest, hand outstretched. 'How do you do?'

The mid-thirties study in masculinity, standing legs astride, cocked his chin as if posing for his adoring, if absent, fans. 'Exceptionally well,' he purred in a silky tone as rich as his dark-chocolate hair. Patting his black velvet jacket front, he added, 'Willoughby Taylor. Soon to be "Sir". A pleasure, no doubt.'

Unsure if he was suggesting the pleasure was hers or his, she smiled non-committally. She had to admit, nonetheless, his eyes were very striking, being bottomless blue lagoons framed by long, dark lashes.

'Evening,' a languid voice said behind her. She turned to find a blond chap whose intricately patterned cravat of surely every shade of blue had escaped from his dinner jacket. The man shook her hand but kept his thumb so tightly pressed to his forefinger, she could grasp little more than his fingertips. She couldn't quite place his age. His features were so fine, they were almost feminine. His floppy fringe and clear hazel eyes giving him a youthful air that didn't fit with the worry lines dogging his forehead. He shrugged.

'No "Sir" in the offing for me. Irrelevant though, given I'm Julius Huish. It's a total mouthful. I'll say that to save you having to cover up that you're thinking it. Everyone does. But it comes in useful, you see?'

'Not yet. But do enlighten me?' Eleanor said brightly.

'Hmm? Oh, another time, perhaps.' He drifted away to the window and stared out at the snow.

Oh, well, Ellie, let's try the next one.

'And good evening. You are?'

She offered her hand to a portly fiftyish man, running an unlit cigar over his thick moustache. He was dressed in full cummerbund regalia.

'Barnabas Musgrave, Esquire,' the man's deep voice rumbled. 'Owner and founder of the renowned Musgrave Insurance Company.' The grey-blonde lady in a lilac taffeta gown sitting at his elbow patted her voluminous updo with a diamond-knuckled hand and tittered into the remains of the brandy she was nursing. He waved his cigar at her. 'My wife, Viola.'

'Esquiress,' she snapped with a smug glance at Taylor. 'Well, I'm not missing out on playing title trumps. It's still ruddy Christmas, remember!'

Eleanor spotted Clifford stiffening at such forceful language, especially from a female. But it had let her catch the woman's accent. Such broad intonation placed it likely way north of even Yorkshire.

Turning, she approached the last person in the room, a vision in vivid orange chiffon languishing on the furthest of the sumptuous burgundy settees. The young woman flicked her blunt-cut dark bob and stared back, offering a finger wave with the hand not twirling a large gin and tonic.

'Hey.' The woman's already high cheekbones rose as she gazed up at Eleanor with intense black eyes. 'I'm Pearl. Pearl Whitwell. And I intend to win that shooting competition. Just so you know.'

'Right. Well, good for you,' Eleanor said cheerily.

'Showing one's hand is inadvisable when sizing up the opposition, I always say.' Taylor slung a finely trousered leg over the arm of the settee he'd slid on to.

Pearl Whitwell threw him a sweet smile. 'Not if one has nothing to hide, *Mister* Taylor.'

Hoping for safer conversational ground, Eleanor gestured at her bulldog. 'This is Gladstone. Who does the other handsome beast in the room belong to?' As Taylor's lips curved into a conceited smirk, she tutted. 'I meant the hunting hound?'

'He's with me. His name's Finbar.' Huish raked his fringe back over his head. 'But it's, I mean, he's rather complicated.'

Trying to disregard her first impressions of the other guests, Eleanor wandered over to admire the enormous holly wreath adorning the ornately gilded oval mirror. Since no one had picked up the conversation, she tried again. 'Perhaps I'm the only one new to Auldwyke Hall?'

'No!' the room all but chorused.

Barnaby Musgrave slipped his cigar into his top pocket. 'It seems we're all at the same disadvantage as yourself, Lady Swift.'

Clifford materialised beside her with a silver tray bearing a larger than usual sherry. 'For fortitude,' he murmured without moving his lips.

The sound of Lofthouse striking the gong in the doorway made her down the sherry in two gulps. The second bringing on a coughing fit that threatened to leak the amber oloroso from her nose.

Chin up, Ellie! At least they all had manners enough not to pounce on you with questions about finding poor Porritt dead.

But then again, she hadn't really learned anything useful yet. Except there seemed to be something odd going on amongst the guests. Perhaps dinner would loosen their tongues.

As she headed for the dining room, she shook her head to herself. *And tighten their manners, Ellie!*

6

Eleanor found the opulently appointed dining room almost as much a feast for the eyes as the stomach. A promising number of lidded salvers filled the far wall, while the grand table was dressed in ivory and silver linen. A beautiful spray of silken spruce and ivy wound around white trumpet lilies and holly berries, making a stunning Christmas centrepiece. She'd dined in some exquisite rooms, but never one hung entirely in silk wallpaper depicting myriad vignettes of impeccably detailed game birds. The burnished bronze, buffed copper and iridescent green of their plumage was echoed in the patterned upholstery of the chairs and the many sets of full-length curtains. Each of which was dominated by a dramatic pelmet, emblazoned in gold thread with what she now knew was the Auldwyke monogram. Since the curtains had not been drawn, she could see the snow being whipped up by the stiff wind that rattled the panes of the French doors. And presiding high over the table in the ceiling was a captivating octagonal stained-glass canopy, each section featured lead-lined images of more game birds flying overhead, even more spectacular against the backdrop of falling snow behind them.

She looked down to find Clifford discreetly restraining Gladstone from scrabbling up onto the chair by her place name. Sensing her butler's meticulous hand in the precisely spaced squadrons of crystal glasses and regiments of cutlery at each setting, she smiled in gratitude as she took her seat. But he gave a discreet nod of approval in Lofthouse's direction in reply. High praise from him, she knew. Evidently, the duke's footman was adept at his duties.

But hopefully not at murder, Ellie!

She dismissed the thought for the moment and glanced around at the seating arrangements. Opposite her, Taylor had abandoned his model-like pose and was tapping the back of his chair impatiently, while on his left, Viola Musgrave faffed with rearranging the taffeta folds of her gown. On his right, Pearl Whitwell looked bored, with her head in her hands and elbows on the table, while Barnabas Musgrave fidgeted on Eleanor's right, muttering about how seats used to be wider. Lastly, Julius Huish sat listlessly on her left, with—

Where's his hound, Ellie?

She glanced around, suddenly realising Gladstone was missing too. Her butler's discreet cough attracted her attention. At the other end of the room he was feeding an eager bulldog with his favourite liver treats. She hid a smile, hoping her butler had brought enough to keep Gladstone occupied for the entire meal.

Surveying the rest of the table, she realised two other places had been set. One at each end.

'Ah, so we'll be eight, not six then?' She winced, hoping she hadn't sounded too eager for additional company.

A flurry of napkins being flapped into laps was the only reply. Lofthouse arrived at her elbow.

'Neither place will be occupied, Lady Swift. One is always laid for his grace, though the master only ever dines alone in his apartment. The other settin' is for his late wife, the duchess.' He bowed his head. 'God rest her soul.'

She nodded, hoping her face wasn't giving away her growing bafflement at the eccentricities running rife at Auldwyke Hall.

'Skillby Moor hare,' Clifford announced, placing a bowl of soup before her.

As the guests genteelly sipped the first course, she fought the urge to be the chatty guest. She needed to listen and observe instead. Someone at this very table might just be the man, or woman, who had dispatched the duke's secretary. After all, unless it was one of the staff, as far as she was aware there was no one else around for miles. Auldwyke Hall was the only house she'd seen since passing through the last tiny village in the valley below. She readied her ears and busied herself with the delicious gamey flavour of the hare, enhanced by the rounds of caramelised onions and baked prune slivers serving as creative croutons.

'The weather's trying to be Christmassy, I suppose,' Viola announced to no one in particular.

'Snow never falls in anyone's best interest,' Barnabas, her husband, grumbled into his bowl.

'Still, we all made it here in time,' Pearl said.

Huish glanced sharply at her. 'In time for what, though?'

Pearl frowned. 'Well, for the shoot. And anything else his grace has planned for us, obviously.'

'Whatever that is,' Barnabas muttered darkly to his laden spoon of prune slices.

Taylor laughed, but Eleanor detected a note of strain behind it. 'A perfectly routine festive time, no doubt, old man. These things always are, I find. Use your imagination.'

Barnabas smiled thinly. 'A man of business never sullies his wits by indulging imagination for even a moment. As I've repeated many times.'

Pearl shrugged. 'Shame for you we're not competing over having the sharpest wits then, Mr Musgrave.'

'No harm in keeping them to the fore, though,' Taylor said. 'Doesn't pay to be unprepared.' He cast a tense glance around the room.

Huish choked on his last spoonful of soup. He shook his head at the glass of water Clifford offered him. 'Hare today. Gone tomorrow. Better to have been immortalised in paint than shot without a chance, I'd say.' The other guests stared at him, and then as a man dropped their eyes. In the awkward silence, Huish cleared his throat. 'Being an artist, as I am, you see.'

As Eleanor tucked into her entrée of quail's egg with duck liver pâté on shredded chicory, she listened intently. The conversation, however, switched stiltedly from a theatre play no one but Huish had seen, to the tedium of long journeys. Eventually, it slewed to an abrupt halt over Barnabas' declaration that he cared little for Yorkshire, finding it still lacking in too many regards.

Eleanor realised it would seem odd if she was silent for the whole meal. And given the painful lulls so far, she felt it churlish not to speak at least occasionally.

'You mentioned you're an artist, Mr Huish? You, at least, must therefore appreciate Yorkshire for her rugged beauty. Are you planning to paint the dramatic landscape while you're here?'

'No, Lady Swift,' he said firmly. 'I'm only here for the... er, the planned activities.'

Viola laughed mirthlessly. 'Naturally. We all are.' She waved her empty glass at Lofthouse.

'And his grace's wine cellar, perhaps,' Taylor added snidely.

Clifford appeared with the third course; brandied crab gratin. She smiled around the table as he left. 'Christmas away from home can be a delightful change, wouldn't you say?'

Barnabas snorted. 'I'd say it's a travesty of lost business time.

Christmas or no Christmas, sales don't walk themselves in through my door. They have to be tempted, lured with a bait, then reeled in.'

'You make your customers sound like dull-witted fish,' Pearl scoffed, twirling her wine glass. 'I'm immune to such tactics, myself.'

'But not above them, maybe?' Barnabas shot back. 'Seeing as you are here!'

Eleanor laughed a little too loudly. 'Perhaps we could go round the table, playing that party game of each telling our neighbour's story? Only you're all way ahead of me there.'

Huish stared at her, then turned back to his crab.

'You've got the wrong idea on that somehow, Lady Swift,' Taylor said hurriedly. 'None of us know anything worth telling about each other. We've none of us met outside of Auldwyke Hall.'

'That's right,' Huish jumped in.

Pearl smiled sweetly. 'Like you, Lady Swift, we're just here for the competition.'

Taylor's jaw hardened. 'With the handicap of having to use our host's guns.'

Huish sighed. 'And little practice with them, Lady Swift, since your "discovery" put paid to that!'

'Really, Mr Huish,' Viola chided. 'It's not fair to blame Lady Swift.'

'I wasn't! What a suggestion!'

Viola pouted. 'It did sound like you were, Mr Huish. Poor Lady Swift. As if finding a dead man wasn't difficult enough.'

Her husband clanged his fork against his plate. 'Hardly a decent subject to serve up at dinner, Viola.'

'I didn't, actually. If you remember, it was Mr Huish.'

'Now look here,' Huish retaliated, 'I was talking about the shoot.'

Taylor pushed his empty plate away. 'Well, at least this

secretary having the bad manners to die while we're all here won't affect the competition.'

Eleanor bristled. 'His name was *Mr Porritt*.'

'Anyway, you're wrong actually.' Pearl smiled sweetly at Taylor, but her tone was acid. 'You see, I heard his grace has been a recluse so long, the rumour in some circles is that he's no longer the one in charge.'

Viola looked up from her plate. 'That's what you said, Barnabas! That you'd heard his secretary, Porritt, controlled the duke and that it was him who decided if favours are granted or not.'

'Nonsense,' her husband huffed. 'The notion of a servant deciding that is preposterous!'

Taylor smirked. 'And besides, the secretary is now dead, so that impediment, if it ever was one, has been removed.'

Eleanor fought a shiver. *Removed, perhaps, Ellie, by someone at this table?*

'Gracious, how insensitive of me. I should have offered my condolences.' She slid back in her seat to get a better view of everyone's face. 'Some of you had probably met Mr Porritt before, of course?'

She suddenly seemed to have the table's undivided attention. Huish toyed with his cravat.

'You maybe didn't know, Lady Swift. But the duke, his grace, has been practically a hermit for the last decade.' He shrugged. 'Or thereabouts, I think I heard. So none of us could have been here before, as Mr Musgrave said. Or have known his secretary. Before he contacted us about this shoot, of course.'

'One would hardly deign to know a servant even if one had, Huish!' Taylor snorted, seemingly unabashed by Lofthouse standing at his elbow with his next course.

Eleanor savoured the smell of the braised partridge in red wine, then speared a honeyed carrot, imagining it was Taylor's head. 'Well, as I'm clearly the new girl, perhaps you'll all be good enough to tell me what I missed by arriving so much later than you all?'

Pearl Whitwell ran her forefinger around the rim of her glass, making it sing. 'Only that whatever your usual form, you'll be at a disadvantage tomorrow, having missed the short practice on the shooting platform we did get. And I believe you didn't even get as far as being measured for your gun? Such a pity.' She smirked a little too gleefully for the sympathetic face she pulled.

Taylor leered at her. 'I'd give you the best of my personal expertise, ordinarily, but not with what's at stake over the next three days.'

'No need to apologise,' Eleanor said genially. 'But three days?'

Taylor shook his head in disbelief. 'Good lord, don't tell me you don't even know how the shooting competition works?'

'No. But I will when you kindly enlighten me.'

Viola tittered into her empty glass, then waved it at Lofthouse, looking rather tipsy. 'On the first day, the twenty-third, Lady Swift, we score a point for every clay pigeon hit. Bang, bang!'

Huish nodded. 'The four highest scorers go through to the next round the following day, Christmas Eve.'

Pearl licked her lips. 'And then the top two fight it out in the final round on Christmas Day, for the grand prize!'

'Which is?' Eleanor said.

Every jaw dropped. Taylor shook his head in disbelief again. 'My dear girl, you are priceless! Surely that's why you're here?'

'My dear sir,' she shot back, 'I'm here to enjoy Christmas at his grace's kind invitation. Nothing more.'

Taylor shrugged dismissively. 'Well, your chance of winning the five-minute audience with him looks slim then.'

'But best of luck, I'm sure,' Viola said with no conviction.

Eleanor was baffled. 'Five minutes with his grace is the grand prize?'

Huish peered at her intently. 'Of course! How else would one ask a favour from a duke? And one as powerful as the Duke of Auldwyke?'

Eleanor's bafflement increased. 'But if the duke has been a hermit for so long, how has he managed to retain such influence that he can grant favours worth fighting over?'

Taylor tapped the side of his nose. 'There are only around a dozen Dukes of England, as you should know, Lady Swift! And the majority of them are directly related to the royal family. Hence, even though the Duke of Auldwyke has been a recluse for some time, his stature and influence is still prodigious. Especially, as I've heard, he still involves himself to some extent in the world of power and politics by proxy.'

'Only,' Huish butted in, clearly irritated at Taylor stealing the conversation from him, 'with the grand prize, the duke's third rule comes into play!'

She frowned, vaguely remembering Porritt on the way from the station to Auldwyke Hall mentioning something about a 'third rule'. Quite frankly, she'd been so stunned by the first two, she'd put it out of her mind.

'The lucky devil who wins,' Huish continued, 'mustn't ever disclose what favour they've asked for or it won't be granted. But rumour has it that several of the elite of society owe their success to one of those favours.'

So that's how the duke entices his guests to give up their other Christmas invitations, Ellie. And how he lures them to come to this remote spot with all its ridiculous rules, when they won't even meet him unless they win his wretched competition.

She shook her head at her dessert of poached pears on a round of baked creamy cheese, topped with hazelnuts. The absent duke had set the stakes high. Very high indeed. High enough, in fact, for murder?

7

Within the first few minutes of meeting Constable Danby, his efficient manner had inspired Eleanor with confidence. As he stepped stiffly off his antiquated motorbike, his boyish face frostbitten, he'd replied politely but firmly to Lofthouse that he was there to do his professional best. And that did not include thawing out in the kitchen with a mug of tea first!

Introductions completed – and now with her thick wool coat and scarf covering her evening wear and boots replacing her satin heels – she led him to the threshold of the fatal storehouse. After unlocking the door with the key he'd got from Lofthouse, he slowly scanned the scene before stepping carefully inside. She assumed coming from such a rural location, his experience in matters of murder would be limited. Unless evil regularly stalked the deceptively festive-dressed moors, she thought with a grimace.

Dismissing that awful notion, she fought off shivers from the freezing damp air as she studied him in the yellow glow of the oil lantern he held up. The look of concentration in his sharp, blue eyes added to the intelligence his calm demeanour suggested. He nodded gratefully as she offered to hold the light.

'If as you're sure, m'lady? But a person who's gone over to the afterlife ain't a sight I'd choose for a lady to witness.'

'Hear, hear!' she caught Clifford mutter behind her.

'Mind,' Danby said, looking at her questioningly. 'You seem mighty calm in the face of such, m'lady?'

Clifford cleared his throat. 'Suffice to say, her ladyship is particularly astute in matters of... this nature.'

The constable seemed to fight a smile. 'I got a slice of that feeling from the off, Mr Clifford, if you'll pardon me saying so. And I'll not bandy bones, but admit it. I've only come across three bodies in my time around here. And each of those were on account of treacherous roads in winter. Still, I know the important thing is to get everything on paper as soon as possible.'

'Excellent,' she said hesitantly, overtaken by a horrible thought. Now that he was about to scrutinise Porritt's body, she was struck by how similar the policeman's broad accent was to the secretary's. And his age. Might they have gone to the same junior school and grown into long trousers together?

Clifford caught her coded look. 'Constable, I wonder if Mr Lofthouse mentioned the identity of the dead man when he telephoned your station?'

'It's more of a room, sir, being as I'm what you might call the rural police beat. But to answer you, yes, Mr Lofthouse did. Mr Porritt, he said. Poor fellow. Word in the village has always been that he worked hard all his days for his grace.'

'You didn't know Mr Porritt personally, then?' Eleanor said.

Constable Danby shook his head. 'We spoke a few times on the telephone when there was a right rumpus over some escaped sheep eating his grace's special roses. And on a few other minor occasions, that's all. Not surprisingly, since the duke is known for keeping fiercely to himself. In the three years since I arrived as an offcomer, I've had nothing serious occur here.' At Eleanor's puzzled look, he added, 'I'm from the nearest proper town, Kirkwell. Fifty-three miles north-west of the village. You'll find that's as good as coming from the moon to the locals.' He gave her a smile. 'So, thank you for thinking to check, but I'm not about to study the body of an old friend.'

She nodded in relief and followed in his slow and careful wake as he halted several times to make notes.

'Hmm. He doesn't seem to have fought anyone for his last breath since there's no sign of a struggle. And no broken glass from these crates. But this mark on his neck is troubling me.' He looked up at her. 'You as much as me, I think?'

She let out a sigh of relief. 'Yes, Constable.'

Danby rose nimbly. 'I don't rightly know what's gone on here, but I do know this lost soul needs a police van to take him to be measured up for his final suit. A wooden one,' he ended with quiet compassion. Clearing his throat, he continued. 'Anyhows, why Mr Porritt would be in here is odd enough. But clad in such a neatly brushed suit, odder still. These crates have got a year's worth of dust and cobwebs over them, which would have ended up over him if he'd come to carry any out. Added to that, I understood all the guests were waiting for him to restart the pre-shoot proceedings?'

'Actually, they were waiting for her ladyship,' Clifford said with a sideways glance at her.

She tutted. 'Hardly my fault, since I was busy trying to rouse poor Mr Porritt after what I thought then was just a fall.'

She waited until Danby had finished writing and closed his notebook before asking what was burning on her tongue.

'Tell me, when you spoke to his grace...' She tailed off at the constable's wide-eyed look.

'I've never spoken to him, m'lady! I didn't expect to either when I arrived here. No one down in the village has spoken to him since he became a recluse. I've seen him pass through in the back of his car, maybe a handful of times at a pinch. But the last time would have been over a year ago or more. Anything needed was handled by his staff, mostly through Mr Porritt here. I remember that last time his grace came through, I heard him coughing fit to bust in the back of that great big car of his. Someone told me he had breathing problems from some infection or other since he were a child.'

The sound of scuffed heavy steps just outside made her turn. Lofthouse hunched his tall form under the door frame.

'I've got a message from his grace, Constable. You are to do whatever needs be done re yon Porritt. As quick as possible. And all of it through me, as his grace's new secretary. Least-ways, as of this afternoon.'

Danby nodded. But standing beside him, Eleanor could sense his discomfort. Over what, she could guess only too easily. Evidently Clifford had noted it too as he stepped forward.

'Mr Lofthouse, perhaps I can save you the numbingly cold task of waiting for Constable Danby to finish here? And then further assist by escorting the gentleman inside to whichever room with a lit fire and more conducive lighting you deem best suited for him to check his notes in?'

'Not a bad offer, Mr Clifford,' Lofthouse conceded readily. He stared avidly upwards, as if mentally walking through the house. 'I should say the small gallery, two doors along from the billiard room I'll go back and do the important work of attendin' to the guests.'

As the footman's footsteps retreated, Danby let out a quiet sigh, which instantly frosted into a white plume. With the onset of the evening, the temperature had been dropping rapidly. Something Eleanor's numb feet had been groaning at for the last half an hour.

'Thank you, Mr Clifford,' Danby said. 'Not that I'm one to ever shirk my official responsibilities.' He shuddered slightly. 'And asking questions of the guests is obviously needed. But they're gentry! And guests of the duke! Crumbs! Like them, his grace is bound to see it as if I'm accusing them of murder!'

Eleanor smiled encouragingly. 'Well, you can start with me.

I've got a title, so I suppose I'm gentry. And if I go first, I'll be able to head off any complaints from the other guests by extolling at length how impartial and courteous you were?'

'That's mighty kind, m'lady,' Danby said. 'But as a policeman, I shouldn't have need of a lady coming to my rescue.' He glanced over at Clifford. 'Though somehow I get the feeling I'll more likely need rescuing from the lady if I don't swallow my pride?'

Clifford's eyes twinkled. 'I should say only if you wish to greet the New Year with your head still attached, Constable.'

Eleanor was still smiling at her butler's mischievous humour as he gestured her through an arched side door which led into the grand house from the snow-covered garden.

'Oh, that's better!' she said in relief, noting Danby nodding too. Despite the lack of heating, the octagonal stone-floored vestibule still felt markedly warmer than the bitter cold of the storehouse they had locked before leaving.

She pointed through the glass-paned door ahead. 'That way, along that old red carpet, is it, Clifford?'

He looked aghast. 'This is Auldwyke Hall, my lady. The mulberry runner is, in fact, an original Wilton carpet of the finest wool.'

She tutted as she took off her coat and scarf. 'I'm sure it is. But at the moment, that's hardly material!'

He sniffed. 'If you say so, my lady. Though, in the early seventeen hundreds, the ninth Earl of Pembroke felt it important enough to smuggle two Huguenot weavers out of the French court to teach their craftsmanship to their English counterparts in Wilton.'

'Meaning, my infallible encyclopaedia on legs?' She followed his gaze down to her snow- and dirt-covered boots and then over to the boot scraper where the constable was cleaning the last from his. 'Gracious, hold your horses, Clifford. I can't tramp all this muck through the duke's house! What were you thinking?'

She took her turn at the boot scraper as Clifford looked on with a raised eyebrow.

Clifford's seemingly uncanny mastering of the house's layout led them through a warren of dark, vaulted passageways until he paused at one door. It was even more ornate than the others they had passed and emblazoned in the centre was what she took to be the Auldwyke family coat of arms.

'The Ashley Room, my lady.'

The room beyond was sumptuously appointed in silver and blue silk, yet it felt forlorn, to her mind. The many panels of its high ceiling were each painted with a portrait of what she assumed were the previous dukes throughout the Auldwykes' evidently long history. The heavy gilt-framed rogues' gallery of more ducal portraits gracing the elegantly clad damask walls gave her the feeling she was being scrutinised by the family ghosts of time immemorial. At least a few paintings were of the children of the various dukes, she assumed, although all bore equally serious expressions, befitting their station in life. One portrait showed what looked like a bespectacled young man in his early twenties studiously reading. Even though he was seated, his confident poise and aristocratic features left no doubt even third cousins or whatever he was were cut from the same Auldwyke mould.

Without warning, she shivered violently.

8

'My lady.' Clifford's concerned voice cut into Eleanor's befuddled brain. 'You must have caught a chill.' He indicated two deep-buttoned chairs. 'Please sit while I tend to the fire.'

Nodding gratefully, she did so.

Pull yourself together, Ellie. It's no time to have a fit of the vapours.

Satisfied the flames he had rekindled would stay alight, Clifford stood up.

'I shall return with warming refreshments in but a minute, my lady.'

He glided from the room. Yanking her boots off and sliding her stockinged feet out to wiggle her toes in the warmth of the dancing flames, she realised Danby was hovering behind her. She smiled, appreciating his chivalry.

'Do come grab a seat by the fire, Constable.'

Instead of joining her, he sat on a stiff-backed wooden settle further away.

'Clifford won't actually bite you if you sit closer to me, I promise.' She patted the other chair.

With a bashful nod, he joined her and perched on the seat's edge, flipping open his notebook as he did so.

'Thank you, m'lady. It'll only be a few routine questions.'

There's nothing routine about murder, Ellie!

After he'd noted her name and address, and studiously looked away on asking her date of birth, he tapped his page. 'If you'd be so kind as to start from when you first met Mr Porritt?'

With her best effort at brevity, she took him through the pertinent facts. From meeting the duke's secretary at the railway station where he'd collected her and her staff, through to the moment she'd realised he was dead.

'That all being within an hour and a half, I think, of meeting the poor man.' She sighed for a life lost.

Danby looked up from his notes. 'I'm sorry you had to be the one to find Mr Porritt, m'lady.'

She shook her head. 'Actually, that unwanted honour falls to my dog, Gladstone.'

'Ah, bloodhound, is he? Fine nose on him, I imagine?'

'Being an overindulged bulldog, with a nose usually only for sausages, Constable,' Clifford said drily, having returned. He stepped back over with a silver tray bearing a steaming teapot and a tiered stand of decorated petit fours.

'Lucky chap. Where is he now?' Danby said.

She pointed towards the window. 'In the old gamekeeper's cottage with the four ladies of my staff.'

'And her ladyship's equally incorrigible tomcat,' Clifford added.

Danby was clearly trying to be professional enough not to show his amusement. 'Pets can lean towards the wayward at times.'

Eleanor laughed. 'Your first assumption was correct, Constable. Clifford was referring to my staff.'

Danby hastily turned his chuckle into a cough. 'So your staff are here as well?'

She nodded. 'Only my gardener and gamekeeper-cum-security guard stayed behind. They don't travel well. And I had to come without darling Kofi, too. He's Clifford's ward. He's spending his first English Christmas with his new best friend from boarding school.'

She didn't miss the wistful look that crossed her butler's face at the mention of the remarkable eleven-year-old Gold Coast boy he had recently taken guardianship of.

'He'll be missing you as much as you are him,' she whispered to Clifford.

Danby looked up from his notebook. 'Can we move on to how you know the duke, please?'

She held her hands up. 'I don't, ridiculously. And it feels even more bizarre now, sitting here, as I couldn't pick him out from among those portraits since I still haven't met him. There was a frightful mix-up, you see. I received an invitation to be a guest at his Christmas shooting party. But I sent the RSVP back saying I wouldn't be attending. I didn't want to appear rude, but I'd never heard of him before and I'm not really into shooting. Although, in truth, it was mostly because I had already made other, very special, plans.'

Danby rubbed his chin with his pencil. 'Yet here you are, m'lady?'

'I know,' she moaned. 'Mr Porritt telephoned me, you see, asking so earnestly what time my fiancé and I would be arriving. Naturally, I felt terrible!'

Danby's brow furrowed. 'Going back a step if you would. Your fiancé's here too? Over with your, er... wayward staff?'

'Fortunately for the gentleman, no,' Clifford said quickly, running his finger around his starched collar. 'Her ladyship's betrothed will arrive tomorrow.'

She smiled. 'The real mystery about the invitation though, Constable, is how the duke even knew I have a fiancé? That he knows I exist at all is confusing enough.'

'So, Mr Porritt never received your reply, is that it?' Danby looked from one to the other.

Eleanor winced. 'Yes. That's why he was so upset on the telephone when I told him I'd declined. I assumed it was my mistake because, well, high society socialising isn't my absolute forte.'

'Ever the mistress of understatement,' Clifford murmured. He tutted pointedly at her lack of boots and turned to Danby.

'In essence, her ladyship's good nature was ambushed by Mr Porritt's plea that his grace's shooting party would be two guests short. And the consequences for Mr Porritt would be anything but festive. Apparently, the annual Christmas shoot is the only event his grace has continued to hold since becoming a recluse, so Mr Lofthouse informed me.'

'And nothing is allowed to spoil it, I got the strong feeling from Mr Porritt's plaintive pleas,' she added. 'And he was so apologetic, bless him. Saying he should have telephoned to confirm earlier, but with all the preparations, somehow it had slipped his mind. Honestly, having met the poor fellow, albeit briefly, he seemed such a nervous young man. No wonder he agreed to my one caveat and arranged for an estate cottage to be free for my staff.' She smiled at Danby. 'All clear?'

'As the moors when t' fog's lifted,' the young policeman replied, a smile playing around his lips. 'So, because of the mix-up with your reply to the duke's invitation, you arrived later than the other guests?'

'Yes. I believe they all arrived early this morning.'

'And when exactly is your fiancé arriving, then?'

'Probably at rude o'clock tomorrow,' she said, feeling sorry for her permanently overworked beau.

Danby glanced bemusedly at Clifford. 'You must have different timepieces down south. Rude o'clock, sir?'

'The mythical time when breakfast is not served for at least another four to five hours. I say "mythical" as her ladyship has yet to see a clock registering such a time.'

Danby smiled again. 'I'll note that as "lark's early", as we say in these parts. Now, Lady Swift, may I take a note of your fiancé's name and profession, please?'

'Of course. Hugh Seldon. He's a detective chief inspector with Scotland Yard.'

'Is he, by crumbs!' Wide-eyed, Danby noted that down.

'It's alright to be secretly surprised at a titled lady snaring a policeman,' she said with a smile. 'It's not the usual way of things, I know.'

Before Danby could reply, a loud knock sounded on the door. Lofthouse loomed into the room. He frowned as he looked at Eleanor.

'Pardon for interruptin', m'lady. I thought only the constable were in here.'

Danby leaped up. 'What is it, Mr Lofthouse?'

'Telephone call. For you. From t' main police station at Kirkwell. You can take it in t' billiard room just along there.' He gestured right out of the door as he disappeared through it.

Danby put away his notebook. 'That's grand news. If you'll excuse me, m'lady?'

'Of course. But how did your superiors know you were here?'

'The moment I finished speaking to Mr Lofthouse I telephoned to say a person had died at Auldwyke Hall, his grace's residence. That's not summat to act on without letting my superiors know immediately.'

She nodded, thinking he was every inch the prudent policeman.

Alone with Clifford, she picked up a sweet treat. 'Poor fellow, all this happening at the duke's house must be very nerve-wracking for him.'

'Yet, he is valiantly doing his duty in the face of it,' Clifford said, determinedly holding a plate underneath her.

She winced. 'Sorry. I forgot. No Gladstone to snuffle up the crumbs before they reach the floor.' She devoured the whole treat in one bite, to her butler's silent horror. She stood and, stepping along the line of portraits, she studied each in turn.

'I wonder if it runs in the family?'

'What, my lady?'

'Not wanting to be disrespectful, but the duke's idiosyncrasies? They strike me as bordering on the... oh, what's the word, Clifford?'

'I do not know, my lady, but I imagine it is unrepeatable.'

Before she could think up a suitable witty reply, Danby returned.

'Good news?' she said hopefully.

He grimaced. 'Um, not exactly. It seems there are no senior officers immediately free to attend to Mr Porritt's death.' At her disbelieving look, he hurried on. 'Things do heat up around Christmas in Kirkwell and the surrounding villages and—'

She raised her hand. 'It's because of the duke, isn't it? No one wants to deal with him, do they?'

Danby's eyes flicked to the door. 'Perhaps you'd be kind enough to talk to my superior? He's waiting on the telephone to speak to you.'

Shooting Clifford a baffled look, she shrugged. 'Alright, but I can't think what good that will do.'

A moment later, much to her butler's evident horror, she was perched on the edge of the billiard table, swinging her stockinged feet.

'Hello? Lady Swift here,' she said into the telephone's mouthpiece.

'Ah, good day, m'lady,' a deep voice rumbled down the line. 'Superintendent Barker here. Good of you to hear me out on this matter.' She held the handset away from her ear with a frown.

'About what? The disgraceful fact that none of your officers are brave enough to deal with a mere duke?'

Clifford pinched the bridge of his nose. 'There's nothing "mere" about the highest honorific title in all of England,' he murmured.

She flapped a hand and risked pressing the earpiece closer again. 'What's that? There's simply no suitable officer free? And my fiancé will be...' She jerked so hard, she slid off the billiard table. 'What about my fiancé?'

Superintendent Barker cleared his throat loudly in her ear. 'Well, Constable Danby informed me he is Detective Chief Inspector Seldon of Scotland Yard, m'lady. And given that this incident occurred on the Duke of Auldwyke's estate, it is most likely that we would have called in the Yard, anyway. So, with your fiancé being set to arrive early tomorrow, I believe, he'll be on the scene quicker than any man I could muster.'

She gritted her teeth. 'Maybe. But Chief Inspector Seldon will also be on holiday!'

'With a murder having occurred in the very house he is staying in? A policeman whose dedication to duty and sterling reputation has travelled as far north as Yorkshire and beyond?'

She had to force her gaping jaw closed before she could speak again. 'You're actually asking me if he will take the case? But I can't contact him. He'll have set off to drive up by now, as you clearly know.' She couldn't temper her frosty tone. 'So, in essence, you're asking me to decide for him?'

Superintendent Barker confirmed he was.

She shared a helpless shrug with Clifford. 'Alright, Superintendent, I agree on his behalf. If, that is, you contact his office and they also agree. In that instance, then he will take the case, I am sure.'

She replaced the handset and groaned. 'Oh, Clifford! Not

only has our supposedly romantic Christmas become a crime scene, but now Hugh will arrive, exhausted from having driven most of the night through perilous snow, to find I've—'

'Appointed him the lead in the most unfestive role imaginable?' He winced. 'Still, chin up, my lady.' He held his hands out. 'There can't be any more disagreeable surprises this Christmas, can there?'

9

Eleanor had never been more grateful for her staff. Sliding into the snug window seat behind the table in the kitchen of the old gamekeeper's cottage, she beamed at her ladies' chirpy welcome. Along with her clearly overexcited bulldog and tomcat, they really were the perfect remedy for the tragic events of the last few hours.

She smiled and leaned back as opposite her Clifford engaged in a tug-of-war with Tomkins for the fringed ends of his smart grey scarf.

Over at the range, Mrs Trotman checked whatever culinary delight was taking shape in the oven. And then returned to the preparation table to resume working her magic with two mixing bowls at once. No mean feat, Eleanor mused, since one was being mixed, the other whipped. Next to her, Lizzie was bent over a pad of paper, using the cleared end of the middle wooden shelf as a writing table. Mrs Butters perched on a stool, sorting through a large holdall of wool, while Polly skipped in, dragging a patched pillowcase behind her. Sitting cross-legged on the floor, she rummaged inside, cooing to herself. Gladstone eagerly assisted by pushing his head into the pillowcase too, doubtless looking for treats.

Eleanor was worried by their collective industriousness. 'Ladies, you have remembered you're supposed to be on holiday?'

'Yes, m'lady,' Mrs Trotman said. 'And the best kind. Christmas!' She waved her whisk.

'All together on another holiday! 'Tis a wonder,' Polly breathed, wide-eyed with delight.

Eleanor looked earnest. 'Well, I hope you can have as wonderful a break here as you would have had back at Henley Hall?'

They all nodded vigorously. 'In this darling wee cottage, how could we nae, m'lady?' Lizzie said emphatically.

Eleanor smiled, reflecting that even stepping through the front door, it already felt more festive here than at Auldwyke Hall itself, despite the grand decorations in the main house.

But then a murder does rather affect the atmosphere, Ellie.

'And the cottage is less "wee" than it looks,' Mrs Butters said. 'There's two bedrooms, perfect for the four of us. And a sitting room with a proper bench table along the back wall. And a fireplace, tucked around the corner.' She pointed down the small passageway. 'So we can stay toasty. And even a box room too.'

Mrs Trotman threw Clifford a cheeky glance. 'Shall we make it up ready, in case you fancy moving in here with us women, Mr Clifford?'

He shuddered. 'Rest assured, ladies, a snow-filled ditch on the moors holds more appeal.' Over Mrs Trotman's huff, he held up a finger, and continued, 'Than spoiling your treat of being trusted to behave unsupervised.'

'Fibber!' Eleanor whispered to him. A thought struck her. 'Hang on, though. I insisted you have plenty of firewood supplied, so why are you all squashed in the kitchen?'

Lizzie laughed. 'We're all that excited to be up here together, m'lady, we've not stopped gabbing to each other!'

Mrs Trotman nodded. 'Being in different rooms wouldn't be at all the same.'

Eleanor's heart swelled with affection at the genuine camaraderie her staff enjoyed.

'Well, I'm impressed at how organised you all are already. We only arrived at the Auldwyke estate how long ago, Clifford?'

He glanced at his pocket watch. 'But five hours and eleven minutes ago, my lady.'

'All of which have been spent tangled in poor Porritt's murder,' she murmured before she could halt her tongue.

Clifford leaned down to lay out a quilted blanket beside her for Gladstone and Tomkins, who were jostling for space on her lap.

She realised the ladies had stopped what they were doing and were gathered at the range. In a blink, the table was set with a generous late supper for six, the centrepiece a platter of Christmas-themed gingerbread biscuits.

Finding it hard to choose what to start with, Eleanor gently batted her pets' pilfering paws out of the way and finally selected a cherry-nosed reindeer with chocolate wellington boots.

'Perhaps, ladies,' Clifford said, 'you might tell her ladyship what plans you've all so efficiently made for your time here?'

'Only the ones that won't make Clifford blush, though,' Eleanor whispered with a wink, rousing more giggles from her staff.

He rolled his eyes good-naturedly. 'Five against one already, I see.'

'Start as we mean to go on, I say.' She picked up the liquorice bowler-hatted gingerbread man, its resemblance to her butler no coincidence, she thought, and waggled it at him.

'Polly, please come to my rescue,' he said in pretend desperation.

''Tis so excitin', sir! We're each in charge of a different compartment!' Polly cheered.

Eleanor peeped over the young girl's shoulder, wondering what kind of chest of drawers or bureau among the otherwise functional furniture she'd missed.

Mrs Butters reached around to cup the maid's chin. 'She means "*de*partment", m'lady.'

'Oh, I see! Do tell.'

Clifford insisted he would play mother with the teapot so the ladies could each speak in turn.

'I'm the Entertainment Elf,' Lizzie said with a giggle, starting them all off. 'Ach, I've a loch's-worth of my grandmother's favourite Scottish Christmas games planned. That'll be totally fun for the others.'

'So we'll learn new things, too.' Polly nudged her friend excitedly. 'And I'm the Festive Fairy, your ladyship. Meanin' I'm to say what's what with all the decorations! I've never been in charge of anythin' afore.'

Eleanor was thrilled for her young maid. 'And a fabulous job you'll do, Polly. Please book me in for a Christmas Decorations Tour of the cottage the minute you've finished.'

Polly nodded so hard she tipped sideways into Mrs Butters, who beamed at Eleanor. 'M'lady, you've an open invitation night and day.'

Eleanor's cook rose to take a cheeky bow. 'And I'm the Noshings Nymph. Food and drinks, mind.'

'And I'm the Sergeant Sprite,' Mrs Butters chuckled. 'Because it's my job to stop Trotters from soaking all her fancy nymph noshings with too much booze!'

'There's the lustre gone from the open invitation then, my lady,' Clifford said playfully.

A knock sounded at the front door.

Lizzie trotted into the hallway and reappeared a few moments later, her cheeks flushed, Eleanor noted.

'Who is it?'

Her maid glanced towards the door, her eyes animated. 'A policeman, m'lady. Says his name's Constable Danby.'

Mrs Trotman poked Mrs Butters in the ribs. 'Ooh, a man in uniform can knock on my door any day!'

Clifford tutted. 'Ahem! Please show the constable in, Lizzie.'

A moment later, Danby followed Lizzie into the kitchen, turning his helmet in his hands. Red-nosed and shoulders dusted with snow, he seemed tickled by something. Then she realised. She was supposed to be a titled lady. And yet here she was, ensconced with her staff in the kitchen, munching a gingerbread chimney, complete with Father Christmas' legs and chocolate boots poking out of the top. She waved the remains of the biscuit.

'You've caught me red-handed, Constable.'

Danby hid a smile. ''Scuse me interrupting, m'lady, but Mr Clifford mentioned as you'd likely be here. And this young lady did say as it'd be alright to come in.' He threw Lizzie a shy glance, then bowled backwards as Gladstone launched himself up the policeman's legs, tongue flailing. 'Ah, the sausage monster, so I've heard. How do, sir?'

Eleanor winced. 'Apologies for my unruly bulldog. He decided some time ago he's above adhering to any kind of rules.'

'Most odd. One wonders where he got the idea.' Clifford glanced mischievously at her.

'Very droll,' she said, enjoying the others' laughter. 'Now, Constable, what can I do for you?'

The young policeman waved his hand. 'Oh crumbs, nowt, m'lady. You've more than helped enough. And mighty grateful I am, too. No, I thought as I ought to come tell you I've done all I can. Including' – he swallowed hard – 'telling the duke's guests about Mr Porritt being...' He hesitated, glancing in concern around the ladies.

Mrs Butters patted his arm. ''Tis alright, young sir. Her ladyship told us the poor fellow had passed. And he might even have been up and done for.'

Danby looked relieved.

'How did the guests take the news?' Eleanor said.

'As well as could be expected from gentry folk being told by a whippersnapper of a rural copper, m'lady. Especially the part about none of them being allowed to leave until further notice.' He cringed. 'It was just as well it wasn't my place to question any one of them. I'd have been fighting my ears getting boxed good and proper, and no mistake.'

Eleanor felt sorry for the dutiful young man, who clearly wanted nothing more than to be worthy of his uniform. 'How much did you tell them?'

'Only as the circumstances in which Mr Porritt died were suspicious and being looked into. And that a senior officer would put them straight on the details in the morning. I didn't want to queer the chief inspector's pitch, so I hope as I did the right thing?'

'Most assuredly, you did,' Clifford said.

'Thank you, sir. And I'll come back up tomorrow with the coroner's van. So, unless I can do owt for you, m'lady, I'll bid you all good evening and slide my way down to the village?'

'Oh gracious! I forgot you're on your motorbike. In the dark and in this weather!' Eleanor said. 'Then, actually, yes, Constable, there is something you can do first.'

He nodded brightly. 'Anything at all.'

'Excellent. Then come and sit down over here. And warm up with lashings of tea and some of these sublime gingerbread fellows. Whatever happens over the next few days, I promise you'll always find it's Christmas in the old gamekeeper's cottage!'

10

Danby looked stunned as her ladies leaped up, the maids scurrying for an extra cup and plate, and Mrs Trotman setting the kettle to boil again. As Mrs Butters ushered him into the seat opposite Eleanor, he smiled. 'Mighty kind, if as you're sure?'

She nodded as, over his shoulder, she caught her cook bumping her hip against a still flushed-looking Lizzie's.

Furnished with a generous mug of tea, Danby wrapped his hands around it and took a grateful glug, dodging Tomkins' white-tipped tail from tickling his nose.

'Dig in.' Eleanor pushed the gingerbread selection towards him. 'They're all the expert handiwork of our Noshings Nymph.'

Danby spluttered into his tea.

'As in Mrs Trotman, her ladyship's cook,' Clifford said, shaking his head.

'Is this always the way of things with Lady Swift, Mr Clifford?' Danby whispered, not quietly enough to be missed by Eleanor's sharp hearing.

'Good gracious, no. Only almost always,' her butler said drily.

'Ah! Much like getting mixed up in bother, perhaps?'

Eleanor shrugged. 'I can't deny it. I seem to have a strange knack for being in entirely the wrong place at the wrong time. But to answer your chivalrously unspoken question, Constable, no, this isn't the first murder I've come across.'

'By a worrying large margin, regrettably,' Clifford added.

'True. Although poor Porritt's must be one of the swiftest dispatches of a victim we've encountered?'

'Indubitably, my lady. Within the eighteen-minute window between twenty past three and twenty-two minutes to four.'

Mrs Trotman slid a mound of hot buttered toast spread with potted meat in front of the disbelieving policeman. 'Well, Constable, least you can be sure us four aprons was here in the cottage all of that time. Our driver must have pulled up at the door afore even her ladyship's did at the main house, I reckon.'

'And we ne'er left and havenae since. Not once.' Lizzie slid her arm into Polly's.

Danby finished savouring a mouthful of toast and deftly whipped his plate out of reach of Tomkins' thieving paw. 'Not to fret, ladies. I'm sure there's no suspicion on any of you.'

'Absolutely not!' Eleanor said. 'But as for everyone else, we've no idea. And won't until Hugh arrives and takes charge.'

Mrs Butters gasped. 'Beg pardon, m'lady. But say it isn't so for the chief inspector?'

Eleanor shared a guilty glance with Clifford. 'He is. Only he doesn't know yet. Poor Hugh, at this moment, he'll be driving up in blissful ignorance, thinking he's about to start a relaxing and unspeakably long-overdue break away from anything to do with murder.'

''Tis just as unfair on you, m'lady,' Lizzie said firmly.

Mrs Trotman nodded emphatically. 'Seeing as his dukeness

poked a fork right in the balloon of your special Christmas plans together.'

Mrs Butters nudged her in the arm. 'Hush, Trotters. Nobody can ruin Christmas. 'Tis the rules.'

Clifford nodded. 'Well said!'

'And not to worry, m'lady,' Mrs Butters continued. 'Us four won't breathe a hint of anything to the chief inspector until you've found a way to break the news.'

Eleanor smiled gratefully. 'Thank you. I still can't believe I've signed Hugh up for this hideous surprise when he thinks he's coming down here for a relaxing, romantic Christmas. My only sweetener for him is that I've had a chance to observe the guests, which might give him a small head start with the investigation.'

Danby pulled out his notebook. 'If it helps, I've not asked anybody for their alibi as Mr Porritt's death hasn't officially been classed as suspicious, as yet. Nor had a chance to write up anything like a report, but you're welcome to take all the jottings I've made so far. Seeing as I'll not be back until the coroner's van brings me tomorrow morning.'

'Brilliant.' Eleanor hid a smile as Clifford quickly produced the miniature fold-out scissors on his pocketknife so Danby could neatly snip the pages free, instead of tearing them out. 'I've obviously met the guests, but have no real idea who may or may not have an alibi yet, dash it!'

'Actually,' Clifford said, 'we do know of a few reliable alibis besides the ladies.'

'We do?' Eleanor and Danby chorused.

Clifford nodded. 'Yes. For the majority of his grace's staff, in fact. Almost all of them were partaking of a brief break before preparing dinner. I was in the kitchen with them, heating her ladyship's handwarmers, ready for the pre-shoot proceedings.'

'Grand. Then, who was missing?' Danby said.

'Let me be certain.' Clifford looked thoughtful. His forefinger twitched across the tabletop as if he was drawing out the kitchen and who was where. 'Mr Lofthouse, the first footman, was absent. As was Mr Bowes, the gardener, for most of the time. He returned to collect Mr Fripp, the under-gardener, and Tosh, the lad-of-all-works, just before I myself went in search of her ladyship. But all the other staff were there for the duration.'

Danby coughed politely. 'Actually, if as I might read the names of the guests out to you, my lady, seeing as my writing is a little illegible, like?'

She shook her head. 'If you want. But, in truth, it looks almost as infuriatingly neat and methodical as my butler's.'

Danby leaned over and leafed through his snipped-out pages. Taking one, he patted the others back into a neat pile. She took Clifford's proffered fountain pen and opened her notebook. 'I'm ready, Constable.'

As he called them out, she wrote each name down:

Lord Augustus Craven, Duke of Auldwyke (no alibi known at moment)

Mr Barnabas Musgrave, Esquire, & Mrs Viola Musgrave – Guests (no alibi known at moment)

Mr Julius Huish – Guest (no alibi known at moment)

Mr Willoughby Taylor – Guest (no alibi known at moment)

Miss Pearl Whitwell – Guest (no alibi known at moment)

As she thanked him, Danby rose. 'Must be going, my lady. It will be a slow ride back, I warrant.'

'Lizzie, please show Constable Danby out,' Clifford said.

Eleanor thanked him again, and he left the room with the ladies' exhortations to be careful on 'that there icy road', a delectable-looking meat pie carefully wrapped for his supper under his arm.

Once he'd gone, Clifford peered over her shoulder and sniffed disapprovingly.

'Hugh is quite used to my spidery writing, thank you!' she huffed.

'It is not that, my lady. Well, not entirely. I was thinking more that once the chief inspector arrives, there will be seven for dinner at Auldwyke Hall. Most irregular to have an odd number.'

'Clifford, everything about the duke is irregular! For instance, I haven't even met him and yet he's supposed to be my host. Now.' She tapped the page. 'How about you list the staff next?'

He nodded, and she wrote them down as he recited them:

Tim Lofthouse – First Footman (no alibi known at moment)

Amos Bowes – Gardener (no alibi known at moment)

Judd Fripp – Under-gardener (alibi – in kitchen until Amos Bowes collected him just before body found – Clifford witnessed)

Tosh – Lad-of-all-work (alibi – as Fripp)

Housekeeper – (alibi – in kitchen – Clifford witnessed)

Cook – (alibi – as housekeeper)

Maids – (alibi – as housekeeper)

She added one more line for completeness:

My ladies – (alibi – all alibi each other as in the old gamekeeper's cottage setting it up for Christmas until I appeared with
news Porritt dead)

She stared at the list. 'It's a start for Hugh, I suppose.' She
ran her finger under the duke's name. 'Have you learned
anything about our mysterious host from eavesdropping on the
staff's chatter, Clifford?'

He raised a brow. 'Eavesdropping? Tsk! I am a butler, my
lady.' He leaned in. 'Thus, I might have made a few discreet
enquiries instead.'

'Good man. And?'

'Apparently, his grace used to be a great socialite, regularly
entertaining at all of his grand houses which are spread across
the country. However, he became a recluse overnight. To the
point of closing up all mansions, except Auldwyke Hall here,
where he has remained ever since.'

'Gracious, what triggered such an extreme change of
character?'

'The death of his wife, my lady,' he said sombrely. 'Evidently, the duchess was killed in a tragic accident at a
Christmas shooting party here at Auldwyke. It was she who
held the love of shooting. Though, the events themselves were
changed in the first year following the duchess' death. From
game shooting across the estate, to clay pigeon shooting from the
purpose-installed platform beyond the west terrace. And his
grace invites only a few select guests. But never attends himself.
That is all I can impart, my lady. To their credit, the staff are
very tight-lipped. It was made abundantly clear his grace does
not like his business to be discussed. Most particularly not with
outsiders.'

She groaned. 'Poor Hugh. That's not going to make his job
of uncovering the murderer any easier!'

11

The following morning, Eleanor's bedside clock yawned that it wasn't even five. But she was already wide awake, fretting over the wretched news she needed to deliver to her fiancé. A familiar tap at the door let her know she'd run out of time. Wrenching back the covers, she jumped out of bed to find her butler in the corridor, facing the other way, holding her moss-green wool coat.

'Amazingly, I'm fully dressed, thank you, Mr Chivalrous.' She winced. 'Dash it, though, Clifford. I can't imagine Hugh is in the best of moods having driven all night?'

He turned around. 'I really couldn't say, my lady. Since the gentleman has yet to arrive.' Without venturing over the threshold, he patted his leg to coax Gladstone out of bed.

She frowned. 'Then why knock for me?'

'Because he will be soon. Constable Danby was most accommodating in helping us to intercept the chief inspector.' He held her coat out until she slid into it.

'Intercepting, Clifford?'

He scooped the snoozy bulldog up, still half-swathed in his quilted blanket. 'My lady, Chief Inspector Seldon is many

admirable things, but at ease in the grand mansion of a duke is
not one of them. The gamekeeper's cottage, however...' He left
that hanging.

His thoughtful plan made her heart swell with affection.
'Oh, Clifford, you're wonderful! To try and smooth the way for
me with Hugh, you asked Danby yesterday to telephone you
here when he saw Hugh's black Crossley motor car pass
through the village, didn't you? So we could pounce on him
before he got to the main house?'

'Perhaps, my lady. However, if I might be excused the indignity of pouncing on anything? At least before dawn?'

A few minutes later, she was scanning the dark, breathing
plumes of frozen breath through her pulled up scarf. The wind
had dropped, but it was bitterly cold. The snow had also
stopped, but what had fallen through the night had crusted with
patches of ice. She was armed with the lantern as Clifford was
hampered by holding her still snoring bulldog in his arms.

Despite the cold, it seemed no time at all before she spotted
the telltale beam of a car's headlights picking out a slow route
along the steep and slippery drive. She skated unsteadily
forward, waving the lantern, semaphoring with her other arm.

Seldon's car came to a stop, gently sliding the last few feet.
His head of chestnut curls poked out of the driver's window, his
deep voice rumbling out into the frozen air.

'Eleanor, you'll catch pneumonia!'

She slipped her way around to his door and rubbed her
frost-red nose on his. 'Morning, Hugh. Gracious, you look
terrible and dashingly dishevelled at the same time.'

'Thank you. I think.' His exhausted but still far too handsome face split into an awkward smile. 'It's good to see you too,
Eleanor. But clearly, I need to have strong words with Clifford.'

'What for?'

'For letting you do whatever you've done! Which must be
something truly terrible for you to be up at this horrible hour.

Normally you only surface when Clifford informs you through your door for the third time that "breakfast cannot be taken just before lunch, my lady".'

She feigned virtuous horror. 'Why, Mr Seldon! I had no idea the two of you regularly discussed my bedroom habits.'

His cheeks coloured. 'What! I... Blast it, Eleanor, I wouldn't ever think of doing so!'

She laughed. 'Shame. But come and tell me off somewhere warmer.'

He smiled. 'Hmm, you're not off the hook yet. But it was a lovely welcome all the same.' He checked Clifford had turned his back and then brushed his lips over hers with a quiet sigh of delight.

'You can turn around now, Clifford,' she said reluctantly, realising Gladstone had started to wriggle in her butler's arms, having been roused by the voice of his favourite policeman.

'Good morning, Chief Inspector.' Clifford stepped carefully up to the driver's window. 'If I might be so bold as to suggest you accompany her ladyship and miscreant bulldog, while I park your car in the stable block? Being, as I am, more familiar with the capriciousness of the icy slope from here to there?'

Seldon slid his long legs out stiffly and stretched his arms above his head. 'That's good of you, Clifford, thanks. Although I get this terror in exchange, I see. Morning, old chum.' He took Gladstone, who was still wrapped in his quilted blanket, from Clifford. Then grimaced at the bulldog's sloppy lick. 'Agh! Every time!'

Eleanor laughed. 'That's deep and devoted love, Hugh.'

'Well, don't you get any of those ideas,' he said jokingly. 'Even though it is Christmas. And it's going to be the best one ever. Because we're finally going to spend the holiday season together.'

She winced. 'Y-e-s. Umm, this way, Hugh.'

At the gate to the gamekeeper's cottage, he looked at her in confusion. 'Not quite the daunting castle I've been dreading?'

'I'll explain later,' she said airily, leading the way to the front door.

Inside, despite the early hour, the cottage's kitchen was wonderfully warm. The table was set for breakfast, a pot of tea warmed on the stove top, and her four ladies were nowhere to be seen.

Seldon laid Gladstone beside Tomkins in their cosy bed and gave the drowsy tomcat a soft ear tickle. He helped Eleanor out of her coat, then shrugged out of his before hanging them on the wooden pegs on either side of the range.

'Right, yes. Ah, tea first!' She fumbled for two mugs on the shelf. Seldon's muscular arms slid through hers from behind and took them from her hands.

'Eleanor, what is it?'

'Ah, it's a marvellous hot drink, made from leaves grown in Ceylon and India mainly...' She tailed off as he turned her gently to face him.

'I mean, what have you done?'

She grimaced. 'Something unthinkable, Hugh. I'm *so* sorry.'

He shrugged. 'Well, whatever it is, you will still be the Lady Swift who captured my heart. So, can we get it over with? It's been a long night.'

She led him to the table by his hand and pressed him onto the window seat beside her. 'It started with the body, you see.'

He groaned. 'Eleanor, tell me I'm just remembering an old nightmare, please? And you're not telling me someone has actually died?'

She winced. 'Do you want me to also fib and say it wasn't within half an hour of me arriving? And that I wasn't the one who found him? And that it isn't—?'

Her last words were lost in the soft wool of his jacket as he pulled her tight to his chest.

'Not again, my love,' he moaned softly into her fiery red curls. 'I can't bear that you saw something so awful. And that I wasn't here to comfort you.' He leaned back and sighed. 'How can I ever hope to be a proper husband to you, Eleanor? Even your dutifully protective butler can't keep you out of trouble. And he's with you all the time!'

'Poor fellow.' She ran her fingertips over his palm. 'But, Hugh, I'm fine, really. Unlike Mr Porritt. Who was murdered.'

Seldon stiffened. 'Murdered? You're sure?'

'I'm positive. I think he was strangled. Clifford agrees. But there's no coroner's report yet because the van hasn't collected the body. And it won't until later this morning. Which is the good news... the only good news.'

Seldon rubbed his hands over his lean cheeks as he jumped up. 'You're right. It is! Because it means I can bundle you into my car and drive you away from witnessing any more awfulness. We're leaving. Right now!'

She slid off the seat, and stepped up to the range.

Time to confess, Ellie.

12

Eleanor took a deep breath. 'We can't, Hugh. For... for several reasons.'

Seldon shook his head vehemently. 'Blast the reasons! And the duke and rules of etiquette and all that. I'm not backing down on this for once.'

'Hugh—'

He rose and strode over to her. 'And I will personally bundle your ladies into the back of my car as well wherever they're hiding at the moment. And they can all perch on Clifford's lap packed in with the luggage and the terrible two under each arm if need be.'

'Clifford will sniff and tut all the way home, you know that,' she said, trying to ease the concern behind his uncharacteristic outburst.

He took a step away from her and held her gaze. 'Eleanor, I gave up attempting to enforce my will on you some time ago. I stopped because I realised you've a fiercely independent spirit and the sharpest intellect I've ever met. And I respect and admire both, truly. But this is different. We are going to be married. I am going to be your husband. One day, at least. And right now, I'm putting my foot down. You are not staying in a house for Christmas where you've just found a murdered man!'

'Alright, Hugh,' she said contritely.

He jerked in surprise, a slight smile playing around the corner of his lips. 'Alright? Just like that, Eleanor? No tirade about being capable of making your own decisions, thank you very much? No argument at all?'

She shook her head. 'No. Not after that impassioned speech. The gruff detective inspector I fell for has never shown his true feelings so clearly.' She smiled weakly. 'But it's not going to be much of a Christmas. Not with me down in Buckinghamshire at Henley Hall. And you stuck up in Yorkshire, here at Auldwyke Hall.'

'Eleanor?' he said guardedly. 'What have you been holding back telling me?'

'Nothing, Hugh. You just haven't given me a chance to get the words out yet. Because first, you buried my face in your chest. Which was deliciously tantalising, by the way. And then you mounted your white charger and declared you'd take on the world for me. Which is still making my heart skip, just so you know.'

His shoulders relaxed, his expression softening with his smile. 'Hmm, unfair and unseemly of you, as always. I don't actually understand how Clifford puts up with it every day.'

'Puts up with what?'

'How you get round us chaps so easily. And turn everything about face to make it seem as if whatever reckless or ridiculous plan you've come up with is sound and sensible.'

She tutted. 'You haven't heard my plan yet. Although it isn't mine at all.'

He cupped her cheeks gently and pressed his nose to hers. 'Then, for Pete's sake, tell me, please?'

'It's about a murder where no one, not even a senior detective, has the guts to go up against one of the most powerful men in the country. A duke, in fact. Except, that is, the most dedicated detective I've ever known.'

He scrunched his eyes tight shut. 'Tell me you didn't, Eleanor?'

She shrugged apologetically. 'I wasn't given the option not to, Hugh. So yes, I'm really sorry, but I might have been coerced into saying you'd take charge of the murder investigation. But only if your office agreed,' she added hurriedly. 'Which maybe they won't?'

He let out a long breath, head back. 'Where is the nearest telephone?'

'Ahem.' Clifford's disembodied voice filtered in from the hallway. 'Unusually, there is one in the cottage, Chief Inspector. But I fancy you may wish no ladies present when you speak to your office? And also, I imagine you will wish to speak to Mr Lofthouse immediately afterwards. So, if you would like to follow me to the main house?'

At the sound of the front door closing behind the two men, Eleanor heard whisperings at the top of the stairs.

'It's alright, ladies,' she called. 'You can come down now. Thank you for giving Hugh and me space to get that over with.'

'Without so much as a cup of tea to sweeten the worst of it, too, m'lady,' Mrs Trotman said, hurrying down. 'That won't do at all.' She turned to the maids and clapped her hands. 'So, hurry scurry, girls! You know what needs doing.'

Gladstone and Tomkins took this as a cue that their best efforts at behaving were no longer needed and bounded out of bed together to join in with the bustle.

Eleanor watched in quiet appreciation of the neat ballet her four ladies performed around the kitchen. Delicious wafts of fried bacon and sausages mixed with those of mouth-watering black pudding. Thick slices of bread were cut fit for an army. And the kettle never stopped singing.

After a short time, the sound of Seldon's deep voice filtered into the kitchen from the hall. Mrs Butters flapped her apron at the others to hurry out.

'You've no need to leave,' Eleanor whispered. 'Safety in numbers and all that, ladies.'

Seldon ducked under the door frame, looking more worn out and drawn than Eleanor had seen in a long time. Which was saying something as he rarely made it home to his small house in Oxford at night, she knew. But on seeing her staff, he shook himself and smiled. 'Good morning, ladies. Apologies for the intrusion.'

'Oh, 'tis no such thing, sir, if you'll pardon me for speaking up so,' Mrs Trotman said, without any of her usual cheeky glances, Eleanor noticed. Not that Seldon had ever registered the effect his dashing looks had on her ladies, or any other women come to that.

'And it's mighty cold out there, but toasty in here,' Mrs Butters said. And with no flushing of her cheeks, as usually happened when Seldon's tall athletic form was within half a mile of her.

The two young maids nodded matter-of-factly and continued with their work. Eleanor caught Clifford's eye questioningly as he bent to give both her pets a well-deserved treat. He arched an ambiguous brow.

'Oh, dash it, Hugh,' she blurted out. 'What's the news?'

'Inevitable,' he said blandly, rubbing his eyes. 'My office confirmed I was put in charge, unbeknownst to me, while driving up here. And as I came off the telephone, the footman fellow, Lofthouse is it? Yes, well, he added the news that the duke has graciously consented to me leading the investigation. So long as' – his expression darkened – 'everything I do is reported to him, Lofthouse, that is, who will, in turn, report it to the duke!'

She slid her arm through his. 'I know that'll be awkward, but the duke seems rather used to getting his own way. Otherwise, you wouldn't be the only detective brave enough to take the case. And I promise not to make matters more complicated for you by getting involved this time. Scouts' honour!'

Seldon's rich chuckle eased her concern he was secretly furious with her. 'Well, I'll believe that when I see it, Eleanor. Which I sincerely hope I do. And if anyone less powerful than the Duke of Auldwyke had attempted to dictate how an investigation of mine was going to be managed, I'd have slapped them in cuffs.'

She wrinkled her nose teasingly. 'I know. You tried it on me the first time we clashed over a murder. I thought it rather forward of you, actually.'

Seldon's glance flicked in embarrassment around the kitchen, but Clifford and the ladies had vanished. 'Eleanor, promise me one thing?' At her nod, he wound his long, strong fingers into hers. 'I need to know we'll still have a proper Christmas together, somehow, even with this wretched murder business? I can't tell you how much I've been aching to spend time with you. And... and I know there's some things we need to discuss. Promise?'

She flapped a hand at her cheeks as if feeling faint. 'After that putting-your-foot-down speech you gave me earlier, I'm tempted to say I won't promise.' As his head fell to his chest, she leaned down into his eyeline. 'But only in the hope Assertive Hugh appears again. I rather like him. In the interim, I promise. And on a positive note, you're not quite solo on this mission. The local constable, Danby, seems a fine young fellow. Very keen. And remarkably efficient given his limited experience.'

He perked up slightly. 'That's a start, I suppose.'

She scrabbled in her pockets. 'He gave me his notes. And Clifford and I made some, too. Which I've got... somewhere.'

Clifford appeared from nowhere and quietly placed her investigation notebook on the table.

'Excellent, both. Thank you.' Seldon rose, rubbing his hands together briskly. 'Now, I need to,' he lowered his voice for the ladies' sakes, 'examine the body!'

13

As Eleanor and Seldon rounded the corner of the house, Danby appeared.

'Good morning, m'lady. And, Chief Inspector?'

Seldon nodded and shook the young man's hand. 'You must be Constable Danby?'

'Yes, sir. Apologies, we're earlier than I thought. Maybe as it's still alright for you to examine the deceased, though? Before the coroner's assistant takes the body?'

'Absolutely. Lead on,' Seldon said briskly.

Danby turned to Eleanor. 'Pardon, m'lady, but in your case, I'll suggest nowt about delicate sensibilities preferring not to be present.'

As they set off after the young constable, Seldon nodded wryly. 'He catches on even quicker than I'd hoped!'

After arriving at the storehouse, he unlocked the door with the tarnished iron key Clifford had passed to him and they stepped inside. Eleanor felt colder than on her previous visit. Bitterly so. The kind of deathly cold only the hand of evil could leave behind. The sight of Porritt's angular form sprawled on the brick floor where he'd lain alone all night made her chest clench with sadness. She closed her eyes and offered more heartfelt words heavenwards for the duke's secretary to rest in peace.

She opened them as the gloomy space was lit by two large lanterns carried by Clifford. He placed them both on nearby crates and slid her heated handwarmers into her thankful palms.

Danby cleared his throat. 'I touched nowt, sir. Not even the body.' His words hung in a frosted plume.

'Good man.' Seldon opened his notebook.

'Would you like me to step out, sir? Give you a tad more room?'

Eleanor was pleased to hear the young policeman emboldened enough to speak up. Seldon slid on a pair of cotton gloves.

'No, Constable. I'd like you to watch. And listen.'

Eager-eyed, Danby nodded. 'Will do, sir.'

Torch illuminated, Seldon crouched to scan the brick floor, then the position of the body. Picking his way over Porritt's legs, his coat sides clasped tight, he sank down and scrutinised the red mark on the dead man's neck.

Eleanor carefully stepped closer. 'It's faded somewhat, Hugh. Receded, I mean.' She squatted down beside him. 'As his vital fluids have pooled in his organs after death, I imagine. But the line is still darker here at the back of his neck. And wider.' She frowned, not having noticed that before.

He nodded. 'As you said in the cottage, definitely murder! Strangled. However, he didn't black out immediately. The position of the body is all wrong. He would have crumpled to his knees. Then landed face first, hands defencelessly by his sides. Or, at most, bent underneath him.'

'So he may have pretended he was dead and gone limp?'

Seldon nodded again, grimly. 'But too late.' He glanced at the door to the storeroom. 'So was the killer waiting for him here? Or did they come in after Porritt?'

She thought hard. 'There was no snow on the floor when I stumbled across his body. Or rather, Gladstone did. Not like the clumps we're leaving now, Hugh, even after stamping our boots before stepping inside.'

He pointed at her. 'Then whatever wretch did this probably crept directly from the house. Across the rear terrace we skirted past, perhaps. Assuming the staff had cleared it as they have already this morning?'

'It was pristinely cleared, Chief Inspector,' Clifford said.

'Or the murderer nipped along from one of the other storehouses, since the glass canopy covers all the walkways?' she added.

Seldon made some notes, then looked up. 'Constable, you and I will search the other storehouses shortly while Lady Swift warms up inside.'

Danby nodded enthusiastically.

'Any intuitive thoughts, Eleanor?'

She hesitated. 'The thing is, as Clifford knows, I usually have to act out how my intuition feels a murder happened.'

'Usually?' Danby muttered. He slapped his hand apologetically over his mouth.

Seldon groaned. 'Though it's disgraceful of me to ask, please show me, Eleanor.'

She nodded. 'Alright. Constable Danby, you're the murderer.'

The young policeman nodded. 'Ready, m'lady.'

'Thank you. And I'm the unsuspecting Porritt.' She bent forward as if looking through the contents of the top crate in front of her. 'Now, as the murderer, you've slunk in and are about to creep up on me, hands raised to throw a rope around my neck.' She turned back to the crates, facing away from him.

Danby coloured. 'Oh, by heck, sir. Suddenly this doesn't feel at all right.'

'You heard the lady, Constable.' Seldon sounded far from happy himself.

'If as you say so, sir.'

Even though the whole re-enactment was a theoretical demonstration at her own insistence, the hairs on Eleanor's neck prickled. After a beat, she caught the barest swish of Danby's coat as he raised his arms. Then, out of the corner of her eye, his hands gripping an imaginary rope descending around her neck.

'Stop! That's it!'

Gratefully, Danby let his hands fall by his sides. She turned to Seldon.

'I think the murder was premeditated. That thicker line at the back of Porritt's neck, I now realise, suggests the murderer fashioned a noose out of the rope. Which takes thought. And also suggests our murderer might be a woman. Or at least not a very powerful man.'

'You could be right,' Seldon said slowly. 'Any male of ordinary strength would almost certainly have been able to strangle the unsuspecting Porritt with just a length of rope. Or even their bare hands, I'd say. He was slightly framed and only five foot seven or eight. And even if our killer was shorter, it wouldn't have been that hard to reach up and throw it over Porritt's head from behind and then tighten it.' He chewed his lip thoughtfully. 'The real mystery is why was he killed when he was? Time was firmly against the murderer. There would have been other people around and Porritt was central to the proceedings, so his absence would have been quickly noticed. So why would the killer take such an enormous risk?'

'And why was Porritt here in the first place? As Constable Danby astutely noted to me yesterday, Porritt would have messed up his smart suit collecting a crate of these Christmas baubles.'

'Ahem, my lady,' Clifford said. 'These are, in fact, the glass "clays" you and the chief inspector will be firing at during the clay pigeon shooting competition. They are very old-fashioned. I have not seen them used for a decade.'

'Shooting competition?' Seldon said.

Ignoring his look of horror, she held up a finger. 'Ah! Then it makes more sense Porritt was in here.' But even as her last words flew out, she shook her head. 'No, it doesn't! Clifford, you said Lofthouse and Bowes, the gardener, were the only staff absent from the kitchen when you were there?'

'Indeed, my lady. But Mr Porritt would surely have delegated the task of collecting the clays to a lower member of staff such as Judd Fripp, the under-gardener, or Tosh, the lad-of all-work. And Mr Porritt disgracefully requested when we arrived that you hasten to the west terrace as soon as possible to join the other guests in being measured up for your gun.'

Seldon raised his eyebrows. 'I'll talk to you both later about that little titbit you forgot to mention. Your point is, though, Clifford?'

'That in any case, there can have been no requirement for any clays on the shooting platform, Chief Inspector. Not only was the light already fading, but Mr Porritt did not specify her ladyship needed her shooting garments.'

Seldon jotted a few lines. 'Then I assume Porritt came here to meet the murderer. Which, unfortunately, doesn't narrow the field of suspects much as he would have known them all to one degree or other.' He snapped his notebook shut and slid it into his pocket. 'Last thing, Constable, I'm going to check for other obvious injuries. Plus the contents of his pockets before the coroner's assistant takes the body away.'

Danby stepped closer to watch, eyes wide as if to ensure he didn't miss anything. 'Now,' Seldon continued. 'Always start from the crown.'

His long fingers traced the contours of the dead man's head. Eleanor watched in quiet dismay, thinking her fiancé's every working day was grittier and mired in more tragedy than she could bear to think of him having to endure.

'Now the torso, then down the legs.' Seldon demonstrated in his ever-efficient manner. 'Lastly, arms and hands. Then pockets. Got it, Constable?'

Danby nodded. 'Drunk every step to memory, sir.'

Seldon rubbed his forehead. 'Actually, you might want to do the same for Lady Swift's insights. I've learned the hard way how effective they can be in cases of murder!'

Clifford caught her eye. 'Haven't we all? Regrettably,' he mouthed.

Her butler's familiar lament took her thoughts back to being crouched with him over the body just as the two policemen now were. 'Oh, Hugh, you should probably know Clifford pilfered something from Porritt's waistcoat.'

Clifford flinched. 'In one's defence, Chief Inspector, it became necessary to liberate one item from the gentleman only. The key to his grace's apartment, which Mr Lofthouse needed.'

'Useful to know,' Seldon said.

Danby's expression brightened. 'Because we need to factor in Mr Clifford must have disturbed a bit of summat about the body, yes, sir?'

Seldon paused in running his fingers down Porritt's left arm. 'For reasons I shan't explain, Constable, I'm confident we don't. Now, the left hand... wait a minute. What's that?'

Danby leaned forward eagerly as Seldon examined the nail of the dead man's index finger.

'It looks like a... piece of thread, sir?'

Seldon nodded. 'The nail is broken, the thread caught in it. I wonder... Oh, thank you, Clifford.'

He took the tweezers her butler had magicked from his bottomless pockets and carefully removed the thread. Eleanor leaned in to get a closer look as he held it up to the light.

'I'd say it's navy-blue wool, Hugh. Maybe from a jumper or a coat.'

'Looks like it, Eleanor. And I can't say for certain, but I'd warrant Porritt was desperately trying to get the noose off his neck and caught the killer's clothing.'

He wrapped the thread in tissue and placed it in his pocket.

'Now, Constable, just the right arm and hand. Which means lifting him slightly. A shoulder each and I'll ease his arm out. Lift... now.'

'He's nowt of a weight, sir, as you said.'

'That's it!'

'Glad to be of help, sir.'

'No.' Seldon shook his head. 'I mean, yes you were, Constable. But not as much as I hope this turns out to be. It was in Porritt's right fist.' He unfurled his gloved hand. Nestling in it was a gold jewelled pendant.

14

Back at the cottage, despite Seldon's protestations, the ladies stepped forward in formation with loaded plates of still warm bacon and sausage, piles of freshly buttered toast and cups of piping tea.

'It would be rude to waste their efforts, Hugh,' Eleanor said innocently.

Seldon threw his hands up. 'Blast it, Clifford! I don't have time. But it's five against one.'

Her butler's lips quirked. 'Welcome to my world, sir. And trust me, it's much less painful to surrender!'

Eleanor forced herself not to protest as Seldon sat, but pushed his breakfast aside to spread Danby's notes and her notebook in its place. After all, he was a policeman first and foremost, she knew.

And the finest there is, Ellie.

A moment later, he waved an amused hand. 'You've included your ladies on your list, Eleanor. Why?'

She slid a fork into his distracted grip. 'For completeness, Hugh. After all, it's important to stay impartial.'

She hastily pretended to be engrossed in her breakfast. In

previous investigations, he'd often lambasted her for her lack of impartiality.

Mrs Trotman appeared at his elbow with a bowl of buttery scrambled eggs, which she spooned beside the fried one he was now absent-mindedly dipping a herby sausage in.

'We was all in the old gamekeeper's cottage together, you see, sir,' Mrs Trotman said. 'When poor Mr Porritt got done for. Bowes, the gardener, dropped us here. But he didn't stay. Had to get back to gardenin', he said. Or maybe as it was shootin'? Mind, he didn't half hare off in the car like the wind. I remember Butters carpin' as he'd almost blown her skirts over her—'

She halted at Clifford's firm look. 'Potentially useful information welcome, Mrs Trotman. Minus indecorous embellishments, however,' he said.

'Spoilsport,' Eleanor mouthed teasingly.

'But news of his haring off is definitely helpful. Thank you, Mrs Trotman.' Seldon jotted a line in his own notebook, then turned back to Eleanor's. Spearing a piece of crispy bacon, he murmured, 'At least there's one's silver lining in this investigation.'

'What, Hugh?'

He looked up and shifted awkwardly. 'No offence, Eleanor. But apart from his grace, none of the guests' names suggest they are actually, ummm—'

'Toffs?' She laughed at his nod. 'Honestly, it felt rather princessy I was the only one with a title. Though that Willoughby Taylor already fancies himself enough without the "Sir" he declared is in the offing, doesn't he, Clifford?'

Her butler tutted. 'If I might be excused this round of character assassinations, Chief Inspector?'

'Excused.' Seldon distractedly accepted more marmalade toast from Mrs Butters. 'Eleanor, you must have some thoughts, no doubt, having already grilled the guests at dinner?'

'No, I didn't, Hugh,' she said primly. 'I observed and listened only.'

Clifford nodded. 'True, if, in itself, unbelievable.'

Seldon made a show of pinching himself in disbelief. 'Still, something must have struck you? Aside from how deliciously delectable each course was?'

'Hilarious, Hugh!' She smiled but it faded to a frown. 'I did notice something, though. Or rather, felt it. Everyone seemed... guarded. As if they were avoiding some topic of conversation. I couldn't wait for the meal to be over, in truth.'

Clifford nodded. 'Remarkably, her ladyship's appetite remained unaffected.'

'No surprise there.' Seldon shared an amused look with him.

Eleanor let it go, always delighted when her two favourite men shared a joke.

Seldon tapped the page of the notebook open in front of him. 'But I assume all the guests knew Porritt had been murdered?'

'Not at that time. And when the conversation came up at dinner, I only echoed what Constable Danby had said.' She leaned over his arm to rifle through the constable's notes. 'Here, he wrote exactly what he told them.'

Seldon read the entry, swallowing his last mouthful of succulent black pudding. 'Good man! He played it perfectly. You too, Eleanor. I initially wondered if the guests were avoiding discussing the murder at dinner out of decorum. But that doesn't wash now. It must have been something else. Hopefully it will come out in the interviews. Now, excuse me while I read Danby's notes from the murder scene.'

To Eleanor's delight, Mrs Trotman took the opportunity to artfully slide more scalloped potatoes and a golden-topped mushroom soufflé onto Seldon's plate unnoticed.

She eagerly accepted the same herself.

'Right,' he said a minute later, absently loading his fork again. 'Having examined the deceased Mr Porritt, I'd now like to build a picture of him while he was still alive. But only if that's not too upsetting, Eleanor?'

'It's fine, Hugh. Anything to help get justice for the poor fellow.' She closed her eyes to replace the unsettling image of Porritt's sprawled corpse with one of him still alive, sitting opposite her in the car on the way from the railway station. 'Well, to start with, he seemed nervous.'

'Or "nervy", m'lady?' Mrs Butters said apologetically. 'The gentleman was most jittersome.'

'A fine distinction,' Clifford said. 'With "nervy" being a state induced by a mental or physical condition. Whereas "nervous" is a response to a situation or other person.'

'Good point, Mrs Butters,' Seldon said appreciatively. 'Hmm, so was he a born worrier or just worrying about something particular? Something that got him killed perhaps?' He jotted a note. 'Other impressions of him, anyone?'

'The gentleman looked as if he ne'er had so much as a minute's fun in his life, sir,' Lizzie volunteered quietly.

Polly tugged the older maid's uniform shyly. 'Not like we do with her ladyship.'

Eleanor smiled at how fervently the rest of her ladies nodded, then laughed at Clifford mischievously shaking his head.

'Not surprising, though,' Mrs Trotman said. 'I wouldn't have fancied his job for all the tea in Yorkshire!'

Eleanor grimaced. 'Nor me. I'd also add he seemed loyal to the duke, Hugh, but also... intimidated by him, I think.'

'Maybe even scared of him?' Seldon waited, pen poised.

She thought for a moment. 'Now you ask, yes. Poor Porritt was almost frantic on the telephone when I told him I'd declined the duke's invitation.'

'Hence us dropping all of our plans for him,' Seldon said without ill humour. 'Ever compassionate, Eleanor.'

'Forgive my suggestion, Chief Inspector, but Mr Porritt's demeanour may have been purely out of respect for his grace's position and title.' Clifford glanced sideways at her. 'The majority see no reason to rail against the class system.'

'I don't rail against it, Clifford. I just think we're all born equal.' She hesitated. Across the seven of them cosied in the tiny kitchen, they represented every class. Her ladies, born of working-class stock, wholeheartedly embraced their situation. She knew little about her fiancé's roots, except his mother was a cook, but his career had rooted him firmly in the middle classes. While her uncle having bequeathed her his title and estate, officially she was upper class. Though she didn't feel it, nor feel entirely comfortable with it, yet. And Clifford? Goodness only knew where he belonged. Perhaps one day she'd discover the truth about her oh-so private butler's life. And his secrets. Clearly having read her thoughts, he glanced away.

'Back to Mr Porritt,' she said quickly. '"Efficient" also springs to mind.'

Clifford sniffed as he topped up her tea.

'What now, Mr Devil's Advocate?'

'Merely an observation, my lady. That a duke's secretary who fails to follow up on not receiving a prestigious guest's RSVP to his employer's most important event of the year cannot be credited with being "efficient".'

'We all make mistakes.' Seldon looked around the kitchen. 'Right, between you all, you've given me an excellent start on the victim's state of mind and character, thank you. Now, what about the duke?'

The ladies all shook their heads.

'Haven't met him,' Eleanor said.

Clifford shook his head as well. 'Neither is that likely.'

Seldon looked incredulous. 'But he's the host!'

'In absentia, sir.'

'What's that? Latin for certifiable?' Seldon grunted. 'Don't answer, Clifford. I'll find out when I interview him. You know, it's fortunate you were in the kitchen at the time of the murder so you can alibi the majority of the staff at the main house. That'll save me a raft of unnecessary questioning. Now.' He finished the last swig of his third cup of tea. 'I'll start the interviews with Lofthouse the footman and Bowes the gardener first, as neither of them were in the kitchen with you, Clifford. Then the guests, and then the duke.' He stood up and looked apologetically down at Mrs Trotman, hovering with another plate of sausages. 'I'm sure breakfast would have been delicious if I'd had time.'

Eleanor's cook laughed. 'Never you mind, sir. The two plates as you did clear without noticin' won't tell tales on you.'

Eleanor tutted. 'Unlike the dark circles under your eyes, Hugh, but, as I know, you're too diligent to agree to even a short rest. Even though dawn hasn't broken yet, how about we walk the long way back to Auldwyke House? Together.' She lowered her voice. 'And talk. About us.'

Seldon ran his hand through his tousled chestnut curls and whispered, 'I'm desperate to talk about us. And... and our future together, Eleanor. But' – he threw his hands out – 'I've no idea how to start!'

15

There was an awkward silence for a moment. Then Eleanor smiled.

'Nor me, Hugh. Maybe we just need to be brave and blurt out what's uppermost in our minds?'

'You left it in the hallway, Chief Inspector,' Clifford called as he glided out of the back door.

Seldon frowned. 'I didn't leave anything?'

He strode out of the kitchen. In a blink, he reappeared. Beckoning Eleanor to follow him onto the front step, he produced a bunch of exquisite red roses tied with a holly-green velvet bow and pinned with a tiny silver heart.

'You? Hopeless at romance? Never!' she breathed.

He ran his thumb tenderly over her chin. 'Well, the thought was there when I bought them before leaving London. But the vase fell over almost immediately, so they had no water. And then I swerved to miss a blasted sheep in the road somewhere past Lancaster and they tumbled into the footwell and my brief-case fell on them. So, I thought them too battered to give you. Evidently, however, your wizard of a butler spotted them while parking my car and worked his magic.' He sighed. 'And now, to ruin the moment, I do really need to return to the main house. But definitely the long way around!'

Seldon lovingly looped his arm around her waist as they set off, the crunch of their boots in the snow summing up the sound of Christmas to her.

'Of course, Clifford's probably made a meticulously scribed list for us to work our way through.' She patted her pockets down. 'He's probably even secreted it in my coat somewhere.'

Seldon smiled. 'Or mine. Knowing his questionable sleight of hand. But I'd prefer we muddle through on our own. Muddling feels familiarly us.'

'Muddling? Downright blundering, I thought, was more my best efforts with you so far. On the personal side, that is.'

'I agree.' He ducked as she swiped at him. 'Can I be ungentlemanly and start first, please? Because I want to apologise profusely, Eleanor. For... for it still taking so long before being ready... financially. To marry you, that is.'

She squeezed his arm. 'Please, Hugh. Don't think like that. I've only got what I have because Uncle Byron kindly left it to me. And, in truth, hung onto it because Clifford manages the household accounts like a ferocious terrier. It's actually something I've been thinking about a lot lately.'

'I'm listening,' he coaxed.

'Well, when I was cycling across the world solo, I was making my own way. Same when I was scouting out safari routes for Mr Walker's wonderful travel company.' She snuggled into his arm to hide her cheeks reddening. 'Quietly, Hugh, I feel a bit lost in life now I'm a titled lady who doesn't have to work. Except for marrying you when we're ready, of course. I've nothing but excitement about that. Now, your turn.'

He took a deep breath. 'Here goes.' He stopped and turned her gently to face him. 'I've been thinking about leaving the police force when we marry.'

Her jaw fell. 'Hugh! But why?'

'To be home at least a few hours a day so I can have a proper life with you, Eleanor,' he said passionately. 'Not a normal one because I don't think "normal" and Lady Swift have ever been introduced.' He hesitated. 'The... the trouble is, police work is all I know.'

'And all you're passionate about. Except me,' she said firmly. 'The force needs you, Hugh. You can't give up what you love. Even for me. We're getting married, not grafted at the hip.'

'I'll mull it over some more, then.' His expression softened. 'But regardless, will you promise, once we're married, to charge down whatever path you want in life without watering it down for me? Unless it's dangerous. And... and even then, I'll try and accept that's who you are?'

'Promise.' She let out a long breath, which he echoed with a whispered, 'So far, so good.' He swallowed hard again. 'Which leaves the other big ones. Like how we'll live, and where. And the question of... children.'

She gulped. 'That sounds like a life I have no idea how to navigate yet.' He drew her into a deep hug. 'Why am I suddenly feeling fluttery?' she murmured into his chest.

'Because both our hearts want to know the answers,' he whispered into her red curls, then pulled her back gently. 'But how about we say it'll all keep until later? But not too much later!'

He kissed her so tenderly she wished he'd never stop.

Linking arms, they crunched reluctantly towards Auldwyke Hall and the ominous façade of the unlit third floor.

16

'Blasted weather!' Seldon gruffed as he slipped and slid towards Auldwyke Hall's imposing main entrance. 'Christmas is already looming and I'm shackled with a wretched investigation I should never have got involved in!' He tightened his grip on her arm as she sighed quietly. 'Sorry, Eleanor. I didn't mean to sound like I'm mad at you. Truly I'm not. I... I just wanted so badly to spend some time with you alone. And I resent anything that is going to get in the way of that.'

She smiled. 'I feel exactly the same, Hugh. But, in truth, you probably have just cause to feel mad at me. Even though I haven't had enough minutes with you yet to be *truly* maddening. I'm saving you that treat for later.' Relieved that he smiled back, she did her best to increase her pace. 'Come on.' She pointed at him. 'Poor Porritt deserves the most brilliant detective in England to find justice for his murder.'

He took a deep breath. 'Let's hope I can live up to that moniker over three hundred miles outside of my normal jurisdiction then!'

'Well, your discovery of that pendant clasped in Porritt's

hand was an exciting development. And that thread under his fingernail. And both after you'd only arrived at Auldwyke Hall a few hours earlier.'

He frowned. 'True. The pendant certainly suggests we were right. Porritt's murderer stopped strangling him before he was quite dead without realising. Porritt would have dropped the pendant as soon as the noose was tightened around his neck had he been holding it.'

'One potential piece of good news then, Hugh. It means we're probably not dealing with an experienced killer.'

Seldon nodded grimly. 'Yes, thank heavens! However, why would Porritt have spent his last few moments on this earth dragging this pendant out of his pocket or wherever he got it from? Which wasn't pulled from the killer's neck as the clasp is still intact.'

'Perhaps it meant a lot to him?'

'Possibly. It seems unlikely it belonged to him. I don't know much about jewellery, but it's a woman's pendant.' He passed it to her.

She examined it. Shaped like a rose, the cupped, intricate filigree gold leaves were clustered around a striking but small emerald and three tiny diamonds set as if they were the first morning's dew. She nodded. 'Looks like genuine precious stones. And pure gold, I'd say. But Clifford will know for sure. Either way, it seems a little expensive for a mere secretary. So, it either belonged to his sweetheart, who was above his station, or his mother came by it, or...'

'Or it's a clue to his killer!'

As they hurried up the wide, curved steps they were met by the first footman waiting in the hallway.

'Mr Lofthouse.' Seldon beckoned with his hand. 'Time is of the essence, please.'

Regardless, the footman stepped over at a stately pace. As

he came to a stop in front of Seldon, Eleanor noticed the two of them were the same impressive height. Holding each other's gazes gave them the appearance of squaring up to each other.

Seldon lowered his voice. 'I need to telephone for more officers to be sent up to assist me in the investigation. But I need somewhere quiet—'

'No can do, sir.'

Seldon's brows knitted. 'Don't say the dratted snow has pulled the line down?'

'Telephone's workin' alright.'

Seldon's jaw tightened. 'Then what's the problem?'

Lofthouse looked smug. ''Tain't my problem, sir. 'Scuse me sayin' so, but by t' sound of things, it's yours. Seein' as his grace has just this minute given his orders.'

Eleanor felt a sinking feeling. She glanced at her fiancé, who uncharacteristically seemed to be about to lose his professional manner.

'What are you saying, man? That I cannot use his telephone?'

Lofthouse shook his head. 'Nay, not that. There's to be no other policemen permitted on the premises.'

Seldon's expression turned thunderous. 'But that will tie my hands in this investigation! Clearly, his grace does not realise the implications. He needs to be told immediately.'

Lofthouse stretched his neck to gain an extra quarter inch over Seldon. 'Sir, there's not a man alive as can tell his grace a thing. Nor go against his wishes. He is the Duke of Auldwyke, in case that's escaped you?'

'No, Mr Lofthouse,' Seldon said through gritted teeth. 'I am well aware of his grace's position. But it doesn't alter the fact his latest wishes fly in the face of law and order!'

'Maybe,' Lofthouse said impassively. 'But that's not an argument as will sway his grace.' He leaned in. 'I shouldn't be sayin' as much, but his grace don't care much for the police. There was a different sort of doin's here some years back that brought a brace of 'em striding in. His grace threw them out on their shiny brass buttons before they'd cleared this 'ere hallway. Then he went straight to the top and got 'em all eatin' humble pie.' Lofthouse shrugged. 'Always does.'

Trying to quell the fuming volcano beside her, Eleanor caught Seldon's eye with a cautioning headshake. She'd had an idea.

'No other policemen permitted on the premises? Those were his grace's actual words, Lofthouse?'

'To the letter, m'lady.'

'Well, we're all clear on that, then. That will be all, Lofthouse.'

She discreetly steered Seldon back towards the front door.

'Thank you, Eleanor,' he grunted as she herded him out to a secluded spot between several enormous, snow-cloaked rhododendrons. 'I lost my professionalism in there, shamefully. No sense butting heads with this overbearing duke, I admit. But I shouldn't have needed you to wade in.'

Her butler joined them, bearing a tray with two steaming cups of rich-roasted coffee.

'You're right on cue, Clifford.' She warmed her hands gratefully around the mug. 'To witness the boot being on the other foot for a change. Normally it's you valiantly striking out up to your underthings to haul me back from locking horns with someone in authority.' She hid a smile at her butler's horror at the indecorous image she'd painted of him. 'This time it was me hauling Hugh back!'

Seldon let out a long breath. 'I can't deny it. But solving a murder is never a one-person job! I need a handful of good men. Especially on an estate this big.'

Clifford arched a brow. She nodded soberly. 'His grace. Again. "No other policemen permitted on the premises," it seems.' She turned back to Seldon. 'But, Hugh, you've missed something significant.'

'Very likely.' He scowled into his coffee. 'But that's hardly encouraging right now!'

'Oh, dash it, that didn't come out the way I intended. I meant you aren't a lone policeman on this case. You've got Constable Danby at least.' She held up a set of crossed fingers. 'With Clifford's permission, that is.'

The two men shared a baffled look. Then her meaning dawned on her butler as he pinched the bridge of his nose, eyes closed. 'Given the dire circumstances, permission reluctantly granted, my lady. However, with strong reservations regarding breaches of decorum.'

Seldon groaned. 'Blast it, you two! What am I missing?'

Clifford cleared his throat. 'Her ladyship is suggesting that since Constable Danby is already on the Auldwyke estate, you cannot be accused by his grace of bringing more policemen onto his premises.'

Seldon laughed. 'That level of devious thinking should be illegal! But keep it up, Eleanor.' His brow furrowed again. 'Hang on, though, Clifford. Why would I need your permission to allow Danby to remain on the case?'

'Because, Chief Inspector, the constable needs to stay on site. If he leaves, his grace may not allow him back. However, his grace would never countenance him staying in the main house. So where else can he stay...'

'But the ladies' cottage,' Eleanor finished for him. 'There's a small spare room.'

'Excellent!' Seldon said. 'But I'd say your concern, Clifford, over him behaving himself is totally unfounded. He seems a fine young man.'

Clifford's lips pursed. 'It was not Constable Danby's behaviour to which I was referring!'

Eleanor stifled her chuckle as Seldon relapsed into deep

thought. He shook his head as if arguing with himself, then threw his hands up. 'Danby will be damned good help. But he has no experience with a murder investigation. He told me so.' He hesitated. 'So, though it's disgraceful of me to ask, especially as it's Christmas...' He looked between them. 'Eleanor, and you too, Clifford, could you bear to assist with the investigation where needed?'

'Unquestionably,' she said immediately. 'Especially as I was the one who mired you in it in the first place. It's only fair you return the favour.'

Clifford held up his hands. 'If the lady wishes, I too will be happy to assist, Chief Inspector.'

She had to fight the urge to hug him for respecting her desire not to be cosseted in cotton wool. 'Who knew Clifford's infuriatingly chaotic approach would come in handy, Hugh?'

Clifford rolled his eyes at her joke. Seldon laughed, looking relieved.

'Eleanor, if you could aid in the interviews, please? And, Clifford, if you could be the one to round up interviewees and be my eyes and ears among the staff?'

The rumble of the coroner's van rounding the corner made the three of them turn. Seldon flagged it down. Danby leaped from the passenger seat.

'Yes, sir?'

'A request, Constable. Not an order. Would you be willing to assist me for the duration of the investigation? It would mean staying here overnight on the estate, though. I don't know if that would work with your normal duties?'

Danby's eyes lit up. 'It'd be a privilege, sir. And no bother. I was told by the top brass on the phone, after you accepted the case, that I was to prioritise my time to assist you in any way possible. All I need do is have any calls to my police room transferred up here to Auldwyke Hall. If as that'd suit?'

Eleanor nudged Seldon. 'Unusually, there's a phone in the ladies' cottage, remember?'

He nodded. 'Excellent! Constable, I want you to search for the murder weapon. Start with the other storehouses first. With everything that's been going on I haven't had time to examine them as I intended, so be on the lookout for anything that could be relevant to Porritt's murder.'

'Right away, sir!'

'Good man. As you're staying overnight on my request, though, I just need to dash and ask Lady Swift's staff personally if they're happy with the arrangement.'

Her fiancé's chivalrous attitude towards her ladies made Eleanor's heart skip.

Danby, however, seemed to fight a smile. 'I'm fully house-trained, if as they ask, sir.'

'Heartening news, Constable,' Clifford said. 'But as I explained to the chief inspector, it is not you I am concerned about!'

In the old gamekeeper's cottage kitchen, Eleanor delighted in watching her ladies' sterling efforts to hide their mischievous glee at Seldon's request.

'It's a fearful cheek on my part, ladies. So, please don't feel pressured to say yes.'

'One extra among us aprons won't be an ounce of trouble, sir,' Mrs Butters said, her bright-eyed look telling Eleanor more than Seldon was picking up. ''Twas a crying shame the box room was going to waste anyhow.'

Lizzie bobbed a curtsey. 'Polly and me will get straight to making it up, sir. Ach, we'll see the gentleman is more 'n comfortable.' Eleanor noticed the young girl colour slightly.

'And feeding up a hard-working constable is the least we can do to help your investigation, sir.' Mrs Trotman quietly bumped hips with Lizzie. 'He'll be in willing hands, and no mistake,' she added with a cheeky glance at the others. Eleanor covered her chuckle up with a cough.

The sound of the ladies' excited whisperings followed her and Seldon out into the hallway where Clifford was waiting.

'I daren't ask,' he said, hands over his ears. But his eyes twinkled.

17

Back in Auldwyke Hall, Seldon paced the passageway leading to the servants' stairs, muttering about wasting time. As he drew level, she caught his arm.

'Hugh! You agreed it's more advantageous to the investigation not to go against the duke. But instead, to cleverly work around his wishes and schedules.'

He rolled his eyes. 'Yes. But that was before I realised I wouldn't be able to start interviewing the guests because they are still languishing over breakfast. And I'm not allowed to chivvy them up! The staff are all too busy running after them to be interviewed either. It's ridiculous!'

'I agree. But your idea to search Porritt's room and office while you're waiting is perfect. It's just quicker to let Clifford work his magic on Lofthouse to get the keys.'

'He shouldn't need to,' Seldon griped. 'And I'm supposed to be in charge.'

'Which you are. But we're learning things run on unorthodox lines up here.'

He smiled. 'Says the expert of precisely that!'

Clifford glided towards them, holding up two keys.

'It didn't take you long to pick Lofthouse's pockets then,' she whispered.

He tutted. 'Categorically I did not, my lady. Now, which room first, Chief Inspector?'

'Is Porritt's office anywhere near the space I've been granted for interviews?' Seldon said. 'Assuming his grace hasn't issued an edict against me having one, of course?'

Clifford's lips quirked. 'Not yet, sir. The small library on the ground floor, adjacent to the billiard room, is at your disposal.'

'Good. Then Porritt's room before his office. So I'm back downstairs and ready when it's deemed my interviews might finally begin. I'll see Lofthouse first. Then Bowes.'

Clifford led them apologetically up the staff stairs. 'The main staircase past the second floor has been blocked off to isolate his grace's quarters, as he occupies the third. Thus this is the only route to Mr Porritt's room on the fourth floor along with the other male staff. All female staff reside on the fifth floor. Obviously, before his grace's self-induced retirement from society, his staff was much larger.'

As they reached the third floor, Eleanor gasped. 'Gracious, there's not even a door from here through to his grace's apartment! How did Porritt get to him, then?'

'Quite, my lady. Access must be via a separate staircase I have yet to discover. But I shall discreetly observe Mr Lofthouse's movements now he is acting secretary to his grace.'

A moment later, he stopped at a plain wooden door furthest along the musty-smelling fourth-floor landing. Seldon slipped on his police-issue cotton gloves, nodding appreciatively to Clifford as he offered Eleanor a pair of his butlering ones. Seldon unlocked the door and led them in.

Her nose twitched as she crossed the threshold. It smelt

fresher inside than in the corridor. Oddly, like a forest at dawn or a basket of newly cut logs. The room was larger than she had expected, too. That warmed her somewhat to the duke. Despite his seeming disregard for his secretary's death, it appeared he'd appreciated his right-hand man enough in life to afford him a reasonable living space. Far better than the shockingly cramped staff conditions she'd encountered in other aristocratic houses. There was also a decent-sized fireplace to heat the room, although it was currently unlit. And several large windows that bathed the room in natural light.

The main furniture was a small chest of drawers and a single bed, dressed in a traditional patchwork quilt over blue cotton, with three folded towels hung over the end and a pair of grey pyjamas on the pillow. A modest, but varnished, writing table stood against one wall. A simple cane chair with a slim blue cushion was ready to receive the man who would never again sit there, she thought sadly.

The desk was occupied by a neat stack of well-thumbed books and a jar, half-filled with pencils, but no pens that she could see. Next to the jar was a simple gilt frame containing a photograph of a kindly-looking, middle-aged woman in a house-keeper's uniform.

Porritt's mother, I bet, Ellie.

In front of it was a small brass vesta case on a chain. Originally used to keep matches dry, this one had been converted to a needle case. She wondered if Porritt's mother had been a dab seamstress, like her own Mrs Butters. She placed the case back down and looked around the rest of the room.

An attractively carved free-standing wood-panel, inset with an oval mirror and painted in the Auldwyke bottle green, seemed to serve a double function, as a washing and dressing screen behind and a wardrobe in front, given it was set with a row of four black iron hooks facing her. Hanging in meticulous order were several crisp white shirts, two pairs of blue trousers, three ties and one set of rather old-fashioned hunting tweeds. She couldn't help but marvel at the impressive lion claws serving as the screen's feet. They seemed an unwarranted extravagance given the rest of the furnishings.

Her nose twitched again, her gaze drawn to a calico curtain that partitioned the far side of the room. Around the edge of which she now saw a cloud of something billowing out.

'Hugh, is that smoke?'

With him on her heels, she raced across the floor and burst through the curtain.

'It's just wood dust, thank heavens! With the light glinting through it, I thought the room was on fire!'

She gazed along the run of clearly repurposed shelves joined and jointed onto equally scavenged but matching legs which made up a long workbench. A rack of six chisels and sheets of various graded sandpaper hung on the wall above. A large open sack was filled with wood shavings, a dustpan and brush resting on top.

But what really caught her eye was the collection of lovingly carved figurines, many of birds. And, among them, the makings of a darling nativity scene part-way through completion.

'Goodness. First impressions don't lie, Hugh. He really does appear to have been the gentle soul he seemed.'

She ran her gloved fingertip along a pair of turtle doves carrying a reed together in their beaks.

Seldon looked unmoved. 'You think so? Just because he enjoyed whittling?'

'No, Hugh. Because of the one abiding theme in everything he's carved. Look closer.'

He peered over her shoulder. 'Er, pigeons?'

'No. Love! Look, there's two initials, *ML*, carved on almost every piece.'

'Eleanor, I'm trying in the romance stakes,' Seldon mumbled, looking abashed.

'And getting it just perfect, honestly,' she said apologetically. She slid her arm through his. 'But I think our tragically departed Mr Porritt was pining for a special girl. And this was his way of releasing his feelings.'

'Poor chap. If you're right. But it seems a leap of imagination, if I'm honest. Looks more to me like he had nothing better to do with his evenings.'

'We'll see.' She waved him back out. 'Get Clifford in here while you and I search through Porritt's things.'

Seldon strode through the curtain. 'Clifford? A third opinion, please. Only try and bail a fellow out, will you?' she caught him add in a whisper. 'I've dug myself a blasted hole again.'

'Well?' she said, after her butler had examined the curtained-off area.

Clifford adjusted his tie. 'I really couldn't say, my lady. Not wishing to malign the gentleman's success in matters of the heart.'

'That's another vote for love, Hugh.'

'Remind me not to ask you to bail me out of anything less serious, Clifford. Like jail!' Seldon muttered.

Even with her scouring under and around every piece of furniture and shaking out each of the books, she found nothing. No hidden notes, no photographs, no diary. Not so much as a scrap of mismatched cloth or a suspicious stain.

'What's this?' Seldon called from across the room.

Eleanor hurried over as he lifted a buttoned cardigan out of the chest of drawers.

'Hugh! That looks like the same wool as the thread you found under Porritt's fingernail.'

'Let's see.'

Seldon laid the jumper down and pulled out the tissue-wrapped thread from his pocket. As he did so, Eleanor's face dropped.

'Actually, if it is a match, that's a pity.'

Seldon nodded. 'Because it means Porritt broke that finger-nail earlier and snagged his *own* clothing with it, not the killer's.'

She leaned forward as he placed the thread on the jumper.

'Blast it! It matches.'

'Wait a minute. Clifford! Pocket magnifying glass, please.'

He strode over and handed it to her. She peered through it at the thread. 'I thought so. The colour isn't quite the same. It's slightly darker. This is definitely not from this cardigan.'

Seldon smiled. 'Good. For once I'm pleased we couldn't identify a clue!'

After leading them back to the main hallway, Clifford gestured respectfully down one passageway with a list of lefts and rights to be followed from there to Porritt's office. 'If I might be excused to assist the staff in Mr Lofthouse's absence, my lady? His grace called for him just as I left.'

'Don't worry. We'll find it,' she said optimistically.

But a good five minutes of dark-oak passageways later, they hadn't. The lack of any natural light, compounded by the posi-tively mediaeval iron sconces housing lacklustre clouded glass bulbs, didn't help. Seldon had returned to muttering about wasting time and she was beginning to think him right.

'Oh, hang on!' She hurried over to the small brass plaque she'd missed seeing the first time in the gloomy light. 'Hugh, it says "Secretary" here.'

'Does it say "Finally" underneath that?' he grumbled, poking one of the keys Clifford gave him into the lock.

'Perhaps, "Later" might be more advisable?' Clifford's measured tone came down the passageway. He cleared the distance to them in elegant long strides and lowered his voice. 'With apologies, Chief Inspector. His grace has instructed Mr

Lofthouse to venture to the village with Mr Bowes in half an hour on some urgent errand. I thought, therefore, you might wish to interview them before searching Mr Porritt's office?'

Seldon withdrew the key. 'Definitely. In case his grace decides to send them on to the Scottish Hebrides or France before I can speak to them! I especially want to hear what light Lofthouse can shed on Porritt's death. Maybe he'll be able to tell me where that pendant came from.'

18

In the library, Seldon unceremoniously shifted the pile of books and yellowed periodicals from the green leather-topped desk onto the floor beside it. With businesslike efficiency he set his notebook and pen on the cleared space. He then pulled up the nearest chair, only to find Clifford had beaten him to it. He frowned at the elegant wing-back Clifford placed at an angle at the desk, watching as he flicked a pristine handkerchief over the seat and the desktop.

'Clifford, I'll be interviewing suspects in here, not entertaining them over a sherry!'

'Indeed, Chief Inspector. With your appointed observer, her ladyship,' Clifford ended pointedly, holding the chair as Eleanor settled into it.

As the door closed behind her butler, Seldon dropped into his seat. 'Why do I feel I've just had my ears verbally boxed for being an unchivalrous bounder?'

She laughed. 'Right now, I only want you to focus on getting justice for poor Porritt.'

He sighed. 'Still, Clifford's right. A chief inspector forever blinkered by murder investigations can't possibly make a thoughtful husband. As I've been worrying.'

She sprawled across the desk to kiss his cheek. 'Nonsense! Besides, I hardly fit the mould of a proficient wife. I can barely boil an egg. And I'll probably set the pan alight trying.'

He smiled. 'Maybe in part to needle your long-suffering butler as well?'

'True. But only on his truly sniffy days when I could dream it was his head I was boiling.'

As they embraced, his rich chuckle made her heart skip. The sound of voices outside, however, made them leap apart. She landed back in her chair with a bump, hastily arranging the folds of her skirt. Seldon tugged on his charcoal-grey suit collar as the door opened abruptly to reveal a sulky-looking Lofthouse and Eleanor's apologetic butler behind him.

'Ah, Mr Lofthouse. There you are.' Seldon beckoned him forward.

The footman glanced at Clifford. 'I didn't need a chaperone, sir. 'Specially seein' as I'm the one who knows this house best now.'

'Nevertheless, kindly knock in future,' Seldon said firmly. He held Lofthouse's gaze as he gestured at the chair on the opposite side of the desk.

'I'll stay standin', sir.' Lofthouse's eyes flicked to Eleanor and back.

Seldon's jaw twitched. 'Lady Swift has kindly agreed to act in the capacity of observer since his grace has forbidden any additional officers being at my disposal.'

Lofthouse shuffled his smartly polished shoes. 'That wasn't my meanin'.'

Eleanor caught Seldon's eye. 'Even though I'm in the room, it's fine to sit as the chief inspector has asked, Lofthouse. Likewise, to say whatever you need to.'

A cloud of self-reproach crossed Seldon's face.

'Thank you, m'lady.' The footman sat squarely, filling the chair with his broad frame.

As Clifford left, Seldon flipped open his notebook.

'Mr Lofthouse, I have some questions I need to ask you to help establish the facts of Mr Porritt's death.'

'But I don't know nowt about it, sir. And, anyways, his grace has instructed me to run an errand in t' village shortly.'

'Number one,' Seldon continued, 'where were you between twenty past three and twenty to four yesterday afternoon?'

Lofthouse shrugged.

Seldon took a deep breath. 'Just take me through your movements from dropping Lady Swift at the entrance to Auldwyke Hall. With as much detail as you can.'

'Well, naturally I went straight to return t' car to stables. And just as I'd had, Amos raced up with t' other, complainin' about bein' more behind than the bullock's tail at gettin' back t' pre-shoot doin's.'

Despite the reason they were all there, Eleanor couldn't help thinking the image his description conjured up was charmingly country-esque. Nor wondering how much of it Seldon was noting down verbatim.

'Amos being...?' Seldon said.

'Amos Bowes, gardener, sir. Old-timer's mostly used to his plants, as they don't ask much of him. Needin' to see to guests had him rattled by half. So I parked t' second car for him. Only then I noticed a scratch on it and grabbed a polishin' suede to buff it out. Then quickly checked t'others. I'm in charge of all his grace's vehicles, you see.'

'Understood. How long would you say you were in the garage? The stables, I mean?'

'Somewhere 'tween... ten or fifteen minutes, I reckon.'

'And where is this building?'

'Past t' memorial garden, sir. Originally, it were t' coach house and stables, but his grace don't keep horses no more.'

'I see. And on leaving the stables, you did what?'

'Went t' kitchen to grab a quick summat warm.'

'What time would you have reached the kitchen?'

'Couldn't say exactly, sir. I've longer legs 'n most and them stables ain't too far, but I weren't quick. Not with snow lying thick on t' path as it was. Amos, Mr Bowes I mean, hadn't got t' clearin' it on account of bein' called to drive after me t' station and back.'

'Three minutes? Five?'

'Nay. Under two, sir. I'm not one as ever takes the long route when there's work waitin' with my name to it.'

'No doubt. Did you see anyone on your way from the stables to the house?'

Lofthouse looked up at the ceiling. 'Not a one. Leastways not until the kitchen. Then all t' staff were there, save for Bowes. It were regulation teatime, though, sir.'

Seldon relaxed his blunt demeanour an inch. 'Mr Lofthouse, do not concern yourself. I'm here to question the events around Mr Porritt's death, not scrutinise the diligence of his grace's staff.'

Lofthouse pointed at Seldon's notebook. 'If as it might be noted all the same, sir.'

'It might. Was the tea ready when you arrived?'

'It was, sir.' The footman pulled a face. 'Barely warm and over-stewed fit for nowt but browning cook's lardy cake. Mind, I still downed it in one. No time, you see? This is his grace's biggest event of the year. There's guests. And they don't look after 'emselves, by crikey.' He blanched as he glanced at Eleanor. 'Beg pardon, m'lady. I didn't mean that to come out so bad.'

'It's fine, Lofthouse.' She smiled encouragingly. 'You'll be of far more help to the chief inspector if you do forget I'm here.'

'And that I'm supposed to be a guest too,' Seldon said a trifle testily.

'Ah, yes.' Lofthouse winced. 'Thing is, as I said already, his grace hasn't a great fondness for, er, police, sir.'

'You don't say,' Seldon said drily. 'Having dutifully downed your tea, what did you do next?'

'Went searching for Porritt. He'd been in a right lather about his grace's schedule runnin' off t' rails.'

'What caused the disruption?'

Lofthouse stared at his hands.

'Was the schedule off track on account of me and my staff arriving late?' Eleanor said.

Lofthouse nodded gratefully.

'Your respectful approach to Lady Swift is appreciated,' Seldon said.

'Might that be noted too then, sir?' The footman pointed at the notebook again.

'Why not?' Seldon's pen shot across the page. 'Now, you went searching for Mr Porritt. Where?'

'His office, for starters. Then outside thinkin' as Porritt must have gone round to t' west terrace.'

'And when you arrived there?'

'Oh, I didn't. Because I heard voices in t' first storehouse. Only when I got there, I found Lady Swift and Mr Clifford. Kneeling over Porritt!'

'How long have you been employed by his grace?'

Lofthouse looked momentarily flummoxed by the change of topic. 'Near eight years. I came in as first footman, straight after the last one were dismissed.'

Seldon looked up sharply. 'Congratulations. However, wasn't it unusual a second footman wasn't promoted to that position?'

'There weren't no other, sir. Just as now, I'm only one.'

Seldon held his hands up. 'Then purely out of curiosity, why is your title *first* footman?'

'Hangover, sir. From when his grace had barrels of staff years back.'

'I see. And why was the footman before you dismissed?'

'Haven't the foggiest. Rarely do.'

'Alright. What can you tell me about Mr Porritt?'

Lofthouse rubbed his chin. 'Well, he'd been with his grace since a lad. Worked his way up. Got given his secretary job 'bout three year back.'

Seldon's pen was poised. 'Did the vacancy come about because the last secretary was also dismissed?'

He grimaced. 'Yes, sir. His name were Derek Stark. He left after a mighty big argument with his grace. But I've no idea what about. It weren't the first row, I did hear.'

'Did he leave with a reference, do you know?'

'Doubt it! He made it clear before he went that he and his grace parted on bad terms.'

'Back to Mr Porritt then. Did he seem to enjoy his work?'

'Best I can say is, he was always on top of things. But he were the sort as never seemed to enjoy anything. And face like a damp blanket left on t' moors most of time.' He hesitated. 'Not meanin' to speak ill of the dead.'

'How did the other staff find him?'

'He didn't mix below stairs. But I couldn't say there's one among us as didn't leastways respect him.'

'Some staff were probably jealous when he was appointed secretary, though? Perhaps even you?'

Lofthouse scratched his nose. 'No, sir.'

'Any enemies you're aware of on the staff or elsewhere?'

'Don't know of any.'

'When Mr Porritt was killed, that being between three twenty and three forty yesterday afternoon, where was his grace?'

'In his apartments, must have been. Same as always. His grace is a stickler for routine.'

'Last two questions. Do the initials "ML" mean anything to you?' He glanced at Eleanor. 'A woman Mr Porritt was romantically involved with, perhaps?' At the footman's shake of his head, Seldon reached into his pocket and unwrapped the tissue. 'Final question then. Do you recognise this?'

Lofthouse glanced at the gold pendant and shook his head. 'No, sir. Is it important then?'

Seldon replaced it in his pocket. 'Thank you, Mr Lofthouse. You've been extremely helpful to police enquiries.'

Lofthouse swallowed hard. 'Might as that *not* get noted, sir? In case his grace gets sight of your notebook?'

As the footman left, Clifford entered, bearing a small tray with two cups.

'There's no time for...' Seldon clamped his mouth shut as Clifford offered the tray to Eleanor, who took one.

'That was interesting, Hugh.' She took an eager sip. 'I thought Lofthouse's story about checking all the cars sounded odd. If he was lying, he'd have had time to murder poor Porritt instead. And then dash to the kitchen.'

Seldon took the other proffered cup. 'And he arrived after you'd left, Clifford?'

'Indeed, sir. That being at five-and-twenty to four precisely.'

'Your habit of living by your pocket watch is often as brilliantly helpful as it is infuriating,' Eleanor teased.

'Mixed compliment notwithstanding, my lady, I had no need of consulting it.'

She slapped her forehead. 'Of course! There must be a clock in the kitchen so the staff can be on time with meals, et cetera.'

'Naturally. A Salter's standard, unbevelled, with different chimes on—'

'Clifford, not now, please.' Seldon sniffed his tea suspiciously. 'But good work, both of you. And I must say, I wasn't convinced by Lofthouse's insistence he wasn't jealous of Porritt being promoted to secretary. Eleanor?'

She nodded. 'I agree.'

He jotted another note. 'Motive-wise, however, jealousy over Porritt's promotion feels weak, as it happened three years ago. I mean, why wait to kill him now? And when there were so many people about?'

'Do you think he recognised that pendant though, Hugh? I didn't.'

'No. He seemed genuine enough about that.'

Clifford topped up Eleanor's tea, then turned to find Seldon had his hand firmly over his untouched cup.

'Thanks, but no thanks. I now understand Lofthouse's grumble about his tea being stewed. Could you fetch Bowes next?'

'As you wish, sir. He is waiting along the passageway.' Clifford half-turned. 'Though, if I might mention, the tea is not, in fact, "stewed". It is orange pekoe, which his grace imports especially. But not for the staff!'

19

As they waited for Clifford to fetch Bowes, Eleanor caught a quiet tapping behind her. She craned around the side of the wing-back.

'Hugh, it's Constable Danby.'

Seldon strode over and unlocked the French doors, letting in a bitter cold gust as the red-cheeked constable stepped inside. Gladstone lumbered over to greet him with scrabbling paws and a flailing tongue.

'Hello again, sausage monster.' Danby patted him on the head, then stood up straight. 'Not wishing to interrupt, sir. But just to say, I've done scouring all the storehouses. And the area yonder. But nowt. Not even a chip off a button came to light, I'm afraid.'

Seldon's brows knitted. 'I expected as much. But hoped otherwise. Thank you for your excellent efforts, anyway, Constable.'

Danby's eyes lit up at Seldon's praise. 'What can I do next, sir?'

'Probably nip to the kitchen for a well-earned drink, I'd

think.' Eleanor hadn't missed how flushed from his exertions the young policeman looked.

Danby smiled. 'Thank you, m'lady, but Mr Clifford saw me right about a half hour back, bringing a cuppa while I was out searching.'

Seldon smiled wryly. 'Good man. I hope it was better than the one he brought me earlier. So, search the stables next. But discreetly. I also want you to check for a scratch having been buffed out on the second car. Which one was it, though? Blast, I didn't ask.'

'The black Wolseley,' Eleanor said.

Danby nodded. 'Stables next, sir. And then?'

'Search the surrounding grounds. And then widen your search using your initiative, of which you obviously have plenty.' Seldon nodded encouragingly as he walked Danby back to the French doors. 'Or your intuition. I'm learning it also has possible merits,' he muttered.

A moment later, Clifford led the Auldwyke gardener into the room and then left. At first glance, Amos Bowes struck Eleanor as being an uncanny double of her own treasured gardener, Joseph. His weather-sculpted face was framed by silver-grey strands of thinning hair, while in his calloused hands he turned a weathered cap. He wore a green wool jerkin with his shirtsleeves rolled up. Conversely, his thick-ribbed socks were pulled extra high, as if trying to replace the wellington boots he'd obviously left on the doorstep.

He stepped hesitantly up to the desk and bobbed his head to Eleanor, then Seldon.

''Twas you as wanted me, sir?' he said in a reedy voice.

'Yes. I'm Chief Inspector Seldon. Are you Mr Amos Bowes, head gardener?'

'That I be, sir. For me sins. Though I ain't committed one. I've never had truck with the law all me life, I swear!'

Seldon's expression remained unmoved. 'Then you won't

mind answering my questions. Where were you between twenty past three and twenty to four yesterday, the window in which Mr Porritt was killed?'

'I was... wait up!' Panic crossed the gardener's face. 'I never killed him! Honest!'

Seldon held up a halting hand. 'I'm not accusing you. Just answer my questions fully and truthfully. And take your time.'

Bowes' Adam's apple wobbled. 'Can't, sir, beggin' your pardon. But his grace has given order I'm to go with Mr Lofthouse t' village.'

Eleanor swore she could see steam escaping from Seldon's ears. He held up his notebook with an uncompromising look.

'Mr Bowes, I am officially conducting a murder investigation which takes precedence over any orders you might have been instructed to carry out. Do I make myself clear?'

Bowes gave a shaky nod. 'As dew on roses at dawn, sir. If you're a gardenin' gentleman, that be?'

'No, Mr Bowes, I'm not. Now, you drove Lady Swift's staff back from the station, following Mr Lofthouse. On arriving at the Auldwyke estate, you did what?'

'Forked off to drop off her ladyship's ladies at the old gamekeeper's cottage. Along with carrying all their cases inside to where as they were wanted.' His harried expression softened. 'Mind, the one as made such a bonny warm scarf on the long trip back from station, I could have kept for takin' to me bed.'

Seldon's head jerked up. 'Watch your tongue, man! Lady Swift's staff—'

Eleanor hid her smile. 'Hopefully, Mr Bowes, my ginger tomcat, Tomkins, behaved himself?'

Bowes nodded. 'Whiskers is always welcome company, m'lady.'

Seldon glanced at Eleanor and rubbed his forehead. 'I see. After dropping off her ladyship's entire entourage, you did what?'

Bowes gathered his thoughts. 'Drove over t' stables, sir. Mr Lofthouse was just done parkin' t' first vehicle. He were good enough to offer and do mine. Then I went t' kitchen to rustle up Judd and Tosh for shoot preppin's.'

'Judd and Tosh being?'

'Under-gardener, that's Judd. And lad lackey, that's Tosh.'

'How long were you in the kitchen?'

'Not long enough to down a mug of tea, more's the pity.' He smacked his lips. 'Cook has her brew down to an art. Has that knack of keeping it hot but it don't overdo until—'

'Mr Bowes!' Seldon said with forced patience. 'Can we move on to more important matters?'

The gardener looked contrite. 'I got you, sir. Well, outside's like the perfect frosty lawn and inside, better nectar 'n honeysuckle to a bee.'

Seldon threw Eleanor a lost look.

She hid another smile, knowing how important break-time treats were to staff. 'The chief inspector has all the details he needs to know about cook's biscuits now, thank you. When did you, Judd and Tosh leave the kitchen, he means?'

'Ah! Right on half a'clock chime of three, m'lady. Everythin' had to be ready for when guests came back out, see? Only we never finished and the guests never did.'

'Why was that?' Seldon said, pen poised.

'On account of Mr Lofthouse's news about poor Mr Porritt. He came out onto terrace wi' a face like a pheasant as been hung too long.'

Seldon leaned forward. 'Think carefully, please. Aside from you, Judd and Tosh, did you see anyone else on the terrace before Mr Lofthouse came out?'

'Not a one, sir,' Bowes said definitely. 'Leastways not after the gentleman and his wife had left.'

'So you did see someone? They were there when you arrived?'

'Aye, sir. Mr 'n' Mrs Musgrave, I been told.'

'How soon after you, Mr Judd and Tosh arrived, did Mr and Mrs Musgrave leave?'

'Soon as they noticed us, sir.' He shrugged. 'Even though we'd all whipped off us caps.'

'How long have you been employed by his grace?'

'More 'n four score seasons.'

Seldon looked up from his notebook. 'Please tell me everything you can about Mr Porritt.'

'He were a worker, sir. And no mistake. Since he were a nipper, servin' as stable lad. Was seventeen when her grace, the duchess, passed. Gettin' t' giddy height of secretary were no more 'n he deserved. Not like the one afore him. Rightly so, he got kicked out for rowin' with his grace!'

'How long ago was that?'

'I'd say about twelve seasons gone.'

'Didn't Mr Porritt strike you as being rather young for such a responsible position?'

'Aye, I s'pose, sir. But what's age matter when you can trust a man wi' your life?' Bowes frowned. 'Though 'tis mighty wrong for me to be speakin' 'bout his grace at all. Can't I be done here, now?'

'Not yet,' Seldon said firmly.

'Then you'll 'scuse me clapping me trap tighter 'n a rabbit snare. His grace won't stand for no one bein' told his business. Especially police!' He stared down at his socks.

Eleanor gave Seldon a placating smile. 'Mr Bowes, I'm not a policewoman. You can tell me instead.'

The gardener turned to her. 'Grief heals in time, folks say, m'lady.' He shook his head sadly. 'Not for his grace, though. It's been terrible knowin' he's turned tighter in on hisself every day since her grace passed over. God rest her soul. Won't even see his own family. Even the best men ain't built for spendin' too long in their own heads.'

She felt a wash of sorrow for the duke. 'It's very sad. What family does his grace have?'

'He *had* two brothers, but one died in the war. T'other, Lord Grayson Auldwyke, his grace ain't seen like all the rest since he shut hisself away.'

'I see. But his grace trusted Mr Porritt, you say?'

'Almost like t' son he never had, m'lady. Mind, he'd watched him grow from a lad into britches, and out of 'em and on into a fine fellow. Course, you know he was born here at Auldwyke?'

'I didn't, no. Perhaps his parents were in service here at that time?'

'That they were, m'lady. Only as his father up and died when he were a nipper. That's when his troubles started, see?'

'Not yet?' she said coaxingly.

'Gossip!' Bowes spat. 'Meanest streak ever bred in folks. Mr Porritt's father weren't even cold in 'is grave before rumours was burnin' fit to set whole village afire.'

'What rumours?'

'That it was Mr Porritt's mother as up and done for his father. But his grace was havin' none of it and told t' whole village and his staff so. Told 'em anyone spreadin' them rumours would have to answer to him!'

'So his grace kept Mr Porritt's mother on?'

'Aye, m'lady. Until she passed just under a year ago.'

She glanced at Seldon, who nodded imperceptibly for her to continue. 'Tell me, Bowes. Were any of the staff jealous when he was appointed secretary to his grace?'

'Not to my knowledge, m'lady.'

'Not even Mr Lofthouse?'

He shook his head.

'Did he have any enemies?'

'Mr Porritt? Can't think he did. Never heard a word of disrespectin' against him among the others. Weren't one for making a drama. Nor riding a high horse over anyone.'

'I see. Well, did he have any lover... I mean, did he have any romantic attachments?'

Bowes frowned. 'Well, there was a lass. Near five year back or more. A maid here. Mr Porritt were right sweet on her.'

Sensing there was more, she waited for him to continue. He hesitated.

'The thing is, m'lady, despite what his grace said, her parents refused to let them become engaged. In the end, they forced her to give up working at Auldwyke. Said they'd rather she got a job elsewhere than marry son of a... well, you know.'

She sighed. 'Unfortunately, yes, I do, Mr Bowes. What was her name, by the way?'

'Mary. Mary Lewes.'

ML, Ellie. The initials Porritt carved on his wooden figurines.

She glanced at Seldon, who inclined his head in acknowledgement that she'd been right. 'Mr Bowes, last question.' She nodded at Seldon, who revealed the pendant. 'Do you recognise this?'

Bowes swallowed and cast his eyes down. 'M'lady, I'm only a gardener. What could I be doin' recognisin' jewellery like that? They don't grow on trees, thou knows.'

Clifford joined them once Bowes had left. He glanced between Eleanor and Seldon.

'Ah!'

'You're right,' she said soberly. 'We didn't get much out of him.'

'Apparently, I was honoured to get anything!' Seldon said with a touch of pique. 'But to keep you in the loop, Clifford, Bowes confirmed Lofthouse parked the car he'd driven the ladies here in. And then went to the kitchen to collect Judd and Tosh, as you'd noted.'

'And confessed he has a soft spot for Tomkins,' she added, trying to lighten Seldon's frustration.

'Then Bowes' word is doubtful,' Clifford said drily. 'Clearly having so little wherewithal as to fall for the wily ruses of a ginger menace.'

Even Seldon chuckled before sobering again. 'Bowes might have had time to kill Porritt between leaving Lofthouse to park the car and arriving in the kitchen to collect Fripp and Tosh, but it would have been a short window.'

Clifford nodded. 'Though we think the murderer went prepared. If her ladyship's conjecture that a noose was used is correct.'

'True. But motive-wise?'

Eleanor shrugged. 'Sorry, Hugh. Not much help there.'

He held up a hand. 'You did plenty, Eleanor. Better than I did. Particularly with Bowes.'

'Thank you. Well, the other staff all have alibis, thanks to Clifford. But one or more might have seen or heard something. So that's an avenue to follow.'

Seldon looked down at his palm. 'But was he lying about recognising this pendant or not?'

'Ahem!'

'Enlighten me, do, Clifford,' Seldon grunted resignedly.

'Even if Mr Bowes had recognised it, Chief Inspector, he couldn't have said so. Not without fear he'd be dismissed for... impropriety.'

Seldon threw his hands out. 'Blast it! What's improper about recognising a lady's pendant?'

As Eleanor rose to lean on the desk, Clifford spun away towards the door.

'Do you recognise the one I'm wearing, Hugh?'

'Eleanor!' Seldon's cheeks coloured as he hissed, 'I can't peer between... there. Not yet, anyway.'

'Shame,' she whispered, turning him completely beetroot.

20

'Excellent suggestion, Clifford!' Seldon said forty minutes later as the three of them herded after an overexcited Gladstone. 'Just as you predicted. The rest of the Auldwyke staff were much more at ease being questioned below stairs.'

Eleanor's heart swelled at his appreciation of her treasured butler. And at his lack of ego in being open to suggestions. She nodded. 'At least as much as could be hoped for when being questioned by a policeman. And a very senior one at that.'

As they continued through the maze of oak passageways towards the small library-cum-interview room Seldon had been granted, she felt a sudden frisson of unease. Pausing, she caught a faint movement out of the corner of her eye.

Clifford, having captured her errant bulldog, whispered, 'Stay, sir!' and glided silently down the hallway. He stiffened as he reached the partly ajar door of the billiard room. Without knocking, he stepped inside.

'Sincere apologies, Mr Huish. And Master Finbar,' his measured voice floated out. 'I was unaware any guests were planning a game. Shall I fettle the shot clock?'

Julius Huish's long-winded air from dinner was nowhere to

be heard as he replied sharply, 'Whatever for, man? The shooting competition doesn't start for ages. And it won't be in here, you fool.'

'Very good, sir.' Clifford's impassive tone didn't falter.

Eleanor grabbed Seldon's arm and hurried him into the interview room. She closed the door behind them. Before she could speak, the clatter of dog's claws on a polished wood floor sounded outside in the corridor, followed by a volley of barking.

She flew out to see a wide-eyed Gladstone rooted to the spot as Finbar, Huish's hound, descended on him, teeth bared.

'Quick, boy!' she hissed. With a rare turn of speed, her portly bulldog shot inside. Just in time for her to close the door as a frothing Finbar reached it.

'Perhaps a few of these might assist, sir.' Through the keyhole, she spotted Clifford stride up and drop several baked liver treats in the hand of the red-faced Huish who was trying unsuccessfully to haul his hound away.

With a mumbled reply, Huish marched off, now being nose-butted by an eager Finbar.

Clifford tapped on the door before stepping into the interview room. He fed Gladstone the remaining treats while ruffling his ears. 'A fine example set, Master Gladstone. I'm always telling your mistress prudence is the better part of valour!'

She ignored the mischievous remark. 'Is Huish a fan of billiards, do you think, Clifford?'

He shook his head. 'Unlikely, my lady, as he seemed unaware a "shot clock" is used to make sure players do not dally too long when it is their turn at the baize.'

Seldon's brow furrowed. 'So he was waiting to spy on us?'

Clifford nodded. 'I imagine so.'

'Well, we'll deal with him later.' He waved towards the desk. She settled into the wing-back chair, not missing he waited until she'd finished before taking his seat.

'Right, a quick round-up on the staff's responses so I can get both of your opinions, please?'

'That under-gardener, Judd Fripp, was a surprisingly garrulous sort, wasn't he?' Eleanor said.

'About roses, slugs and unmentionable fertiliser, overly so, yes!' Seldon shook his head. 'Honestly, before this case is solved, I'll have learned enough to open a blasted plant nursery.'

She laughed. 'Best stick to being a policeman, Hugh.'

'I might.' He looked away and flipped through his notebook. 'So, key points then?'

She sat back thoughtfully. 'Fripp confirmed what Bowes told us earlier about collecting him and Tosh to go around to the west terrace. He also confirmed it was not long before Lofthouse told them the news of Porritt's death, so Bowes would definitely have had time to kill Porritt first.'

'Agreed.' Seldon made a note, then looked up. 'I couldn't get anything much from that lad, Tosh.'

Eleanor pictured the startled freckled-faced boy in clearly hand-me-down britches held up by patched braces. 'He looks barely fifteen. He was definitely awestruck facing a scary London police detective.'

'I'm not scary.' Seldon frowned at his open notebook. 'Mostly.'

'I do know Tosh was taken on with Mr Fripp,' Clifford said. 'Though the under-gardener is not his guardian in any official capacity.'

Eleanor sighed. 'Another orphan?' It was something she and Clifford had in common. 'Like you and darling little Kofi?' She smiled at the image of the two of them poring over engineering diagrams together whenever Kofi was at Henley Hall.

'Um, moving on?' Seldon said, waving an apologetic hand. 'Which leaves the housekeeper, cook and maids?'

'If Clifford hadn't seen them all in the kitchen during the

time frame Porritt was killed, I'd almost think they'd agreed in advance what they would say,' Eleanor said.

'There was no discernible difference in their responses, certainly.' Seldon flipped through his pages. 'They all seemed to have found Porritt efficient and generally reasonable.'

Over at the hearth, Clifford paused in stoking the fire. 'And they dealt only with Mr Lofthouse and Mr Porritt. Never his grace. In fact, they all joined after his grace became a recluse.'

Seldon rolled his eyes. 'Lucky them! I'm beginning to think they've got off lightly. Next. Any new motives for Porritt's murder? There's none to my mind.'

'Nor mine. Only Lofthouse. And we've all agreed that jealousy over Porritt's promotion feels weak.' Eleanor failed to keep the frustration from her tone.

Clifford coughed. 'Dare I suggest patience, my lady?'

She smiled sweetly. 'Depends if you want to see Christmas Day with your head still attached?'

Seldon chuckled again. 'Let's hope we find plenty of motive in one of the guests. On that note, would you fetch the Musgraves please, Clifford?'

A minute later, he introduced the couple. Barnabas Musgrave, his expression an equal mix of fury and uneasy curiosity, marched up to Seldon's desk, leaving his wife, Viola, trailing in his wake.

'You've got a nerve. Issuing a summons to us!' he growled. 'Myself and my good lady are guests of the Duke of Auldwyke.'

'So am I,' Seldon said smoothly.

'Being sent here to make accusations against a respectable businessman like myself does not qualify you as a guest, Sergeant!' he sneered.

Seldon nodded coolly. 'I agree, Mr Musgrave. But the printed invitation Lady Swift and I received from his grace several weeks ago *does*. And it's *Detective Chief Inspector* Seldon. Of Scotland Yard.'

The Musgraves stared at each other, then both seemed to register Eleanor for the first time.

'You haven't had a chance to meet my fiancé before now,' she said. 'Only Gladstone here.'

'Well, this is a fine "how do you do" way to meet,' Barnabas grumbled, glaring at Seldon and then her bulldog, receiving a cheeky tail wag in reply.

'Your fiancé's a policeman, Lady Swift? How unusual!' Viola failed to cover up her titter as she folded herself into a chair, faffing with the numerous layers of her lavender day dress. 'So you're sitting in on us being interrogated because you can't bear to be parted from him. How sweet!'

'No, Mrs Musgrave,' Seldon said firmly. 'Lady Swift has kindly agreed to act in the capacity of my observer during interviews.'

Viola's sulkiness evaporated as her hungry gaze roved over Seldon's handsome face.

'Of course, we'll be glad to help, Chief Inspector,' she purred.

'Not that we know anything about anything, Viola.' Her husband plonked his robust form onto the other chair with a grunt, his black moustache twitching. 'Which makes this a waste of my time. And a downright impudence with it.'

Seldon ignored the remark. 'Would you please tell me where each of you were between three twenty and three forty yesterday afternoon? Mrs Musgrave?'

'Ladies first. A proper gentleman,' she cooed. 'I was on the terrace waiting for the shoot practice to start again. With Barnabas, of course,' she added at her husband's glare.

'That's right. We were together. The whole time,' he said assertively.

Seldon smiled thinly. 'Rather cold to be standing outside for twenty minutes, wasn't it?'

Eleanor noted they both turned away from each other. Viola

adjusting her dress, while her husband inspected his unlit cigar, holding it up to the light.

'Barnabas and I are from Cumbria, you see?' she said after a beat, as if that explained everything.

Seldon's head shake made it clear it didn't.

'We're quite used to fresh air up there, you know,' Barnabas grunted. 'It's not a crime to be outdoors, is it?'

Seldon's lips pursed. 'No. But murder is. So what happened while you were on the terrace?'

'Oh, nothing of interest, I don't think,' Viola said. 'Did it, Barnabas?'

'No, Viola. It was just us two. Taking the air.'

Seldon made a note. 'Where were the other three guests?'

'Dulling their wits in the drawing room.' Barnabas frowned. 'Least, two of them were there all the while. One of them left, I believe, at some point. But I was hardly paying attention to them.'

'Mrs Musgrave?'

'Barnabas is right, of course, Chief Inspector. I've learned over the years that he always is.' Her voice held a tinge of bitterness, Eleanor thought.

Seldon frowned. 'Did you see anyone else while you were on the terrace?'

'Only staff,' Viola said dismissively.

'Which staff precisely?'

'Staff are staff,' Barnabas snorted.

'I did notice that gardener person passing with a crate of those ancient glass clays,' Viola added hastily at Seldon's look.

'Aged about sixty, silver-grey hair, weathered face?'

'Yes, that's him. I saw him again later with another gardener-type and some urchin.'

Seldon leaned forward as her husband brandished his lighter. 'Mr Musgrave, I'll thank you not to smoke without checking all ladies present are happy first.'

He grumpily replaced the cigar in his jacket pocket. 'And I'll thank you to get this nonsense over with!'

Seldon ignored him again. 'When was it you saw Mr Bowes a second time, Mrs Musgrave?'

'It was just before his grace's order came for us to go back into the drawing room.'

'How long have you known his grace?'

'Known him?' Viola faltered. 'I mean, his grace has been holed up here for a decade. Or thereabouts, didn't we hear, Barnabas?'

'What my wife is trying to say, Inspector,' Barnabas said impatiently, 'is that we don't. We simply received an invitation. And one doesn't refuse opportunities. I'd never have built up my business empire acting any other way. The fact our host is less present than the fog that I wish would swallow this wretched county has come as a very unwelcome surprise, I can tell you.'

'And don't I know it,' Viola muttered, not quietly enough for Eleanor's sharp hearing.

'What did you know of Mr Porritt, the duke's secretary?' Seldon said.

'Neither I nor my wife knew anything about him. We'd never met him before.'

'Mrs Musgrave?'

'What Barnabas said, obviously, Chief Inspector.'

'Last question then.' He slowly unwrapped the tissue in his palm, exposing the pendant. 'Do either of you recognise this?'

Eleanor frowned as the woman shook her head. Had a flash of recognition passed across her face?

'And you, Mr Musgrave?'

He stood up. 'No, Chief Inspector. And as that was the last question, this interview is obviously at an end!'

As the Musgraves left, Clifford entered. Seldon let out a

sigh. Gladstone scrabbled up his legs and curled a consoling tongue into his ear.

'Yuk! Really, old friend?'

Clifford lifted the bulldog down. 'Apologies, Chief Inspector. It's Master Gladstone's best effort at decorum. A consequence of example, perhaps.' He glanced mischievously at Eleanor as he held out a pristine handkerchief to Seldon.

She laughed. 'Shall we concentrate on the case? It's obvious the Musgraves didn't join the other guests because they were arguing.'

Seldon frowned. 'Where did you get that from?'

'Only everything about their body language to each other. But I would never carry an argument over to the next day. Especially at Christmas.'

'Unless it's with a senior policeman trying to stop you from getting caught up in a dangerous situation?'

'Well, obviously. If he's going to be that pig-headed,' she said innocently.

Seldon shook his head ruefully. 'Not since he's learned to listen better. Now, what about the pendant?'

She shrugged. 'I wasn't quite sure if either of them had seen it before.'

'Me too. But they did add something useful Bowes didn't tell us. That he passed them on the terrace with a crate of the clays for the shoot. He never mentioned that. Why would he leave that out?'

Her eyes widened. 'More to the point, Hugh, where did Bowes get the clays from? Because if it was the storehouse...'

'Exactly.' Seldon nodded grimly. 'He'd have seen Porritt's body!'

21

The new layer of pure white snow crunching under Eleanor's boots on the way back to the old gamekeeper's cottage made murder feel a thousand miles away. The frosty air also helped crystallise her thoughts, while Gladstone's clumsy efforts to gambol ahead through the deeper patches brought a smile to her face.

Feeling reinvigorated, she followed Seldon and Clifford into the warm kitchen to receive an ecstatic purred welcome from a delighted Tomkins.

Her ladies hurried into a line and curtseyed.

'Please don't stop what you're doing,' she said too late, spotting the piles of wool, felt, lace, fir cones, holly, string and paper filling the table. 'It all looks wonderfully Christmassy.'

Mrs Butters squeezed the youngest maid's arm. ''Tis her doing, m'lady. She's in charge.' She winked at Eleanor behind the young maid's back. Clifford turned to Polly.

'Well done, Festive Fairy. You've organised a veritable factory of Christmas decoration making.'

His praise clearly meant the world as Polly bobbed excitedly on her toes. 'Thank you, Mr Clifford, sir. 'Tis such a treat.'

He nodded, then gave the barest flick of a finger. In a blink, Eleanor found herself cosied up beside Seldon on the window seat, her bulldog and tomcat snuggled either side of them. A section of the table had been cleared for their notebooks, while her ladies were spread around the other seats, busily crocheting, weaving, gluing and cutting.

Clifford set down a platter of warmed mince pies dusted with icing sugar and seven steaming glasses offering wafts of cinnamon and cloves.

Mrs Trotman put her hands on her hips. ''Pologies, m'lady. But this Spoilsport Sprite 'ere,' she nodded at Mrs Butters, 'hasn't let me add a second dose of my rhubarb brandy to that yet.'

'Just as well!' Seldon muttered.

Even Clifford's lips quirked as Eleanor and the ladies burst into laughter.

'In the inimitable words of one of England's literary greats, my lady, "There is nothing in the world so irresistibly contagious as laughter and good-humour."'

'Oscar Wilde?'

'Charles Dickens. From *A Christmas Carol*.'

Lizzie clapped her hands. 'Ach, we're so looking forward to Mr Clifford's promise to read it to us by the fire of an evenin', your ladyship.'

Eleanor's heart swelled with affection as treasured memories of her butler reading fairy tales to her as a lost and lonely nine-year-old orphan flooded back.

'It wouldn't be the same if you weren't among the gathering, my lady,' he said gently, clearly having read her mind.

Overcome by the lump in her throat, she nodded, busying herself with her notebook until she could trust herself to speak. 'Right. What have we learned from the Musgraves?' She bit into the sumptuous buttery pastry of her mince pie with a moan of pleasure.

'Um, perhaps we should wait?' Seldon looked around at the ladies.

'Don't mind us aprons,' Mrs Trotman said. 'Won't be the first time.'

Clifford tutted. 'Quite. Given her ladyship's propensity for attracting deceased persons.'

'Like an aged spinster attracts cats. Or have I mentioned that before?' Seldon said innocently.

'Yes, you rotter!' she cried, joining in the collective amusement.

Seldon quickly sobered. 'Well, let's leave aside what we learned about Bowes until we can reinterview him and concentrate generally on motives first.' He held up his hands. 'None so far to my mind though, blast it! You, Eleanor?'

'I agree. I certainly didn't get the feeling the Musgraves had argued with poor Porritt. Nor held a grudge against him. But, like Bowes, if we don't have a motive yet, at least we do have opportunity. The Musgraves suggested either Huish, Taylor, or the charming Miss Whitwell left the drawing room around the time Porritt was murdered. So, did one of them sneak away, kill Porritt and return?'

Seldon shrugged. 'As yet, we don't know.' His brows knitted. 'If Taylor, Huish or Whitwell left the drawing room at the time Porritt was murdered, then the other two must be covering for them as neither have come forward with the information.'

Clifford looked up from the intricately folded papers he was snipping at with his pocketknife scissors. 'I can understand if it were the Musgraves covering for each other, Chief Inspector, being husband and wife, but why would Mr Huish, Mr Taylor or Miss Whitwell do so? Unless they also wanted Mr Porritt dead, I suppose?'

Seldon shook his head in disbelief. 'We haven't even got a decent motive for one of them wanting him dead yet, let alone all three of them! Not that I've had a chance to interview them

yet. Which I shall remedy straight after this.' He absently took a
bite of a pie. 'Mmm. Investigation aside for a moment, these
mince pies are too good, Mrs Trotman, thank you.'

Flushed-cheeked, Eleanor's cook beamed at him. 'Pleasure,
sir.'

'Well, Hugh,' Eleanor said. 'I still feel the Musgraves are
holding back about something.'

He looked thoughtful. 'It might just be a natural reaction to
a murder and being interviewed?'

Clifford spread his arms, revealing a lengthy paper-chain
garland of intricate winged angels which he handed to an awestruck
Polly. He stood and bowed at the round of applause from the rest of
the table, Seldon even joining in. As he did so, however, he knocked
one of Mrs Butters' balls of wool off the table with his elbow.

'I'm sorry, Mrs— Tomkins, no!' Seldon lunged after the
tomcat, too late to stop the last of the wool from being unwound
across the floor by eager ginger paws.

''Tis no matter, sir,' Mrs Butters said, blushing as Seldon
apologetically returned with the now unravelled ball of wool.

He shook his head. 'No, it was clumsy of me.' He held his
hands up straight, several inches apart. 'How about you untan-
gle? I'll wind?'

As she took another mince pie, Eleanor noted her housekeeper checking for Clifford's nod of permission before bash-
fully agreeing. As she ate it, she marvelled at how adept her
fiancé seemed at wool winding.

'Actually, what you said about having no motive for anyone
so far isn't quite right, Hugh.'

'I meant ignoring the rather weak one we have for Lofthouse, Eleanor.'

'I wasn't talking about that, Hugh. I'm talking about the
guests, including the Musgraves. They do all have one possible
motive in common for wanting Porritt dead.' She turned to Clif-

ford. 'You remember the conversation Miss Whitwell started at dinner about his grace?'

He tutted. 'Shameful as it was, yes, my lady.' He turned to Seldon. 'Miss Whitwell inferred that it is rumoured his grace has been alone for so long, he is not completely compos mentis, Chief Inspector.'

Eleanor rolled her eyes. 'What Clifford is too respectful to say, Hugh, is it's apparently rumoured that the duke has entirely lost the plot. And therefore, for some time, his secretary has decided whether the winner of the annual Christmas shoot has their favour granted or not. And it seems it's a once-in-a-lifetime opportunity if they are.'

Seldon's eyebrows rose. 'The sort of once-in-a-lifetime opportunity worth killing for?'

She nodded. 'Very possibly. And I'm sorry I didn't mention it before. But we've been so caught up since you've arrived, it slipped my mind.'

Seldon was looking thoughtful once more. 'Is this the same shooting competition I knew nothing about until five o'clock this morning? The one you and I still have to compete in shortly? By order of his grace?'

'That's the one.' She shared a wince with Clifford. 'However, silver linings and all that, Hugh.'

He smiled and murmured, 'Yes, Eleanor. I get to spend more time with you.'

'Actually, I meant we'll be able to observe and listen out for anything the other guests might let slip.'

The whole room turned as a knock sounded at the front door. Being nearest, Lizzie leaped up. There was a brief delay, then she returned, scarlet-cheeked. ''Tis, er, Constable Danby, my lady.'

She smiled as the young policeman appeared in the doorway, hands behind his back as if walking the beat. His cheeks

also looked unusually suffused. She charitably put it down to
the cold, but had a suspicion otherwise.

'Welcome. Come to check your temporary digs in the
cottage, have you?' She caught the ladies' excited expressions.

Danby shook his head. 'Wouldn't dream of checking 'em,
m'lady. It's such an honour to work with the chief inspector, I'd
have lain the whole night in an old bath on the moors if need be.
And besides, there's things to be done.' He looked apprehen-
sively at Seldon. 'Begging your pardon, sir. Not meaning to
suggest owt.'

'Like what?' Seldon said, only then seeming to realise his
hands were still wound with wool. He nodded gratefully as
Eleanor relieved him of it. 'We were discussing the few interviews we've managed to do so far, Constable, while, er, assisting
the ladies.'

Danby stood straighter. 'Then maybe as I might have
summat of help, sir. Seeing as I found... this!' He held up a thick
wet rope, tied as a noose.

'Excellent work!' Seldon was beside him immediately,
Eleanor on his heels. 'Where did you find it?'

'In the ornamental pond. I took the initiative to drag a
branch along the bottom of it. And lo and behold, this come up
on the end of it.'

'Constable, you're proving invaluable,' Seldon said, causing
the policeman's chest to swell. Seldon took the rope and studied
it. 'No chance of fingerprints with it being soaked through. But
it's the murder weapon, I'm sure.'

Eleanor felt a wash of sadness. 'Porritt might not have been
an angel, but he didn't deserve to die with that around his neck!'

Danby regarded the noose eagerly. 'So who killed him? And
why?'

'We don't know yet,' she said determinedly. 'But, between
us all, we will find out.'

Seldon nodded. 'Next step, then. We'll interview Taylor,

Whitwell and Huish. And afterwards, compete in this blasted shooting competition in line with his grace's orders and see what we can find out there.' He took a deep breath. 'Then have the Christmas treat of interviewing a reclusive, police-hating duke who I'm beginning to think is just a figment of everyone's imagination!'

22

Back in their impromptu interview room in Auldwyke Hall, Seldon strode back to the desk. 'Right. We're ready for the next interviewee, Clifford.' He stared at the tray in front of him. 'What's this?'

'Ahem! You may be ready, Chief Inspector, but regrettably, your next interviewee is not.' Clifford restrained Gladstone's greedy scrabble up the front of the desk.

Seldon rubbed his forehead as if trying to contain his exasperation. 'Did I not make it clear I would interview either Miss Whitwell or Mr Taylor next?'

'Indeed. However, the former is selecting her second wardrobe change of the morning in her room. And the latter is completing his self-appointed assessment of his grace's extensive cigar collection in the smoking lounge.'

'This is ridiculous! Call Julius Huish then. Forget I said I'd make him sweat by seeing him last after he was lurking in the billiard room.'

'As you wish, Chief Inspector. However, Mr Huish is currently at the lake, ostensibly running some energy off his hound. Though, it rather appeared he was attempting to escape the ill-mannered creature.'

Seldon threw up his hands.

Eleanor frowned. 'Hugh, I know how hard you're trying. But we agreed to work around the duke's guests as the path of least resistance so as not to anger him any further.'

Seldon waved at the refreshments. 'By having a picnic, apparently!'

Clifford's lips quirked. 'Hardly, Chief Inspector. It is nowhere near substantial enough to be called a "picnic". Not by her ladyship's standards. That would require wheels to transport it.'

She joined in Seldon's burst of laughter, pleased frustration hadn't completely overtaken his sense of humour. 'You terror, Clifford! What paltry offerings have you brought instead? Given that all we've had to eat is mince pies, delicious though they were.'

'Quail Scotch eggs, Wensleydale cheese and beetroot crackers, my lady. Also miniature Yorkshire puddings with potted partridge and rosehip confit. Paltry enough to devour in a short fifteen minutes. By which time, Mr Taylor will have deigned to saunter along.'

Seldon pointed at the array of teapots. 'Hardly sets the tone for interrogating him about murder.'

Clifford stepped away to offer Gladstone a roasted bone by the fire.

'Hugh, stop fussing,' she whispered. 'Pretend we're at the Ritz Hotel for a romantic Christmas treat, as my wonderful butler clearly intended. And before you know it, we'll be back to murder talk all too soon.'

Seldon sighed. 'I'm sorry, Eleanor. To you too, Clifford. It all looks great.'

And it was. Moreishly so, she enthused over the breadcrumbed and seasoned sausage meat cosseting the rich yoked quails' eggs. Not to mention the creamy nutty taste of the cheese and the flavoursome gamey partridge served in traditional Yorkshire batter puddings. Seldon munched keenly without a word, looking increasingly amused by her constant raptures.

'And a favourite among our specialty teas, madam?' Clifford was playing his part as a Ritz waiter perfectly. 'Darjeeling? First or second flush?'

'Second, for me,' Eleanor said. 'That spiced fruitiness in the background is sublime.'

'Or "muscatel", in tea parlance.'

She patted Seldon's arm. 'You see, so much to learn, Hugh. Best to stick to being the best policeman ever. Now, what tea would you vote for?'

'Hmm.' Seldon shrugged at his cup and then pointed at the nearest pot. 'That one. If I had to. Because it's the only one that tastes even a bit like a proper everyday brew.'

Clifford cleared the desk. 'Chinese congou, sir. However, fear not, whilst at Auldwyke Hall, the odyssey for your perfect cup is far from over.'

He glided away and closed the door behind him.

'I'm going to remember this as the most absurd murder case ever!' Seldon muttered.

'Mr Taylor,' Clifford announced a little while later.

Taylor's affected rangy stride as he entered the room made Eleanor wonder if his ego was even more bloated than she'd feared. Or if he'd sat on something akin to a cactus.

'What ho, Lady Swift!' he said silkily. 'Fancy you and I being called together. Rather sweetens the inconvenience, eh?'

'We haven't, Mr Taylor.' She gestured at Seldon, who fixed him with a stern gaze.

'Mr Taylor. I am Chief Inspector Seldon. In charge of the

investigation into Mr Porritt's murder. Lady Swift has agreed to act as an observer.'

'But only when she heard I was next up, I'll warrant,' Taylor stage whispered.

'Mr Taylor,' Seldon said firmly, 'I'll thank you to remember your manners and why you are here. Which is to answer my questions. Now, kindly take a seat so we can start.'

Taylor shrugged. 'Alright. No need to lose your shirt so quickly.'

Pinned by Seldon's uncompromising gaze, he lounged back in the chair nearest Eleanor and slid his right ankle up over his left knee, tapping his foot in her direction.

She fixed him with an even more uncompromising glare. 'Chief Inspector Seldon is not only a detective with Scotland Yard, he is also my fiancé.'

Taylor's face was a picture. 'Ah! I see. The lady and the policeman, is it? Then, welcome to the fray of Christmas at Auldwyke, old man!'

'Chief Inspector is fine, thank you,' Seldon said smoothly. 'Now, full name and address, please?'

'Willoughby Edgar Taylor. Soon to be "Sir". Of 14a Cavendish Mews, London. Kensington, you know.'

Seldon nodded. 'I do know it. It's just over the boundary and therefore actually in Hammersmith.' He made a note. 'So, Mr Taylor, where were you between three twenty and three forty yesterday afternoon?'

'In the drawing room,' Taylor said testily, clearly unhappy at having been çaught out. 'Trying to stay sane waiting for the shooting practice to restart.'

'You seem very certain of the timing?'

'Do I?' Taylor stretched languidly. 'Well, that's because I was watching the clock like a hawk.'

'Why?'

'Because all the while, the bally light was fading! Practice makes perfect, as the saying goes. But when one is banned from bringing one's own gun, it's critical!'

'You didn't leave the drawing room at all?'

'No. I was poised, ready to be called when the last guest had finally arrived. Being Lady Swift. Alone.' He shot Seldon a smug look.

'Were you, Mr Taylor? Alone in the drawing room?' Seldon said, raising his voice slightly over Gladstone's crunching on his bone.

Taylor grinned. 'Chaps like me rarely are, you know. Miss Whitwell was also there. And Huish too, unfortunately. It was because of her I went in, actually.' He caught Eleanor's eye. 'But only to be chivalrous. She was too cold outside.'

'It's the chief inspector who wants to hear what you have to say, Mr Taylor,' she said pointedly.

Seldon waited for Taylor to look back at him. 'And in the drawing room, you each did what?'

'Sat and chatted together. Not that Huish has anything much to say worth listening to. I should take him with a hefty dose of strong, coarse mustard when you grill him.' At Seldon's sharp look, Taylor shrugged. 'Just being helpful.'

'Are you?'

'Of course. I'm answering your questions like a good boy, aren't I?'

Seldon ignored the comment. 'Did the three of you stay together for the full twenty minutes in question?'

'Think so,' Taylor said, with a tinge of boredom. 'But you know, if a lady goes off to powder her nose, a proper gentleman doesn't remark upon it. You might want to note that.'

'Are you saying Miss Whitwell left the drawing room?'

'No.'

'And during the time you were in the drawing room, did anyone else come in?'

'No.'

'Did you see anyone outside?'

'Did I, um...?' Taylor stared up at the ceiling, tapping one hand on his thigh. 'Yes, the Musgraves on the terrace.'

'Did either one, or both of them, leave at any point?'

'Yes. Both. But as I said, I was watching the clock, not spying on fellow guests, so I've no idea where they went or for how long, if that's what you're going to ask.' He folded his arms. 'I can't help saying, but by dragging us in here one by one to tattle on each other, you're making a shocking show of the shooting festivities.'

'Murder is the most shocking show, Mr Taylor. Now, did you see anyone pass the terrace?'

Taylor's lips twisted into a smug smile. 'There can't have been anyone who passed because the Musgraves were on the terrace. At least, most of the time. And me, Miss Whitwell and Huish were in the drawing room, and Lady Swift, and yourself, had yet to arrive, remember?'

'The question was not limited to guests. I said "anyone".'

'And who else is there? The duke? That's a laugh.'

'Is it?'

'Yes. But only if you're fun at parties. Which I suspect you're not.'

'So I've been told.' Seldon glanced at Eleanor since she had accused him of precisely that when they first met. 'You were saying about his grace?'

'I only meant he wouldn't have passed because he doesn't leave his ivory tower, does he?'

'How long have you known his grace, given you are so well acquainted with his habits?'

Taylor started. 'What? I don't. Know him, that is. Everyone knows the duke is a recluse, except you, it seems, Inspector.' He leaned forward. 'And it's not cricket to try and trick a chap.'

'Never played cricket,' Seldon said dismissively. 'So, if you are not acquainted with his grace, why did you accept his invitation?'

'Because one does, Inspector. In *our* circle.'

Looking unfazed, Seldon continued. 'Going back to the actual question. For clarity, did you see any members of staff pass the terrace?'

'I wouldn't have noticed one if they did!' Taylor scoffed.

'That's a no. For clarity.'

'What did you know of Mr Porritt?'

'Nothing. Never met him before. But he seemed efficient enough, I suppose. Terrible taste in ties, mind.'

'Last question, Mr Taylor.' Seldon unfurled his hand. 'Do you recognise this?'

Taylor blinked hard as he looked at the gold pendant. Eleanor noticed him leaning forward, almost imperceptibly. 'No.'

'You're absolutely sure?'

'I said "no", Inspector.'

'That will be all for now. Thank you for coming.'

'The pleasure was all yours,' Taylor said with a snide smile. He eased out of the chair and gave Eleanor a courtly bow. At the door, he turned back. 'Oh, actually, there is one thing I almost forgot, Chief Inspector.'

Seldon jerked up from his notebook. 'Yes, what is it?'

'A friendly word of advice. It's rather rotten of a chap to drag his fiancée through a murder investigation, old man.'

The door banged shut.

Eleanor grimaced. 'Want me to dash off so you can shout rude words you wouldn't dream of in front of me?'

Seldon let out a long breath and smiled. 'Almost. But I'll settle for shamefully hoping it turns out to be him.'

'Good man. He was obviously holding something back, I'd say. And I'm pretty sure he was lying when he said he'd never seen that pendant before, so maybe you'll get your wish!'

23

Clifford knocked and stepped into the interview room, closing the door behind him.

'Where's Miss Whitwell?' Seldon said suspiciously.

'Unfortunately, not with me, Chief Inspector. Evidently the lady is at her, ahem, ablutions.'

'What? At this time of day?'

'Indeed, Chief Inspector. If it suits, Mr Huish is outside, however?'

Seldon threw up his hands. 'Clifford, I'd take his dog for questioning at the moment!'

'Very good, Chief Inspector. I'll fetch him in.'

With his cerulean cravat, tightly belted blue tweed jacket and matching trousers tucked into his long tan boots, Huish had all the hallmarks of a man dressed for sport. But with none of the spirit for it.

He also seemed very nervous, Eleanor thought. He gave her a wan nod of acknowledgment, then recoiled as Gladstone trotted up with his half-munched bone, tail wagging.

Seldon stood up, his tall athletic frame dwarfing the more slender-built artist. 'Good morning. Are you Mr Julius Huish?'

Huish nodded and sank into the chair Seldon indicated. 'And you're the detective who's going to save us, are you?'

Seldon sat down and opened his notebook. 'What do you think I need to save you from, Mr Huish?' he said blandly.

'This evil fiend stalking the halls of Auldwyke... er, Hall!' he whispered dramatically.

Seldon glanced at Eleanor and away. 'Are you a fan of the more... lurid crime novels, perhaps, Mr Huish?'

'No. Well, maybe a little.' He shrugged. 'Alright, I admit it. I find them hard to resist. I've a whole bookcase full, in truth. One isn't supposed to confess to such things, I know. But it's just that I feel as if I'm trapped in one! In the middle of the wild Yorkshire Moors in a godforsaken Gothic mansion. And without my host even appearing to explain what the dickens is going on when a man was found murdered. Even if he was one of the staff. It's still unnerving.'

Eleanor flinched as someone, or something, out in the corridor hurled itself at the closed door. Seldon caught her eye and frowned. In a blink, the door flew open and Finbar, Huish's hunting hound, sprang over the threshold, hackles raised.

'Finbar, no!' Huish cried, shrinking back and curling his legs up in his chair.

Eleanor leaped up in unison with Seldon to dash toward Gladstone, who was now quivering by the fire, his bone hanging loosely in his jowls. As Finbar advanced on him with a low growl, Gladstone dropped the bone and retreated slowly.

Clifford strode in and pursed his lips at the sight of the cowering Huish and Gladstone's bone now in Finbar's jaws.

'Master Finbar! Stand down. And drop that bone!'

With a meek gruff, the hound let it fall from his jaws and lay down with his head between his paws.

'That's better.' Clifford dropped a liver treat by the hound's nose. 'Chief Inspector, my sincere apologies. I momentarily stepped but a few yards from the beast to assist one of the maids.'

'It's not for you to apologise,' Seldon grunted. 'Nor to babysit this hairy menace. Mr Huish, your dog needs controlling!'

'I know,' Huish muttered weakly. 'But you try. He won't listen to me.'

'He will to me, sir,' Clifford said firmly. 'For the duration of the chief inspector's questioning, I shall make sure of it.'

'Thank you, Clifford,' Eleanor called as he left with the subdued hound.

With them all back in their seats and Gladstone snuggled into Eleanor's lap, Seldon tapped his notebook. 'Mr Huish, where were you between three twenty and three forty yesterday afternoon?'

'Oh, timings, I see. Yes, detectives always need ask, don't they? Well, I was with Miss Whitwell and Mr Taylor. Chatting in the drawing room. Do you know if he tells me once more he's got a "Sir" coming to him, I might be tempted to...' Huish coloured.

'You might be tempted to what?' Seldon waited, pen poised.

Eleanor watched the two men hold each other's gazes in fascination. Having fallen for Seldon's calm self-assurance and brooding, reserved manner, she found it a treat to see how effective it was in his work. Huish, conversely, looked like a rabbit mesmerised by a snake. 'I... I only meant tell him he sounds as if he were a stuck phonograph record. Nothing... violent. If that's what you were thinking?'

'You seem very sure where you were between those times yesterday, Mr Huish. How is that?'

'Oh, because it came up in conversation. Afterwards.' He tugged on his cravat.

Seldon stiffened slightly. 'After *what*?'

'After we learned about that Porritt being found dead. The

footman came to tell us. And to say we'd been ordered to stay in the drawing room by his grace until it was time to go and dress for dinner.' Huish let out a huff. 'You see what I mean now about how unsettling it's been? Once Taylor had stopped sounding off to Miss Whitwell and me about the shocking way it had been handled, we got to talking about things. And I think one of us mentioned how lucky it was we'd all been together all the time.'

Why would that have been lucky, Ellie? No one except Loft-house and the duke knew Porritt had been murdered until later on.

Seldon looked up from his notebook. 'Mr Huish, did you remain in the drawing room for the entire twenty-minute duration?'

'I just said so, didn't I?'

'No.'

'Sorry. I did. Stay there the whole time, I mean.' Huish blinked rapidly as if to add to the contriteness of his tone. 'Next question?'

'Did you see anyone outside during that time?'

'It was bitter. And the shoot practice was on hold, Inspector. Everyone was very fractious about it when Mr Porritt said he had to go and collect... er, well, Lady Swift, of course, as it turned out to be.' He grimaced. 'I say, Lady Swift, you must have got out of the car and walked straight in on the fellow's corpse.'

She hid her shudder at the memory. 'Mr Huish, the chief inspector is the one who is asking the questions.'

'Oh, yes. Did I see anyone outside?' He tapped his fore-head. 'Yes. Mr and Mrs Musgrave stayed on the terrace, Chief Inspector.'

'And did either one, or both of them, leave the terrace at any point?'

Huish fiddled with his cravat. 'I think so. But after a while I sat on the Morris pomegranate print settee, facing away from the window, so I couldn't see if they'd just stepped off for a moment and then come back.' He looked up. 'Do you know, some philistine had left a jasmine print cushion among the pomegranate ones? Dreadful!'

Eleanor caught a muscle flinch in Seldon's lean jaw. 'How do you know the duke?'

'His grace?' Huish's eyes widened. 'Me? Know him? How could I? He's a recluse. But he sent me an invitation for his Christmas shoot. And etiquette being what it is, one couldn't say no.'

'His grace had obviously heard something of you to warrant the invitation. What might that have been?'

Huish groaned. 'My supposedly illustrious heritage is all I can imagine. Not my art, sadly. My family name, you see, still carries something of a notable weight, Chief Inspector. But only because England lives, thrives and dies on old glories.'

'I see. What do you know about Mr Porritt?'

'He was the duke's secretary, that's about all. Seemed competent enough. Everything was running smoothly until he disappeared. Died, I mean.'

'Was murdered, you mean,' Seldon said matter-of-factly. 'Anything else? Did you chat to him?'

Huish shook his head vehemently. 'I didn't chat with him, no. But I'm an artist. All people I encounter are subjects to me, whether or not I like them. To capture someone in oils, my mind has to harness their most essential characteristics. Words don't always reflect correctly. Art transcends words. Perhaps you're an art lover, Chief Inspector?'

'No. Last question. Do you recognise this?' Seldon held out the gold pendant.

Huish wrinkled his nose. 'Can't say I do.'

'Thank you, Mr Huish, that will be all for now.'

As he stepped out, Clifford stepped in and closed the door.

'I have located the lady, Chief Inspector. Or rather relocated her. To the passageway outside.'

Seldon jerked upright. 'Miss Whitwell? Well done, man.'

Eleanor gave her butler a teasing look. 'Lucky you'd packed your dashing charm in your valise, Clifford.' At his tut, she added, 'To temper Finbar, I meant.'

Seldon smiled. 'Clifford, your mistress is incorrigible! Now, before you show Miss Whitwell in, we've got two discrepancies so far.'

Eleanor nodded, eyes bright. 'Yes. Earlier the Musgraves insisted they never left the terrace, but Huish and Taylor both recall they did. The Musgraves also mentioned Huish, Taylor and Miss Whitwell were in the drawing room, but that one of them left at some point. Whereas Taylor and now Huish have both insisted they never left the drawing room. So, if they are telling the truth and the Musgraves aren't, that only leaves Miss Whitwell. Which means she, along with the Musgraves now, would have had the opportunity to kill Porritt.'

Seldon nodded. 'So let's hear what she has to say about—'

The door flew open again. Gladstone cowered in Eleanor's lap, but instead of Huish's hound, Pearl Whitwell stood on the threshold, hackles raised.

'I don't like to be kept waiting!' Her tone was as sharp as the cut of her dark-bobbed hairstyle. Her bold scarlet jacket and long skirt seeming to declare danger was in the air. She marched up to the desk and looked Seldon over hungrily. 'Oh, but then again, maybe I do. What's your name?'

'I am Chief Inspector Seldon,' he said coolly. 'And kindly wait next time until you are asked to enter, Miss Whitwell.'

She shrugged and turned to Eleanor. 'Hey, you.'

'Hey yourself,' Eleanor said rather over brightly. 'I don't believe you've met my fiancé?'

Pearl spun back to gaze at Seldon with a pout. 'I don't have to have an audience, I'm sure?'

'Lady Swift is kindly acting in the capacity of observer.'

'Oh, well.' She dropped into the chair in front of the desk and folded her arms. 'Can't we get started already?'

Seldon opened a new page in his notebook. 'Certainly. Now, yesterday afternoon, between three twenty and three forty—'

'I was in the drawing room which adjoins the west terrace. With Julius Huish and Willoughby Taylor. It was cold outside. And the shoot practice had been halted. Infuriatingly.'

Seldon frowned. 'Please answer the questions as I ask them, Miss Whitwell. Not before. Now, what did the three of you do in the drawing room?'

'Talked. Generally. But mostly we carped about the fact we were losing practice time while we waited for Lady Swift to arrive.' She turned to Eleanor. 'We talked about you too. Wondering what you'd be like. I was closest, of course.'

Seldon called her attention back by tapping the desk. 'Miss Whitwell, did any of you leave the drawing room during the twenty-minute window between three twenty—'

'And three forty, I know. No. The three of us were still there when the footman came to say the secretary was dead.' Eleanor and Seldon exchanged a glance. 'And,' Pearl continued, 'therefore the darned shoot practice was postponed. It was the final straw!'

'Murder always is,' Seldon said gravely. 'Did you see anyone outside while you were in the drawing room?'

'The Musgraves. They were on the terrace. But I've no idea if they stayed the whole time, before you ask me.'

'What made you think I was going to?'

'Taylor. He slid up to me as I came downstairs, saying he thought you'd got them in your sights after his little chat with you.'

'For your information, Miss Whitwell, I am asking questions of everyone at Auldwyke Hall. What do you know about Mr Porritt?'

'That's he's dead.'

Seldon waited a moment, then made a note and looked up. 'Mmm. Interesting. Moving on—'

'No wait,' Pearl said, looking less assured now to Eleanor's mind. 'I'd never met him before yesterday morning, so his being dead is the only fact I know. And that he was the duke's secretary. Which probably explains why he seemed so organised. It's a pity some of the guests weren't also.' She glanced meaningfully at Eleanor.

'Anything else about Mr Porritt?' Seldon said firmly.

'He wasn't for me. At all.'

'Do you mean you felt he treated you differently to the other guests?'

'No, Inspector. I meant he wasn't my type. I like tall, sporty-looking men.'

Seldon's jaw twitched. 'I repeat, Miss Whitwell, please keep your answers relevant to the questions I ask. Now, how do you know his grace?'

'Seriously? I don't know him. I've been here over twenty-four hours and he hasn't so much as waved from the end of a shadowy hallway. It seems he doesn't leave his apartments on the third floor. Surely you've grasped that, at least?'

'Then why are you here at Auldwyke Hall?'

'To win the shooting competition. Obviously. I like to win. And I fully intend to.'

'Why would his grace have invited you particularly, Miss Whitwell?'

'Lucky name out of the hat? To make up the numbers? I don't know. And neither do I care. Now, I need to get ready for the first round.' She flounced up.

Seldon rose and pointed firmly at her chair. 'Miss Whitwell,

I haven't finished. Which means you are not done here yet. Please retake your seat.'

Reluctantly, she sat back down. 'How many more questions are there, for goodness' sake?'

'That depends.' Seldon held out the pendant to her. 'Do you recognise this?'

'That? Hardly. Too gauche for my tastes.' She cocked her head petulantly. 'Now can I go?'

As the door closed loudly behind her, Eleanor turned to Seldon. 'So the Musgraves insist Huish, Taylor or Whitwell left the drawing room around the time Porritt was killed. But all three deny it, Huish and Taylor counter-claiming it was in fact the Musgraves who left the terrace.'

He nodded thoughtfully. 'So who's lying? One of them? Or the Musgraves? And why?'

24

Changing for the competition had felt a fiddlesome waste of time to Eleanor. It was true she was keen to wear the new fern tweed belted jacket and matching culottes now swishing at her long leather-booted shins. But she was bursting to get on with observing the other guests. So as Seldon tugged her gently to a stop, leaving the others following Lofthouse towards the shooting range, she huffed.

'Hugh, please save whatever list of cautions you're itching to give me.'

'I haven't got a lecture, Eleanor,' he said resignedly. 'Mostly because I know it will only spur you to stubbornly do the opposite.'

She adjusted the brim of her sage felt hat with the sporting feather in the leather band. 'Probably. What is it then?'

'I need to tell you something.' Her heart skipped as he held her hands out on either side with a tender smile. 'That you look too radiant and beautiful for words. Particularly with the end of your cold nose matching your irresistible fiery red curls.'

She laughed. 'Likewise, Hugh. I've never seen you in sporting togs before. You look positively delicious. Especially in those three-quarter length knickerbockers.' She gestured down his russet tweed ensemble, which ended in thick ribbed socks hugging his divinely built calves. The colour intensified his chestnut curls and gorgeous brown eyes more than she wanted to resist. 'Where did you pilfer all that from?'

'I didn't pilfer anything, Eleanor! I'm a policeman, remember? Which is also why I didn't ask any questions when your butler thoughtfully appeared with them as I'd brought nothing suitable, not surprisingly.' He tugged at the fabric. 'But they aren't knickerbockers!'

'Ah, there's no mirror in your room, I see,' she said, fighting a smile.

'Clifford? Help a fellow out, please?' Seldon called behind him.

Her butler appeared as if by magic. 'Yes, Chief Inspector?'

'What is the name of these ridiculous trouser things again?'

'"Breeks", in shooting parlance.'

'And in pantomime parlance?' she said teasingly. 'Now, come on. Everyone else will already have arrived.'

'Such a familiar lament,' she caught Clifford mutter.

The shooting range itself was a complete surprise. She'd been too preoccupied focusing on Porritt's murder to pay it any attention. The long, free-standing stone platform, rising eight feet, was adorned with an exquisitely carved garland of intertwined roses. Twelve hip-height columned plinths were regimentally spaced along its impressive fifty-yard length. A red metal pail, emblazoned in gold with the Auldwyke coat of arms, stood smartly at the foot of each plinth. Wider, balustraded wings flanking each end of the platform added extra grandeur.

'Gracious, this looks rather serious, chaps,' she whispered as she climbed the last of the steps, gripping her heated handwarmers in her pockets. 'Surely we could have just spread ourselves out across the grass?'

Clifford tutted. 'And negated the element of "fair play" the precisely designed shooting positions provide? Besides, I am minded to think his grace instructed his architect to model this as a memorial tribute.'

'To his poor wife, of course. How sad he can't bring himself to join us even briefly.' She felt Seldon's fingers squeeze her shoulder.

She tuned in to the fact that the other guests all seemed to have bagged a plinthed position along the platform and were staring at her, tapping their shotguns.

'Lovely day for it, with the wind having dropped and the sun coming out,' she called chirpily.

With Seldon following, she hurried over to where Lofthouse was deep in conversation with Bowes. Beside them, three tall and formidable-looking metal trunks stood on end, their open fronts revealing they were purpose-made cases for an array of different shotguns mounted in polished wooden racks.

'Bowes is more the expert, m'lady,' Lofthouse said, stepping to one side. 'Havin' served on all his grace's shoots. Long afore they was changed to clays, rather 'n game.'

'I should say a twenty bore for Lady Swift,' Pearl called to Bowes. 'So many advantages for the slender-framed female.'

'I'll check my options, but thank you for the thought, Miss Whitwell,' Eleanor said brightly, trying not to stare at how strikingly masculine the woman's outfit was. In her Norfolk jacket and sporty 'breeks' as Eleanor now knew they were called, there was no mistaking she had dressed to improve her chances by dispensing with any feminine clothing or decorum. Something Viola evidently wasn't bold enough to emulate given her heather high-collared top coat and pleated skirt which finished at her stout-booted ankles.

It didn't take Eleanor long to choose a gun. The ones Bowes gave her to try from the first two trunks felt either unpredictably light or capriciously awkward. The second from the last trunk, however, had her nodding confidently after firing a test shot.

'Perfect, thank you.'

Bowes' weather-sculpted brow furrowed as he tugged on his grey scarf. 'Beg pardon for sayin' but he's a twelve gauge, m'lady. Not even a midway sixteen. Meanin' as he's got a kick like a furious donkey. And he's gettin' on for near thirteen ounces heavier 'n the lighter twenty gauge.'

She nodded. 'Which explains why it feels like the two of us might understand each other. You see, even though it was a while ago, I'm only used to the weighty, bull-spirited old rifle I had out in the South African bush.'

She'd learned to shoot there some years ago, as a necessity, while scouting safari routes in the wilds for Thomas Walker's prestigious travel company. But that had been mostly for the worst-case scenario of facing a hungry lion or charging hippo. Thankfully, she'd never had to use in earnest what she'd learned.

But her words to Bowes hadn't been missed by the others. Not judging by their poorly concealed glee at her being at such a disadvantage.

'Well, good luck all the same, Lady Swift,' Pearl said unconvincingly.

'South Africa! Pointless place,' Barnabas grunted. 'No business opportunities in sand, swamps or scrubland.'

'Can we please get started, for goodness' sake?' Huish called impatiently from his shooting position on the platform.

Viola nodded vehemently, making her high-crowned lilac felt hat wobble. 'We're all standing about getting cold feet.'

'Good! Competition nerves give one a helpful edge,' her husband said, earning himself a glare.

'I'm sorted gun-wise too, now, thank you, Mr Bowes,' Seldon called.

'Well, I'm bally well handicapped by mine!' Taylor grouched. 'I always use a Boss and Company, over-and-under barrel. Not this Holland and Holland side-by-side I've been lumbered with here.'

'Like all of us have, Taylor,' Huish shot back.

Barnabas snorted. 'I'd say these firearms are about as responsive as museum muskets. And I'm a left-handed shot, to boot. Most unfair!'

'Plus, we've always favoured Purdeys for our guns,' his wife added.

Eleanor smiled genially. 'Well, given that I'm a shotgun novice, that at least levels the playing field somewhat. More sporting. Which is the essence of competition, don't you agree?'

'No, Lady Swift. It's to win!' Pearl said scathingly.

'Actually, I agree, Lady Swift. Which is why I'll share a nugget of invaluable information to be sporting toward the novice.' Taylor stepped over and ran his hand along her gun. 'You see, with a fully choked barrel as you'll have, eighty-five per cent of the shot will be delivered within a forty-inch diameter at forty yards. So just point and fire. You'll be fine.'

His eyes flicked to Seldon before he turned and strode back to his firing plinth.

'Disgraceful tactics. That is categorically not so, my lady,' Clifford murmured. 'Only seventy per cent of the shot will. And within a thirty-inch diameter.'

'Willoughby the worm, I see!' she murmured back.

Seldon frowned. 'Absolutely. Thanks, Clifford. Let's get this nightmare over with then.'

Eleanor took firing position number four to have the empty number three between her and Pearl in position two. With Taylor not far off in position one and Huish on her right in position five, she was near enough to closely watch all three guests. Positions six, ten, eleven and twelve were empty. Seven, eight and nine were occupied by Seldon and the Musgraves, who had swapped places after Viola had kicked up a fuss. Purely to be next to Seldon, Eleanor mused, as the woman openly preened her hair and batted her eyelids at her completely unaware fiancé.

Clifford stepped over with a smart leather bag filled with cartridges.

Eleanor nodded towards the gardener and under-gardener. 'So those cannon-like things Bowes, Fripp and Tosh are wheeling to the edge of that shallow pit are going to chuck out our glass ball targets, I guess?'

He checked her cartridges thoroughly as he said, 'Indeed, my lady. They are the "traps", one placed either side of the shooting range. Both are of significantly vintage stock as are the glass balls being used as "clays". The trap itself consists of a weighted base supporting a tensioned, spring-coiled arm which is adjustable to create differing angles of trajectory. The long lever is hand operated to release up to three glass ball targets or "clays" on a competitor's cry of "Pull!" Mr Lofthouse is standing in Mr Porritt's stead as judge at the scoreboard, with myself acting as second adjudicator in case of contested judgements. A misfired clay will be declared a "no bird". A target missed, a "miss". And one hit, ahem, a "kill".'

'Unfortunate in the extreme, given what happened to poor Porritt,' she said grimly. 'But with the echo of the gunshot, how will Lofthouse be sure if a target is hit?'

'Because the glass clays are filled with a silver-grey powder. The explosion will therefore be easily observed.'

'But how many shots do we each get? And at how many clays?'

'That is information as yet unknown. But I believe we are about to be enlightened.' He gestured to where Lofthouse was marching to the central point behind the firing plinths, arms raised to attract everyone's attention.

'Ladies and gentlemen, in accordance with his grace's orders, today's competition will run as a royal flush. Over halfs.

Fired in braces to the orphan clays. Movin' to double rise. Standard, varyin' twenty-two throughout.'

As if that made everything clear, he marched back to the scoreboard. Evidently it did to the other guests who busied themselves loading their guns and perfecting their stances.

Seldon strode over, ostensibly to collect his bag of cartridges from Clifford. 'Please tell me you can explain what in blazes all that was about?' he hissed.

'Aside from baffling gibberish?' she added.

'Quite.' Clifford arched a sympathetic brow. 'Each competitor will have one hundred glass clays. Fired from the traps, two at a time, except the twenty-fifth and fiftieth balls, which will be fired alone. The first fifty clays will be fired from one trap only. The next fifty from two traps simultaneously at opposite sides of the range. The angle of trajectory will vary with every firing, but within a consistent arc of twenty-two degrees either side of the central line. That being indicated by the two posts mid-field.'

Eleanor's brow knitted. 'Which I hadn't even noticed. Talk about being thrown in at the deep end. I want to miss as few as possible, though.'

Seldon shook his head disbelievingly. 'Lady Swift, do you ever not charge after every challenge like a proverbial rhinoceros?'

She lowered her voice to a whisper. 'Not when I want to goad a murderer into revealing if they killed Porritt in order to get an audience with the duke. Or make sure their favour was granted, Hugh.'

'Point taken,' he said soberly.

'Remember, my lady. Chief Inspector. Only the top four today go through to tomorrow's second round.' Clifford bowed from the shoulders as if to leave.

'Wait!' she hissed. 'Any tips up your infallible sleeves?'

His eyes twinkled. 'I suggest, my lady, hitting as many glass clays as possible.'

She smiled sweetly. 'Ah! Not aim at your head rather than the target in the hope of blunting your razor wit, then?'

'No, my lady. However, in all seriousness, try to avoid the natural temptation to close one eye on looking down the gun's sight. Availing yourself of all your peripheral vision will allow you to spot and track the clay's trajectory earlier. Good luck.'

She shared a look with Seldon as Clifford strode away. 'Our level best each? For poor Porritt, Hugh?'

He nodded and retired to his shooting position.

'First half. Begin!' Lofthouse hollered.

25

A hush fell over the shooting party. Eleanor stared out at the blanketed field, the snow deadening all sounds, as if nature was holding its breath along with everyone on the terrace. She breathed deeply and reminded herself that whatever happened, it was still Christmas!

'Pull!' Taylor cried, making her jump. She fought the urge to watch the glass clays fly across the sky and studied him instead. All signs of his normal swagger were gone, replaced by intense concentration, his gun tightly gripped as he stared along the barrels. He suddenly jerked the stock to his cheek, the crack of two shots tearing the air.

'Two misses!' Lofthouse declared.

'Oh, hard cheese, Taylor,' Huish called with more than a hint of delight.

Taylor scowled.

Pearl adjusted her stance for the umpteenth time, looking like a taut tigress waiting to pounce. The stock of her gun was already held fast to her cheek.

'Pull!'

'Two kills!'

She glanced smugly at Taylor.

Huish, up next, looked around nervously. 'I say, give a chap some quiet, would you?' he demanded testily.

Definitely betraying his nerves, Ellie. No one was speaking anyway.

She didn't know if it was his nerves again, or his lack of skill, but he missed both clays. Looking dejected, he pointedly turned away from the other competitors.

You're up, Ellie!

Grateful her pocket handwarmers meant her fingers weren't cold, she slid a cartridge into each barrel and closed it with a snap. Left foot forward, she found her natural point of balance. Taking her time to mount the butt comfortably into her shoulder, she pressed the walnut stock against her cheek and whispered, 'Work with me, friend.' Reminding herself of Clifford's tip to keep both eyes open, she took a deep breath.

'Pull!'

The flight of the glass clays seemed so much faster than it had with the others. Before she could register how indistinct their shape was, they had passed the centre of the field. Trying to follow them without swinging the gun wildly ahead or behind their trajectory took every screed of calm she could muster. She fired. Once. Even expecting it, the vicious recoil from the first discharge seemed to punch into the second. Twice. A cloud of silver-grey powder unexpectedly popped in the sky.

'A miss,' Lofthouse declared. 'And a kill.'

Pearl glared at her. 'A novice, Lady Swift? You expect us to believe that?'

'After nailing only your second clay?' Taylor put his hands on his hips.

'Genuinely, I am,' Eleanor said truthfully, forcing down a wash of triumphant delight. She had other, more important things to concentrate on. Her fiancé was up to shoot. She snapped her gun open and emptied the spent cartridges into the red pail at her feet. With the intense blasts in her right ear still making her grimace, the acrid cordite smoke stung her eyes.

Seldon's first round was hampered by two "No bird!" judgements from Lofthouse. There was a collective muttering of annoyance from the others while the trap was checked.

'Being a police detective, you'll be a crack marksman, no doubt,' Barnabas growled.

'Not at all, Mr Musgrave,' Seldon said smoothly. 'I never carry a gun. I've seen the worst they can do. Too many times.'

Pearl smiled slyly at Eleanor as she called out to him, 'Chasing down murderers with just your truncheon at the ready, Chief Inspector. How brave.'

Seldon ignored her and retook his position. 'Pull!'

He scored two misses, which he waved off. But she caught him slapping his forehead, a sure sign he was furious with himself.

Viola's demeanour made Eleanor blanch as she readied her gun for firing. With the hard set of her jaw and steel-eyed look, she had the air of a woman imagining she was squaring up to settle a score. She, too, missed both targets, releasing a loud flurry of colourful words. Clifford shook his head to himself in disapproval.

Her husband, who had been watching her shots like a hawk, threw his hands up. 'For pity's sake, Viola. What were you playing at?'

'I wasn't "playing", Barnabas! Let's see you do better.'

'Couldn't do any worse!'

Missing both, it seemed he couldn't do any better either.

It was only then it struck Eleanor. As a couple, they had two chances to win. But did they have the same favour in mind to ask from the duke? The Musgraves seemed at odds over everything. Maybe the favour itself was what they had rowed about on the terrace when Porritt was murdered?

The tension mounted as the first half continued. Taylor found his stride and led for three rounds. Then lost it to Huish, who then had the look of a dog with two bones. Eleanor managed to stay within four shots of the lead score, with Seldon only just behind her. Irritatingly, Pearl kept one ahead of Eleanor at every turn. The most delighted, however, seemed to be Viola, who stole a march, overtaking her husband. It didn't last, as hurt masculine pride pushed him into overtaking her in the next round.

By the latter rounds, Eleanor had got her eye in and her natural competitive spirit made sure she hit two clays in a row. This earned her a muted flurry of begrudging applause, except from Seldon, who gave her a rousing clap.

By the midway point, they were in joint fifth place. Behind Huish in fourth, Barnabas in third, Pearl in second, and Taylor in the lead.

Much to Eleanor's delight, a break was announced. She eagerly indulged in the hot coffee and brandy snifters being served by Lofthouse. Along with finger sandwiches of smoked salmon, egg and watercress, cucumber and mint, and roast beef and horseradish served by her own butler. The large plate of sliced Christmas cake looked decidedly inviting, too. Seldon joined her, teasingly rolling his eyes as she waved for Clifford to add more sandwiches to the dainty serving he'd mischievously given her.

'Hearty commendations so far, my lady. Chief Inspector,' he murmured.

'On the scores, yes. Not progress on the suspects, though,' she whispered back. She nodded at the steps where she'd spotted several competitors getting together. 'Hugh, you stay here and keep an eye on the Musgraves. I'll take Huish, Taylor and Whitwell.' She instructed Clifford to guard her refreshments and followed the three discreetly down the stairs, and ducked out of sight around the corner.

'Intimidating my eye! He's only a wretched policeman,' her sharp hearing caught Taylor say.

'Who can cause us serious trouble!' Huish shot back.

'Alright. But stop griping,' Taylor grouched. 'It's simple. We all just need to stick to the same story. That'll fix everything.'

'Men, honestly!' Pearl hissed scathingly. 'I bet you were both so busy buffing your egos through each of your interviews, you missed the real danger entirely.'

'Which is?' Huish muttered.

'It's not that chief inspector we need to worry about,' she snapped. 'It's his wretched fiancée! Now, let's get back before it's noticed. But separately.'

Eleanor hurried back up the stairs, trying to walk nonchalantly across the terrace. The Musgraves were sitting at either end of a bench, as if the other had something contagious.

Seldon, then Clifford, joined her. She jerked her head backwards. 'Watch Huish, Taylor and Whitwell when they return. I'll tell you why later.'

'Second half begins,' Lofthouse announced as Bowes stationed himself at one trap and Fripp with Tosh stationed themselves at the other on the opposite side of the range.

Seldon appeared beside her with a groan. She nodded.

'I know. The path of the glass clays was unpredictable enough before. And now they'll be flying from both directions as well. Dash it!'

By the mid-point of the second half, she was finding it increasingly hard to concentrate on observing her suspects and trying to improve her score. Miraculously, however, she remained in the top five. Which felt like more pressure she didn't need.

As her next round arrived, she blotted out anything other than becoming one with her shotgun. Her fingers sensed a partnering spirit beyond the cold steel, while her shoulder appreciated the reassuring fit of the butt nestled snugly into it. And her cheek found the stock a soothing balm to her charged emotions. She fired twice.

'A kill,' Lofthouse declared. 'And another kill! Lady Swift is now in fourth place.'

'Another double hit for Lady Swift. Pick your game up, will you, Viola?' Barnabas fumed.

'Contested!' Pearl called in a spiteful tone. She flicked self-consciously at her dark bob as Clifford stepped over to her.

'Might I enquire contested on what grounds, Miss Whitwell?'

'On the grounds... we were led to believe she's a novice!'

Her transparency was embarrassing, the others giving her cutting looks.

Clifford glanced at Lofthouse who shook his head. 'With apologies, overruled, Miss Whitwell.'

Eleanor had to will herself not to react as she caught Pearl's death stare after Clifford's retreating form.

There's a woman who would kill to win this competition, Ellie.

'Five pairs of clays apiece remaining,' Lofthouse announced.

Eleanor smiled at Seldon encouragingly as his turn arrived. He was now in sixth place and needed every score he could get.

'Miss,' Lofthouse declared. 'And a kill.'

That puts him fifth, Ellie!

The last two rounds were nail-biters. Huish seemed to have succumbed to the pressure as he dropped below Eleanor, pushing her up to third. Barnabas was repeatedly rounding on his wife, despite his own score now placing him second to last. And then in Seldon's final round, he hit both of his targets, which leapfrogged him over Huish. She cheered loudly, ignoring Clifford's horrified flinch.

'Royal flush. Completed,' Lofthouse announced.

The group broke out into loud chatter.

The footman called everyone to order by semaphoring his arms.

'Qualifiers for tomorrow are Mr Taylor with 81 clays. Miss Whitwell with 79. Lady Swift with 64. And Mr Seldon with 62.'

The Musgraves turned to each other. For the first time seeming to be united, albeit in acrimonious disappointment. Faces flushed, they made a poor job of consoling each other, given every other word was a criticism. Huish, conversely, made her shiver as he looked daggers at Taylor.

She shook her head. Feelings were running high. High enough, perhaps, for another murder?

26

'Please say that again, Mr Lofthouse?'

'If as you want, sir. But it won't change owt. Them's his grace's orders.' Seldon opened his mouth to reply, but before he could, Lofthouse hurried on. 'He'll grant you a five-minute audience on the half hour afore dinner gong this evenin'. Not one moment longer. Nor earlier.'

For a moment, Eleanor was sure Seldon would explode. Instead, he nodded calmly. 'Excellent!'

Lofthouse recoiled. Brow furrowed, he looked almost... disappointed, Eleanor thought. Dismissing him with a nod, she threw Clifford a mystified shrug, receiving only his ever-impassive look in reply before he also left.

'Excellent, Hugh?' she said, once they were alone. 'Gold star for controlling your temper. And maintaining your composure. But, dash it, now the investigation is on hold for hours! So how is his grace's latest edict in any way excellent?'

Seldon spun her gently by the shoulders and slid her jacket on. His deep voice tickled her ear as he murmured, 'Because I shall put the time to a truly important matter instead.'

'What could possibly be more important than solving Porritt's murder?'

He shook his head. 'Not more important than seeing justice is done, obviously. Nor more urgent. But it's up there. I know we haven't searched Porritt's office yet, but finishing our conversation has to be top priority as well. Our conversation about our future together, remember?' he whispered.

'Oh, yes! Where shall we go?'

'Who cares?' He laced his fingers into hers.

They stepped out the front door to find the snow falling lightly and Clifford deep in explaining the intricacies of Auldwyke Hall's architecture to a disinterested, but dapper-looking Gladstone, snug in his quilted tweed coat. The bulldog seemed much more interested in what was in the oval green leather case next to him.

'Ah, Clifford. We're off out.' Seldon led Eleanor down the steps. 'We'll be back in time to interview his grace, obviously.'

'Very good, sir,' Clifford murmured. 'Very good, indeed.'

Having no plan, they let their boots take them around the snow-covered driveway past the east side of the house. They continued up the slope behind to the start of a wood, populated with ancient oak and elm trees.

'I haven't got any sausages, old friend.' Seldon lifted the bulldog's scrabbling paws down from his borrowed shooting breeks. 'Hang on!' He gaped at Gladstone, then stared down at the lead in his hand. 'How in blazes did I miss us bringing him along?'

Eleanor laughed and tapped the green leather case her bulldog was trying to reach that was hanging from his shoulder.

'My wonderful scallywag butler, of course. You were rather preoccupied. But I didn't see him do it either.'

They linked arms and set off down the meandering path through the forest, enjoying Gladstone gambolling and sniffing around them. With the sun shining weakly, the swathes of red holly berries they passed made the wood seem particularly Christmassy. Even the birds seemed to sing with festive glee.

A weathered swing gate blocked their path. After wrestling to open it, Seldon gave up. 'The latch is rusted shut and frozen to its mounting. We'll have to turn back.'

She shook her head, laughing. 'You city boy! Once we're married, how are you going to manage being lord of the manor in the rural wilds of the Cotswolds if you're defeated by a sticky gate?'

His brow furrowed. 'I didn't know I was going to be. Or that we'd live there. Not for certain, anyway. Nor, how I can ever be anything "of the manor". Especially a lord.'

She winced. 'Oh, gracious! It was a joke. A bad one. I'm sorry. But that's what we're here to talk about.'

She nudged aside a thick clump of snow-frosted nettles to reveal a wooden step to the side of the gate. 'It's a stile. And as Gladstone knows, you simply lift this slotted part up to let him through.'

'I think it's designed for less portly ones,' Seldon said with a chuckle, helping her bulldog wiggle his way through while she stepped over.

Leaping over the gate with one hand on the top bar, he landed beside her, then cupped her chin. 'Eleanor, enough torture. Let's make our plans without any more misunderstandings.'

She nodded emphatically. 'Most of our past conversations have been misunderstandings, really.'

'With heavy doses of murder talk mixed in as well, unfortunately.'

She sighed. 'It would be wonderful if we could banish misunderstandings and murder from our conversations with each other. Especially once we're married. But the only way to reduce the amount of time we spend talking about murder at the moment is to solve poor Porritt's.'

'And the only way to reduce the amount of time we spend misunderstanding each other at the moment is to be brave and carry on talking. Especially about our future together.'

He pulled her to his chest. 'Just imagine, if for the next four years and nine months neither featured in our conversations?'

She laughed. 'For four years and nine months? I didn't know you'd been counting?'

The steeply descending path forced them to pause the conversation as the going was icy and too narrow to walk side by side.

'Sounds like tumbling water,' she said after a while. At the bottom, they were greeted by the enchanting sight of a waterfall cascading down the rocks into a clear green pool, encircled by centuries-worn stones now turned to shingle. A small wooden footbridge crossed the pool, with lush, elfin ferns sprouting between the craggy stones below. The smaller trickles of water had frozen into myriad icicles resembling Jack Frost's fingers. By the side of the pool, soft emerald moss covered the snug hollow in a boulder that had fallen from the hillside eons ago, offering an inviting-looking love seat.

Seldon held Gladstone firmly around the middle while he lapped at the water. 'I've rescued you from foolhardy swimming before, old friend. And that looks freezing.'

Before she sat, he insisted on clearing the snow off the impromptu seat and laying his jacket down. Once the two of them were settled with Gladstone cuddled into her side, he nodded.

'You first? Or me?'

She looked around, shaking her head slowly. 'You know, Hugh, it's such a fairy-tale place and the last few days have been so...'

'Stressful?'

She nodded. 'I know we need to have a serious chat soon.

Very soon. But could we, maybe, just enjoy the moment here and talk about less... weighty matters?'

He nodded, already unbuckling the picnic case and pulling out a Thermos flask. Pouring a cup of delicious-smelling mulled wine, he handed it to her.

She took it, glad of the warmth. 'Hugh, what's your naughtiest memory growing up? I've asked you a lot of things, but never that.'

He rolled his eyes teasingly. 'Naughtiest? Trust you. Ah! I know.' He grimaced. 'To my shame, when I was twelve, I really didn't like one of our neighbours. So I snuck into her garden and switched all her washing on the line for our other neighbour's washing.'

She laughed. 'Not the worst crime.'

'Hmm, it was when our neighbours were the retired Reverend Potter and Miss Trixie Delight. Of dance hall fame. So her washing was mostly... indescribable.'

'Hugh, that's priceless! I'll never lose the image of you grabbing Trixie's underfrillies in your hot, clammy hands.'

He shook his head. 'Hot and clammy is right! You have no idea what illicit lacy bits do to boys of twelve!'

Once she'd stopped laughing, he pulled out from the bag a tin of savoury herb crackers and roasted walnuts. Plus a waxed paper pouch containing a selection of cheeses and another of baked meaty treats for Gladstone.

'Best memory of growing up, next, you've never told me?' She savoured a moreish cracker as her bulldog devoured the treats.

He thought for a moment. 'Helping my mother do the laundry she took in, between cooking jobs.'

She leaned forward eagerly. 'I don't remember you ever mentioning that.'

'It was a lot of extra work.' Her heart squeezed as his eyes misted over. 'But I loved it, because it was just the two of us.

She used to dream aloud. Of having a cosy home. Some pretty things. Enough money not to worry.' He swallowed hard. 'I never managed to get her any of those things before she died.'

She hugged him. 'Oh, Hugh, it wasn't your responsibility. Where was your father?'

'He died when I was six. Just passed away in his sleep one night. He was a wonderful man. And my hero. He still is.'

'That's why your mother went into service, then? You mentioned that once. And that she was dismissed unfairly.'

'Yes. When I was ten. It was the night we were thrown out I made up my mind to become a policeman. Even at that age, I understood she was being used as a scapegoat. And that she had no one to turn to for help.' He smiled as she squeezed his hand. 'Mine is far from a sob story, Eleanor. After a time of moving here and there, we always had a decent enough roof over our heads. And food. Because Mother was a cook. I... I just wanted more in life for her.'

'I wish I could have met her. What was she like?'

He smiled. 'A big and generous heart wrapped in brisk practicality.'

'Like you,' she said genuinely. 'That's why you've got kind eyes, and hands, too.'

He turned his hands back and forth. 'I have no idea what you mean.'

'No. Just as you've no idea how divinely handsome you are.'

He shook his head. 'I think we need to get you an eye test, Eleanor.'

She slapped his arm. 'You're hopeless! Next question. Is it too much to ask what you dream of, Hugh?'

'Of course not! However much it makes me blush. As it likely will. We're going to be married, after all, Eleanor. One day, at least. I want it to be that you can ask anything. Anytime.' He took her hand in his. 'I dream of you and me. Of me keeping you safe. And making you happy. And watching you grow into whatever you want to be. Of me somehow being the best husband since husbands were invented. Which is still less than you deserve. And I dream of... our family.'

'Oh, Hugh! How did I ever believe you were short on feelings?'

'Because I carped repeatedly on about being a policeman. And feelings have no place in that world.'

'So you learned to strangle them.' She winced. 'Oh! Bad choice of words, sorry.'

'Unfortunate. But accurate. Eleanor, I meant what I said about leaving the police force. I want us to have a proper life together.'

She snuggled into his neck. 'Please, just think it through. Better still, talk it through with me when we have more time. And I'm sorry again about my lord of the manor remark. That was insensitive.'

He kissed the tip of her nose. 'Don't apologise. I'm under no illusions. I fell for a rhinoceros and that's that.'

'Rotter!' Her smile faded. 'It's a tricky one though, isn't it? Where we'll live, I mean. Your house holds such important memories for you, I know. Even though you've been careful not to mention it.'

'As Henley Hall does for you, my love. We've never acknowledged how much we have in common in one way. But blast it, shut up, man!' He thumped his leg. 'I don't want to spoil things.'

'Then let me say it quickly. Albeit years apart, both our spouses died at the hand of another. And we both helped find justice for each of them. Although, there the similarities end. My marriage wasn't much of a one, given it only lasted a few months.'

He pulled her tighter. 'Please believe me when I say I've finally moved on from my earlier chapter in life. Completely.'

'Me too. It's time we both built a new life, Hugh.'

'Together. At Henley Hall.' At her gasp, he nodded. 'Yes, because I know you still feel your beloved uncle's spirit there. And, because the most endearing thing I've seen blossom in you over the years of getting to know you is that you've finally found somewhere you can call home. If I wouldn't be intruding on that, of course?'

Her eyes welled up. 'Don't be daft. You're the last thing missing to make it perfect.'

'Now,' he said gently. 'How about we take a break and walk? And then it's my turn to grill you!'

27

Eleanor navigated the footbridge's unevenly spaced planks with care. Behind her, Seldon carried Gladstone across for fear he'd tumble into the pool, there being no sides and the wood icy underfoot. The path out of the enchanting dell led them up and around the back of the waterfall, through a forest of ferns and broad-leaved ivy. As they neared the top, it felt as though they were climbing into a different realm. The greenery thinned dramatically, surrendering to knee-high acres of snow-bonneted heather.

'Gracious, this is equally beautiful in its own way.' Eleanor stood mesmerised by the magnitude of the white blanketed Yorkshire Moors which rose and dipped to the faraway horizon, only one isolated half-ruined hut puncturing the skyline.

Seldon slid his arms over her shoulders and pointed. 'Looks like we can return via that track.' She followed his finger as he traced the line of a descending drystone wall ahead. 'That rising smoke must be from Auldwyke Hall's chimneys beyond the treetops down there. This snow is getting heavier. But I wouldn't go back now even if I was frozen to the bone. I've got you to myself for a few hours, Eleanor. For the first time. Ever, I think.'

'Alone except for my rather hapless chaperone, of course.'

She pointed at Gladstone's furiously wagging tail sticking out of a patch of heather. He jerked his head up at his name, the peak of snow on his nose tumbling off as he woofed his agreement that this was far too much fun to end yet.

'If you're sure, Hugh?' At his nod, she waved him on. 'Then that little barn, just the other side of the track over there, looks a romantic spot to devour the rest of our picnic in.'

He laughed. 'You're supposed to be too smitten to think of eating!'

Up close, the barn was made of grey stone, no more than twenty feet in length and less than half that in width. Its steeply sloped roof was covered in a blanket of freshly fallen snow. At one end an ancient iron bell sat in a short stone frame, while at the other, a weathered gable porch shrouded an arched wood door. The door looked as if it had been hewn from King Arthur's round table itself. She pointed at one of the windows.

'It's stained glass. Mary and Joseph cradling the baby Jesus. It's a tiny chapel, not a barn. Perhaps we'd better find somewhere else?'

Seldon shook his head. 'You said you liked Assertive Hugh. Well, he's here. And he definitely wants to go inside.'

She was surprised. He'd never given the impression of being overly religious.

'What for?'

He clipped Gladstone's lead onto his collar and nudged her forward in silent reply.

She turned the pitted iron ring on the door. It creaked open with a wail of rusted hinges. Bowing her head, she stepped inside. Her breath caught. The Lilliputian house of worship was peppered with baskets of dried flowers and neat stacks of exquisitely embroidered prayer kneelers. Four petite pews were set on either side of the short flagstoned nave. The simple font had clearly been a labour of hand-sculpted love that had started with a rock straight from God's green earth itself. While the diminutive altar of dove-grey stone was bathed in the pale sunlight streaming through the nativity window. But it was the modest pulpit that caught her attention most. Built of unadorned wood panels, with a polished shelf serving as the lectern, it was raised only by the height of one flagstone.

'What a beautiful chapel this is,' she breathed.

Seldon coaxed Gladstone to sit and then stepped to the altar. He beckoned her to join him. Taking both of her hands in his, he whispered, 'I want to stand here with you, just as we will in whichever church we finally take our marriage vows in. So I can dream of it constantly until it's actually our wedding day.'

Her heart skipped. 'So do I, but we'd never hear the vicar over Clifford's constant tutting if I turn up like this in tweed culottes with stout boots and a feathered hat.'

He shook his head. 'Just as you do now, you'll look too beautiful for words in whatever you choose.'

'Bless you, children,' a rich-timbered voice called.

They broke apart guiltily. An elderly man with a head of grey hair framing a deeply lined face above a clerical collar stood before them. The creases around his animated grey-green eyes suggested to her his formidable tone wasn't a reflection of his disposition. As did the cheery, cherry-red bobble hat he wore.

As if to confirm her thoughts, he let out a rumbling chuckle as Gladstone, rather than staying as commanded, shuffled on his belly along the stone floor towards him.

Eleanor smiled apologetically. 'So sorry. We didn't mean to intrude.'

He held up his hands. 'This is God's house, dear lady. Intrusion is not possible. Welcome you be. I am Reverend Yeadon.'

For the first time, she noticed over his black cassock he

was wearing a bibbed calico apron. A wide pocket spanned the top, with three square ones below. From all of them cascaded loops of different coloured wool; cardinal red led the procession through its rosy brethren to seasonal oranges and celestial golden yellows. The lower pockets continued with all of nature's greens, through ocean teal and turquoise to sky and violet blues, ending with Bishop-worthy purples and indigo.

'Still, we've clearly interrupted you, Reverend,' she said, enjoying his evident delight in kneeling to pat the wrinkled jowls of her now soppy-eyed bulldog.

'Not at all. Company is always a pleasure.'

Seldon gestured at Eleanor. 'This is my fiancée, Lady Swift. I'm Hugh Seldon.'

Reverend Yeadon shook their hands warmly. 'I assume you are both staying at Auldwyke Hall as guests of his grace?'

She nodded.

'Ha! Then he won't miss me keeping you both up here for a short while to chat and meet my good friend, Mr Ruddock. It was he who told me you were here.' He folded his hands across his apron. 'If you can bear to indulge me, that is?'

'We'd be delighted,' she said genuinely, finding something irresistible in his manner. It was only then she had a pang of doubt about the vicar's lucidity. She glanced around. There was no one else in the chapel who could have alerted him to their being there.

Reverend Yeadon motioned for them to follow him into a tiny room furnished with two stools, a lidded coal scuttle with a cushion on top and a miniature pot-bellied stove. The only other item was a wooden frame, which was home to an exquisite half-finished tapestry. He closed the door, untied his apron and hung it on the one hook in the wall.

'Do take a seat. Both of you, I insist.' After they were seated on the stools, he sank onto the coal scuttle and adjusted his bobble hat. 'I might even have a quart ounce of tea left somewhere.'

'Actually,' Eleanor said, 'we've a simple picnic with us if you, and your, er, friend would care to help us finish it?'

'Verily, dear lady! Our Lord has seen fit to send you here with refreshments and the grace to share them. Who am I to cast that aside?'

As Seldon unpacked the picnic, she chatted.

'Your congregation must be a thriving, tight-knit group, I imagine? Seeing as they trek so far off the beaten track to your services.'

'Would that I had one, dear lady,' Reverend Yeadon said in a wistful tone.

'Oh! But you have so many prayer kneelers.'

'Yes. But they are my gift to other ministers when theirs fall into disrepair. And my diversion to keep busy while serving Our Lord in my thoughts alone.'

She gaped at him. 'You've made them all yourself?'

He nodded and pointed at the wool cascading from his apron hanging on the hook, then at the half-finished tapestry. 'Wool is so much sturdier and comforting to devout knees than embroidery thread. Plus, I do a line in bobble hats for winter wear.' He smiled, tapping the ribbed cuff of the one he was wearing. 'But yes, since his grace became a recluse years ago, my sermons have been delivered to a congregation of mostly one.'

'Mr Ruddock?' she ventured. Before he could answer, she started at a fluttering sound beside her. She turned, as a stout, red-breasted robin landed by her shoulder.

'Allow me to introduce Mr Ruddock, a stalwart member of my congregation,' Reverend Yeadon said. 'Forgive his lack of manners. And his inability to shake hands.'

'Oh, I see, then you're not...' Eleanor's cheeks coloured.

'Going mad, cast away up here in the wilds of the Yorkshire Moors?' He chuckled. 'No, dear lady.'

Gladstone seemed entranced by the bird. All the more so when it fluttered over to sit on his head and tease a hair from between his ears.

Seldon held out the savoury crackers and cheese selection. 'Can I ask what his grace becoming a recluse had to do with you losing your congregation?'

'Of course, young fellow. I once had the privilege of being the spiritual guide and mentor to his grace's staff. And guests, whenever entertaining was the order of his week. Plus a few villagers who wished to gawk at the high and mighty, as they seemed to them. Well, everything changed when his grace shut himself away. And without him attending here, his staff no longer came. Likewise his guests, since none were invited to Auldwyke.'

'Except for the annual Christmas shoot, as we have been?'

'I believe so. But only from the shots I've heard. And the extra smoke rising from the Auldwyke chimneys.'

'Then, it's a wonder your beautiful little chapel is still left in commission, if you'll forgive me saying so.' She broke off a tiny corner of cheese for Mr Ruddock. The robin took it keenly.

'Not a wonder, dear lady. Salvation. Courtesy of his grace.'

She was desperate to ask more, but feared it would be rude.

Reverend Yeadon smiled at her. 'An open heart gives an open face, and yours is like a picture book. Let me tell you what you're yearning to ask. His grace saved this little chapel from decommission by taking on the cost of repairs and upkeep. He also funds an annual stipend for myself, so long as I stay in the rectory. It's a small cottage just over the hill. You can't see it from here.' He sighed. 'I'm very blessed.'

Seldon caught her eye and nodded encouragingly.

'Reverend, can I ask when was the last time you saw his grace?'

'Of course, my dear. Christmas Day. Same as every year since.'

'Since?'

'Since her grace passed on to Our Lord. Every year, on the anniversary of that day, his grace comes here to attend a private sermon, delivered by myself. And then sits by her grave until the sun has long set. The duchess is buried in the little grave-yard behind this chapel, you see.'

Seldon cleared his throat and busied himself giving in to the robin's pointed chirp by crushing the last piece of walnut in his hand and holding it out for him.

'Does his grace walk up for your annual sermon, Reverend?' Eleanor said casually.

'Goodness, no. His health prevents him from doing so, now even more than before.'

'So Mr Porritt has driven him here in recent years?'

'Yes. He always waits respectfully in the car. I remember him attending services as a lad in short trousers! How I delighted in seeing him grow into such a fine young man.'

'Will he be buried in the graveyard here, too?' Eleanor said sadly.

Reverend Yeadon frowned. 'I would not know until the time comes. Hopefully, many years hence if the Lord sees fit.'

Eleanor's insides clenched. 'Perhaps you haven't heard?' she said quietly. 'Mr Porritt passed away yesterday.'

Reverend Yeadon's face creased. 'Young Porritt? Oh my! He will be in my prayers tonight.'

Eleanor took a deep breath. 'Forgive me being so blunt, but he died at the hand of another.'

Reverend Yeadon looked ashen. 'So he...'

Seldon looked sharply at him. 'Did you happen to meet Mr Porritt recently?'

Reverend Yeadon sighed deeply. 'Yes. Yes, I did. Once or twice. He... he wanted to ask my advice. In confidence.'

She leaned forward. 'Mr Seldon is actually a chief inspector and is investigating this terrible crime. Can you tell us of any reason someone would want Mr Porritt dead?'

Reverend Yeadon hesitated. 'No, no, I... I can't. By sanctity of my vow.' He let out a long breath. 'But I will tell you, he was a troubled young man of late. A deeply, deeply troubled young man. With the very best of intentions, mind.' He shook his head sadly. 'Intentions which, it seems, proved fatal!'

28

Helping interview a suspect was usually fraught enough to Eleanor without the awkwardness of being incongruously dressed. And the full-length moss-green silk dress she'd put on for dinner felt incongruous indeed. And the duke, being an unknown quantity, was exacerbating her nerves further. Seldon, tugging on the cuffs of his black velvet evening jacket, told her he felt the same. He sighed and ran his thumbs gently across the delicate sea-green embroidery along her scalloped neckline.

'You looking so beautiful in this new gown makes it even worse, Eleanor. I should be giving you a proper Christmas. Not dragging you into a murder investigation, blast it!'

'You're not dragging me, Hugh. I got you into this mess, remember?' She smiled, wanting to tease his usually tousled curls out of the strident combing he'd inflicted on them. 'But thank you for noticing my gown is new. I'm impressed. But like you, I'm keen to get this interview started.' They shared a grimace. 'And over with,' she added for both of them.

Seldon frowned. 'Where's Clifford? He abandoned us here over five minutes... Ah, finally!' he grunted as her butler appeared around the corner.

'Well?' she urged. Clifford arched a knowing brow. She rolled her eyes and smiled sweetly. 'Point taken. Hugh and I need to take a deep breath and play ball with his grace like good little children and overlook all his eccentricities.' She leaned forward and hissed, 'Although his shocking disregard for keeping people waiting is outrageous!'

'Notes the mistress of such,' her butler murmured.

She winced. 'Fair enough. But in my defence, I don't do it on purpose. I just find it hard to always be on time.'

Seldon interrupted them. 'What in blazes is happening, Clifford?'

'The other guests have retired to their rooms to dress for dinner, Chief Inspector. The staff are all deep in the meal's preparations. And Mr Lofthouse is on his way to escort you both to his grace's apartments.'

'But why have we been forced to wait in the gloomy depths of this wretched maze of a house?' Seldon gruffed. 'Eleanor hasn't even had a seat.'

'Quite,' Clifford intoned. 'However, all will be revealed. Ahem, literally.'

The footman's heavy footsteps halted Seldon's reply. Like Eleanor, he stared both ways along the passage as they stopped with no sign of the footman.

'Quickly, please. His grace won't stand for bein' kept waitin'.'

Lofthouse's voice made Eleanor jump. She turned, clutching her chest on finding him standing close behind her. A section of the oak panelling was actually a cleverly disguised door. On the other side, an intricately carved wood staircase spiralled steeply up into the shadows.

'Any more conjuring tricks we should expect, Mr Lofthouse?' Seldon said crisply.

'No. This way.' The footman turned back briskly to the stairs.

'Good luck with his grace,' Clifford murmured to Eleanor. 'And in ascending those stairs elegantly in evening heels!'

Hindered by needing to hold the folds of her gown, she held firmly onto the stairwell's thick capping rail with her other hand as she followed Lofthouse. At the top of the three flights of stairs was an octagonal landing, adorned with a crimson rug with the Auldwyke coat of arms emblazoned in gold. In front of them was a formidable black oak door flanked by two statues on marble plinths; on the left, a rearing boar. And on the right, a majestic stag.

Lofthouse made an unnecessary meal of producing the iron key she recognised as the one Clifford had lifted from Porritt's jacket in the storehouse. To her surprise, he slid aside the covering plate of the lock without knocking, inserted the key and turned it.

'Approaching now, Your Grace,' he called, sounding like a respectful foghorn.

On the other side of a wide expanse of pale marble flooring were several doors. Through the only open one, she just caught sight of a shadow crossing the floor.

'Five minutes only, m'lady. And, sir.' Lofthouse closed the main door behind him as he left the apartments.

Alone, she and Seldon nodded to each other.

'Here goes,' he muttered.

Her satin heels and his smart dress shoes echoed across the marble as they crossed the floor and entered the far room.

'Good evening, Your Grace.' She looked around.

Only a sharp hiss from the veritable tree burning in the vast cowled fireplace answered.

They were in a spacious sitting room with a deep-vaulted ceiling, lit only by the furthest of three chandeliers, leaving most of the room in shadows. A dramatic curved bank of floor-length windows flanked by railed shutters filled the end wall. Beyond, she could see the inky backdrop of the Auldwyke estate grounds and, beyond that, lay only the desolate moors. The windows rattled as if the blizzard now raging outside was trying to force its way in. Two burgundy-dressed settees faced each other like opposing factions across a thick ivory carpet runner in the centre of the room. The only other seating was a judge's bench with tall sides which would not have been out of place in a courtroom. It was set at an angle, facing the windows. Beside it, a lion-clawed free-standing mirror stood glaring at them.

She frowned, gazing around the carved walnut furniture lining the walls. No doubt Clifford would have delighted in detailing what constituted bureaus, commodes, secretaires, and credenzas. All she saw was a forest of forbidding dark wood. And no host.

A portentous off-key chime of the half hour from a clock hidden somewhere out of view made her brow furrow even further.

Then she noticed it. A movement around the high-side of the bench seat. A gnarled oak tree of a man with a thatch of grey-white hair that ran down to his equally thick whiskers appeared slowly, with the expression of a thunderclap. He was dressed in a sombre ash and ebony striped evening robe that ended below his black-suited shins and matched the looped cravat tucked tightly inside the wide shawl collar. She realised he'd been silently watching them in the deliberately angled mirror.

'Good evening. Though, I do not appreciate the intrusion,' he said in an unexpectedly rasping voice for such an aristocratically large frame. As he came closer, Eleanor noticed his clearly once majestic shoulders were stooped and his breathing laboured, which perhaps accounted for the silver-handled cane he was leaning on. His deeply lined brow and ghostly pale complexion suggested he was in his early seventies. Though the razor-sharp intelligence burning in his piercing hazel-eyed glare

and his lightness of step made her think she could be ten years
out in her estimation.

'You are Lady Swift, I understand?' he said to her, ignoring
Seldon.

'Yes. Delighted to meet you, Your Grace. However, we have
no wish to intrude.' Eleanor threw Seldon a soothing look.

'And I am grateful for your time, too, Your Grace,' Seldon
said. 'I just have a few questions regarding the murder of Mr
Porritt.'

The duke leaned forward on his cane, looking Seldon over
as if he were something he'd find in the sludge at the bottom of
his ornamental lake. 'I am the Duke of Auldwyke! Which
means I answer to no one. Most especially not to jumped-up
policemen from Kirkwell who think they can impress me by
daring to brazenly appear on duty in evening wear!'

'Your Grace,' Eleanor said more tartly than intended, but
too bristled on Seldon's account to rein in her words. 'This is
Chief Inspector Seldon. Of Scotland Yard. He is, in fact, not on
duty by choice. He is your guest, accompanying me as my
fiancé.'

'Your fiancé!' The duke's bushy eyebrows met in disdain. 'A
titled lady and a policeman, engaged? Whatever next!'

'Marriage. A devoted and happy one, too,' she said firmly.
Then faltered.

But when, Ellie?

29

Rallying herself, Eleanor looked the duke in the eye. 'Refreshing, isn't it? If one chooses to be enlightened, of course.'

'I choose as I see fit,' he growled wheezily. He rounded on Seldon. 'Whoever you are, I want this matter completed swiftly and kept quieter than silence itself. Do you understand me?'

Seldon nodded. 'I do, Your Grace. But I can't do either of those things without cooperation. Yours included.'

'Sit!' the duke commanded, breaking into a coughing fit.

Eleanor stepped to the carafe to pour him a glass of water, but stepped back at his dismissive wave. She sat on the settee, Seldon then perching on the other end, flicking open his notebook.

The duke sank onto the edge of the furthest settee. 'Now, Inspector, your five minutes is disappearing fast. And I will not tolerate guests late to dinner.'

Eleanor fought the urge to point out to the duke that as he never joined his guests, he wouldn't know if they arrived an hour after the gong. Or if they'd danced the fandango between courses.

Seldon looked up from his notebook. 'Do you have any idea why someone would want to kill Mr Porritt, Your Grace?'

Outside, the storm renewed its assault, pummelling the windowpanes with fierce gusts.

'No.'

'You seem very certain.'

The duke scowled. 'Being of entirely sound mind, why wouldn't I be? And I do not appreciate your inference otherwise.'

'No inference intended. But as Mr Porritt's long-standing employer, I need to know how much you knew about him.'

'He had only been my secretary for three years or thereabouts. Quiet in his habits. Ardent. Efficient. He arranged everything, including the guest list for this shoot, as he did last year. That shows how efficient I thought him, and how much I trusted him to do his job. And that's all I can tell you.'

Seldon's pen shot across his page. 'Did he ever discuss anything about—'

'Inspector! Porritt was a member of my staff. I would not have tolerated him discussing anything at all with me except what was needed for him to carry out his duties. And he knew it unquestionably. By Jove, he knew it!'

Seldon's brow flinched fleetingly. 'Moving on. Where were you between three twenty and three forty yesterday?'

The duke's expression turned thunderous. 'And you'll have me believe there's no inference in that insolent question either?'

'Yes, Your Grace,' Seldon said smoothly. 'A purely routine question. And one I have asked everyone in this house. To establish the whereabouts of all. So, you were where, please?'

The duke harrumphed grumpily. 'If you must know, I was in my office. As I always am every afternoon. Unlike those who choose to spend their time in unwarranted interruption of others, I am a man of precise habits which I apply purely to my own business.'

'Thank you,' Seldon said, rising above the jibe. 'Did you see or hear anything out of the ordinary between those times?'

'No. I wasn't idling my time staring out of the window, but busy at my desk, naturally.'

'I see. Your office is where?'

The duke jabbed a finger at the opposite door to the one they'd come in by. 'The room adjoining this one.' He gripped his cane tighter. 'Inspector, I am tiring rapidly of your questions.'

'I apologise, Your Grace. But I am trying to discover who murdered your secretary, Mr Porritt.'

The duke stared back dispassionately.

Eleanor couldn't stop herself from adding, 'The very same young man who grew up on your estate. As a result of your kindness.'

The duke flapped his hand, but his gaze dropped to his robe sash, which he busied himself adjusting.

Seldon reached into his pocket. 'I'd like to know if you recognise this?' He stepped around to the duke and opened his hand to reveal the gold pendant Porritt had been clutching.

Another coughing fit seized the duke. Seldon fetched him a glass of water.

'Do you recognise it, Your Grace?' Eleanor said, once the duke had sipped enough to recover his breath.

He shook his head without even looking again. 'No. And I—'

The huge central window exploded into the room with a spine-chilling *boom*. Eleanor and Seldon instinctively ducked behind the settee as the wind howled into the room, blowing a frenzy of whirling snowflakes and glass shards with it. The duke, his brow thunderous once more, merely stared at the jagged rock which landed a split second later between the settees.

'Looks like a single rock,' Seldon shouted above the wind. 'But stay put while I check, Your Grace.'

He hunched his way along the side wall to the end of the bank of windows, lashed by a wall of wind and snow. Just as he started to straighten up, a volley of missiles flew through the broken window and smashed in clusters of more shattered glass.

Eleanor's arms were a rash of goosebumps. She stared mesmerised as the wind whipped up what looked like whirling dervishes of smoke from the debris.

Then she understood. There was no mistaking the stinging in her eyes and throat as the smoke reached her. Nor that smell!

'Cyanide!'

Eleanor's warning cry turned into a hacking cough as the deadly gas invaded her throat.

'Hugh!' she screamed.

With her eyes and lungs burning, she groped her way over to the catatonically wheezing duke. Through the pounding in her ears, she caught an ominous whoosh.

'Watch out! More missiles!' she cried again, grasping for the thick runner rug. Hurling it over the duke, she cowered, hands over her head as more explosions showered her in broken glass.

'Eleanor!' Seldon yelled from somewhere across the room, retching violently. 'Get out. With the duke. Now!'

She hesitated.

There's no time, Ellie! Do as he says.

Before she could move, over the whistling of the wind, she heard the screech of the solid wood shutters being rolled in front of the shattered windows. And just in time. The dull sound of more missiles hitting the outside of the shutters made her shudder.

Ignoring every fibre of her body that begged her to check her fiancé was alright first, she tried to stem her own violent coughing as she grasped the now worryingly breathless duke. She winced in pain, the rug thick with sharp glass shards.

Throwing it off, she dragged him to his feet, pressing him down to keep him in a crouched position.

'Got him, Hugh!' she yelled. 'Tell me you're alright before I—'

She got no further as she doubled over gasping. Closing the shutters had shut out more cyanide missiles from landing in the room, but it had also shut out most of the wind. The wind which had diluted the cyanide by whipping it into the air. Now it was forming a solid wall of death between her and the door to safety.

The duke turned his head weakly, his eyes running.

'Leave me, woman! Get out!' He collapsed onto his knees, wheezing horribly.

'No!' Eleanor grasped the duke's arm and pulled, but she couldn't lift him. She gasped as she felt her lungs constrict violently.

It's too late, Ellie.

30

A rug flew over her bowed head, smothering the rising gas in front of her. A hand shot out and grabbed the duke's other arm.

'Hugh!'

Together, they hauled the duke up, and propelled him out of the room into the hallway. Seldon slammed the door shut behind them. They leaned against the wall in the hallway, drawing snatched breaths of clean air, the sound of pounding feet coming from the stairs.

Someone hammered on the outside door of the apartment.

'My lady!' Clifford's anxious voice called, muffled by the thick oak.

Eleanor propped the coughing duke up as Seldon staggered unsteadily to open the door.

Clifford strode in. 'My lady, are you hurt?'

'I'm okay,' she managed between retching and spluttering. 'We all are. Just about.' She gestured for him to help aid the duke.

Seldon returned to her side, still coughing, with Danby behind him.

'Eleanor.' His throat sounded sore, as if it had been rubbed down with glasspaper, just as hers felt. 'We all three need to get out of our clothes and get into a bath or shower immediately! And' – he swallowed with difficulty – 'drink milk. It might help a little.'

He turned to Clifford and Danby. 'There's no time to explain. Except to say there was an attempt on the duke's life.'

Clifford spoke up. 'Constable Danby and I will pursue the attacker.'

Without a word, Danby followed Clifford out of the door. As the sound of their footsteps flying down the stairs rang out, Lofthouse appeared in the main doorway.

'What is goin' on in his grace's apartments? You've none of you t' right to be...' He tailed off, realising the duke was present.

'Everything's alright, Mr Lofthouse.' Seldon cut the footman off before he realised things were far from alright. Swallowing with difficulty, he continued. 'Someone broke his grace's window with a rock or two. A peevish protest over losing the shooting competition, nothing more. His grace—'

'Is fine!' The duke rallied himself enough to stop coughing for a moment. 'Lofthouse. Your... presence is... not required. Now get out!'

The footman bowed. 'I'll be going, Your Grace.' He shot Seldon a look. 'To tell guests 'n staff his grace is fine.' He spun on his heels.

'No. I'll do that in a while,' Seldon spluttered.

'Aye, and leave me fendin' off angry guests who has no clue what's occurrin'? I don't think so!' Lofthouse muttered, stomping off.

Seldon squeezed Eleanor's arm discreetly. She turned to the duke. 'I used to be a nurse, Your Grace, so you'll be fine in my hands. Where is your bedroom?'

Between another coughing fit, the duke glared at her. 'You will not... I repeat... not... enter my bedroom! The infernal—' He broke off, overtaken by more coughing and retching.

Eleanor steered him forcefully towards the bedroom door. 'Save your breath, Your Grace.'

After administering to the duke, Ellie had hurried to her room, stripped and bathed, while Seldon did the same in his. Returning to the duke as quickly as she could, she checked his breathing was restored enough to leave him to sleep alone. As she slipped out of the bedroom, Clifford appeared. The look on his face said everything. She joined him outside the entrance door to the apartments, trying to hide the still sporadic croak to her voice.

'This is no time for fussing about decorum, Clifford. You're the only one who knows I was in there, for goodness' sake.' She folded her arms, instantly regretting it as the cuts to her fingertips reminded her that she'd grasped the rug through shattered glass.

'That will be the cause of my secondary nightmares only, my lady.' He produced his hip flask and uncorked it. 'Yet another protracted battle over the serious effects of shock going unheeded by my mistress will be the first.'

'Not this time,' she said, realising her legs were shaky. 'I confess, brandy, mint humbugs, throat salve and whatever else you can muster from your wizard's jacket will be gratefully received.' She managed an impish smile. 'A restorative hug if you like.'

'Ahem.' He ran a horrified finger around his starched collar. 'Here comes the chief inspector. And salvation.'

Seldon strode a trifle unsteadily up to them, rubbing his throat and looking drained. At his enquiring look, Clifford shook his head. 'Constable Danby's still scouting for any clues left behind, Chief Inspector. But whoever it was, was long gone before we got down there.'

He sighed, running his hand through his hair. 'I didn't expect them to hang around.'

She blanched. 'Are you alright, Hugh?'

'Always.' He smiled, but it faded quickly. 'And you?'

'Fine.' She cleared her throat and winced. 'Fine enough, really.'

'And the formidable duke?'

'Comfortable enough. But he needs medical attention. And soon. I've no idea how much of that stuff he inhaled.'

Or you, Ellie. Or Hugh.

Seldon grimaced. 'I tried to ring for a doctor, but the line's dead. Lofthouse informed me that this infernal blizzard brought it down. And I can't imagine for a moment that anyone could get up or down here by road now. It was touch and go hours ago when I arrived by car.'

Clifford cleared his throat. 'I fear I have to disagree with Mr Lofthouse, Chief Inspector. I noticed the line down some distance from the house while looking for his grace's attacker. Or attackers. But judging from the way it had been cleanly severed, I think it most certainly the work of man, not nature.'

She let out a deep breath and took another sip of brandy. She passed Seldon the flask and waited until he'd taken a few sips as well.

'Hugh, we need a plan. Someone wants the duke dead.' She shook her head soberly. '*Really* wants him dead! Cutting the phone line and subjecting him to such a... a calculated, malicious attack.' She looked up, real fear in her eyes. 'I'm worried they'll try again.'

'Almost certainly,' Seldon said grimly. 'But with the duke refusing to allow me any more men, what on earth am I supposed to do about it? There's only me, Clifford and Danby to guard him, blast it!'

'Now wait, I can do a shift too.'

'No, you cannot, Eleanor.'

Clifford nodded in agreement. 'Categorically not, my lady. Perhaps instead, Chief Inspector, you could suggest to his grace...' He tailed off at the look on Seldon's face.

Eleanor grimaced. 'I think Hugh's right, Clifford. His grace won't change his mind, despite the danger he's obviously in. We've all seen first-hand how stubborn he is. I suppose it comes from everyone giving him everything he wants without question pretty much from the moment he inherited the title, if not before.'

Clifford nodded. 'I agree, my lady. However, it is not an impossible situation. If I might suggest, Chief Inspector, Constable Danby takes the hours of the day when I am needed to assist with interviews? Then I can cover the bulk of the nights so he can rest.'

'With me doing whatever I can in between.' Seldon shook his head and sighed. 'It's the best we can do. Although, whether it will be enough...' He shrugged. 'Anyway, thank you, Clifford. I'd be lost without you.'

'Me too.' Eleanor risked an affectionate nudge to her butler's suited elbow. 'However, until we catch the murdering wretch who now seems to have the duke in his sights, I doubt any one of us will get a wink of sleep!'

Especially as your throat still feels as if it's been sandblasted in a furnace, Ellie.

31

Eleanor's prediction proved accurate. It was a long and fretful night. At three a.m. she finally ceded to Clifford's brandy nightcap and retired. But her fears over when and where the killer might strike next dashed any chance of sleep.

If he, or she, strikes again, Ellie.

Her throat, as predicted, also kept her awake. But the duke's worried her more. Which is why she lay down for only a few hours before returning to check on him. The attack had obviously badly affected his already impaired breathing. Hopefully, only temporarily. But with the snow having cut the house off, there was no way of getting him to a doctor or hospital. She'd need to call in on him every three or four hours from now on. Lofthouse had insisted the key to the duke's apartments be returned to him, but Seldon had refused to hand it over and Lofthouse had surprisingly relented, rather than tackle the duke about the matter in his weakened state.

Having left the duke and Auldwyke Hall in the gloomy light of early dawn, she tramped with Clifford through the knee-high snow to the old gamekeeper's cottage.

'Now, my lady. How many of your cook's delectable crumpets shall we fetch for toasting?' he said as he opened the front door.

Eleanor brushed the snow off her clothes in the hall. 'Given that it's Christmas Eve, heaps!' Her stomach gurgled in unladylike agreement.

As she walked into the toasty sitting room, Mrs Trotman put her hands on her hips. 'I'd warrant more like a mountain, Mr Clifford! Likewise, all the toppings to go with them from the pantry. Only they're actually pikelets, which is some kind of Yorkshire crumpet.'

As Polly hurried after Clifford to fetch the breakfast fayre, pursued by Tomkins and Gladstone, who had leaped from their beds at the word 'pantry', Eleanor noticed the tree.

'A Christmas tree! And just look at your darling little crocheted nativity figures!'

Even though it was clearly a fallen bough of spruce, it gave the cottage the perfect festive feel.

Mrs Trotman nudged Mrs Butters, who opened her mouth, then hesitated. 'The thing is, m'lady... well, we don't want to overstep. Only seeing as Chief Inspector Seldon's not allowed any extra men except Constable Danby, we girls were hoping—'

She broke off as Clifford returned bearing a large woven wicker tray. Polly froze in the doorway with her smaller one.

'Hoping you might... help, perchance, Mrs Butters?' he said.

Eleanor's four ladies nodded enthusiastically.

'If only as a washboard,' Polly whispered.

Clifford's lips twitched. 'Perhaps a "sounding board" might be more helpful to her ladyship, Polly.' He turned to Eleanor. 'If that would suit, my lady?'

She nodded in relief, accepting her notebook from him. 'Gracious, absolutely. Your thoughts are very welcome, ladies. Now, I'll fill you in on what exactly happened yesterday evening and last night. And the parts Clifford missed too, as he was caught up elsewhere.'

Lizzie and Polly poured the teas while Clifford buffed the toasting forks, before handing them one each. Eleanor dived to her knees in front of the fire, spearing the pikelets, which looked similar to crumpets, only thinner. Holding them out to the crackling flames, she composed her thoughts.

'Right then, about last night's, um, incident.' She didn't want to use a dramatic word like 'attack'. Especially with Polly there. 'Clifford and Constable Danby discovered that someone had moved two of the traps used in the clay pigeon shooting competition onto the lawn area just beyond the terrace below the duke's windows. One of which they loaded with rocks to break the windows. The other with the glass clays, but ones they'd maliciously tampered with.' She frowned. 'Oh, but you probably can't quite picture what I mean?'

The four women looked at each other shiftily.

Clifford coughed. 'Actually, my lady. If I might interrupt to offer the ladies a well-deserved commendation?'

'Always. But what for?'

'For hiding in the trees beyond the shooting platform in order to support yourself and the chief inspector in the first round of the competition. Miraculously, for such an often rebellious gaggle, without being heard. Or seen.'

'Except by you, Mr Clifford, it seems,' Eleanor's cook huffed. 'Bah! How are we ever going to get a trick past you?'

'I really couldn't say, Mrs Trotman.'

Eleanor laughed. 'Well, you do know what I mean then, ladies. And thank you for braving the cold to cheer us on. It means the world, genuinely.'

Pikelets toasted to a golden brown, she sat back down, torn between her cook's sublime jam, marmalade, lemon curd or roasted nut spread.

Lizzie linked arms with Polly. 'Ach, it were lucky the terrible person as wanted to frighten the duke last night didnae think to do the same at the shooting competition earlier, m'lady.'

'Good point, Lizzie,' Eleanor said. 'Although, the clays last night were filled with what we believe is prussic acid. Which would be effective only in a confined space. Particularly so, if one already had breathing difficulties like the duke, as it irritates the throat and lungs.'

Polly put her hand up.

'It's fine to speak up in front of the mistress on this occasion,' Clifford said. 'Her ladyship wishes to hear everyone's thoughts, remember?'

Polly nodded vigorously. 'But that's why I'd better leave, Mr Clifford. So as you won't keep things back from the others by bein' careful what you say with me here, same as usual. Even though I'm growing up, only just a bit behind Lizzie.'

Eleanor had never seen her ever-composed butler lost for words before. Nor heard her youngest maid sound older and wiser than her seventeen years.

Clifford half bowed. 'I stand corrected, Miss Polly Patton. Please stay. As part of her ladyship's team.'

'Thank you, Mr Clifford.' Polly's expression couldn't have been prouder. 'Because I don't think the gas was meant as just to scare, was it?'

Eleanor shook her head. 'No, Polly. We think it was intended to, well, kill his grace.'

'Then lawks, how is he?' Mrs Trotman said.

'He's recovering. Slowly. But without proper medical attention. The telephone line is down and the road impassable.' She failed to add that the phone line had been maliciously cut. There was no point in worrying them further. 'Lofthouse, the footman, tried to reach the village in the car. And Constable Danby on his motorbike. Both vehicles are still stuck where they slid off the road.'

Lizzie choked on her tea. 'Is he... are both gentlemen alright, m'lady?'

Aha, Ellie! So Lizzie is sweet on Danby, it seems.

'They're both fine,' she said smoothly. 'Constable Danby is scouring the lawns again with a torch right now for any clues about last night's attack. Lofthouse was preparing the breakfast room when I left. And Hugh is guarding the door to his grace's apartments. And his grace himself is well enough to still be impossibly stubborn.'

'Brays one donkey about another,' Clifford murmured mischievously. He raised his voice. 'His grace is indebted to her ladyship for saving his life, or, ahem, should be! With quickness of thought, she flung a rug over him for protection against the gas-filled missiles.'

'Tsk, Clifford! I didn't "fling" anything over him. He's a duke.' Winking at the ladies, she whispered, 'I hurled it over him after I'd wrestled him to the floor.'

Mrs Trotman grinned. 'Then perhaps that is why his grace didn't seem as grateful as he might last night, my lady?'

Once the laughter had died down, Mrs Butters spoke up. 'Does everyone over at the big house know someone tried to kill the duke, m'lady?'

Eleanor shook her head. 'Hugh only told Lofthouse someone threw a few rocks through the duke's window. Possibly after losing the first round of the shooting competition. Then we spread that version of events ourselves to the guests and staff. I think Lofthouse guessed there was more to it than that, but he seems to be keeping his own counsel.'

Mrs Trotman rolled her eyes. 'Lummy, I bet that drew some choice words from them as had lost, though!'

Eleanor winced. 'The most choice from Mrs Musgrave. It's a good job Clifford wasn't there to hear her.'

'What did you do then, m'lady?' Lizzie said.

'Hugh and I discreetly asked each of them where they'd been at the time of the attack while Clifford and Constable Danby equally discreetly searched their rooms.'

Clifford pursed his lips. 'Regrettably, we did not find anything incriminating.'

Mrs Trotman gazed at him innocently. 'Not even among the lady guests' drawers of underfrill—'

'Mrs Trotman!'

Eleanor hurried on. 'Actually, as Clifford was in the kitchen at the time of the attack, he was able to alibi three of the staff, which is a start.'

'So which staff haven't an alibi, Mr Clifford?' Mrs Butters said.

'Mr Lofthouse, Mr Fripp, and Mr Bowes. They—'

A knock at the front door halted the rest of his reply.

Lizzie leaped up. 'I'll go.'

But a moment later, she returned, looking rather pale as she whispered to Clifford, 'He says his name is Mr Lofthouse!'

Eleanor strode out to the hall. 'If you've come for Clifford to help with anything, Lofthouse, I'm afraid I need him a little longer.'

The footman shook his head. 'Nay, not that, m'lady. I've a message from his grace.'

She reached for her coat hanging on the wooden pegs, fearing his breathing had worsened enough to defeat his obstinacy. 'I'll come now.'

Lofthouse shrugged. 'If as you wish, but it won't start for nigh on two hours.'

'What? You can't mean the shooting competition?'

'Aye, m'lady, I do. His grace's orders stand. Everythin's to continue exact as scheduled. Anyone still in the running takes part, or leaves. Immediately!'

'They'll have trouble. The roads are impassable!'

'That's as maybe. Good mornin', m'lady.'

As she watched him stomp away through the deep snow, she frowned, suspicious he had actually come over to learn what they were up to.

Back in the sitting room, a plate of newly toasted pikelets dripping with butter awaited her. The ladies were whispering together at the tree as they hung up woven yarn stars and angels, cinnamon sticks, threaded berry strings, and felt snowmen. They hurried back over.

'You were 'bout to tell us what the guests were doin' when the rocks and gas was sent flying through the window, m'lady?' Mrs Butters said.

She nodded. 'They all claimed to have been in their rooms preparing for dinner.'

Clifford stroked his chin. 'Mr and Mrs Musgrave alibied each other again?'

'Yes. Taylor and Huish also alibied each other.'

Clifford's brow flinched. 'Hmm, collusion, maybe?'

'Possibly. But without Miss Whitwell this time.'

'This time?'

She groaned. 'Dash it! We haven't had a minute without some drama or other for me to tell you.'

She quickly relayed the clandestine conversation she'd heard during the break in the shooting competition between Huish, Taylor and Pearl.

Lizzie frowned. 'But even if the guests were where they said, m'lady, it doesnae mean as one couldn't have snuck down. And set up the traps on the lawn and then snuck back.'

Mrs Trotman rapped on the table. 'Wait! It would have taken more than just a few minutes to move and set them traps up, fire them, and then race back upstairs unseen.'

Eleanor grimaced. 'That's true.'

Mrs Butters clucked her tongue. 'Whoever did it is a brazen menace, alright. 'Twas a risk to think no one would hear a big window like that breaking on the floor below and look out to see what was what.'

Mrs Trotman frowned. 'Who would have known his grace would have been there at that time, though?'

'Any of the staff, or guests,' Clifford said. 'His grace is a gentleman of admirably punctual habits.'

Polly looked thoughtful. 'Who would want his dukeness gone, do you think, your ladyship?'

She sighed. 'I wish I knew. What's making it more baffling is the difference in method.'

'Modus operandi seems at odds between the two deaths, indeed,' Clifford muttered thoughtfully.

Polly shuffled in her seat. 'I give my word not to need a hanky, Mr Clifford, if as you might say how that poor Mr Porritt passed over?'

Eleanor sensed his discomfort, but he answered her. 'Mr Porritt was strangled. With a noose. But in every other regard, his death seemed to have been a spur-of-the-moment act.'

Suddenly, she felt an overwhelming urge to check Danby was alright. She glanced up at Clifford who, as usual, seemed to have read her mind.

'I think, ladies, we will have to leave you for a while.'

She rose. 'Don't worry. We'll be back shortly. And we'll bring Constable Danby with us. I'm sure he must be frozen by now. And starving.'

She noted Lizzie's cheeks flush as she headed for the door.

Policeman or not, Ellie. He's just a young boy and there's a murderer running loose out there!

32

On the second floor of Auldwyke Hall, Seldon leaped up from the heavy oak chair that looked as if it had been sequestered from a mediaeval castle. He stared at Eleanor and Clifford in surprise.

'I've another hour guarding his grace's door until Danby's due to take over. So, to what do I owe this visit?'

Eleanor nodded. 'I know, Hugh, but I'm worried about the young fellow. I thought we might both go and make sure he's alright. It's fearfully cold out there. And—'

'And her ladyship has, for once, been prudent, Chief Inspector. She has not gone charging off on her own into the gloom.' At Seldon's disbelieving expression, Clifford nodded and gestured down the stairs. 'Exactly. If I might therefore relieve you?'

Leaving Clifford on guard, Seldon led Eleanor out of the house by the main door, around what seemed to be a memorial garden and on past ornamental hedging shrouding an old coach house and stables. As they passed the kitchen gardens, he turned to her.

'I know Danby was going to start around this area, so I

expect he'll be somewhere up ahead, knowing how thorough he seems to be.'

Eleanor yanked the hood of her cloak up against the soft snowflakes, wishing she was in the mood to enjoy their festive magic as they settled on her lashes. As they went, Seldon swept his torch in an arc, checking either side to see if there was any sign of Danby. She did the same with the torch Clifford had passed to her, hoping to glimpse the young constable.

Soon enough, after climbing a steep slope and descending the other side, she caught sight of another torch beam off to the right just ahead of them.

As they approached, Danby emerged from the dark, surprise on his eerily-lit face.

'Didn't expect to see you, Chief Inspector, m'lady?'

Seldon saved her blushes by explaining he just wanted to check up on anything Danby had stumbled upon, but she wasn't listening. On the opposite side of the rough path to the two men, her torch had picked up a thick copse. And, she was sure, a movement!

'Hugh! There!' she whispered fiercely. She pointed into the copse. 'Something... or *someone*, just snuck in there.'

Seldon and Danby hurried forward as stealthily as they could, waving her back. They pushed into the bushes and were soon swallowed up, only the beams of their torches partially visible.

A moment later she almost screamed as a form darted out of the copse and shot across the path in front of her. Feeling foolish for raising the alarm, she pushed into the copse.

'Boys! It was only a fox!'

At the lack of response, she penetrated deeper into the bushes, looking for the others' torchlight. But everywhere was dark. As she swung her beam around, she was joined by Danby.

'I think the chief inspector's come out the other side and doubled back, m'lady. That's his torch beam coming... m'lady?'

She spun around as Seldon pushed through the bushes behind her.

'Look!'

Seldon chuckled. 'Another fox? Or maybe a badger, this time, Eleanor?'

She shook her head. Despite the grey-white clouds above and the pristine blanket underfoot, it was ominously dark where the canopy of hazel, hornbeam and hawthorn branches had grown thickly together. However, she trained her torch beam on an eight-foot-high bank of winter-scarred brambles threaded with ivy. Aside from its thorny branches sprouting at all angles, it seemed a peculiarly symmetrical shape for such overgrown vegetation. That had first drawn her attention. Then she'd seen it. A glimpse of aged brick.

'I think it's an old shed. But look! Around the door.'

The three of them hurried up to it. A rotten door hung by one rusted hinge, a mat of hoary creepers tightly woven across it holding it up. But around the door her torch picked up the fresh ends of a recently cut creeper.

'Well done, Eleanor,' Seldon breathed. 'Let's see what we've got here.'

She held her breath as she followed him over the dipped stone threshold.

Inside, broken gardening tools, old boxes, tea chests, garden pots and heaps of sacking lay along three of the walls. She glanced at the fourth.

The shiver that overcame her wasn't from the biting cold. Nor the icy ivy tendrils growing down through the hole in the roof that flicked at her cheek. It was what was lying on the bench.

She stepped tentatively over. A pair of worn gardening gloves, a jar of powdered potash, a metal funnel, a paring knife, a lantern, candles, an old tobacco tin and a rusted drum were laid out in front of her. The tin, on close inspection, was stuffed with spent wax ends, while on the drum she could just make out the words, 'rat poison'.

But it was the crate in the far corner of the bench that made the hair on her neck stand up. It was half full. Of glass clays.

Seldon tilted the rusted tin back on its rim with the end of his pen. 'Feels almost empty.' He shook his head. 'With his breathing already impaired, his grace really wouldn't be here but for you, Eleanor.'

'*Us*, Hugh,' she countered. 'Hmm, I'll bet that large jar isn't filled with potash then, but the original powder contents of the glass clays. And those wax ends aren't from the candles, but are the original seals dug out of the stopper tops. Look.' She pointed at the finger-width neck of a glass clay that had not been tampered with.

Seldon scrutinised the lantern. 'You're right. There are candle wax splatters all around the base here. The wretch used this flame to melt new stoppers into place once they'd poured the deadly contents inside using that narrow-necked funnel.' He stared thoughtfully at the tin of rat poison, a heavy frown on his face.

She nodded. 'Even if the killer's lungs had been in top health, pouring out that amount of poison in a confined space like this was highly dangerous.'

'Might that be as how they did it, m'lady?' Danby pointed under the bench. He'd been so quiet she'd almost forgotten he was there.

With Seldon beside her, she whipped up the hem of her cloak and crouched to look. The war-issue gas mask hanging by its strap on a protruding nail made her insides churn with memories she'd rather forget.

'I just spotted there's three more inside this tea chest behind me,' Danby said.

'As if this wasn't already macabre and sinister enough,'

Seldon muttered, staring at her anxiously. He helped her up, discreetly squeezing her arm as he did.

'What are you thinking, Hugh?' She noted Danby leaning forward to pay attention.

Seldon looked around again. 'I'm thinking I want to search this place thoroughly. But I don't want to tip our hand to the murderer so they realise their hideout has been discovered.' He tapped his chin. 'But given the attack thankfully failed last night, on reflection, I think it's unlikely they'll return here and try the same method again, so let's do it.'

He instructed Danby to scour the shelves while he took the likely spider-infested drawers and remaining tea chests. Insects of the eight-legged variety were one of Eleanor's few weaknesses.

That only left her the bench area and an old iron pot-bellied stove languishing in the corner. She opted to start there, but the door was jammed. She peered down the broken-off stack. Gingerly sliding one hand inside, she hoped there was no hairy-legged nightmare waiting to run up her arm.

'Hugh!' she breathed, yanking her arm back out. 'There's something in here, but I can't quite reach it.'

He was beside her in two strides. Hunching down, he yanked the door open with a grunt and reached in.

'I'd say that's an old gamekeeper's bag,' she said.

He undid the buckles on the green canvas holdall he'd pulled out and opened the flap.

She gasped. 'Hugh! It's a jumper. Navy blue! And wool!' Without a word, from his pocket he pulled out an envelope. From inside he produced the original thread they'd found under Porritt's fingernail. After studying it carefully for a moment, she nodded.

'It matches!'

33

Seldon nodded slowly in reply. 'It does. I'm certain now that whoever strangled Porritt is the same person who tried to kill the duke last night.' His expression darkened. 'Which means we need to totally reassess Porritt's murder!'

Danby glanced from one to the other, confusion on his face.

Eleanor ran her hands down her arms. 'You're right, Hugh. The guests only arrived the morning of the twenty-second, the day Porritt was murdered. It would have been a gargantuan task to get this... this "bomb-making factory" together in that time. Especially without being missed by the other guests.'

Seldon moved back to the bench and looked over what she had now dubbed the 'bomb-making' equipment. 'All normal enough items. Probably all on the premises already. But not necessarily here.'

'Still, the murderer would have needed to unearth it all. And discover this hideout too on that first night after Porritt was murdered. None of the guests are familiar with the estate.'

'And we're a goodly way from the shooting platform,' Danby said, catching on. 'And wouldn't they have needed to have a check of the traps afore making the "bombs"? If as it's not interrupting to say?'

Seldon shook his head. 'Not at all. Chip in, Constable. We need all the help we can get. After all, I'm sure none of us thought we'd be doing this on Christmas Eve!'

Eleanor stared up through the hole in the roof with a frown. 'The fact that this obviously took some planning should suggest it was a member of staff as they know the estate well and could have arranged all this at any time. Lofthouse or Bowes come to mind, obviously, since neither has an alibi for when Porritt was murdered, or the duke attacked.'

Seldon frowned. 'It should. But what do you say, Danby?'

The constable scratched his head. 'Bowes is the more likely culprit. Being the gardener, he'd have the most knowledge and opportunity. But' – he looked from one to the other again – 'I've a feeling I'm missing something?'

Seldon nodded. 'The problem is, you see, we haven't a decent motive for either Lofthouse or Bowes. And even if we had, why would they kill Porritt or attack the duke when there's a whole raft of guests here for the shooting competition? It only happens once a year, after all. Why not wait until they'd gone?'

'To have more people to throw suspicion on?'

Seldon grimaced. 'Possibly. But something still seems off.'

Danby's eyes widened. 'I get it. Your experience tells you, sir, that things just don't stack up?'

Seldon nodded grimly. 'We've either got the wrong suspects. Or...'

'Or, sir?'

'Or,' Eleanor finished for him, 'we're missing a major piece of the puzzle!'

Seldon nodded again. 'Exactly. So, a renewed search, everyone, please. Seeing as this place is our best hope of unearthing that piece of the puzzle at the moment.'

She suggested they swap where they'd looked previously, even though that left her with the spidery piles of sacking and the tea chests. Letting out a long breath to rally her courage, she—

Seldon caught her arm gently. 'Do that again.'

'What? This?' She let out another long breath.

'There!' He pointed at the wafts of silver-grey powder that had swirled up from the bench.

Danby shrugged. 'Isn't that just spilled powder from when the glass clays' original contents were emptied out?'

'In which case, Constable, why didn't this particular patch of powder puff up into the air like the rest?'

Eleanor whipped Seldon's pen from his hand and pressed the end into the powder he'd pointed at. They shared a look as they heard a slight crunching noise.

'Glass!'

Danby's brows knitted further. 'Yes, sir. But the murderer likely just broke a glass clay in their haste to swap the contents.'

Eleanor bobbed down and scoured the floor around the bench. 'Ah! Here's two pieces.'

Seldon bent down and picked up the items using his handkerchief. He traced the curve of each shard with his fingertip. 'Are they both from a glass clay or not?' He frowned. 'With Auldwyke Hall cut off by the snow, I can't send them for analysis. Or call a glass expert.'

'Yes, you can!' Eleanor said.

Seldon nodded slowly. 'Of course! Constable, please relieve Mr Clifford and tell him how to find us.'

While they waited, she and Seldon resumed their search. But by the time Clifford arrived, they'd discovered nothing new. Seldon led him over to the bench and swiftly explained the situation.

'Not good at all,' Clifford murmured, surveying the bomb-making equipment. He slid his pince-nez onto his nose and pulled out his pocket magnifying glass. She watched as he moved the magnifier over a glass clay in the trug, then the suspect powder. After a considered study of the two broken pieces in Seldon's handkerchief also, he nodded.

'The one on the right is a fragment of a glass clay, Chief Inspector.'

'And the other?'

'A fragment of a spectacle lens. Likewise, the ground glass here on the bench.' He took his pince-nez off. 'I suspect the perpetrator we seek inadvertently set a crate down on their spectacles in their haste.'

Seldon frowned. 'How can you tell it's from a pair of spectacles?'

'A simple matter of refractive error, sir. Measurable thanks to the ophthalmoscope created by the renowned Ferdinand Cuignet in 1873. If memory serves—'

'Clifford,' Seldon said, weakly. 'Perhaps the short version? There's a good chap.'

'My apologies.' Clifford offered Seldon the magnifying glass. 'In short, under magnification, you can see scratches on the convex, or outer curve of the glass clay shard, but not the inner. But, on the other piece, fine abrasions on both sides.' His lips pursed. 'Due to cleaning the spectacles with an inappropriate item as opposed to a soft polishing cloth, I would surmise.'

'So our murderer wears spectacles? Good work, Clifford.'

'However, not all the time. They are, or were, for reading only.'

Seldon eyed him doubtfully. 'I don't want to appear sceptical, Clifford, but how can you be sure?'

Clifford produced a pair of needle-nosed tweezers from inside his coat, along with what looked like an outsized, leather-bound postage stamp. He opened what Eleanor realised was its cover, revealing a miniature book, and held it out for Seldon to read.

He stared at it. '"Money… can't buy…" What's that?' He shook his head. 'I can read it, but it's almost as hard as reading Eleanor's writing.'

'Quite, Chief Inspector,' he said drily. He held up the fragment of glass between the tweezers for Seldon to look through. 'Try again.'

'Alright. "Money can't buy a happy life, or a peaceful death." What the dickens?'

Clifford nodded. 'Indeed. Charles Dickens. A miniature version of *A Christmas Carol*.'

Eleanor nudged his elbow. 'Which you're reading so you are word perfect when you treat the ladies and me to your distinguished narration. You softie.'

'So our murderer wears glasses for close-up work. Well done, Clifford,' Seldon said. 'Is that near- or far-sightedness? I can never remember.'

'Far, Chief Inspector. "Hyperopia" in medical parlance. Though not exclusively. The same blurring effect is a not uncommon symptom of ageing, known as "presbyopia". Wherein near vision is increasingly reduced by the lens of the eye losing its elasticity, so to speak.'

Seldon folded his handkerchief carefully over the piece of spectacle lens. 'So our murderer could be any age. And any gender. Marvellous!'

'Have you seen Lofthouse or Bowes wearing reading spectacles, Clifford?' she said.

'No, my lady. But the situation for such has hardly arisen.'

Seldon waved his hand. 'No matter. We'll devise a way to check each suspect's ability to read with or without spectacles.'

'But not now, Hugh. Because they'll all be getting ready for the second round of the shooting competition.'

He shook his head disbelievingly. 'It can't still be on?'

'It is!' She steered him towards the door. 'But in the mean-time, how about we search Porritt's office? We got interrupted before, and maybe that missing piece of the jigsaw will miracu-lously turn up there!'

34

As Seldon unlocked the door to Porritt's office, he waved to Clifford.

'Please stay. In case I need to call on your... special expertise. While I look the other way, of course.'

'Ahem, I can't imagine what you mean, Chief Inspector. However, as you wish.' He patted his jacket front conspiratorially.

Eleanor stepped past him into the office. 'Since you've evidently come to Yorkshire dubiously equipped, Mr Scallywag, it's lucky for you Hugh didn't pack his handcuffs for this Christmas holiday.'

'Forgive my having missed the "Christmas" and "holiday" elements to date, my lady,' Clifford said drily, following behind. 'Hence my coming prepared.'

'Point taken. So then, let's hurry and solve this awful matter before it's too late to even toast in the New Year, let alone Christmas!'

She stopped in the middle of the room, needing to understand Porritt. To get a sense of the young man she'd met barely an hour before finding him so mercilessly dead. And where better than here? In the very room where he'd likely spent most of his waking day labouring over his duties, given he'd been the duke's secretary.

'Poor fellow,' she muttered, grateful her blessings meant she would never have to answer to a man as irascible as the duke to be sure of a roof over her head.

She slowly scanned the space before her. Her first thought was that it was austerely functional. A worn leather-topped desk sat in the middle of the room, a roll-top writing bureau off to one side. Glass-fronted bookcases and chests of drawers formed an almost continuous line around all four walls. Each shelf and drawer was labelled, and filled with what looked like a century's worth of hefty ledgers and record books.

'I imagine the duke's business and financial records are filed in here, somewhere.'

'Of course!' Seldon thumped his forehead. 'Blast it, where's your head been, man?' He strode over to her. 'Hmm, that's where it's been,' he murmured.

'Focus, Hugh!' she whispered. 'Then we'll have more time for the thing we're both desperate to get on with.' She raised her voice. 'You're thinking the same as me, I bet? That Porritt might have been murdered over information he knew about the duke's finances or business dealings?'

Seldon stroked his chin. 'Possibly for blackmail.'

'Or insider knowledge perhaps, Chief Inspector?' Clifford said. 'Being forearmed of the investment plans of a gentleman of his grace's wealth would enable a savvy person of significantly lesser means to coat-tail those investments. And thus substantially increase their own financial stock.'

Seldon pointed at him. 'Excellent thinking.'

'Wait though. The Musgraves,' Eleanor said aloud, even before her thoughts had crystallised. 'And Pearl Whitwell!'

'Go on.'

'At dinner the first night, Pearl mentioned a rumour in some circles. Over his grace having been a recluse so long, it was thought his secretary ran everything. Including deciding if the winner of the shooting competition was granted their favour or not. The Musgraves had heard the same.'

'So you told me before.' Seldon waved his notebook. 'You're thinking then the murderer challenged Porritt over promising to grant that favour and didn't like his answer?'

'It's a possibility.'

'Likewise, another premise based on that same rumour,' Clifford said. 'But not the competition prize. Instead, that the murderer sought to pressure Mr Porritt into investing a portion of his grace's funds in an enterprise which would benefit the murderer more than the duke?'

Eleanor nodded. 'Again, possible. The Musgraves spring to mind. After all, he's a businessman, as he's constantly harped on about it.'

Seldon opened his notebook. 'Right. I'll interview them straight after we finish here. That is, if his grace hasn't conjured up any more edicts to stop me by then, of course. Now, we'd better get started searching. But for what, exactly, I don't know.'

Eleanor glanced around. On the desk, she noted a type-writer already loaded with a sheet of paper with the Auldwyke crest and, beside the telephone, a tiered letter sorter with neatly stacked correspondence. A fan of buff-brown fronted files were labelled 'schedule for sweeping of chimneys', 'maintenance of boilers', 'maintenance of water pumps' and so on, through to guns and cigar humidors. Her eyes glazed over. The tightly filled pages of an open diary caught her eye.

'It's a good thing Porritt's writing was so neat and tiny, otherwise he'd never have fitted his endless tasks into his diary.' Seeing a youthful version of her own treasured butler in Porritt, she threw Clifford a grateful look. 'His grace was lucky to have found someone so trustworthy. Just as Uncle Byron was to have found you. And as I am, thankfully.'

Clifford's lip twitched. 'Thankfully, my lady? How fortunate one of us considers it such.'

Seldon chuckled. 'On that note, Clifford, if you would cast your expert eye over the records and ledgers? And, Eleanor, if you could take the bureau while I search the desk?'

She nodded, only to find the roll top and drawer locked. Clifford glided over, taking only a moment to work his magic. She rolled the now unlocked top open.

'Golly!' She gazed at the small, but lovingly carved, wood figurine. Ostensibly a paperweight, it was a couple's hands intertwined, the fingers of one larger and stronger than the ones it encompassed. She shook her head sadly, the initials 'ML' on the base leaving her in no doubt this was another representation of the love Porritt craved as he carved.

As Clifford stepped over to assist Seldon as the main desk's drawers were also locked, she returned her attention to the task before her. The multitude of small square pigeonholes running along the back of the desk were filled with tradesmen's bills, sorted into categories according to goods or services supplied. All were marked 'paid' and meticulously dated.

Seldon waved a bundle of what looked like letters as she bent to open the bureau drawer.

'The current guests' RSVPs are all here, tied with a ribbon.'

She frowned. 'In which case, I still don't understand how he failed to receive mine.'

She dismissed the thought and pulled the drawer open, thinking it had a peculiarly familiar aroma. It was filled with innumerable keys of every conceivable design, alongside a notebook which detailed the corresponding locks each fitted.

With a sigh, she upturned the wastepaper basket and perched on it gingerly to stare at the bureau. There was nowhere else to look.

'Speak to me, Porritt,' she whispered.

Returning to the bureau, she pulled the pigeonholes out to

see if she could discover a secret hiding place behind. Nothing. She tried to do the same with the drawer, but it stuck. Out of frustration, she yanked harder and then gasped as the whole key compartment lifted. It wasn't a modified drawer at all, but a precisely fitted insert. She lifted it out and froze at the item hidden underneath.

'No wonder I recognised that smell!'

'What have you found?' Seldon hurried over.

She brandished an envelope. 'It's my perfume!'

'Oh, good work.' He stopped, looking a little crushed.

'Hugh, what's the matter?' she whispered.

He tugged a hand through his curls. 'I just didn't realise you dabbed your perfume on your letters to... to other people.'

She smiled. 'I don't, silly. But the bottle I keep in my handbag somehow spilled when I cycled down to the village to post it. Along with the card I posted to you at the same time, to say I was missing you dreadfully.'

He smiled. 'That was the best treat to come home and find on the mat. I...' His brows knitted. 'But why did you send Porritt a letter? What was it about?'

She opened the envelope and pulled out the card inside as Clifford joined them. 'I didn't send him a letter, Hugh. It's my RSVP! The one Porritt insisted he never received, but as the envelope seal is broken, had obviously read!'

She passed him the card. His eyes widened as he read it. 'I don't understand. It's unequivocal that you weren't accepting the invitation, Eleanor. But Porritt hid it and pretended he'd never received it. Why on earth?'

They all stared blankly at each other, deep in thought. Clifford broke the silence.

'He obviously wanted, no, *needed* her ladyship's presence for some, as yet, unknown purpose.'

'And I think it's not too fanciful to assume,' Seldon said slowly, 'that that purpose had something to do with whatever got him killed.' He turned to her. 'Eleanor. Think, please. What exactly did he say when he telephoned you and you told him you'd declined?'

She closed her eyes. 'That he hadn't received my RVSP.' She held up the card. 'So naturally he'd assumed I, we, Hugh, were coming. Because, especially to someone of his grace's standing, it's quite unforgivable to forget to say one isn't coming.' She frowned. 'Or to decline at all, actually. Porritt mentioned it's very rare anyone ever has.'

'What else?' Seldon coaxed.

'Er, that his grace would be hugely indebted if we dropped everything and hastened up here. As would he. He was honest, if very respectful to the duke. Even when he hinted he'd get it in the neck for having let it slip his mind to telephone me the week prior to confirm.'

Seldon grimaced. 'Hmm. That sort of slip-up is not how his diary and notebook suggest he attended to his duties. They're like the impossibly meticulous way I've seen you work, Clifford.'

He half bowed. 'Thank you, Chief Inspector. And I agree with your assessment.'

Seldon threw his hands out. 'Then why would he have wanted you up here so badly, Eleanor?'

She shrugged, totally flummoxed. 'To make sure the numbers weren't short?'

Clifford raised a brow. 'My lady, a single telephone call would have had half the country biting Mr Porritt's arm off for the chance to be at his grace's annual Christmas shoot.'

Seldon shook his head in exasperation. 'What, then, is so unique about Lady Eleanor Swift as a guest to Porritt that even the monied set can't match?'

Clifford peered sideways at her. 'Being mistress of the indecorous? Of faux pas? Of the unorthodox?'

She put her hands on her hips. 'All of which you secretly

delight in, you terror! Otherwise you'd have nothing to chide me over. Or...' Her eyes widened. 'I think I've just realised what's unique about me!'

The two men leaned forward eagerly.

'What, my lady?'

She shook her head. 'Not what? *Who!*' She reached back into the drawer and pulled out a bulldog clip. It was holding what looked like a series of clippings from various newspapers. 'You, Hugh!'

Seldon stared at the headline of the top clipping, his brow creased. '"Detective Chief Inspector Seldon arrests Chelsea Killer,"' he read. He took the clippings and leafed through them, shaking his head. 'They're all about cases of mine. Some dating back over a year. And... the last one's from the *Oxford Gazette* mentioning our engagement!' He handed them back to her. 'Blast it, Eleanor! Would you please explain?'

'Hugh, listen. When Porritt telephoned, I remembered being amazed that he knew I was engaged. And he mentioned you several times. Then in the car from the station, he asked again when you were arriving.' At Seldon's lost look, she took him by the shoulders. 'Hugh, Porritt couldn't have cared less if I came or not! It was you he was interested in.'

Looking unconvinced, Seldon glanced at Clifford. 'What?'

'As the clippings go back at least a year, Chief Inspector, one wonders if Mr Porritt had identified yourself as the man he needed. And then later looked for a, ahem, acceptable way for you to appear as a guest at his grace's Christmas shoot.'

Seldon stared between Eleanor and Clifford, who were both resolutely holding his gaze.

'Two against one, I see.' He held up his hands in surrender. 'Alright. I'll go along with your theory.' He shook his head. 'Just when I thought things couldn't get any more blastedly confusing though!' He frowned. 'In which case, maybe you weren't the only guest Porritt put pressure on to attend,

Eleanor? Maybe he used strong-arm tactics on one or more of the other guests, too?'

'Brilliant, Hugh! Let's get them all back in that interview room and give them a stiffer grilling than last time. Starting with the Musgraves together as we agreed. Given their behaviour at the shoot, they'll probably turn on each other!'

He nodded. 'However, we still have no idea why Porritt wanted me down here, assuming you and Clifford are right. And as I said before, I'm convinced whatever it was, it got him murdered. So, unless we want history to repeat itself, we'd better tread carefully!'

35

Having insisted she check on the duke first, Eleanor then hurried back to the library.

'Are we still interviewing in here?' Seldon said, on catching sight of her. 'No edicts from his grace to the contrary?'

She shook her head. 'Only because he is asleep, thankfully. But his breathing has definitely improved from last night.'

'Excellent. On all counts. In which case, Clifford, could you please?'

Her butler returned quickly with Mr and Mrs Musgrave, who were both wearing their sporting outfits from the shooting competition. And very dark scowls.

With a discreetly mouthed, 'Good luck!' Clifford closed the door behind him.

'I appreciate you both coming.' Seldon gestured at the two seats across his desk.

Instead of sitting down, Barnabas marched stiffly up to him. 'I dare say you do! Particularly as it's Christmas Eve. However, to say you are chafing my patience to its bitter limit, would be an understatement!'

'Thank you for pointing that out,' Seldon said impassively. 'So...' He pointed at the seats again.

Barnabas' moustache quivered. 'Is that all you've got to say for yourself?'

Seldon held his gaze. 'Unless either of you wish this to take longer than necessary?'

Barnabas spun around and plonked himself down heavily, earning a glare from Viola, who was still fighting with the pleats of her heather-hued skirt. Seldon waited until she was finally settled before sitting.

Barnabas tapped the desk. 'If this is about those rocks thrown through his grace's window, I didn't do it. And neither did my wife.'

'That's right,' Viola added hurriedly. 'We aren't harbouring any sour grapes over not making the second round of the shooting competition. We've stayed on here to be good sports. I mean, we could have simply driven off after dinner last night.'

'As far as the end of the driveway before getting stuck in the snow, yes.' Seldon looked up from jotting something down. 'However, the attack on his grace is not the reason for me asking you here.'

The couple glanced nervously at each other.

'Then I hope it's not that murder business again,' Viola said disdainfully.

'It is. Particularly the story you and your husband told me about not leaving the terrace during the twenty-minute window in which Mr Porritt was killed.'

'Are you calling my wife and I liars?' Barnabas snorted.

Seldon gestured at his notebook. 'I'm letting you know that you were seen.'

'Oh, ruddy heck,' Viola muttered.

Seldon nodded curtly. 'The truth this time. Both of you.'

Eleanor fought the urge to give her fiancé a round of

applause. He'd only implied he knew something incriminating about them, but it had hit the target!

'Look, if you must know,' Barnabas said, 'we didn't join the other three in the drawing room because my wife and I had had a bit of a tiff. Then we both went for a walk to cool off. Separately, that is.'

Viola smiled tightly. 'A brief storm in a teacup. Nothing more.' She turned to Eleanor. 'You understand how it is with men, Lady Swift. They see black and swear it's white. They—'

'So you both left the terrace,' Seldon interrupted smoothly. 'Where did you go, Mr Musgrave?'

'Good lord, man, do you think I was taking notes?' Barnabas growled. 'I was trying to calm down. So, all I can tell you is I walked around.'

'It is in your best interest to try and be more specific, but as you wish. Mrs Musgrave?'

She slapped on a compliant expression. 'Honestly, Chief Inspector, I was just walking and... thinking. I can't—'

'Mrs Musgrave,' Seldon said sternly. 'Please remember that I have an eyewitness.'

Barnabas glared at him. 'I fail to see what you're trying to make of this, except to try and embarrass me and my wife. Really, Inspector.' His tone turned smug. 'If you were a gentleman, you'd have done the decent thing of taking a wife a long time ago. Then you'd know, it's hardly unusual to have an argument after being married for twenty-odd years.'

Seldon looked up from his notebook. 'Your marriage is odd in what way?'

Eleanor bit her lip to hold in her cheer. He was too professional to retaliate to the insulting remark levied at him. But human enough to quietly needle the man responsible.

'Not our marriage!' Barnabas blustered. 'The time frame. It's twenty-ish years. Specifics are not important.'

Seldon looked at Viola. 'I rather believed ladies thought remembering things like that very important?'

'They do, Chief Inspector,' Viola said in a sulky tone, throwing her husband a daggered look. 'Most especially when it comes to remembering anniversaries!'

'Noted.' Seldon caught Eleanor's eye fleetingly. 'Now, Mr Musgrave. As you returned to the terrace, what did you see in the drawing room?'

Barnabas bit his lip. 'The other three coming back in. I... I hadn't remembered it until now. When you mentioned us stepping back onto the terrace, I visualised it. Imaginations play tricks, you see.'

Hmm, says the man who lambasted Taylor that a businessman never sullies his wits by indulging in imagination, Ellie!

'That's where you're wrong, Barnabas,' Viola snapped. 'Only Mr Taylor and Miss Whitwell came back into the drawing room.'

Barnabas rounded on her. 'No, Viola. I distinctly saw that fop, Huish, too. And Miss Whitwell. I definitely noticed her.'

'Naturally, you noticed her!' Viola said tartly.

Seldon held up his pen. 'Both of you. Think carefully as to who was and who wasn't already in the drawing room? And who came in?'

Barnabas waved his hand dismissively. 'It's as I said.'

'Although you'll find my recollection more accurate, Chief Inspector,' Viola said smugly.

Seldon made another note. 'Moving on. Why are you here? Mr Musgrave first, please.'

Barnabas snorted. 'Because you had the nerve to send for us again!'

Seldon sat back and folded his hands, his expression uncompromising.

Viola clucked at her husband. 'Barnabas, a little cooperation won't kill you.' The sharpness of her tone made Eleanor wonder if she'd wanted to add, 'But I might!'

Mr Musgrave's nostrils flared. 'Alright. We are... we were here in the hope of winning the wretched shooting competition. Why else?'

Seldon narrowed his eyes. 'After all my years as a detective, do you really think I'd believe you gave up spending Christmas with family or friends to spend it here, among total strangers? Knowing your host is a complete recluse? And most particularly, that neither of you had a chance of winning the competition?' he ended pointedly.

The Musgraves both opened their mouths. Then closed them again without a word.

Bullseye, Ellie!

'What is your point, Inspector?' Barnabas finally grumbled.

'The truth about why you are really here,' Seldon said firmly.

He shrugged. 'Curiosity. That's all.'

Viola turned to Eleanor. 'It's hardly every day that one is invited by a duke, is it?'

Eleanor smiled sweetly. 'But your husband told me long before you were eliminated from the shooting competition that your coming down here was a complete waste of time. Over the sublime quails' eggs with duck liver pâté, I believe it was.'

'Barnabas did no such thing!' Viola snapped.

Eleanor tapped her forehead. 'No, you're right. It was over the delectable brandied crab gratin that he declared it was a "travesty of lost business time". You were most emphatic, Mr Musgrave.' She held his death glare. 'And it was over the quails' eggs that you declared vehemently how much you disliked the county of Yorkshire. And yet you still came. You both did. Just out of... curiosity?'

Barnabas leaned forward and rapped on the desk. 'Yes! And Yorkshire doesn't improve on reacquaintance, either!'

Eleanor tried to keep her face neutral. *So they've been to Yorkshire before, Ellie. Or did he mean...?*

She leaned forward this time. 'Yet you still came *back* to Auldwyke Hall!'

It was a hopeful ploy. But the Musgraves' wide-eyed expressions showed she'd scored an ace. Seldon's fleeting smile told her he knew it too.

'Mr and Mrs Musgrave, I am now officially cautioning you both,' he said.

'On what charge?' Viola flustered.

'Wasting police time and attempting to pervert the course of justice, for starters.' He raised his hand as Barnabas started to protest. 'I'll give you one last chance. Now, as Lady Swift said, this is not your first visit to Auldwyke Hall, is it?'

For a moment Barnabas hesitated, then his shoulders sagged in defeat. 'No. The second. The first time was a Christmas shoot, too.'

Viola shrugged. 'We didn't win then, either.'

Seldon's face was impassive. 'When exactly was that?'

'Oh, some years ago.'

'I warned you, Mrs Musgrave. Now—'

She waved a panicky hand. 'Ten years ago.'

Eleanor felt a frisson run up her spine. She exchanged a glance with Seldon, who then held Viola's gaze.

'The Christmas shoot when his grace's wife died?'

Viola nodded reluctantly.

'Why did you lie about it?'

Barnabas glowered at him. 'Oh really, Inspector! This has no bearing on anything that's happened on this present shoot.'

'That is for me to be the judge of,' Seldon said sternly. 'Mrs Musgrave?'

Viola's eyes flashed. 'Oh no, Chief Inspector. That's Barnabas' tale to tell!'

'Viola, have a heart!' Barnabas pleaded. At her cold look, he hung his head. 'Very well. At the previous Christmas shoot, I admit it... it was foolish of me, but I... I fell for the duchess.'

Viola scoffed. 'Foolish, he says! The two of them had an affair under my very nose!'

Eleanor could see Seldon was fighting to keep his disgust from showing.

'We didn't!' Barnabas protested. He held his hands up. 'But... but only because the duchess was having none of it.' He let out a long sigh. 'My wife has never believed that nothing actually happened between us.'

'So you have both met his grace before?' Seldon said levelly.

Barnabas nodded dispiritedly. 'That's the whole truth, Inspector. We've no more to tell you. Now, if you'll excuse us, we need to finish preparing to watch the second round of the shooting competition.'

Viola snorted. 'Not that it isn't a foregone conclusion who'll win again...' She tailed off, her husband staring at her in horror.

Seldon glanced at Eleanor. She nodded discreetly.

'Mrs Musgrave. Who do you favour to win the next round, then? I mean, between Mr Taylor and Miss Whitwell, of course,' she said. 'After all, you must have a reasonable idea, having seen them compete at this year's shoot. *And* the one before. Although, that was ten years ago, wasn't it?'

Barnabas rose hastily. 'Perhaps I wasn't clear, Inspector. I have nothing further to say. And neither does my wife.'

'One last thing.' Seldon picked up Clifford's miniature Dickens book. 'Does the inscription in this mean anything to you?'

Mrs Musgrave's lips moved as she read the highlighted text with difficulty. 'No, Inspector.'

Her husband took it with bad grace. Then reached into his shooting jacket and pulled out a pair of reading spectacles. Scanning the line, he snorted. 'What is this parlour game nonsense?'

'Thank you. That will be all, Mr Musgrave.'

Once Clifford had shown the Musgraves out, Seldon turned to him.

'Before I trouble you to call Taylor, Huish and Miss Whitwell, Clifford, you need to know that your mistress was inspired, and wonderful! That was a surprise development. And possibly a major breakthrough.'

She beamed, genuinely delighted. Then smiled impishly.

'You'd best watch out, though, Clifford. Hugh's taught me a line in deviousness the like of which will let me trump you remorselessly in our future squabbles.'

He flashed Seldon a pained look. 'If I had offended you, Chief Inspector, you only had to say!'

36

Seldon was still praising Eleanor's ingenuity as Clifford's familiar knock sounded on the library door.

'Wow me again, Eleanor, please,' Seldon whispered softly, quickly pressing his lips to hers.

As they pulled away, she sighed. 'The thing is, after that kiss, Hugh, I shan't be able to think straight until you do it again!'

She hastily sat down as he called, 'Come!'

Taylor swaggered in first, followed by Julius Huish and Pearl Whitwell. Eleanor fought off the uncharitable thought that Taylor really was a bloated peacock and dug out her best imitation of her butler's impassive expression. Prancing up to the desk, he ran his hand over his dark-chocolate hair and gave her a sly grin.

'What ho, Lady Swift. Here you and I are, thrown together again.'

'With, if you remember, Chief Inspector Seldon, my fiancé?' she said pointedly.

He turned to Seldon and shrugged. 'I'm a natural sportsman. What can I say?'

'Nothing, thank you. Unless it's answering my questions,' Seldon said with perfect composure.

'Nothing at all would be a treat for everyone,' Huish muttered. He stepped around Taylor to face Seldon, raking his floppy blond fringe from his eyes. He was the only one of the three not dressed in shooting wear but a French navy wool suit which made his cornflower cravat seem even more vivid. 'A question first, Chief Inspector. Why have you called all of us at the same time?'

'No. My question first, Mr Huish. Why could you not have left that troublesome hound in your room?' Seldon pointed at Finbar, who was straining on his lead, teeth bared.

Huish bristled. 'Because, in case you've forgotten, Chief Inspector, there's a murderer in our midst. Finbar here is my insurance.'

'What makes you think you might be in danger?' Seldon said blandly.

'What? Oh, well, you know how murdering types can be. One taste and they're overcome with bloodlust. And then no one is safe!'

'Oh, you'll be no use to us if you don't find some backbone, Huish!' Taylor hissed.

Eleanor pursed her lips. It seemed the three of them were still persisting in ganging together, but tempers were fraying. At least between the two men. Which puzzled her all the more that Pearl was so uncharacteristically quiet.

Clifford stepped forward. 'Chief Inspector, since my offer to mind Master Finbar during your questions was declined, perhaps an improvised muzzle might assist?'

'Definitely, thank you.'

Clifford turned to Huish. 'If you will relinquish your cravat, sir?'

Huish's indignant protest was cut short by Seldon's raised

hand. 'Do it or I will charge you with possession of a dangerous animal.'

'Outrageous. It's silk, you know,' Huish mumbled, at least having the gallantry to turn his back from Eleanor and Pearl as he undid his top button and unwound his neckwear.

With one of Gladstone's liver treats as a bribe, a few deft flicks of Clifford's wrists had the hunting hound subdued. She hid her smile as he mischievously tied off the muzzle with a theatrically foppish bow at the back of the dog's head.

Pearl scowled. 'Can we get on with it now?'

'Certainly, if you would sit, Miss Whitwell?' After she'd done so, Seldon gestured for the two men to follow suit, then looked at the three with a steely-eyed stare. 'To answer Mr Huish's question candidly, I'm interviewing you as a group because of damning information that has come to light.'

Taylor clapped lazily. 'Bully for you, old man. Though worming out dirt on others is the basic tenet of your job, isn't it?'

'It's called collecting intelligence,' Seldon said coolly, 'And it's Chief Inspector.' He leaned on the desk. 'Question one. Why did you lie to me about having been at Auldwyke before?'

Eleanor watched their reactions carefully. Huish shuffled in his seat, while Pearl studied the weave of her Norfolk shooting jacket. Taylor, however, frowned at the pair of them.

'You conniving wretches!' he spat.

Pearl flicked her blunt-cut dark bob. 'Whatever the inspector has on you, he didn't get it from me.'

'Nor me,' Huish huffed.

'Why do you assume my question was directed only at Mr Taylor?' Seldon said.

Pearl blanched.

'Now look here! What is this?' Huish demanded.

'A murder investigation,' Seldon said firmly. 'And there's already enough cause to see each of you in serious trouble.

Especially as I know you lied when you insisted you'd never been to Auldwyke Hall before.'

Eleanor smiled to herself at how Seldon had phrased the question so it could be addressed to any of them. Or all of them.

Huish leaped up. 'Alright, I was here before, I admit. But so were those two.' He pointed to Taylor and Whitwell.

Taylor got to his feet and rounded on him. 'You fool!'

'Sit! Both of you,' Seldon barked, already on his feet, his broad frame making them cower backwards.

Once the two men had resumed their seats, he sat himself and picked up his pen.

'Mr Taylor, more lies will only go even more badly against you.'

'How? I haven't done anything,' Taylor said belligerently. He flinched away from Seldon's hard stare. 'Alright. Maybe I was here before. Is that a crime?'

Seldon ignored his question. 'How long ago were you here?'

Taylor shrugged. 'Ten years, I guess.'

Seldon glanced fleetingly at Eleanor.

'Miss Whitwell?'

She looked at him smugly. 'I didn't lie before about being here. You never asked. You only asked how I knew his grace.'

Taylor's mouth dropped open.

Eleanor bit back a smile. She was right. He'd never actually asked any of them.

'I'm asking you now, Miss Whitwell,' Seldon said smoothly.

Pearl sat back in her chair. 'It's nothing to do with you, Chief Inspector. The murder of Porritt may be, but how I chose to spend my past Christmases is not.'

He held her gaze. 'Your answer was particularly ill-advised. All the more so as I didn't ask if you had been here before at Christmas.'

Pearl glared at Eleanor. 'Really, Lady Swift, whatever do you see in a man who likes to deceive women?'

'I don't, Miss Whitwell. All the deception I've witnessed hasn't been from the chief inspector's side at all.'

Pearl sat back huffily.

Seldon turned to Huish. 'When were you previously at Auldwyke? And why?'

He squirmed in his seat. '"When" is easy enough. "Why" is not really something I wish to divulge.'

Taylor slapped him on the shoulder. 'Don't worry, Huish. I'll divulge it for you. Just as you dropped me in it earlier. You see, Inspector, ten years ago while here at Auldwyke Hall, we three rather overindulged in his grace's cognac. Which resulted in each of us confessing—'

Seldon halted him. 'Thank you, Mr Taylor. But I believe Mr Huish is ready to tell his own tale now?'

'If I must,' Huish grumbled. 'But before I do, Chief Inspector, I need your assurance that this won't reach his grace's ears?'

'The details of my investigations are only ever passed on to strictly necessary parties.'

'Is that a yes?'

'Yes. Get on with it!' Pearl snapped.

Huish's shoulders slumped. 'Alright. I was here ten years ago. On the pretext of attending the Christmas shoot.'

'What were you really here for, Mr Huish?' Seldon said.

'The... the duchess was a staunch patron of the arts. Particularly up-and-coming artists, as I was at the time. She loaned me a sizeable sum to set up a small gallery in London's prestigious Piccadilly area. So, when she invited me to Auldwyke Hall at the end of my gallery's first year, I couldn't possibly refuse. Even though I was dreading it.'

'I take it your gallery hadn't proved very successful, then?' Eleanor said.

Huish shook his head glumly. 'No. It was a debt-ridden albatross around my neck. I thought I'd kept it hidden from the duchess, but when I arrived, she gave me a hideous dressing-down and accused me of taking the money under false pretences. Which I hadn't! That's all there is to tell,' he ended abruptly.

Eleanor wasn't convinced. 'I'm surprised the duchess didn't demand you repay her immediately.'

Huish jerked in his seat.

Seldon flashed her a grateful look. 'Mr Huish, did the duchess demand her money be repaid?'

He winced. 'Yes. But I didn't have it. Not a shilling. Then... then she died in that unfortunate accident. I worried his grace knew about his wife having loaned me the money and would demand it back himself. But he never did.'

'Not yet,' Taylor murmured nonchalantly.

'Why do you think you were invited this year, Mr Huish?'

'Honestly, I've no idea.'

'Then why did you come?'

Huish swallowed hard. 'My curiosity got the better of me. And my fears, I'll admit. I'd only have fretted all of Christmas wondering if I hadn't come.'

'Thank you, Mr Huish.' Seldon looked up from his page. 'Mr Taylor, I am interested to hear your confession next.'

He shrugged. 'Who said I've anything to confess?'

Seldon pointed at him. 'You did. Only this time you won't need to decimate his grace's cognac supply first.'

Taylor scowled. 'It really isn't any of your business, Inspector.'

'Murder makes everything my business.'

Taylor frowned. 'Alright, I lied! I was there too. The duchess was one of those darned women who somehow found out your darkest secrets!' He spun around to Eleanor. 'Why do women always want to poke about in men's affairs?'

'I can assure you, Mr Taylor, I have absolutely no desire to do any such thing. Particularly in your case,' she said coldly.

Taylor mumbled something even her sharp hearing couldn't catch, then took a deep breath. 'Inspector, I'm a bastard.'

'Mr Taylor!' Seldon thundered.

'No! In the proper sense of the word, I mean. I was born a few days before my parents married.'

'"Illegitimate" would have been a more appropriate term with ladies in the room,' Seldon gruffed. 'What was the problem with the duchess having found that out, however?'

'Because, being born on the wrong side of the blanket, as the expression is, means if anyone found out, I'd lose my inheritance. It would pass immediately to my younger brother.'

'I see.'

'No, you don't, actually.' The smug peacock Eleanor wanted to knock off his preening perch had returned. 'Because it doesn't matter now. The duchess is dead. As is my brother. France. During the war. And Pater's on his last legs. Hence, "Sir" is very much in the offing for me.'

Seldon's head was bent over the copious notes he was making. 'Miss Whitwell, are you still standing by your ill-advised response that you have not been to Auldwyke Hall before?' He looked up. 'Or have you realised the seriousness of the consequences?'

'The former,' she said forcefully, looking away.

'As you wish.'

'I'll tell, Inspector,' Taylor sneered. 'Seeing as the lady wants to play coy.'

Pearl's lips twisted into a gloating smile. 'And what are you going to tell him? The lie I told you when you were too drunk on cognac to know otherwise, you fool?'

'I'll take that as a further admission you were also here ten years ago, Miss Whitwell.' Before she could protest, Seldon rapped on the desk. 'Listen! All of you. I have eyewitness accounts, so think before you answer. Why did you all lie about staying in the drawing room between three twenty and three forty on the afternoon Mr Porritt was murdered?'

Huish swallowed hard. 'Eyewitness? Who?'

Taylor gritted his teeth. 'That ruddy stuffed shirt, Barnabas Musgrave, I bet! I'll have it out with him, alright.'

'Meaning, Mr Taylor?' Seldon said.

'Don't get excited, Inspector. I'm not going to punch the living daylights out of him. But him and his wife are up to their necks in this mess too. They just thought they'd stay aloof rather than join us three in working out what the heck was going on.'

'What was going on?'

'None of us knew!' Huish cried. 'That's why we split up in the drawing room.'

Whitwell and Taylor groaned.

'Nice going, you idiot,' Pearl snapped.

Huish folded his arms defensively. 'Oh, face facts! The chief inspector knows too much already. I'll tell him because I'm not willing to risk the hangman's noose for something I didn't do!'

'Tell me what, Mr Huish?' Seldon said.

'That the three of us left the drawing room and split up. To find that Porritt fellow. To ask him what in blazes was going on with us all being the same guests as the Christmas shoot ten years ago.'

'I see. And what did he say?'

'Nothing!'

'None of us found him.' Taylor stared between the other two. 'At least that's the story they told me.'

Eleanor spotted Huish's fists balling.

'Last question.' Seldon pulled out Clifford's miniature copy of *A Christmas Carol*. 'Does the inscription in this mean anything to you?'

Pearl took it. '"Money can't buy a happy life..." What rot, yes it can!'

She passed it to Taylor, who glanced at it. '"Or a peaceful death." Doesn't mean a thing to me.'

'The next page, Mr Huish, please?' Seldon said.

Huish, too, read it without putting on any reading spectacles.

Seldon dismissed all three of them. As the door closed, he dropped back into his seat. 'That was—'

The door reopened and Pearl hurried in.

Seldon shook his head. 'Miss Whitwell! I have asked you before to knock and wait to be called in.'

'Yes, Chief Inspector,' she said in little more than a whisper. 'And you asked me a question I couldn't answer in front of Huish and Taylor. But if it's just the three of us...'

Seldon nodded discreetly to Eleanor. 'In that case, take a seat, Miss Whitwell...'

37

Pearl sat rigidly in front of Seldon and Eleanor, winding a handkerchief between her fingers.

'I'll be honest this time,' she said breathlessly.

He met her gaze dispassionately. 'To date, you've been anything but, Miss Whitwell. What has prompted your sudden change of heart?'

'Because I don't know who to trust any more.' Two tears rolled down her cheek. 'And I'm terrified.'

Eleanor knew how much Seldon's gentlemanly nature struggled when faced with a woman in genuine tears.

Though no more followed the first two, Ellie?

'Terrified of who?' she said, trying to keep the scepticism out of her voice.

'Of all of them!'

'Do you mean the other guests?'

'Of course I do! One of them must have killed Porritt. Over something to do with why we were all invited here again, I'm sure. It's too much of a coincidence. But I can't escape because the snow has cut us off. So we're trapped in this awful house. With a murderer!'

'Whom the chief inspector might have caught by now if everyone, including you, hadn't repeatedly lied,' Eleanor said firmly.

Pearl nodded contritely. 'True, I suppose. But you must both see why I did, surely?' She buried her face in her handkerchief.

Seldon gave Eleanor an encouraging nod to keep going.

'Honestly, Miss Whitwell, no.'

'Let me explain why I lied to you, then.' She hugged her shoulders. 'Taylor was telling the truth when he said the duchess was one of those people who made everyone else's business theirs. Hideously true, in my case.'

Eleanor frowned. 'What did she find out about you that was so awful?'

'Who I really am.'

Eleanor shared a quick look with Seldon. The flinch of his brows told her that had surprised him as much as her.

'Who are you really, then?'

'An embarrassment to the world! My mother gave birth to me... in prison.'

That couldn't have been further from what she'd expected. Despite her earlier scepticism, Eleanor's heart clenched.

'I grew up in prison until I was four,' Pearl continued. She looked at Seldon who had taken his eye off his page for a moment. 'I know, even then, the law said babies must leave at nine months. For some reason, they let my mother keep me so I was looked after by her and the woman who shared a cell with her. Two career thieves drawn together behind bars. There's no bond stronger!' She laughed mirthlessly, then quickly dabbed at her eyes with a handkerchief. 'Eventually, the woman was released, but my mother still had a long time left to serve. So, she let the other woman take me with her.' Her face coloured. 'I was brought up to steal. By her. Then by someone else when she got caught and sent inside again. It was inevitable I'd go that way too. Back behind bars.'

'So you've been to prison,' Eleanor said in an understanding tone. 'But if you served your sentence and learned your lesson, albeit a harsh one, if stealing was all you'd been shown, you don't deserve any censure afterwards.'

Pearl's eyes flashed. 'You try telling the world that, Lady Swift! My birthright was nothing more than a hateful curse. I wish I'd never been born,' she ended in a shrill whisper, before burying her face in her handkerchief again.

'It can't have been easy,' Eleanor conceded, even more grateful her own childhood had been only difficult, not desperate like Pearl's. 'But can you tell me what bearing this has on the matter in hand?'

She sniffed. 'After my second stint in prison, I was determined to claw my way out of the gutter. So, when I was finally released, I crafted a whole new background; name, family, achievements, acquaintances, friends, the lot. And persona. I made it all as far away from the truth as possible. And I studied how the other half lived like my life depended on it. Which is how I slowly established myself in better social circles. And eventually, high society.'

Eleanor nodded in understanding. 'I imagine you were delighted to receive the first invitation to Auldwyke Hall, then?'

'Until the duchess pulled me aside and told me she'd worked out what had been niggling her about me.' Pearl's jaw clenched. 'Being a duchess, naturally she'd been involved in good works. And guess where one of her charitable inspection tours had been?'

Eleanor winced. 'The last prison you were in?'

Pearl nodded glumly. 'I don't know how she recognised me, but she did.'

Eleanor fought a frown. The duchess raking up Pearl's past felt unseemly. Particularly as she'd been a guest.

'Do you know why the duchess told you she was aware of your previous life?'

Pearl's eyes glinted. 'Yes! Because she wanted to warn me off stealing the silverware and her jewels! The cheek of the woman! She'd been born with a silver spoon in her mouth. Whereas I...' She broke off into sobs.

'Take a deep breath.' Eleanor stepped over to the table. Returning with a glass of water, she held it out. 'After that had happened, why did you come again this year?'

Pearl sipped the water before replying. 'I was drawn by the prestige of it, of course. Like a moth to a flame. And anyway, the duchess was dead. And the duke a recluse, I'd heard. So it seemed perfectly safe, I wouldn't be exposed again this time.'

And where better to snare a wealthy husband than at a duke's estate, Ellie?

'Thank you, Miss Whitwell,' Seldon said crisply.

She scowled at him. 'It's the truth, I swear.'

'Do you recognise this?' Seldon held out the gold pendant.

She shrugged. 'You asked me that before.'

'I see. So it was a brief change of heart, telling the truth, Miss Whitwell.'

'Wait!' Pearl laid her hands on the desk. 'I'm sorry, Inspector. *Chief* Inspector. Lying and being evasive has become a habit. I do recognise the pendant. And I did before. But I haven't been able to remember where from. Honestly.'

With Pearl gone, Clifford slid in with a tray bearing tea and cake.

'Thank you, Eleanor.' Seldon smiled wearily. 'Hysterical ladies and their troubled emotions are still my Achilles' heel. I can't trust my judgement not to be affected.'

'I know, Hugh.' She frowned. 'But I'm not entirely sure she wasn't playing us. At least in part.'

Clifford arched a questioning brow.

'Her life, and sob story,' Eleanor explained. 'Although, honestly, if even half her description of her early life is true, my heart goes out to her.'

'Mine too,' Seldon muttered.

'Unless the lady turns out to be the murderer,' Clifford said pragmatically.

Seldon rubbed his hands over his sleep-deprived face. 'Yes. I've still no idea who it is, blast it!'

'We will, Hugh.' She pretended to whisper behind her hand, 'Only we'd best buck up before my butler here accuses me of being "uncharacteristically defeatist".'

Clifford's lips quirked. 'Spoilsport. It was on the tip of my tongue.'

Seldon chuckled, then shook his head. 'Take no notice of me, Clifford. It's just tiredness.'

Eleanor was staggered. He never confessed to feeling tired. And then it dawned. He had arrived the morning before, after driving all night. And he'd insisted on taking a long shift in the small hours guarding the duke. And like her, he'd missed the second night's dinner altogether after the attack on the duke. She shook her head. Having to guard the duke night and day was already starting to tell. Not just on Seldon, but on all of them.

She noticed his eyes fixed on the tea tray.

'What's that delectable-smelling treat, Clifford?'

'Yorkshire parkin, my lady. A traditional oatmeal-based gingerbread made with black treacle.'

'Sounds too delicious for words. Heaps for Hugh. And me, please. Right, we've learned lots in the last half an hour.' She tapped Seldon's notebook. 'Hugh, recap for all our benefit. Especially Clifford, who hasn't been in on the interviews.'

Seldon nodded as he finished a mouthful of parkin and took a long swig from his cup. 'Main developments then. All the guests were here ten years ago at the Christmas shoot when the duchess died.'

'Save for yourself, Chief Inspector, and her ladyship.' Clifford topped up Seldon's tea.

She shook her head. 'That's not the most puzzling thing, though.'

Seldon looked at her quizzically. 'What is, then?'

'That the guests all basically admitted they had a motive to kill the duchess! But she died in an accident. Whereas, we've still found no motive for any of them killing Porritt. Who was actually murdered.'

He frowned. 'You're right. It's all the wrong way around, blast it!' He started flicking through his notebook, missing that Clifford was topping up his cake again. 'What connections do we have?'

'The same guests. The same event.' She felt like she was floundering.

'Ten years between events, though...' Clifford murmured. 'Might I ask if any of the guests have admitted to being cajoled by Mr Porritt to attend this year?'

'Dash it, Hugh! We only asked the Musgraves that.'

'Yes, but only because of the revelations you helped me drag out of the others. It's not too late. We can still ask the other three.'

She nodded. 'I'll subtly question them at the rapidly approaching second round of the shooting competition.' She spotted the amused look Seldon and Clifford shared. 'You rotters! I can be subtle.'

'No. But you're definitely the most intelligent and shrewdly intuitive rhinoceros I've met.'

She laughed. 'Not much of a compliment, Hugh, you toad. Especially when it's really your way of working the conversation around to your ulterior motive.'

'Eleanor!' he whispered, cheeks flushing.

'Not that, silly! I meant you want to call on my feminine intuition without me teasing you mercilessly...' She gasped. 'Hugh! Ulterior motive!'

'What about it?'

'It seems Porritt invited all the guests down this year with an ulterior motive. Maybe the duke or his wife did the same ten years before?'

Seldon steepled his fingers. 'It's a good thought.' He frowned. 'But how do we find out?'

'Well, we can't question the duke yet. He's not strong enough.'

Seldon grimaced. 'And when he is, he probably won't be any more helpful than the last time! Hmm. It's still worth pursuing. Clifford, please can you bring Lofthouse in for a few questions?' He drained his cup, then sniffed it tentatively. 'And what in blazes have you given me?'

'Lapsang souchong and ginseng.'

'Which could be voodoo medicine since I've never heard of either!'

'They very well may be, Chief Inspector.'

Clifford took the cup and glided out of the room.

Ten minutes later, Lofthouse stood in front of them, frowning.

'If as you'll 'scuse me sayin', sir, I've no time now for what-ever this is. I'm not in footman's tails for good reason.' He gestured down his green outdoor jacket and corduroy trousers. 'Second round of shootin' competition has to be got ready. And I'm tryin' to be me, and Porritt!'

Seldon held his gaze. 'And I'm trying to ensure neither you, nor anyone else, goes the way of Mr Porritt!'

Lofthouse blanched. 'Well, if you put it like that, I can prob-ably manage a few minutes.'

'Or more, if I need,' Seldon said firmly. 'Now. You're the second-longest serving member of staff here, yes?'

Lofthouse scowled. 'Aye. And thanks for rubbin' it in. I'll be out on me ear for bein' too old to be in service long afore I can measure up to Porritt's years of workin' here, I know.'

Eleanor mentally filed that away as an odd thing to seem jealous about.

'The current guests, Mr Lofthouse,' Seldon said. 'Had you seen or met any of them before this year's shooting event?'

'Nay a one of 'em, sir.' He leaned his square frame forward testily. 'Who's been sayin' as I have, then?'

'No one, Mr Lofthouse. Are you aware of who was a guest here at the time the duchess died?'

'God rest her soul. Nay, sir. Why would I though? I told you, I've been here only eight year.'

'Can you tell me anything about the duchess' death?'

Lofthouse shrugged. 'I don't know nowt. Day I joined here I were told loud and clear that it were never to be talked about.'

'But over the years, among the staff, I'm sure—'

'You're sure of nowt where her grace's passin' is concerned, sir!' Lofthouse said. 'The only one as would know is Amos Bowes, seein' as he was here then. But he'll not go against his grace's orders.'

Seldon held out Clifford's miniature book. 'Does the inscription in this mean anything to you?'

Lofthouse pulled out a pair of bent-framed spectacles and hunched over the book. After a moment, he jerked upright. 'I read it, but it means nowt to me. Now, might I be released to crack on with me actual duties?'

'Murder is everyone's duty, Mr Lofthouse,' Seldon said coolly. 'But yes, you may leave. Please send Mr Bowes to me immediately, however.'

'Amos? But the shoot! He's needed—'

'Immediately, Mr Lofthouse!'

As the footman hurried back down the corridor, Eleanor turned to Seldon. 'Well, we've found our second spectacle-wearer. Now all we need to do is work out if either of them are the murderer!'

38

Helpfully, Clifford had anticipated Seldon would want to see Bowes and had him waiting as Lofthouse stalked out of the library. However, the Auldwyke gardener seemed reluctant to enter.

'Don't dally in the doorway!' Seldon called, beckoning him to the desk.

Bowes looked around nervously. 'Beg pardon, sir, but Mr Lofthouse—'

'Is under my authority regarding staff I wish to question until this investigation is concluded,' Seldon said brusquely. 'Now, come in, man!'

Bowes jumped as Clifford closed the door behind him. He bobbed his head and shuffled forward in his socks, tapping his weathered cap against his leg. 'Here I be, sir. And, m'lady. But for why, I'm at a loss.'

'Then I'll tell you why. It's about the lie you told me.'

Bowes' face fell. 'Lie, sir? I wouldn't have dared to tell an untruth to a gentleman. Not even if he is a policeman.'

Eleanor winced as he stood there, seemingly unaware he'd

rubbed salt into Seldon's irritation, that the police had little to no standing in the eyes of guests and staff alike.

'Mr Bowes,' Seldon said, 'don't waste my time, please. You were seen.'

'Oh lawks!' Bowes muttered to his socks.

'Exactly. Within the twenty-minute window in which Mr Porritt was murdered. Yet you omitted to mention you collected a crate of glass clays before you picked up Mr Fripp and Tosh from the kitchen.'

Bowes' hand gripping his cap trembled. 'Must have slipped me mind, sir. Bein' as I'm donkey's long in the tooth.'

Seldon shook his head. 'I'm in no doubt your mental faculties are working well enough. You didn't mention it to me before because to collect those glass clays you would have had to have gone to the storehouse. The very one Mr Porritt was murdered in!'

Bowes looked as though his knees would give way. Or his heart, Eleanor feared, given the ashen colour of his face.

'But.' Bowes jerked around to her. 'M'lady, I thought the world of Mr Porritt. Genuine I did. He were but a nipper when I started here. And he were nothin' but good and fair to me. I wouldn't never have hurt one hair on his head.'

'Then explain how you got those glass clays without seeing his body?' she said. 'Or killing him yourself!'

He nodded glumly. ''Tis to me shame to have fibbed, m'lady. Only 'tain't the worst of it.' He took a deep breath. 'I never went to the storehouse to get that crate of clays, on account of havin' another store of 'em.' He sighed. 'His grace'll have Mr Lofthouse rip me head clean off me shoulders when he hears. And right he'll be too, seein' as I been takin' them for... for other purposes.'

She frowned. 'For your own purposes, you mean?'

He hesitated, turning his cap in his hand. 'In a manner of speakin', m'lady, yes. Only that afternoon of the pre-shoot preppin's, I came over all of a panic and decided to sneak 'em back soon as I could. So I pegged it to me old tool shed and grabbed one crate to add to the barrow Fripp and Tosh was to take to the shooting platform. Then I raced as fast as I could manage to collect the pair of 'em from the kitchen so as I wouldn't be missed.' He shook his head sadly. 'I reckon as me mind is unravellin' quicker 'n a roll of twine.'

Eleanor's brows knitted further. 'Why do you say that?'

'On account of havin' lost track of how many crates I had left to return. There bein' one less 'n the three I'd thought.'

Her insides clenched. 'Where is your old tool shed, Bowes?'

'Beyond the back wall of the kitchen gardens, m'lady.'

That's on the way to the 'bomb factory', Ellie!

Seldon nodded encouragingly for her to continue.

'Bowes, have you returned all the crates of glass clays now?'

The gardener hung his head. 'No, m'lady. There's still one missing.'

'Forget about it,' she said firmly. 'Do you understand?'

'Clearer 'n lacewings I encourage to eat the greenfly on his grace's memorial garden roses.' He ran a trembling hand over his few remaining silver-grey strands.

Standing there in his socks, he reminded her again of Joseph, her own treasured gardener back home. She bit her lip.

He's still a suspect, Ellie.

'Bowes, why were you stealing the glass clays?'

He hesitated again. 'To... to give to me daughter, m'lady.' He threw his hands together pleadingly. 'Only she don't deserve to be in trouble for me badness.'

'She probably won't be. Why does she want them, though?'

'On account of bein' poorer 'n a church mouse no matter how hard she scrubs for others, poor girl. So she's been paintin' the glass clays I've given her to sell in Kirkwell at Yuletide market for folks to hang on their Christmas trees. They look just like the real thing, painted up all pretty like. And she earns a few pennies so she can have some sort of Christmas for herself.'

'I see.' She glanced at Seldon, who tapped his notebook. 'Bowes, you need to answer the chief inspector's questions now. About the shoot when the duchess died.'

He looked aghast. 'But m'lady, we's not allowed to even mention that, on his grace's orders.'

'No. And you're not allowed to steal glass clays from his grace either, but you did,' Seldon said in an uncompromising tone. 'However, I'm willing to look on that leniently if you answer me honestly about the Christmas shoot ten years ago.'

Bowes sighed. 'I'll say as much as I can, sir. Without tellin' his grace's business, mind. I'll not dishonour the gentleman to anyone. Not even if it means swinging for it.'

'Which the murderer will do. Remember that.'

'Oh lummy!' Bowes mumbled.

'Are you aware the current guests are the same ones who were at the shoot when the duchess died?'

'Yes, sir.'

Seldon made another note on his page. 'Didn't you think it strange the same people were invited?'

'Sir, I'm only the gardener. 'Tain't my place to question anything his grace sees fit to do. Besides, I imagined he'd ordered Mr Porritt to arrange it as a memorial shoot for her grace's anniversary of passin' over.' He turned to Eleanor again. ''Tis terrible to think his grace has holed hisself away for ten long years over it.'

'It is, Bowes.' She felt a wash of sadness. 'But were there any guests at that shoot ten years ago who aren't here now?'

He scratched his head. 'Not that I know of, m'lady. Seemed bit short of numbers that year too, now I think of it.'

'But his grace wasn't a recluse then. He didn't have any family come? Or his oldest friend, say?'

'Nope. The old guard, as it were, came for the other shoots

and parties. And family-wise, it would only have been his grace's younger brother.' He shook his head. 'But small dogs in tall weeds is rarely chompin' to be so.'

Eleanor wished Clifford was there so he could translate for them. 'Meaning, Bowes?'

'Nothin' disrespectful, m'lady. Only that bein' the second son, the gentleman had the sound sense to go off and make a life of his own.'

'Yes, of course. Well, thank you, Bowes. That might save me putting my foot in it with his grace when I check on him again after this.'

His jaw fell. 'Are you meanin' what I thinks, m'lady? That his grace has let you inside his solace?'

'If you mean his private apartment, yes, Bowes.'

'Stands to reason,' he said, then snapped his mouth shut.

'Why?'

'Beg pardon', m'lady, but wild horses couldn't drag it out of me. It's no bearin' on poor Mr Porritt up and bein' done for, I swear.' He turned back to Seldon. 'Am I done now, sir?'

Seldon shook his head. 'No, Mr Bowes, you are not. Do you know how the duchess died?'

'Stray shot from one of the guns caught her. Course, it was a proper game shoot back then, with everyone out in the field. It were her grace's favourite thing in all the world. Made tragedy seem harsher 'n ever, to my mind. But stray shots do happen, sir. Hazard of the sport, see.'

Seldon looked over at Eleanor, his eyes troubled. 'Well, thankfully, the competitors in this year's shoot will be safely standing in a line, on the platform, behind the angle of fire.'

Bowes grimaced. 'Speakin' of that, sir, I'm needed—'

'In here still,' Seldon said. He held out the miniature book as he had with the others. 'Does this inscrip—' He caught Eleanor's quiet headshake. 'Bowes, do these words mean anything to you?'

He shrugged. 'I'm not a man as ever went to school and learned reading and the like, sir. Wouldn't know if that's even words you're showin' me.'

As Bowes hurried out, Lofthouse knocked on the open door.

Seldon frowned. 'What is it?'

He stepped inside. 'I've a message from his grace, sir.'

'Of course you have,' Seldon said wearily. 'What now?'

'Second round of shooting competition is to start in fifteen minutes.'

Eleanor leaped up. 'But you told us we had two hours when you came over to the old gamekeeper's cottage, I'm sure?'

'Aye, I did, m'lady. Only his grace has moved it forward, considerin' t' weather's on turn. Fifteen minutes.' He turned on his heel and marched out.

Clifford returned as Lofthouse left.

She flapped a hand at him. 'Yes, yes, Mr Fusspot, I still have a good fifteen minutes to hurl myself into my shooting togs. So, let's quickly run over where we're at with our suspects first, including what we learned from grilling Lofthouse and Bowes.'

Seldon nodded. 'Right, staff, then guests. What do you think about Bowes as the murderer, Eleanor?'

She thought for a moment. 'I'm fifty-fifty, actually. On the positive, it's possible he might have been bluffing about not being able to read. But on the negative, if he is our killer, why did he confess to stealing those glass clays? And he seemed very convincing about giving them to his daughter to sell.'

Seldon made a note. 'True. Next?'

'Lofthouse. On the positive, he wears reading glasses. On the negative, his only motive still is wanting revenge for being passed over when the duke made Porritt secretary, not him. But if so, why did he wait three years to exact his revenge?'

Seldon nodded. 'I agree. The guests then?'

'We've only got a couple of minutes left, so let's take them together. On the positive, we've uncovered that they all lied about their alibis, so all had an opportunity to kill Porritt. On the negative, we haven't unearthed a single reason for any of them doing so!'

'However, they all had a motive for the death of the duchess,' Clifford murmured. 'If that was also, in fact, murder.'

Eleanor gasped. 'Gracious, yes! Maybe that's why Porritt invited them all back here this year? To expose the murderer! Or maybe even blackmail them?'

'Then why invite them all?' Seldon said. 'And why invite us? Sorry, *me*, as you keep insisting, Eleanor?'

'And why wait ten years?' Clifford added.

She threw her hands out in exasperation. 'Maybe they all killed the duchess? And they all killed Porritt?'

Clifford pinched his nose. 'My apologies, Chief Inspector. I have tried unsuccessfully to deter her ladyship's penchant for penny dreadful novels!'

Seldon laughed. 'Try harder, perhaps. That last theory was definitely in the realm of wild fiction!'

Clifford pulled out his pocket watch. 'If I might be excused to relieve Constable Danby for, ahem, a five-minute respite from guarding his grace's door?'

She nodded. 'Absolutely. Poor fellow has probably had his legs crossed for hours now.'

Seldon held his hands up hopelessly at Clifford's pleading look. 'We might both have to face the fact that on this investigation, decorum is a lost cause!'

With Clifford gone, Seldon pulled her into an embrace.

'I know you're too stubborn to stand down from the shooting competition, but promise you'll be extra vigilant?'

She reached up to kiss his nose. 'You as well. You're precious to me too, you know.'

'Am I?' He grinned. 'I like that. A lot.'

They jumped apart at a knock on the door.

'Er, come in,' Seldon said, tugging on his jacket cuffs. 'Ah! Constable. I'll deal with whatever this is about, Eleanor. You stop worrying about missing glass clays and go get changed so you're warm enough for the shoot.'

Danby held his hands up apologetically. 'It's not a case of missing clays, that's maybe the biggest matter just now, sir. On my way down the stairs, I overheard Mr Lofthouse saying as there's a missing competitor.'

Eleanor's mind whirled. 'Who is it?'

'Mr Taylor, m'lady. He's simply vanished!'

39

Seldon stared at Eleanor. 'The wretch has fled! Blast it! I should have foreseen this.'

She spotted the footman disappearing towards the servants' stairs.

'Lofthouse!'

As they hurried up to him, he frowned. 'Perhaps you've not seen there are bell sashes for callin', m'lady?'

Seldon stared at him sternly. 'What's this about Mr Taylor having gone missing?'

'Just that, sir. Came up blank when I went lookin' everywhere for him to announce shooting competition is startin' earlier.'

'*Was* starting earlier,' Seldon said firmly. 'First, I need to search the premises for Mr—'

'Twenty-minute extension, sir. That's his grace's last concession on messin' with t' shoot schedule.'

'But that's preposterous! The competition can't go ahead,' Eleanor cried in exasperation. 'Taylor was in the running.'

'Hence his grace's givin' an extension, m'lady. So Mr Huish

can get ready to take his place as he was lying fifth, if you recall?'

With Lofthouse gone, Clifford glided over.

'Chief Inspector, I took the liberty of discreetly checking Mr Taylor's room the moment I heard of his disappearance.'

'Excellent. And?'

'The gentleman's things I observed when Constable Danby and I searched his room after the attack on his grace are still there. Save, that is, for his travelling tweeds. And his overcoat.'

'Dash it! Sounds like he's definitely skipped then,' Eleanor said. 'He was in his sporting togs when we interviewed him. What do you think we should do, Hugh?'

He threw out his hands. 'In the twenty minutes until the competition starts?'

'Ahem, sixteen now.' Clifford closed his pocket watch.

Seldon ran his hand through his curls. 'Blast it! Ridiculous though it is, we'd better compete, Eleanor. At least that way, his grace won't shut us down completely.'

She started for the front door.

'Ahem, sporting togs are required, my lady.' Clifford sniffed.

On the shooting platform, the snow was falling in light flakes that settled on her lips and melted in rivulets down her neck, despite the biting cold of the air. She gripped her heated hand-warmers in her pockets and tried to rally some concentration.

Lofthouse raised his hands. 'Given t' weather, his grace's orders are this round of competition will run as follows; in braces, down the line, doubled, pair on report.'

She turned to Clifford. 'What was Lofthouse's mumbo-jumbo this time?'

'Names will be drawn from a hat as to who competes against whom in each pair, my lady. Twenty-four clays will be taken in each half. On the cry of "Pull", only one clay will be released. The second will be released as the competitor fires at the first. Targets will be fired from a single trap. However, down the line means that competitors must, literally, move "down the line". To the next shooting position along. In this case, after every two targets.'

She grimaced. 'So we'll never get our eye in! And we've only forty-eight targets, not a hundred like before, to get the hang of it, too.'

'However, it will be considerably quicker with fewer targets and three fewer competitors, my lady.'

'Good. Because the quicker this nonsense is over, the quicker we can get on with searching for Taylor,' Seldon said ardently.

Clifford collected their guns from Bowes and checked neither had been tampered with.

'Goodness!' she murmured. 'If we're expecting foul play on only the second round, the third could turn into a pitched battle!'

Clifford's reply was halted by Lofthouse holding a black top hat above his head.

'Pairs will be as follows.' He reached up with one hand and rummaged inside.

Eleanor crossed her fingers. 'Oh no, Hugh! I've just thought. Actually, we don't want to be a pair, of course. Because then we'd be competing directly against each other!'

He looked disappointed. 'I hadn't thought of that.'

'Still, we have to do our best. For poor Porritt. To keep up the pressure to flush out his killer if the grand prize is what prompted him being murdered.'

'Well, by disappearing, Taylor has rather singled himself out as our leading suspect now. You're right, though. Until we have firm facts, we do whatever we can.'

'Pair one. Lady Swift,' Lofthouse announced, reading from the first two pieces of paper he'd unfolded. 'And

Mr... Huish. Pair two therefore, Mr Seldon and Miss Whitwell.'

She breathed a sigh of relief. 'Good start.'

Clifford caught her eye. 'You are first, I believe, my lady.'

She stepped up to the plinth more confidently than she felt. Looking through the now lightly falling snow, she noted the path that allowed the firing trap to be wheeled to the centre of the field had been roughly cleared. Evidently the piled-up bank of snow on either side was deemed sufficient cover from exploding glass for Bowes and Fripp. And for Tosh, whose frost-bitten face appeared between them.

Then she saw a flash of movement off on the right, among the trees.

It must be the ladies, Ellie! Come to cheer you and Hugh on again.

Not wanting to give them away, she pretended to be limbering up and gave a discreet wave in their direction.

Sliding a cartridge into each barrel, she snapped the gun shut. Raising it to her shoulder, she whispered, 'We've really got our work cut out this time, friend.' But the butt just didn't seem to quite fit as before. And the walnut stock felt like an unresponsive slab. Settling in as best she could, she found her point of balance.

'Pull!'

Trying to track the targets through the falling snow was even harder than she'd feared. And she could only make out one. Of course! The second would only be released when she fired at the first.

Bang! With everything at stake, she'd forgotten the power of the shotgun's recoil. She fumbled her finger back onto the trigger, just in time to catch her second target sailing down into the snow.

'Two misses,' Lofthouse called.

'Oh, bad luck!' Viola smirked, sounding anything but sincere.

Huish seemed as tense as a coiled spring as he took his stance.

'Pull!'

Eleanor watched the trap release, rather than Huish aiming. He fired. She watched the trap again intently as another clay shot out.

Aha! So that's the angle it flies, Ellie.

'One miss. One kill.'

Huish threw her a smug look.

'Well done,' she said genuinely. Hitting anything in these conditions was a miracle, to her mind.

Having moved to the second plinth, she was encouraged that it felt little different to firing from the first. Lofthouse's call of, 'One miss. One kill,' backed this up. By the fifth, she was feeling less daunted. Her score was three to Huish's four. By the end of the seventh, she'd caught him up with both their scores standing at eight.

Seldon stepped over. 'You're doing brilliantly! What's the secret?'

She quickly passed on what she'd learned so far.

She scored another kill at plinth eight. But so did Huish. Nine was a horrible angle to shoot from, but she held her nerve and was rewarded with 'Two kills,' from Lofthouse.

Huish's nerve obviously didn't hold as he missed both his targets. As the shooting progressed, they were never more than a point apart until at the end of the first half, she was trailing Huish by twelve to his thirteen.

The next pair stepped up. Her heart stopped as Seldon fired first. She needn't have worried as he nailed his second clay. Surprisingly, Pearl missed hers, giving Seldon such a murderous look, Eleanor shivered.

By the third plinth, Pearl had scored three, while Seldon

was still stuck on one. As the pair worked their way along the line, Eleanor's spirits soared and plummeted. By the eighth, Seldon was six behind Pearl, finishing the first round a disappointing nine to her fifteen.

'Not to worry, Hugh,' Eleanor whispered as they met at the refreshment table, where Clifford was serving small glasses of brandy.

Pearl refused any, pulling a bottle of water from her jacket pocket with a snide, 'Sharp wits win.'

Eleanor shrugged, finding the inner warmth her first sip brought very welcoming. She called over her shoulder, 'Won't you join us, Mr and Mrs oh—' She broke off, spotting the Musgraves had left already.

'So much for being good sports by supporting those of us remaining in the competition,' she muttered.

'Which I wish was over before it had even started,' Seldon muttered back, downing his brandy in one.

'Second half begins,' Lofthouse announced.

'However this ends, we'll have tried our best, Hugh,' she said.

He brushed his hand over hers. 'Yes. And I'll have had the chance to watch you looking so beautiful in this snow. Now, go show them how to do this, Lady Swift style!'

'Alright.' She picked up her gun and hastened over.

'One kill. One miss!' Lofthouse declared at her first effort.

'Not good enough, Ellie!' she muttered, despite Huish missing both of his.

At the fourth plinth, she gave herself a second talking-to. Successfully, as Lofthouse announced, 'Two kills.'

Huish scored the same at the next, however. She wasn't surprised. Having unexpectedly been given another chance, he was more aggressively focused with every shot.

By the midpoint, she'd dropped a hideous two points behind. And then another one.

As she was taking her stance for the next, Huish strolled up to her.

'No hope for you now, Lady Swift,' he murmured in a mocking tone. 'But at least you had a bash at playing with the big boys.'

'Foolish mistake, Mr Huish,' she muttered as he sauntered away.

'First pair ends!' Lofthouse announced ten minutes later. 'With the scores at sixteen to fourteen. The winner is Lady Swift!'

Clifford gave her a discreet thumbs up as Seldon broke into a rousing round of applause. She caught Huish's eye and smiled sweetly. He opened his mouth as if he was going to speak. Then closed it and stomped away.

'Apologies, Chief Inspector,' she heard Pearl purr as she and Seldon took their places for their second round. 'I'm afraid I'll have to unleash everything I've got on you now.'

'I wish you luck, Miss Whitwell,' he said dispassionately.

To Eleanor's dismay, she trumped him with one hit at the first plinth. And the second. At the third, his frustration with himself kicked in, she thought. He was back on the scoreboard. Eleanor watched his every shot. And Pearl's, who seemed increasingly stimulated, almost unnaturally so. She dismissed the thought, given the woman's repeated mantra – she had come there to win, after all. By the seventh, Pearl was leading by six points. By the ninth, only by four.

'Everything to play for, both of you,' Eleanor called sportingly.

'Hardly!' Pearl snapped. 'I'm not losing this for anything!'

With only four targets left, Eleanor was biting her nails for Seldon to manage just one more double kill.

'Second pair ends!' Lofthouse announced ten minutes later. 'With the scores at nineteen to fifteen. The winner is Miss Whitwell!'

Dash it, Ellie!

Seldon turned to his opponent. 'Congratulations. You're very single-minded, Miss Whitwell.'

Pearl smiled smugly. 'I've beaten you once, Chief Inspector. I'm sure I can do it again.'

What does she mean by that, Ellie?

At that moment, Seldon scooped her arm into his and it no longer mattered.

40

As they reached the rear of Auldwyke Hall, Clifford appeared and waved them inside.

'Somewhere safe from interruptions to form a plan, perhaps?'

'Good man.' Seldon's brow furrowed as he followed Eleanor into the small anteroom set with one snug high-backed bench seat and a warm-glowing brazier. 'Though, how you got here before us, I can't work out.'

She laughed. 'I can. On his wizard's broomstick.'

Clifford's lips quirked. 'Hardly, my lady, a broom is not for riding around on in public view! However, "hocus pocus".'

With a flourish, he produced two steaming mugs of coffee from behind his back.

Seldon threw his hands up. 'Do that again. And conjure up Mr Willoughby Taylor, would you?'

'Would that I could,' Clifford said soberly.

Eleanor sipped her coffee gratefully. 'It's a blow that we can't leave the duke's door unguarded, Hugh. But, there's still three of us free at any one time. However you want to man, and woman, the search,' she ended pointedly.

Clifford and Seldon exchanged a look of resignation.

'Of course we'll all search, Eleanor.'

'Thank you, chaps. Now what's our plan?'

Seldon thought for a moment. 'Hmm. We have to assume Taylor hasn't actually been able to leave due to the snow. Because if he has, then it's too late, blast it!' He started pacing, absent-mindedly glugging his coffee. 'Danby would be good to cover the grounds, as he's already searched some of it looking for the murder weapon, among other things.'

Eleanor nodded. 'And Clifford knows the house better than us. Although, like the grounds, there must be a dozen or more places to hide in the Hall.'

Seldon turned to her butler. 'Clifford?'

'True. But it seems unlikely Mr Taylor could be hiding on the third floor with the duke.'

'One out of five ticked off already, then,' she said encouragingly.

'One out of six, my lady, if you will forgive the correction. There are six floors, as the servants' hall is below ground. However, given that below stairs is always a hive of activity, it seems unlikely again that Mr Taylor would have chosen that area. Plus, I have been in and out of there a great deal myself since he was last seen.'

Seldon nodded. 'Right. We'll ignore that floor as well for the moment.'

'Would you therefore like me to search the fourth floor, sir? That being the male staff's quarters?'

Seldon nodded. 'Definitely. And the fifth.'

Clifford ran his finger around his starched white collar. 'But, sir, that is the province of the female staff!'

'Who will all be busy downstairs with their duties,' Eleanor said. 'Besides, after you rootled through Mrs Musgrave's and Miss Whitwell's underfrillies before...'

Hands over his ears, in two horrified strides, her butler was gone.

She peeled off her shooting jacket now the brazier's warmth had fully thawed her out. 'How about you do the first floor and I do the second, Hugh? It's the one I know my way around best.'

'Um, like that?'

'What's wrong with my sage cashmere jumper?'

'Nothing. In fact, you look too... enchanting to be searching Huish or Barnabas Musgrave's rooms.'

She smiled. 'Alright. But watch out Viola and Pearl don't both grab you when you march into theirs.'

He shrugged. 'Why would they?'

'Hopeless!'

Seldon opted to take the staff stairs. Eleanor hurried, with only one wrong turn, to the vast marbled entrance hall. Being greeted by the magnificent Christmas tree, however, brought a wash of yearning for the romantic break this was supposed to have been with her fiancé. Craning her neck back, she stared up at the angel looking down serenely from the higher branches.

'Tell poor Mr Porritt we're trying our best to get justice for him,' she whispered.

Darting over to the umbrella stand, she seized the stoutest walking stick available and set off. Her Bartitsu martial arts training might be a little rusty, since she'd learned it even before the suffragettes brought it to general attention, but it had got her out of sticky situations before.

The first door she opened led into an unoccupied morning room, exclusively for ladies, she thought, given the rather over-bearing pink velvet, flower motifs, and proliferation of recliner seats. The next one was a stridently masculine version of the first, swathed in minimally varying shades of business-like grey and stiffly buttoned leather chesterfield armchairs. But equally with no Willoughby Taylor. It dawned, he wasn't likely to be openly sitting in any of the main rooms. Having no idea what lay beyond the numerous doors ahead, however, she pressed on. A blue drawing room with a lavish painted ceiling and a yellow one without came and went. Taylor wasn't hiding behind any of the settees, nor any of the enormous curtains. Nor on the galleried landing in the grand library. She hurried back down the carved spiral staircase and, on a whim, went to the vast ornate fireplace, having spotted the tall figurines in relief that formed the side panels. Pressing and poking in all sorts of places her butler would have been tutting in horror at, she drew another blank. No secret hidey-hole appeared. None of the oak panelling swung inwards. And Taylor hadn't secreted himself up the chimney, as her sooty hands testified.

The end of the passageway turned sharply right, with two doors facing her. She rattled the handle of the first, then hurried to the second to thwart any escaping fugitive. She needn't have bothered. It was the ballroom. And it was as thoroughly empty as it was forlornly forgotten. It saddened her that the duke had lost so much heart. He clearly never intended to entertain again. A music room was next, followed by a small writing room with nowhere to hide. And then a reading room of tall, open bookcases and a vast circular velvet seat with a central post that could have seated sixteen Taylors. She only wanted one. But there were none.

Other rooms came and went until she found herself back in the portrait gallery where she'd first been interviewed by Danby. The former dukes of Auldwyke looked down on her in seeming disapproval. She grunted at them and crossed into the portrait-free billiard room. Which, unfortunately, was also murderer-free.

Not that you should automatically assume Taylor is the murderer just because he's either gone into hiding or fled Auldwyke Hall, Ellie.

About to abandon the search as a lost cause, she jerked to a stop on hearing a sneeze.

She whirled in a circle, willing the perpetrator to give themselves away again. They did. She hurried to where the second sneeze had come from; a sliver of light between two sections of oak panelling at the far end of the room. Walking stick raised in one hand, she flattened herself against the wall as...

'Summat you need, m'lady?' Lofthouse emerged, frowning at her impromptu Bartitsu stick.

She quickly lowered it. 'Ah! Yes. Actually, er, have you seen Mr Taylor yet?'

'Nope. I've not tried lookin' again.'

'Well, if you do see him anywhere, let the chief inspector or Mr Clifford know, please.'

She tried to surreptitiously peer into the room he'd emerged from.

''Tis just prep room for dinin' things, m'lady. If you leave by that door yonder' – he pointed across the room – 'you'll be back off the grand entrance hall.'

This time the sight of the Christmas tree was enhanced by Seldon standing under it.

'Eleanor, thank goodness.' He strode over to her. 'I couldn't find you anywhere.'

'Just as I couldn't find Taylor anywhere.'

'Nor me, blast it! This house is even more of a warren than your Henley Hall.'

'It'll be *our* Henley Hall someday, Hugh.'

At that moment, Danby appeared, looking flushed and breathless.

'You're supposed to be guarding the duke!' Seldon barked.

'Beggin' your pardon, sir. But Mr Clifford didn't find Mr Taylor, so he relieved me and asked I search the storehouses, garages and the like.'

'Ah! Then good work, Constable. You didn't find Taylor, I suppose?'

'Not a sign, sir.'

Eleanor caught Seldon's eye. 'If you're not too famished, Constable, could you bear another hour of guarding the duke's door?'

'With pleasure, m'lady. I'll send Mr Clifford down to join you.'

As Danby left, Seldon raked his hand through his hair. 'I should never have let Taylor's disappearance happen. I—'

She grabbed his arms. 'How could you possibly have stopped him, Hugh? His grace high-handedly forbade you from calling in more police officers on pain of the investigation being immediately shut down. And even if you had decided to risk going against his orders, the wretched telephone line is down and the roads are infuriatingly impassable. Clifford said the Auldwyke estate covers two hundred and forty acres. And' – she halted his protest with a finger to his lips – 'aside from you and me, there's only Clifford and Constable Danby we can trust. And we've all been further hampered by you three chaps having to dutifully keep an unbroken guard on his grace's door and me having to nurse the stubborn old buzzard!'

He managed a smile. 'All true. If an unladylike way of putting it.'

'Hmm, I did leave out that a certain detective chief inspector might have let slip he quietly hoped the murderer would turn out to be Taylor?'

'To my shame, yes.'

'Well, he's unlikely to have got far with this snow.' She grimaced. 'Unless he planned it in advance, of course.'

Seldon held out his hands. 'Whether he did or not, Willoughby Taylor has somehow vanished off the face of the earth!'

41

Eleanor rubbed her eyes. She needed a brief respite from murder, prussic acid attacks and vanishing suspects. It was still Christmas Eve, after all. And looking at the dark lines under her fiancé's eyes, so did he. Clifford, however, seemed to already have something in mind.

Without explanation, he led them out of Auldwyke Hall and towards the old gamekeeper's cottage, the soft white flakes falling around them.

As they passed the front of the cottage, he turned to Seldon. 'With sincere apologies, Chief Inspector, for the pantomime you are about to witness.'

Puzzlingly, rather than going inside, he skirted the cottage's tiny garden, leading them along a path for a short distance, the sound of merriment increasing with every step.

As they rounded a corner, Eleanor gasped. The sight that met her eyes made her want to hug her butler for being an even bigger closet softie than she'd realised. He'd clearly gone above and beyond to make sure the rest of her staff had a holiday they would never forget. And for all the right reasons.

The ladies were straggling up the steep slope in front of

them, rosy-cheeked and elated, their coats and long skirts covered in snow as they dragged makeshift sledges behind them. In the one pulled by Mrs Butters, her bulldog and tomcat were riding in style on a thick blanket. Like Seldon, she roared with laughter at the sight of her beloved pets, both dressed in red and green knitted all-in-one suits and matching woolly bobble hats tied under their furry chins. Gladstone woofed exuberantly on seeing them, setting Tomkins off yowling.

As her staff neared the top, Eleanor and Seldon grabbed an arm each to stop Polly sliding back down.

'Ladies, I don't suppose you've got a sledge spare?' Eleanor said, desperate to join in the fun.

All eyes swivelled to Clifford, who stroked an imaginary beard as if mulling the idea over.

Polly gaped at him. 'Sir, surely like dippin' in the sea in bathing suits, and partyin' in the kitchen of Henley Hall, 'tis against the rules to go sledgin' with the mistress?'

He peered sideways at Eleanor. 'Most assuredly, Polly. But since the former events have disgracefully already taken place, and on more than one occasion, sledging this once will hardly make the world stop spinning.'

'Even though I've passed the grand age of thirty, I've never been sledging!' Eleanor said, overcome with childlike joy.

Seldon shook his head teasingly at her. 'And you ragged me for being a city boy! Stick with me. You're in for a treat.' He looked apologetically around her staff. 'Oh goodness, only if I won't be intruding on your fun, of course, ladies?'

'Lawks, you could never intrude, sir. 'Twill be our pleasure!' Mrs Butters said breathlessly.

It was only then Eleanor realised Seldon was still dressed in his shooting wear of form-fitting jacket and breeks which emphasised his shapely calves, and trim waist below his broad shoulders.

Mrs Trotman threw her a cheeky glance before turning to

her butler. 'You'll have to look the other way to stop all the starch meltin' out your collar, though, Mr Clifford. Seeing as the grandest snow carriage we have for her ladyship and the chief inspector is the long tin bath over there.'

He pinched the bridge of his nose, but nodded.

'And you'll have to double up close with one of us aprons, Mr Clifford, for we've no more sledges free after that,' Mrs Trotman continued. 'So which d'you fancy? Taking your chances with Lizzie or Polly on a tray, though it'll be a tight fit? Or joining me or Butters on the side of an old tea chest we found?'

Clifford shuddered, but his eyes twinkled. 'Surprisingly, none of the above, thank you, Mrs Trotman.'

The tin bath was soon given a rope handle like the other sledges, and lined with two of the softest picnic blankets ever made. Eleanor jumped in, followed by Gladstone and Tomkins, who cuddled excitedly into her lap.

'Race to the bottom. Ready, steady...' She watched Seldon help the ladies line up their sledges, before giving each of them a helpful starting push.

'Go!'

Checking no one was looking, he leaned in to brush his lips over hers. 'Is the lady ready to make this even more of a ridiculous Christmas than I thought possible?'

'Ready and waiting, sire. Only get a move on. The ladies are going to win!'

Hurtling down the slope was exhilarating. And hilarious. But mostly too magical for words. Seldon snuggled in behind her with his arms wound around her waist was so tantalising, she wished they could stay just like that forever.

In their heavier, more aerodynamic sledge, they shot past Mrs Butters and Mrs Trotman before overtaking Polly and Lizzie, who were shrieking with delight.

Despite this, at the bottom Eleanor declared it too close a finish for anything but joint winners all round.

'Next race!' she cried.

Seldon carefully stacked all the other sledges into the bath behind Tomkins and Gladstone and chivalrously started dragging them up the slope. But by the halfway point, he came to a groaning stop and turned around.

'You traitor!' He chuckled at Eleanor, who had stealthily snuck back into the bath.

The next run down seemed faster. Maybe they were already getting the hang of the slope and their impromptu sledge? Not so for her maids, who spun off into a deep drift and fell head first into it. Much to their evident delight.

Before they could catch their breath to start their way back up to the top after the fifth race, Eleanor spotted Clifford walking down the edge of the slope. At regular intervals, he was driving wooden stakes covered in rags into the ground. At the bottom, he lit the first one.

'Burning torches to light the sledge course!' Eleanor breathed, catching Polly trying to hold in her tears at the extra festive magic the dancing flames added.

'Refreshments await,' Clifford called.

Seldon offered to light the other torches so he could return to the top of the slope to ready the refreshment table. Clifford handed the matches to Seldon, who waited for him to start off before stepping over to the ladies and whispering something to them.

'What are you up to, you toad?' she said as he rejoined her, the ladies hurrying to catch Clifford up.

'Oh, just a little payback for your scallywag butler catching me out before with his sleight of hand.'

As the ladies drew level with Clifford, who was hampered by dragging the bath behind him, they all pretended to slip, toppling him into it.

'Allow us to pull you, Mr Clifford. For bein' so clumsy!' Mrs Trotman called as the four of them grabbed the rope and hauled him upwards.

Good-naturedly he didn't leap out, but cradled the happy Gladstone and Tomkins, waving to Eleanor and Seldon as if he was royalty, which had them all roaring with laughter.

Having lit all the torches, at the top she caught Clifford on his own and murmured, 'Thank you for being the best sport ever. And for this magical time together... as family.'

He gave her a rare smile. 'As the eminent Charles Dickens noted, my lady. "For it is good to be children sometimes, and never better than at Christmas, when its mighty Founder was a child Himself."'

The chestnuts toasting on an oven tray over a pail of burning coals smelled as heavenly as they tasted. The tall glasses of hot chocolate, topped with a generous peak of whipped cream and cocoa dusting, were equally delicious. As were the golden sausage meat and thyme lattice pastries. The snow was falling harder now, making the perfect festive chocolate box scene. And the run of flaming torches down the slope really was the icing on the Christmas cake. Although Eleanor managed three slices of that as well, before checking everyone was full and declaring it was time for the next round of races.

After four more downward runs, Clifford stared up at the sky as they scrambled up the slope once more.

'Perhaps that last run had better be the final one for tonight, my lady?' he said apologetically.

'For us old aprons, it had better be,' Mrs Butters panted. 'My knees will have given up bending at all by the morning if I don't.'

Mrs Trotman nudged her. 'Not to worry, Butters. That nice young Constable Danby can carry us both up the stairs.'

'Ahem!' Clifford said.

Eleanor laughed. 'Perhaps you're right, Clifford. The light

has all but gone and the snow really is starting to come down hard. It might bury us all before we reach the bottom of the slope again!'

Her young maids' crestfallen faces, however, told her one more race was definitely needed.

Clifford took Tomkins and Gladstone into his arms and pretended to whisper in their eagerly twitching ears, 'Gentlemen, I fear this will be a most lawless and desperate run.' In his distinguished toastmaster's voice, he declared, 'Winner will be the overall sledging champion. Competitors ready! On the count of three... three!'

'You terror!' Eleanor laughed as they all scrambled to set off. Perhaps it was the extra hard shove Seldon had given their bath? Or the wind at their backs? Whatever it was, they were careering down faster than ever, eyes streaming with the cold air rushing past. Then, without warning, three-quarters of the way down, their tin bath swerved violently off to the left.

'Brace, Hugh!' Eleanor cried as they headed towards a snow bank.

The sudden stop as they hit it jerked her forwards and then back on top of Seldon who had also been knocked backwards.

'The simple pleasures really are the best!' she said contentedly. She'd have been happy to stay like that all night, but everyone needed to get back to the cottage while they could still see their way.

As she sat up and climbed out of the bath, she noticed something sticking out of the bank. At first in the gloom, she thought it was a branch half-buried in the snow. But as she peered more closely, she realised...

'Hugh! That... that's not a branch. It's an arm!'

42

Eleanor leaped out of the sledge.

'Tell me I'm hallucinating!' she muttered desperately as she dropped to her knees in the snow.

But there was no mistaking the icy cold of the hand she had inadvertently grasped.

She just beat Seldon to press her fingers to the disturbingly greyish-white wrist she had initially mistaken as a fallen tree branch.

'Eleanor, no!' he cried, gently pulling her arm back. 'Let me.'

'We're too late, Hugh,' she said through chattering teeth, overcome with shivers from the shock. 'Whoever that poor soul is, they're dead. Very dead.'

She jumped up and semaphored urgently to Clifford. Immediately he started down towards them in long, loping strides.

'Are you alright, m'lady?' Mrs Butters called from the bottom of the slope.

'Oh lord, the ladies,' Seldon mouthed.

Eleanor mustered all her calm as she turned to the four of

them. They were peering up at her, hands over their eyes to shield out the constant snowflakes.

'We're fine. Just stay there a minute,' she called back.

Clifford reached her, his expression filled with concern.

'We've found... someone,' was the best explanation she could manage.

She felt Seldon's arm around her waist. 'Eleanor, please sort the ladies for me.'

She nodded. 'You'll need some of the torches.'

'And a shovel, my lady,' Clifford said soberly. 'There's one by the refreshment table. I brought it in case we needed to clear any snow for the sledging.'

Two minutes later, she had dispatched Polly and Lizzie to the old gamekeeper's cottage with Gladstone and Tomkins. And had broken the news as gently as possible to Mrs Butters and Mrs Trotman. The two women were adamant they wanted to help, so the three of them returned carrying torches and Eleanor clutching the shovel as well.

Seldon, who'd been scouring the snow with Clifford's pocket torch, gaped at her, his eyes darting to her cook and housekeeper.

Clifford slid the shovel from under her arm. 'Her ladyship's judgement is sufficiently sound on this occasion, Chief Inspector.'

''Tis the least we can do, sir,' Mrs Trotman said determinedly.

Still looking uncomfortable, Seldon began to dig as Eleanor and the ladies spread out, holding their flaming torches. It took all of Eleanor's resolve not to drop to her knees and frantically scoop the snow away. That arm. It belonged to a person. To let them lie even a moment longer in their icy tomb felt wrong. Heart-wrenchingly wrong.

About two feet down, a jacketed torso appeared, the fabric threads packed with snow. The world might have stopped spinning for all Eleanor was aware. Everything was silent, save for the sound of Seldon's gloves crunching down into the crystallised white.

Her insides clenched at the blue-white face he exposed.

She nodded to herself. 'Willoughby Taylor!'

Seldon sat slowly back on his heels. 'And he's been strangled. But what would he have been doing down here?'

Clifford looked thoughtful. 'If I might propose a theory, Chief Inspector? That Mr Taylor did not die here. But was strangled up on the path where it joins the top of the slope and was then disgracefully pushed over the edge. A rolling stone may gather no moss, as the Syrian writer, Publilius Syrus, suggested back in the first century. But a rolling body would create a large enough avalanche to hide it comprehensively. Certainly until more falling snow finished off the job.'

'Good theory.' Seldon rose quickly and held his hands out for Mrs Trotman and Mrs Butters to relinquish a torch each. 'Ladies, I can't bear to let you stay any longer. Please go immediately to Polly and Lizzie. I don't think you are in any danger, but the four of you are to remain together, please. And lock yourselves in. Understood?'

'Yes, sir.'

'Commendable poise, ladies. Well done,' Clifford said.

Seldon looked at Eleanor, eyes troubled. 'I wish you'd go with them.'

She shook her head. 'I can't, Hugh. I owe Taylor an apology. And the only way I can make amends is to catch his killer. So, what do we do next?'

He sighed. 'I've grossly insufficient manpower. And womanpower,' he conceded with a wan smile. 'And even if I had more reinforcements, with the light all but gone and the snow increasing and covering evidence by the minute...' He let out a long breath. 'The truth is, this case is getting away from me. And dangerously quickly.' He cast an eye in the direction of

Auldwyke Hall. 'And I still need to protect the duke, not to mention any other innocent parties.'

Eleanor jumped up. 'The duke! I must check on him soon. His breathing is still not what it ought to be.'

Seldon thought for a moment. 'Right! We finish digging out the body and put it somewhere safe until I can have another look properly in daylight.' He glanced around. 'I'll just have to risk disturbing, and missing, something critical here.'

'There is a lockable outhouse at the cottage, Chief Inspector,' Clifford said.

'Excellent.'

It wasn't an elegant hearse that transported Taylor to his resting place for the night. But Eleanor took the small comfort that without the tin bath to lay him in, and the picnic blanket Clifford respectfully draped over him, it would have been worse.

The door locked, Clifford returned to the cottage, while Seldon and Eleanor headed for the main house.

As they entered the grand hallway and made for the duke's private stairs to the third floor, she turned to him.

'Hugh, listen. As I have to tend to his grace anyway, why... why don't I try asking him again what he knows about what happened ten years ago on the last shoot?'

Seldon shook his head. 'Thank you, Eleanor. But as the detective in charge of the investigation, that really should be my job.'

She winced. 'I know. But his grace is the one who's made it impossible for you. And given his feelings about policemen...'

As they neared the top of the stairs, Seldon whispered, 'Look. I'm still not sure. I feel such a heel, you questioning the duke alone.'

She pointed to Danby pacing in front of the black oak door

leading into the duke's apartment. Seldon strode across to the young policeman.

'Good man for staying alert up here. But unfortunately, there's been a development...'

Before he could change his mind, she left him to fill Danby in as Lofthouse appeared, took the key from Seldon, and let her into the duke's apartment as arranged.

Once inside, she took a deep breath, then called out, 'Approaching now, Your Grace. It's Lady Swift.'

'Then unapproach!' the duke's voice rasped from the bedroom. 'You've no business in here, young woman!'

She rolled her shoulders back. 'I hope you're decent, Your Grace, because I'm coming in to tell you I have.'

She turned the handle and stepped in, half-expecting his walking cane to come flying at her head. The floor-to-ceiling shutters were closed and bolted, she was pleased to see after the previous attack, the only light coming from a gold lamp at either end of the room. But it was enough for her to make out the heavy flock curtains around the four-poster bed were drawn back, revealing that it was empty.

'Your Grace!' she said firmly, looking around. 'You're not supposed to be out of bed.'

She spotted him leaning against a chair, his silver-handled cane hanging over his wrist. Dressed in a black velvet dressing gown with a pewter quilted shawl collar and matching piping, he was wearing suit trousers over his pyjama bottoms.

'And you shouldn't be in here to see that I'm not!' the duke blustered, his bushy, grey-white eyebrows meeting in a ferocious line across his deeply lined brow. He broke off into a fit of coughing.

But much less than before, Ellie.

'Honestly, Your Grace, I wish I didn't need to be in here. Trust me, battling with a fractious peer of the realm is not how I planned to spend my Christmas. Especially when I'd already declined his gracious invitation.'

For a moment she thought he was going to bellow at her, but then she saw his piercing hazel eyes looked more curious than thunderous.

'Declined my invitation, did you, by Jove?' He swung his cane down to the floor and stepped over to her. Again she was struck by how light of step he seemed for a man of reduced breath and advanced years. And by how majestic his impressive frame must have been when he was younger.

'Turning down the most prestigious invitation of the year. Finding deceased persons. Getting engaged to a policeman. Challenging a duke in his own bedroom! What kind of a titled lady are you?'

She shrugged. 'One who inherited her title from her beloved uncle, who bequeathed her a beautiful home. But forgot to include a manual on how on earth she's supposed to behave as a lady. Now.' She waved at the chair. 'Please at least sit down, Your Grace, while you continue to inform me of just how much I'm a disgrace to the aristocracy.'

His eyes narrowed, but he stepped over to the wing-back and sat down, gripping his cane between his knees. He hesitated for a moment, then waved for her to join him. She walked over and settled in a moss-green corner chair, the only item apart from a dark-mulberry rug that injected a modicum of colour in the otherwise mournful room.

He held her gaze for an uncomfortably long minute. And then another. Just when she was about to cajole him into letting her check his pulse and temperature, he tapped his cane on the floor again.

'Fractious, you said I am?'

She nodded. 'Honestly, yes. But I didn't mean to offend you.'

'I should think not. I am the Duke of Auldwyke,' he gruffed.

'Are you sure?' she said gently. 'Because I understood he used to be quite the different man.'

His gaze dropped to his lap as he let out a long breath, which, given his impaired lungs, wasn't much more than a dry rattle. 'So I was. So I was...'

She sat quietly, hoping she'd succeeded in penetrating his armour, if only by a pinprick.

The hard stare now boring into her skull suggested she hadn't.

'Lady Swift, I tolerate you being in here for one reason only; you saved my life the other day. I acknowledge that.'

She waved his acknowledgement away. 'I'm just pleased you survived, Your Grace. That we all did.'

'However,' he continued, 'you've no idea what it means. My letting you in. Here.' His breathing seemed to shorten. 'I haven't permitted a soul to enter since...'

'Since your wife died, Your Grace?'

He nodded.

'It's fearfully late to offer my condolences,' she said softly. 'But I understand how hard it is to lose someone that precious.'

'You remind me of her,' he murmured. 'Not least by your fiery spirit and forthrightness. And your... compassion. That's really why I permitted you to come in. So I could believe... just a moment... she wasn't gone.' He coughed, rose unsteadily, and turned away.

Perhaps that's what Bowes meant when he said it stood to reason the duke had let you into his solace, Ellie? And maybe why Porritt was staring so intently at you in the car?

The duke spoke, his back still to her. 'I know my wife married me out of duty, not love. And that... that the life she had was not the one she would have chosen. I was acutely aware of that. Which is why I allowed her anything she wanted. Like her shoots and art patronage. If she didn't have enough to keep her occupied, she had a habit of... getting herself involved in other people's business. Out of boredom, I suppose.'

So that's why she knew so many details about other people's lives, Ellie. It was nothing malicious. Ironically, she probably never intended to profit from any of it.

He turned back, a haunted look in his eyes. 'But I married her out of love. I loved her with every fibre of my being. It's why I can't leave Auldwyke. Because it would mean leaving... her.' He suddenly straightened up. 'But good heavens, that's enough of that! Kindly ignore my rambling.'

She floundered for an artful way to keep the conversation going where she needed it to. 'Was this year's annual Christmas shoot planned as a ten-year anniversary of your wife's passing perhaps, Your Grace?'

'Of course not!' he barked, relapsing into a fit of coughing.

She stepped forward, then back. She wished he'd let her attend to him, but she knew it was pointless at that moment to insist.

Recovered, the duke waved his cane. 'Why would I have wanted to highlight how long I've been without her? Porritt organised everything for the shoot, as usual. Including the guest list. My only interest was to have the event run as it does every year.' The strength of the duke's voice weakened as he stared over her head. 'So I can stay up here and listen to the shooting and the party below. And... and imagine my wife is down there, being the centre of everything, just as she always was.'

She expected his wistful look to switch back to cantankerous again, but his gaze seemed fixed behind her. She turned. On the wall was a portrait of a striking woman in her late forties, holding a shotgun, a scattering of game birds at her feet. Looking every inch the aristocrat in her green tweed shooting attire, her head of copper curls shone in the sunlight streaming through the trees.

'That's your wife, isn't it, Your Grace?'

'Yes.' His tone was distant.

Eleanor's breath caught. The duchess was wearing a gold pendant. She spun back around.

'You said you didn't recognise the pendant my fiancé, Chief Inspector Seldon, showed you, Your Grace. And yet your wife there...' She tailed off, watching his expression.

The duke nodded slowly. 'I recognised it, yes. It was my wife's. A beloved aunt of hers gave it to her.' For a moment he said nothing, the only sound in the room the ticking of an unseen clock. Finally, he looked up at her. 'The last time I saw it, she was wearing it. On the final day of the annual Christmas shoot ten years ago.' He lifted his hands and studied them. 'Just before I killed her.'

43

'He did what!?'

In the library-cum-interview room, Seldon stared at Eleanor in disbelief while Clifford arched an astonished brow.

She nodded. 'You heard correctly, Hugh. The duke admitted the pendant you found in Porritt's hand was his wife's. And that the last time he saw it was on the last day of the shoot, ten years ago. She was wearing it. Then he dropped the bombshell that he'd killed her. And then he basically threw me out.' She sighed. 'So, what can we do?'

'About the duke having killed his wife?' Seldon sat back and let out a long breath. 'Nothing! As well he'll know. It was, as you said, ten years ago. We've no proof and any there was I'm pretty certain he will have made sure was destroyed. Even if we could unearth something he'd overlooked, he'd simply claim Trial by Peers and most likely walk away free.'

She groaned, having forgotten about that aristocratic loophole. Any member of the House of Lords had the right to be tried, not in an ordinary court, but by his peers. All of whom were automatic members of the High Court of Parliament. Even without being cynical, it was unlikely the duke, one of the most powerful aristocrats in the country, would be convicted. Of anything.

'However we feel about it, we need to focus only on Porritt and Taylor's murders,' Seldon said firmly.

She grimaced. 'I see that. But suppose Porritt knew the duke's secret? And maybe tried to blackmail him? The duke would have had plenty of reason to kill Porritt then.' Her words tumbled out. 'Think, Hugh. That could explain why the duke refused to have any other policemen on Auldwyke property. Remember, he thought you were just a run-of-the-mill inspector from Kirkwell? No wonder he's thrown so many obstacles in your path after finding you're from Scotland Yard. And why he insisted the shooting competition continue unaffected.'

'To make it as difficult as possible for the chief inspector to solve Mr Porritt's murder?' Clifford said.

'Precisely. And to disguise it as just more eccentric behaviour.'

Seldon rose and ran his hand around the back of his neck. 'I'm sorry to be blunt, Eleanor, but you're wrong. Both of you. Porritt was not blackmailing the duke. I'd stake my career on it.'

'A bold claim, Hugh.' She folded her arms. 'But I fail to see how you can be so sure?'

'You wouldn't if you'd seen the troubles my mother had for the rest of her life after she was falsely accused of theft and dismissed from service.'

'When you were just ten,' she said softly, reliving the sadness she'd felt for both of them when Seldon had confessed to her down by the waterfall.

'Yes. That stigma never actually died, Eleanor. Well, Bowes told us the duke stood up for Porritt's mother when rumours were rife she'd had a hand in the death of her husband.' He swallowed hard. 'No one stood up for my mother. Let alone a duke!' He placed his hand on his heart. 'If they had, I would have been loyal to them until death. No matter what!' He ran a finger around his shirt collar and cleared his throat. 'Besides, who attacked the duke if not Porritt's killer?'

'Most disappointing!' Clifford muttered. With lightning speed, he unlocked the French doors and shot outside. 'Running now will not spare you, young man!' Eleanor heard him call out in his sternest tone. The one that had made her quake as a nine-year-old. And still did.

'What is it?' Seldon strode to the door with her close behind.

'Rather a case of *who*, Chief Inspector.'

Clifford stepped back in, leading a cowering boy by the sleeve of his frayed shirt.

'Tosh!' Eleanor stared at the Auldwyke's lad-of-all work.

'What were you doing out there?' Seldon barked. 'Speak up, boy!'

The lad's face was ashen behind his freckles, his eyes wide with fear.

Eleanor caught Seldon's eye and gestured to let her try. 'I'm confused, Tosh. Perhaps you can help me?'

His gaze lifted an inch from his scuffed boots.

Having got his attention, she continued. 'During my time at Auldwyke, all I've seen of you is a hard-working member of the team.' She bobbed down to his height. 'Without your efforts, I wouldn't have been able to get as far as the last round in the shooting competition.'

He raised his eyes a little more and blinked at her.

'And Mr Clifford here hasn't reported catching you slacking even once.' She shrugged. 'And he is not one to be lenient over that. So what am I to think about you skulking outside the door of a private conversation between guests of his grace?'

'I... I didn't mean no harm, m'lady,' he stammered.

'Alright, I believe you.'

He let out a long breath.

'However, you need to tell the truth about what you were actually doing out there. Don't be afraid, Tosh.'

The boy hesitated. 'Mr Porritt was always good to me, m'lady. They said someone up and done for 'im and you are trying to catch whoever did it. It weren't right for 'im to go like that. He was only tryin' to do right.'

She fought down her own wash of emotions. 'No, Tosh, it wasn't. It was very wrong. But who was Mr Porritt trying to do right by?'

He clapped his hand over his mouth.

'It's alright, I'll say it for you. It was his grace, wasn't it?'

He looked away, shaking his head.

'Tosh, please listen to me. I understand you're scared. But if you know something, and you can be brave enough to say, it could help Mr Porritt be at peace. And it could help us find out who killed him.'

'And make sure they're properly punished,' Clifford added.

The young lad tugged on his shirt cuffs. ''Tis what Mr Porritt said to his grace, m'lady. Only I wasn't meanin' to listen.'

Over his shoulder, she caught Seldon's encouraging nod. 'It's okay, Tosh. When was this?'

He bit the inside of his cheek. ''Bout two seasons back. Mr Porritt always brings the car round to t' back of house when his grace needs go somewhere.' He scratched his neck. 'He's a stickler of a gentleman for not likin' any folk to see 'im, is his grace. Don't make no sense, that, though, do it, m'lady?'

'Actually, yes it does, Tosh. But neither of us want to tell secrets we don't need to, so you'll have to trust me. Now, what happened?'

'I was runnin' be'ind on me duties, so ran round the back way for bein' quicker to t' reach t' trap down to t' coal cellar. Only I'd forgot his grace would be leavin'.' His breath shortened, clearly feeling the panic all over again. 'So I threw meself down be'ind the shrubs.'

'And you heard Mr Porritt say what to his grace?'

'Mr Porritt said as he was wrong 'bout bein' the one as did for his wife. And he could prove it.' He looked up, puzzlement in his eyes. 'But everyone always said as it was an accident?'

Her breath caught. 'Go on. What did his grace say to that?'

'He said as Mr Porritt would be thrown out if he so much as mentioned it again.' His lip trembled. 'Like I'll be now, for tellin' his grace's business. But I came 'ere, and I told you, m'lady, 'cos wi'out folk like Mr Porritt, and Mr Fripp, I'd a been left in the workhouse.' His eyes filled up. 'But... but I don't want to be sent back there.'

It took all her resolve not to pull him into a hug. Clifford stepped forward to her rescue. 'Tosh, nothing you have done or said this evening will result in you being sent back there. Neither are you in trouble. You can trust her ladyship unquestionably on that. Now, off you go and do not repeat any of this conversation to anyone. Understood?'

The boy nodded and made good his escape.

As Clifford closed the French windows, Eleanor whistled.

'Well, that's put the cat among the pigeons!'

44

Seldon stopped pacing the room and held his hands up. 'I don't have your knack for showing empathy, Eleanor. Even though I feel it too, sometimes. But I wish I had. That's another questioning session you had to do on my behalf.'

She nodded. 'Although how many times do you think I've needed Clifford's silver tongue to bail me out when I've got it hopelessly wrong? He probably keeps a record of all my blunders to delight in chiding me over one day.'

'Regrettably not, my lady.' Clifford's eyes twinkled as he waggled his leather notebook. 'Due to insufficient pages to record them all.'

Seldon laughed. 'Thank you, Clifford. We can't afford to lose our sense of humour.'

Eleanor drew her knees up underneath her in her favoured wing-back chair. 'I'm still trying to work out why the duke threatened to dismiss Porritt. You'd think his secretary saying he could prove he didn't kill his wife would have endeared Porritt to him like a son. But even unanswered, it's further proof I was wrong about Porritt blackmailing the duke,' she added quickly to save Seldon any more discomfort at needing to point it out.

'Perhaps it explains his grace's confession to you, my lady?' Clifford said thoughtfully. 'Maybe he did not mean he killed his wife *literally*. But morally. Perhaps he believes the stray shot which killed her came from his gun?'

'It could be. Guilt like that might drive a man to become a recluse,' Seldon said. He hesitated. 'Eleanor, it's shameful of me to ask, but do you think you could...' He tailed off at her headshake.

'His grace is not going to say another word to me about that subject. Trust me!' She grimaced. 'Or about anything, in fact, given the way he all but threw me out of his bedroom.'

Clifford tutted quietly.

'I know. Hardly chivalrous of him,' she said innocently.

Before Clifford could reply, Seldon interrupted.

'If we believe his grace's admission that the pendant is his wife's, and the last time he saw it was around the lady's neck just before she died, then...?'

Her hand flew to her mouth. 'Gracious! Porritt must have taken it from her lifeless body.'

Seldon nodded. 'Which means Porritt's murder is definitely somehow related to the duchess' death. I repeat, however, our only concern has to be the murders of Porritt and Taylor.'

'We hear you, Hugh. Let's think why Porritt would have had the pendant on him in that storehouse then? He can't have carried it about with him for the last ten years.' Her eyes widened. 'You know, I think Porritt pulled out the pendant in his dying moments to tell whoever found him his murderer was the same person who killed the duchess ten years before.'

'Of course!' Seldon thumped his forehead as he'd done too many times recently, to Eleanor's mind. 'Why can't I see the woods for the trees?'

'Because you haven't slept, Hugh. Not for more than, what, three hours at a stretch since you arrived? You've been surviving on my wily butler's magic tea potions.'

'All of which have tasted quite awful, actually, Clifford,' Seldon said apologetically. 'But on a positive note, this means whether or not his grace was responsible, I'm convinced the duchess was murdered.'

'And by someone who was at the shoot back then,' Clifford said soberly. 'And who is at the shoot now.'

'Of course!' she cried. 'That must be why Porritt invited the same guests. He wasn't sure which of them killed the duchess, but was desperate to prove to the duke that the duke wasn't responsible.'

Seldon looked at Clifford.

'It's beyond plausible, Chief Inspector. And not a hint of a penny dreadful plot either of us could highlight, unfortunately.'

Seldon smiled at her. 'Eleanor, you're brilliant! Let's pursue this avenue and hopefully we'll get some proper progress. So, Porritt invites all the same guests down, intending to expose the murderer of the duchess somehow?'

She rapped the desk. 'Hugh, that's why he was so anxious to have you come. So you could help expose and arrest the murderer!'

'I wish he'd had the sense to say so.'

'He never got the chance, poor fellow. I think the killer arrived at Auldwyke Hall to find the same guests from when he killed the duchess. Smelling something fishy from the off, he, or she, followed Porritt to the storehouse and confronted him. And we know the rest,' she finished sadly.

Seldon nodded. 'Which would explain one mystery then; why the murderer risked killing Porritt with all the guests here. He realised he had to silence Porritt then and there. Before the plan to expose him, or her, worked.'

'But the identity of the killer still eludes us,' Clifford said.

'And why they then attacked the duke,' Seldon added.

Eleanor wanted to cheer they'd got a good way towards finding out why Porritt was murdered, but something felt off.

Very off. She stiffened as the mist cleared. 'Hang on! Supposing we're reading it all wrong?'

Seldon and Clifford stared at her.

'Suppose... just suppose Porritt never *was* the intended victim? And that it was the duke all along?'

Seldon frowned. 'Please explain, Eleanor?'

'Suppose Bowes *did* take the glass clays? But to fill with poison, not to give to his daughter. Because he intended to use them on an attack on the duke from the start. But Porritt discovered him stealing the clays while I was changing into my shooting togs the afternoon I arrived, and Bowes was forced to kill him.'

Seldon rubbed his chin. 'It fits. Bowes would certainly have known about that disused shed we found the bomb-making equipment in.'

'But if I may point out, we still have no motive, my lady,' Clifford said. 'Why would Mr Bowes want to kill his grace?'

Eleanor nodded. 'I knew you'd ask that. And I know we don't have the answer. Not yet.'

Seldon nodded. 'But if we did, I'd be clapping handcuffs on Mr Bowes right this minute! We've ascertained that Porritt's death is directly related to the duchess' and the only member of staff here now who was at the shoot when she died, excluding Porritt, was Bowes. And we've ascertained within reasonable doubt that whoever killed Porritt was also responsible for the bomb-making equipment we found, as the thread from Porritt's fingernail matched the one found in the shed. As it was Bowes who stole the glass clays used in the attack...' He held his hands out.

Eleanor winced. 'I agree. In principal. But something is niggling me. Like glasspaper on bare skin.' Her shoulders slumped. 'And actually, Taylor's murder is making me all the more confused.'

'Perhaps we should consider the question then; who would have benefited most from killing Mr Taylor?' Clifford said.

'Julius Huish!' Eleanor blurted out. 'It would have been his only way to get back into the shooting competition.'

'Taylor wasn't the only competitor left in,' Seldon said.

'No, Hugh. But Taylor was far more of a threat to winning than I could ever be. Which suggests, if Huish is our killer, that maybe the rumour was right about the duke losing control, and Huish killed Porritt because he wouldn't guarantee him his favour from the duke if he won?'

'Well, if Huish did kill Taylor to get back into the competition, it didn't do him any good, seeing as you trounced him in the second round.' Seldon spread his hands on the desk. 'I'll admit to you both, I'm closer to my wits' end than on any recent case. The murderer is still on the loose. And anyone could be their next victim. Which is why I'd like to clap Bowes in handcuffs before we find out he's got another stash of cyanide bombs somewhere for some purpose we're not aware of!'

Eleanor leaped up. 'Good lord! I hadn't thought of that!'

Seldon held his hands up. 'I was half-joking, Eleanor.'

She swallowed hard. 'I know. But I'm not!'

45

'Hurry!' Eleanor called over her shoulder as she ran out of the interview room. There was no time to explain. Even though she had no idea if the terrible thought that had come to her a moment before was utter nonsense or not, she couldn't risk it.

She heard Seldon and Clifford's feet pounding behind her.

'The Christmas tree. Which way?' She whirled in a circle at yet another crossroads of dark oak panelling. Why did the Auldwyke passageways have to be such a confusing maze?

'Right. And right again,' Clifford called back.

In the grand entrance hall, she skidded to a stop. Pulse racing, she stared upwards, suddenly feeling totally unprepared for the daunting task. The stately Christmas tree rose to the third floor, but was only decorated up to the second. She'd known that. But she had underestimated the number of baubles that made up the breathtaking display that cascaded down the branches like a glittering waterfall.

Breathtaking could be literally what some of them are, Ellie. And fatally so.

Seldon's hand gripped her shoulder. 'Eleanor, what's going on?'

'The Christmas baubles, Hugh!' she panted. 'Bowes said his daughter turned the clays he'd stolen into decorations by painting them ready for hanging on Christmas trees. But which tree? And what were they filled with? Harmless powder or more cyanide? He might have been telling the truth. But he might also have been lying. And even if it isn't Bowes, if you remember Bowes told us that he was still "missing" a case...'

Seldon's eyes widened in horror. 'You think...' He glanced at the tree. 'That some of the decorations might be—'

She nodded grimly. 'The missing clays filled with more prussic acid! I don't have an answer as to why whoever attacked the duke might want to do such a thing, but—'

Seldon held up a hand. 'You're right, Eleanor. We've still no idea exactly why Porritt and Taylor were murdered and an attempt made on the duke's life. We could just be dealing with a lunatic with a grudge against everyone here.'

She nodded grimly. 'Maybe they were besotted by the duchess and blame *everyone* for her death? I know it's all speculation, but—'

He held up his hand again. 'But we can't take the chance.' He surveyed the tree quickly. 'There must be hundreds of the blasted things.'

'Actually, just under a hundred, I calculate, Chief Inspector,' Clifford said. 'And there are three of us.'

'It could be four?' She looked hopefully at Seldon.

He shook his head. 'We can't take Danby off guarding the duke's door. The killer might be waiting for this very opportunity.'

'Or even manufactured it, Chief Inspector?'

Seldon grimaced. 'Possibly. So we'll have to stick with us three. And I suggest we don't specify to anyone else exactly what we suspect. If we're right, we need as little panic as possible.'

'And if I'm wrong, Hugh?'

'Let's deal with that when it happens. The first thing to do is to get this area cordoned off. But how, blast it? It's the main stairs.'

Eleanor shook her head. 'I don't think we can. We'll just have to warn anyone off who appears.'

Clifford held out three large pristine handkerchiefs.

'Thank you. But even with these as a breathing shield...' Seldon started to tie his over his nose and mouth. 'Be very careful. Both of you. They will only delay the effect of poisoning for a brief time.'

'You too, Hugh.' Her fingers fumbled to secure the handkerchief in place. 'And we can't pull the hooked closures off the bauble necks to check inside. It will release any gas.'

'Blast it!' Seldon grunted. 'You're right, Eleanor. We'll have to scrape off a small section of the paint and see what's inside each bauble. Proper decorations should be empty. Anything at all inside is bad!'

They all nodded in agreement.

'Do you have a knife, Chief Inspector?' Clifford asked.

Seldon yanked his hands back out of his jacket pockets. 'No. I'm still in blasted, borrowed shooting clothes.'

Clifford passed him a small pocket knife. 'And for you, my lady.'

She took the larger pocket knife he held out. 'Thanks. Now, Hugh, you take the ground floor as you're tallest and can reach the branches. Clifford, if you take the first floor, I'll take the second.'

She darted up the stairs. Leaning over the second-floor balustrade, she faced the gossamer-winged angel.

'The first time we met, I thought you were presiding over an enchanting celestial waterfall of light and hope!' she muttered. 'But now, I fear it's one of darkness and death!'

She opened the longest blade on Clifford's penknife, grabbed the nearest bauble and started scraping.

'I say, what's all the ruckus?' a laconic voice said.

She carried on scraping without looking up. 'Huish, get out of here!' She cursed how muffled her words were behind the handkerchief.

He leaned against the balustrade. 'Bit terse. What happened to Mister? Or even Julius?' He bent down. 'What on earth? What peculiar party game have you got going on there?'

She elbowed him away. 'It's not a game. Get out of here, dash it! I'll explain later.'

'Didn't have you pegged as a drama queen,' Huish said in a miffed tone, wandering on along the landing.

The paint on the bauble was so frustratingly militant she was getting nowhere. She forced herself to muster some calm and scrape a small area methodically. After a minute, she held it up to the vast chandelier's light.

Empty, Ellie. No prussic acid!

'All good so far,' Seldon's voice bellowed up to her. 'But only managed three!'

'Better than my one!' she called down. Grabbing another bauble, she lost her grip on the penknife, which slipped from her hand and speared the carpet in between a set of men's dress shoes. A pair of silver satin heels stopped nearby.

'Were you bitten by Father Christmas as a child, Lady Swift?' Barnabas said in a sardonic tone.

'Oh, Barnabas. How witty of you,' Viola tittered, slurring her words slightly.

Eleanor gritted her teeth. 'Please hurry downstairs. It's not safe here. The—'

'Auldwyke Hall not safe?' Barnabas scoffed. 'That's hardly news. Or me and my wife wouldn't have to suffer the indignity of your fiancé—'

'Dash it, will you get out of here!' Eleanor cried.

'Ooh, testy, isn't she?' Viola slurred.

You'll just have to ignore them, Ellie.

She grabbed another bauble.

'Her butler's at it too,' Huish called up.

'I advise you to vacate the immediate vicinity, Mr Huish.' Clifford's voice came from the floor below. 'For your own safety. And no, I cannot expand on my reason.'

Obviously bored, the Musgraves moved on, leaving Eleanor fighting the sharp pine needles for more baubles. Wishing she could just smash the wretched things to check inside, instead she dropped to her knees and patiently scraped some more.

'Miss Whitwell. Pity, you've missed half the show.' Barnabas' voice echoed from the ground floor.

'Why? What's going on?'

'It appears Lady Swift and her entourage are providing tonight's entertainment!'

Another empty one, Ellie, thank goodness.

Leaning out as far as she dared to snare her next decoration, she knocked a lantern off the branch as she did so.

'Watch out!' she cried over the rail.

She held her breath as it bounced down through the branches. Thankfully, the candle flame inside was extinguished by the time it hit the floor, the glass case exploding into a sea of fragments.

Dash it, Ellie.

Lofthouse appeared and glared up at her. 'What in heck's name is a goin' on, m'lady?'

Admittedly, he had a point. Seldon was standing amid a scattering of discarded baubles, paint scrapings, and broken glass. Her butler had made it a fair way up the stairs, leaving a trail of his scraped efforts on every step. And in their makeshift face shields, the two of them looked like desperados. Which meant she must, too.

Before she could work out what exactly to say, Bowes hurried up from the direction of the servants' hall in his socks, brandishing a dustpan and brush.

'I heard smashin', Mr— Cor, lummy, who broke Christmas?'

'Lady Swift!' the assembled guests chorused.

Lofthouse crunched away over the glass. 'Wait till his grace hears of this!'

She held her hands up apologetically and called after him. 'I'll pay for all the damage, naturally.'

Oh, Ellie, what a mess!

46

They were a subdued group of three that trudged through the snow, away from Auldwyke Hall's grand entrance. It wasn't their collars and scarves pulled up high against the whirling snowflakes that curtailed any conversation.

Eleanor sighed again. What was there to say? She'd made a mess of things. And a laughing stock of her two favourite men in the whole world. Seldon had summed it up for all of them as she'd reached the bottom of the stairs after finally checking the last few baubles.

'Can we just get out of here?' he'd muttered wearily.

She glanced at Clifford a few yards ahead, valiantly leading them through the shallowest sections of snow, which was still up to her calves. Seldon was, unusually, languishing behind, despite having by far the longest stride. No doubt trying to quietly stomp out his frustration over the debacle she'd added to their already disastrous progress to date. Wading fitfully through this endless blanket of white felt a rather pointed metaphor for everything they'd been doing since the moment she'd found Porritt's body.

She realised her eyes were stinging. The hood of her cloak

had whipped back over her head in the wind. She tugged it over her soggy red curls, hunched her shoulders and willed this whole trip to Auldwyke to be over.

Pull yourself together, Ellie!

Mentally shaking herself, she wiped the snowflakes from her eyes again and focused on trying to follow in Clifford's footprints to make the going easier. But no matter how much she lengthened her stride, she couldn't match his longer-legged gait and abandoned it. As she went back to finding her own best way forward, something niggled her thoughts.

'For heaven's sake, brain, be quiet!' she grumbled. 'You've caused enough trouble for one day.'

The old gamekeeper's cottage looked more like a fairy-tale gingerbread house than ever as they trudged up the path. The comforting orange glow from the candle lanterns lit in both of its eyebrow dormer windows seemed to promise not everything was rotten at Auldwyke.

The eager welcome from her ladies further lifted her spirits and felt like being wrapped in a soft wool blanket. Which she soon was, cosied up with Gladstone and Tomkins on the two-seater settee by the crackling fire in the sitting room. She couldn't help smiling at her bulldog, who, despite the warmth, refused to relinquish his new all-in-one Christmas suit. The tall glass comfortingly hot in her hand wafted soothing aromas of cinnamon and nutmeg, while whispering the festive season was far from over. Even Seldon's troubled expression seemed to ease as he settled into the Windsor chair on the other side of the fire.

Clifford was trying hard too, she realised. He said nothing as the ladies bustled about the room, draped in woven garlands of holly and spruce or coloured paper chains, which added more much-needed cheer. The only thing marring the scene was the reminder of her blunder in the corner. The Christmas tree which, in truth, her ladies had decorated adoringly with darling homespun figures, stars and angels.

Oh! And Taylor's body in the outhouse, Ellie.

'Chaps, I'm so sorry,' she said earnestly.

Seldon shrugged. 'It's not your fault, Eleanor. I agreed we should check the baubles.'

'We all thought it prudent, my lady.' Clifford held out her investigation notebook. 'However, hurling a decorative lantern at Mr Lofthouse's feet...'

Seldon almost smiled. 'And mine!'

She noticed the ladies staring at each other in confusion.

She winced. 'I, er, might have instigated a slight decimation of his grace's Christmas tree.'

Mrs Trotman pointed at her pets. 'Can't be as bad as the mess the terrible two made of ours earlier, m'lady.'

Lizzie nodded. 'Master Gladstone dug the tree out of its pail altogether. And then helped Tomkins steal all the crocheted snowmen and Father Christmases. We still cannae find half of 'em. Nor the angel.'

Clifford caught Eleanor's eye as he pinned up a garland along the window. 'I stand corrected, my lady. Since your resultant destruction has been trumped by a wilful bulldog and tomcat.'

She couldn't help laughing.

'That's better!' Seldon ran his hand over the arm of his chair. 'We'll never solve this if we let a minor setback, like looking total fools in front of the entire...' He tailed off at Clifford's quiet cough. 'I meant, um.'

She shook her head. 'What you said, Hugh. And you're right.'

He nodded, but his brow furrowed as he turned to her staff. 'Ladies, are you sure you don't mind hearing all this?'

Polly put her hand up, waiting for Clifford's nod she could speak up. 'No, sir. If as you don't mind. 'Tis more of a comfort to know what's happenin'.'

'I can see that,' Seldon said in a kindly tone. He held up his glass. 'And thank you for whatever this concoction is. It's delicious.'

Mrs Trotman beamed at him. ''Tis buttered rum, sir. With my special secret ingredient.'

Clifford raised a warning finger. 'Beware, Chief Inspector. Likely, more rum!'

As the laughter died away, they all savoured their drinks for a moment.

Seldon sighed. 'Alright. So far, the killer has run rings around us. So, we need a new approach. New thinking. And fast!'

Eleanor snapped her notebook shut and closed her eyes. 'Completely fresh. Like the pure white blanket of snow out there.'

'I should have been able to eliminate some of the suspects by now, blast it!' Seldon muttered as he turned the pages in his notebook.

'We have. Willoughby Taylor.' She winced. 'Poor fellow. And the duke. Although, to be fair, with his difficulty walking and breathing, we never seriously considered him a suspect.'

Seldon nodded. 'Taylor's body is my next port of call. To examine it again for any clues I missed. But I'm not holding out much hope there.' He held Eleanor's gaze. 'Nor that this investigation will definitely be concluded. You might as well know now.'

'But you just said, "new approach, new thinking!"'

'Yes, but I do this all day, every day, Eleanor, remember? I have to be realistic.'

She nodded. 'Yes. But I don't.'

He smiled. 'I hoped you'd say that!'

She smiled in return. 'So, to our new thinking. Start us off, Hugh.'

He thought for a moment. 'If we're starting anew, then we need to go back to the very beginning of the investigation and work out what we've missed. Back to the moment you found Porritt's body in the storeroom, Eleanor. By retracing our footsteps—'

'Hugh!' she gasped. 'Say that again.'

He frowned. 'Which part? The "retracing our—'

'Footsteps! Yes! That's what's been bothering me since we left the main house just now. I tried to walk in Clifford's, but I couldn't because his stride is too long.'

The two men exchanged a confused look.

She jumped up. 'Hugh, you said we needed to go back to the beginning of all this. To when I found Porritt's body in the storeroom. Well, once I had, Clifford appeared and then Lofthouse, who then left to tell the duke. He then returned, told us what the duke had decreed and what he, Lofthouse, had done about it, and then left again after securing Porritt's body in the storeroom. After that, I left Clifford and came over here to let the ladies know what had happened. It was snowy underfoot, so I walked in a set of someone else's footprints to make it easier. But they quickly veered off in the wrong direction.'

Clifford stepped over, his expression intent. 'They must have been very fresh footprints, my lady. It was snowing when you left me.'

'That's my point! We know all the guests were in the drawing room at Auldwyke Hall, on his grace's orders via Lofthouse. Likewise, the staff were all assembled in the kitchen.'

'And us aprons was all in here, m'lady,' Mrs Butters said.

'As we had been since Mr Bowes dropped us off,' Lizzie added.

'Plus, the footprints were too big to be any of yours.' Eleanor drained her glass.

'And' – Clifford topped it back up – 'they can't have been Mr Lofthouse's as we both saw him come from the house to the storehouse. And then leave the same way.'

She nodded emphatically. 'Exactly.'

'Could they have been Constable Danby's?' Seldon said.

'No, Hugh. He hadn't arrived from the local village yet. Lofthouse was instructed not to ring the police until after dinner on his grace's orders, so as not to inconvenience his guests.'

He scratched his head. 'What does that all mean, then?'

She took a deep breath. 'That the footprints must have been made by someone else altogether. Someone not at Auldwyke Hall. Or in this cottage.'

Seldon's brow knitted deeper. 'I feel we've been running this entire investigation back-to-front!'

'And inside out, Hugh! All this time, we've been looking for a killer *inside* Auldwyke Hall. One of the staff or guests. Or even, initially perhaps, the duke himself. But the murderer came from *outside* the Hall all along. Not inside!'

Seldon's eyes widened. 'I see what you're getting at. Porritt was murdered in the outside storehouse. The attack on the duke came from the lawn *outside* his windows. And Taylor was murdered on the path near our sledging slope. Again outside.'

'And the clay "bombs" were made outside the main house, in that forgotten shed,' Clifford said.

Eleanor nodded again. 'Plus, the footprints I just mentioned were also obviously made outside. All of this explains why we could never quite settle on any one of our suspects as the guilty party. They either had a motive, but an alibi, or no alibi, but no real motive either.'

Seldon's brow furrowed. 'But how does that work with our theory that all these events are somehow connected to the death of the duke's wife then? We were sure the killer must have been at the Christmas shoot ten years ago. Or how did they kill the duchess? But one of the current guests, or Bowes, would have remembered or let slip that someone who was there then isn't here now?'

She closed her eyes to picture the shooting party, as it must have been back then.

'I mean,' Seldon continued. 'How can you miss someone—'

Her breath caught, her eyes flying open. 'No one missed them! Everyone noticed that person missing! Even you and me, Hugh. But no one mentioned it, because they're *supposed* to be missing.'

Seldon and Clifford shared a mystified look.

'The duke's previous secretary. Derek Stark!'

Clifford's brows rose. 'Of course, my lady. He would have been in charge then, just as Mr Porritt was this year.'

'And we know he was dismissed after a row with the duke, almost certainly without even a reference, according to Lofthouse, so he had a motive. At least for attacking the duke.'

Seldon shook his head. 'Brilliant, Eleanor! And he'd have known the estate grounds well enough.' His elation quickly faded. 'Now all we need to do is find out where he's hiding before he kills ag—' He glanced up sharply.

She frowned, then slowly her eyes widened.

'Hugh. Do you think...?'

He nodded grimly. 'I do!'

47

Yorkshire was at her most raw. Eleanor couldn't decide if the dark, the cold, or the wind was her worst enemy. She finally decided it was all three. The impenetrable darkness made it essential to use a torch, which then potentially alerted the killer to her presence. The bone-chilling cold sapped her concentration, and the biting winter wind made her eyes stream, just when she needed them most.

And the same held true for Seldon and Clifford, now crouched either side of her.

In these conditions, the trek out towards the chapel up the steep snow-bound track had been arduous enough, the path being no more than a ragged scar between the endless moors of shivering heather. Having to then strike out along the wind-battered treeline had been exhausting. And fraught with concern they'd be seen, even though they kept the use of the torches to an absolute minimum.

The one positive was that the snow had finally abated. Although how long until it started up again was anybody's guess.

But she had something else on her mind. Something more

worrying. A still small voice in the back of her head whispering that something was wrong. A voice that had become increasingly urgent since leaving the cottage.

A chink of moonlight broke through the fast scudding clouds. The silhouette of the remote stone hut she'd noticed with Seldon on their walk to the waterfall and chapel came into focus in the weakly pulsing fingers of light. At the same time in the bleached moonlight, the shadows of the wildly swaying trees performed a dance macabre on the virgin snow.

She ducked back down, waving Seldon and Clifford into a huddle. 'No window on this side. Door must face the other way.'

'In the lea of the prevailing wind. Makes sense as it is a bothy. A type of refuge, a last resort against the elements,' Clifford said.

'Very apt,' Seldon murmured. 'Because this is definitely our last resort.' He squeezed Eleanor's hand in the dark. 'And our trump card, yes?'

'I hope so. We couldn't think of anywhere else the killer could be hiding out.' Her insides clenched. 'But with Constable Danby needing to guard the duke's door, we've left the other guests and staff horribly exposed if we're wrong.'

'Decisions are never easy when murder is involved,' Seldon said gravely.

Clifford nodded. 'Dwelling on the Christmas tree... episode can only blunt your wits, my lady. Just when they are needed most.'

'I know. But honestly' – she tapped her forehead – 'something started niggling up here as we left the track.'

'Flash of light on the snow,' Seldon hissed. 'Far side.' His confident tone faltered. 'But have they slunk into the bothy...'

'Or out into the dark?'

She swung one of the three shooting competition shotguns

Clifford had 'liberated' from the Auldwyke armoury off her shoulder.

'Only one way to find out!'

In previous encounters of this nature, she'd rarely gone armed. However, Seldon and Clifford had both insisted, given the man they were hunting had already killed three times, and attempted a fourth. The feel of the shotgun in her hand should have been a comfort, but as she slunk through the thick snow, it felt only a testimony to how dangerous a foe they were up against.

As they reached the back of the hut, Seldon tugged Eleanor's coat sleeve. He pointed along the right-hand wall, then gestured for Clifford to take the left one.

The lack of windows was a godsend as she stealthily followed Seldon. Assuming the murderer was inside, of course. The moonlight, which had been so helpful in letting them assess the bothy, now refused to creep back behind the clouds. Which left them spotlit against the hut's wall. If the killer was outside, hidden among the trees, he could pick them off like a clay pigeon shoot. Easier, in fact, she knew now from experience.

At last the clouds swamped the moon and she could breathe more freely. Although she was sure the crunch of snow under her boots would betray her presence long before she reached—

Seldon interrupted her thoughts. 'I'm going to check he's inside,' he breathed in her ear. Creeping around the corner, he instantly returned. 'I saw him through the window. He's there, with his back to the door. Perfect. And Clifford's in position. Stay behind me.'

The moon, as if in a last act of defiance, flitted into view for a moment, making his face glow ghostly white above his dark clothing.

Her breath caught. *Ghosts, Ellie!*

'Hugh!' she hissed urgently.

But too late.

The door caved inwards at Seldon and Clifford's joint kick. They rushed in, with her on their heels.

'Police! Put your hands up!'

The seated figure facing the wall flinched momentarily, the lantern on the bench beside him flickering in sympathy.

'I said, hands up!' Seldon barked, a disconcerted frown clouding his features.

The clump of heather burning in a rusted pail on the stone floor spat a glowing ember at Clifford's feet. He stamped on it.

'We're armed. And there's three of us,' he growled.

'It wouldn't matter if there were a hundred of you,' the figure clad in a hooded green overcoat said calmly, closing the book in his hand. 'You've no business with me. I'm just a traveller sheltering from this wretched weather.'

Seldon's frown deepened. He lunged forward to grab the lantern as the figure shot out an arm towards it. 'I am Chief Inspector Seldon of Scotland Yard. And I am officially arresting you for the murders of Mr Neville Porritt, and Mr Willoughby Taylor. And the attempted murder of his grace, the Duke of Auldwyke. Who you used to be secretary to, Mr Derek Stark!'

The figure laughed darkly as it rose. 'I know of his grace, of course, but I don't recall working for him. I think I'd remember. And as for those other two unfortunate people you mentioned.' He turned around, his hazel eyes glinting as he unhooked his spectacles. 'I have no idea who they are.' He glanced at Eleanor and Clifford. 'You see, Chief Inspector, you've got the wrong man.'

Seldon kept his gun aimed on him. 'I don't think so! You...' He shot a look at Eleanor, who was nodding, a pained expression on her face. 'Eleanor? What...?'

She swallowed hard, wishing the niggle that had dogged her thoughts as they left the track had become clearer sooner. 'I'm sorry, Hugh, but he's right.'

A flash of triumph crossed the man's face.

Seldon's forehead creased in puzzlement.

'Do you mean this man is *not* the murderer?'

She shook her head vigorously. 'No, no! He's definitely the murderer. Only he is being quite truthful when he says he isn't Derek Stark. And that he's never worked for his grace.'

Seldon shot Clifford an enquiring look. But her butler merely raised an eyebrow, looking equally lost. 'I'm listening, Eleanor,' Seldon said calmly, making her heart swell with his belief in her.

She took a deep breath, trying to find the words for what had become clear only a few moments before.

'I need to go from when his grace confessed, wrongly, that he killed his wife, the duchess. That struck me as a turning point in the investigation. It was then I was sure that his grace, not Porritt, had been the intended target all along. Porritt's death was merely needed because you' – she grimaced at the man in front of them – 'realised he was about to expose you, not the duke, as the duchess' real killer. Which is why, despite the risk with so many people around, you had to act.'

Their captive bolted for the door, only to be grabbed by Clifford, and pressed firmly back down onto the bench with the barrel of his shotgun.

'Manners! Whoever you are, you will sit and listen to what the lady has to say,' Clifford barked. He nodded for Eleanor to continue.

She gathered her thoughts again. 'With his grace having become so reclusive in recent years, Porritt was in charge of sending out the invitations to this year's annual shoot. And he was determined to pay back the debt he felt he owed his grace for standing up for his mother against rumours she had a hand in his father's death. So, despite being told he would be instantly dismissed if he even mentioned the duchess' death, he set out to prove his grace was blameless. By inviting everyone who was here ten years ago to this year's shoot. Where he would expose the real killer – you!' Swallowing her disgust, she continued. 'And to do this, he intended to enlist the aid of a certain chief inspector from Scotland Yard.' She gestured at Seldon.

'What rot!' the man sneered. 'The duchess died in a shooting accident. Everyone knows that. Except you, apparently!'

She nodded slowly. 'Actually, he's right again. She did die by accident.'

Seldon was fighting a deep frown. 'Not murdered?' he murmured to her.

She shook her head sadly. 'This wretch shot the poor woman by mistake, I'm sure. The shot was intended for the duke.'

The man's eyes roved around the room, clearly looking for ways out. But Seldon and Clifford stepped nearer, training their guns on him again.

'Are you really going to listen to more of this ridiculous fairy tale?' the man snorted.

Seldon nodded grimly. 'Yes. And so are you.'

Having got everyone's attention once more, she continued. 'Actually, strangely, he's right yet again, only this time he doesn't realise it. There is a fairy tale involved here. The one thing we weren't right in thinking was that Porritt had been murdered purely to cover up a past event; the duchess' death. In fact, Porritt was also murdered to cover up a *present* event. Or at least this wretch here hoped it would be; the successful murder of the Duke of Auldwyke!'

She caught Clifford and Seldon's shared look of bafflement again. 'Charles Dickens' *A Christmas Carol* pointed it out to me. Just before we burst in here. Like Scrooge, the Ghosts of Christmas Past and Christmas Present could only show Scrooge the result of his completed actions. It was the Ghost of Christmas Future who showed him the result of his future actions!' She pointed at their captive. 'You see, this cold-hearted wretch yearned for what he saw as his future. A future he believed had been unfairly snatched from him by a mere anomaly of birth.' She shook her head in distaste. 'As Bowes said, you really are a small dog in tall weeds, aren't you, Lord Grayson Auldwyke!'

Seldon stared at her.

She winced apologetically. 'It's an untimely introduction. However, meet the Duke of Auldwyke's younger brother, whose portrait I saw the very first day I arrived, hanging in the Ashley Room.'

48

For a moment, Eleanor was sure the man in front of them would attempt to flee again. His eyes flicked from her to Seldon, then Clifford, before fixing on the door behind them. Sensing it too, the men took a step backwards, shotguns raised, blocking the only way out completely. The fight seemed to leave him. As if finally accepting he was caught, he collapsed back onto the bench.

'It's true. I am Lord Grayson Auldwyke.'

'Lord Grayson,' Seldon said sternly. 'I must warn you that anything you say can, and will, be used against you in a court of law. Your confessing may go in your limited favour, however.'

The man scowled. 'Like I care now. Might as well be hung for a sheep as a lamb. Or a lord as a... lady,' he muttered, staring evilly at Eleanor. Before she could respond, he laughed curtly. 'I never liked my brother. In fact, I loathed him. Typically, he was too stupid to realise it.' His expression clouded. 'Have you any idea what being the second son means in an aristocratic family like ours?'

'Tell me,' Seldon said dispassionately.

'A life sentence of being immaterial, unimportant. Second.

For everything! That's what. Being given a pittance to live on while your older brother lives like a king!' He laughed bitterly. 'My older brother didn't even have the decency to die in the war. But what he did do was steal my one love away from me. And made her... his duchess.' He convulsed as if the notion nauseated him. 'Can you imagine the agony of knowing another man was making love to the only woman who made your life worth living? Can you?'

Eleanor didn't miss Seldon swallow hard. She stepped forward.

'So you decided you had as much right to all your older brother had as the Duke of Auldwyke. And decided to get them by murdering him!'

Lord Grayson's voice shook. 'What other way was there? And yes, I wanted all the good things that went with the title Duke of Auldwyke! But more than that, I wanted... her! She loved me, you see. But it was her family's wish that she married my brother, naturally. They wanted her to take the title Duchess of Auldwyke. A title I should have given her! So when my loathsome brother invited me to the annual Christmas shoot ten years ago, I saw my chance. And I took it.'

Seldon's look of revulsion was replaced with a frown. 'But you can't have accepted the invitation! Otherwise one of the guests, or Bowes, would have mentioned you were there then, but not now.'

'True, *if* I'd attended. But I cancelled at the last minute. Feigned an urgent business matter. Even bought a train ticket to the south coast, the opposite direction to here, and set up my alibi. Then I paid someone to buy me a ticket here to Yorkshire. I knew my illustrious brother would never let on that one of his prestigious invitations had been declined.'

'Did you hide out here in this shelter then, too?' Eleanor said.

'No. I booked into the coaching house in Kirkwell. Under

an assumed name. And in disguise, of course. Then I hired transport. There wasn't much snow around that year, so it wasn't too hard to drive up here. But... but then the unimaginable happened,' Lord Grayson ended in a whisper. 'I... I killed the woman I loved.'

Eleanor's heart squeezed fleetingly at the evident but unexpected anguish the man displayed. Then she gasped. 'You... you gave her the pendant, didn't you?'

His eyes darkened. 'Yes. I gave it to her to remind her that whatever her marriage vows said, she was still mine! She wore it even after she married my brother, pretending it used to belong to a beloved aunt who died around the same time, so it was of sentimental value.'

In a heartbeat, Lord Grayson's sorrow spun back to rage. 'My wretched brother has always kept to a fatuously strict routine in everything. So I predicted his every move from the few shoots he'd deigned to invite me to previously. Proper shoots, by the way. Not this clay pigeon nonsense! He liked to blast the game as it flew out from being roused by the beaters. Not to wait until they were high in the air. So, I hid in the thicket at the edge of the shooting area and waited.' He rubbed his face in his hands. 'It should have gone perfectly! One barrel from me. And down my brother would go. His death forever deemed nothing but an accident from a tragic stray shot. And... and then I'd have installed *my* duchess in a dowager house on the estate.'

'Lord Grayson, did you aim and fire, killing the duchess, but with the intention of killing your brother?' Seldon failed to keep the disgust from his voice.

'Yes,' he murmured in a faraway tone.

'What went wrong?' Eleanor said quietly.

He closed his eyes. 'I didn't know that she'd tripped and ripped her cloak. Nothing would interrupt her shooting. She was fanatical about it. So instead of waiting for a servant to fetch another from the house, she'd borrowed...'

'Your brother's?'

He nodded. 'I heard the shots near to the edge of the thicket. Saw his cloak swishing within close range and thought it was him. I... I fired.' He clamped his hand over his mouth. 'It was only when a beater dashed over and pulled back her hood, I realised the horror of what I'd done. I've relived it every day since.'

'Why did you kill Mr Porritt?' Seldon said.

Lord Grayson pointed at Eleanor. 'She's already told you, more or less. I forced him at gunpoint to confess what he was up to. Then strangled him. Someone would have heard a gunshot,' he said matter-of-factly.

Eleanor's thoughts flew back to what Bowes had told her about Porritt's years rising up the staff ranks at Auldwyke. 'Porritt was the beater who ran to the duchess after you shot her, wasn't he?'

'Yes. Although I didn't know that then. He was just another scruffy youth, to my mind. But when I confronted him in the storehouse, I recognised him. I didn't know he'd risen to being my brother's secretary. Just before he died, he realised I was the one who killed the duchess. He had no idea until then.'

She shook her head at the bitter irony. They'd been wrong. Porritt had never known who had killed the duchess. He had invited all the original guests, thinking the killer must have been among them, but he never was!

'Porritt didn't invite you this year, did he?' Seldon said. 'We found all the invitations and RSVPs on his desk. So why did you come?'

Lord Grayson shrugged. 'I came because I overheard a drunken fool in Savini's bar in London mention he'd been invited by the Duke of Auldwyke to his shoot this year. Out of curiosity, I bought the idiot a few more drinks, and he confessed he'd been invited before. Which surprised me. My brother always pompously maintained the honour of attending his Christmas shoots was so great, he'd never invite anyone twice. Then I found out the idiot had been at the shoot when' – he gritted his teeth – '*she* had died! With that, and it being the tenth anniversary of her death, I became suspicious. Something fishy was afoot. Possibly dangerously so for me.'

'It wasn't just the anniversary of her grace's death that made Porritt bold enough this year. I see that now,' Seldon said. 'The death of his mother meant he no longer needed to keep quiet for fear she would be sacked along with him and turned out with nowhere to live.'

Eleanor nodded. 'And before, no one would have listened to him anyway. Not as a lowly servant of what, likely only seventeen? He bit his tongue for almost ten years. But when he finally felt he could face broaching the subject with his grace, he was threatened with instant dismissal.'

Lord Grayson smirked. 'That was a stroke of luck I hadn't predicted.'

'No.' Eleanor shuddered with repulsion. 'You letting his grace think he had killed his wife for all these years was crueller than if you had put a bullet in his heart.'

Lord Grayson shrugged coldly. 'I would have shot my brother this time if I could have. Like the first time I tried to kill the fool. But he'd barricaded himself away from the world and I couldn't reach him with a bullet. But after killing the secretary, Porritt, it felt fitting to finish what I'd started ten years ago. So I came up with the idea of the clays filled with poison gas launched from the traps. I knew my brother's breathing was bad.' He threw Eleanor another look of loathing. 'And if you hadn't interfered, it would have worked!'

'I'm sorry to have spoiled your murderous plan, Lord Grayson,' she said coldly. 'By the way, the drunk man you say you overheard. Was that Willoughby Taylor, by any chance?

The man you then cold-bloodedly murdered on the path up beyond the old gamekeeper's cottage?'

'Was that his name?' Lord Grayson said vaguely. 'He stumbled on me when I was scouting out the ground for another attempt on my brother's life. It seemed he wasn't as drunk as I thought as he remembered my face, even though he couldn't quite place where he'd seen me before. So he had to go. I dispatched him with another rope, laid him over the shooting trap, and wheeled it up to where I could push him off, never to be found until the snow had thawed. Only, irritatingly, I assume you did find him somehow?'

Eleanor suddenly wondered how she was going to break the news to the duke that his own brother was responsible for the death of his secretary and one of his guests. Not to mention the attempt on his own life.

Or that his own brother killed his wife, Ellie!

'Tie Lord Grayson's hands behind his back, would you, Clifford?' Seldon said grimly. 'And make it suitably tight. He's got a long trek through the snow to Auldwyke Hall with three shotguns at his back. And then an even longer one to the hangman's noose.'

49

Staring down the barrel of a shotgun wasn't how Eleanor had pictured spending Christmas Day morning only a week ago. At least it answered her own question when she'd first arrived; would anything run on orthodox lines at Auldwyke Hall? Apparently not, as his grace's latest edict via Lofthouse had been that breakfast would be taken after the last round of the shooting competition.

She readjusted her stance, trying to ignore how hungry she was, even though she'd managed to grab a bite to eat with the ladies before hoofing it over to the shooting platform.

'Oh, well. Expect the unexpected, Ellie!' she muttered as she tried to focus.

'Notes the mistress of such,' Clifford murmured as he checked her cartridge case. Straightening up, he discreetly gestured to the edge of the treeline where her four ladies had surreptitiously appeared to cheer her on.

'Oh, Clifford, thank you,' she murmured back, overcome with affection that he'd burnt his precious rule book on etiquette to ashes on this occasion.

In the centre of the shooting platform, Lofthouse raised his arms. Silence fell.

'Before we commence the second, and final, round of this year's shoot, scores after the first round are seventy-eight to seventy-seven. Three-point lead needed to win. As Miss Whitwell leads, she will fire first. Hereon in, I, not the competitors, will call "Pull!"'

Another change, Ellie!

'Good luck!' she called to Pearl, who was poised like a hungry tigress at the next shooting stand to hers. She doubted she'd heard.

Leaping off the spectator bench, Seldon raised a double set of crossed fingers.

Lofthouse held his hands high again. 'In line with his grace's orders, last clays will be rapid fire, any of either quartering, looper, teal or incomer.'

'What does that gibberish mean!' Eleanor gulped. But as Clifford stepped forward to explain, she waved him back.

It means hit the dashed things, Ellie!

'Pull!' Lofthouse called without warning.

Bang! Pearl recoiled from her shot.

'Pull!' Lofthouse called again.

Bang! Eleanor grimaced at the ringing in her ears.

How many times she and Pearl fired and reloaded, she couldn't have said. She was too busy giving her all. Thus she jumped as Lofthouse called out, 'Competition complete!'

The collective intake of breath from the other guests on the spectator benches made her realise, they too were on tenterhooks. Seldon shrugged to her, biting his fist. Clifford, however, avoided her gaze.

Ah, well! Good try, Ellie.

'Final scores. Eighty-six to eighty-three. Winner is...' Lofthouse paused theatrically, clearly enjoying his moment, 'Lady Swift!'

'Hurrah!' Seldon cheered, leading the rousing round of applause.

'Oh gracious,' she muttered, catching Clifford's quiet thumbs up to her. And her ladies dancing in a circle with their arms looped.

Pearl strode over, her blunt-cut black bob adding all the more ferocity to her clouded expression. But to Eleanor's amazement, her face broke into a tired smile. 'Not bad for a novice, Lady Swift.' She offered her hand. 'What's your secret, then?'

Eleanor laughed. 'Simple, Pearl. I just wanted to beat you. But not for the reason you think.' She smiled enigmatically in silent reply to the woman's puzzled look.

Huish spearheaded the congratulations from the others by turning to Seldon, who now had his arm looped around Eleanor's waist.

'Chief Inspector, you're engaged to an amazing sportswoman. And amateur sleuth!'

'Or an obstinate rhinoceros,' Seldon teased. 'I wonder which?'

'Well don't start up in business against me, I beg you, Lady Swift.' Barnabas Musgrave chuckled.

His wife pulled Eleanor into an unexpected hug. 'Jolly good for you, my dear. You've taught us all a lesson we won't forget this Christmas.'

Huish nodded. 'The footman fellow said the roads have been cleared enough to make it to the village. None of us fancy hanging on any longer at Auldwyke for luncheon, I'm afraid. Christmas or not. Instead, we're all going to grab a quick bite of late breakfast and then hotfoot it down to the station and hop on the first train.'

Eleanor waved them off, wishing everyone a 'Happy Christmas!'

Alone with Seldon and Clifford, she sighed. 'As if his grace hasn't had enough go wrong. His guests aren't even staying for lunch.'

Seldon shrugged. 'After all that's happened, I can't exactly blame them. His grace won't even join them.'

'Especially,' Clifford said gently, 'as his grace banned all further visits from even Mr Lofthouse after he delivered the chief inspector's news regarding his younger brother's murderous exploits.'

'Imagine your own brother being behind everything that has gone on here. Including killing your wife and trying to kill you.' Seldon let out a long breath. 'Poor fellow, I suppose that will be the last straw that sees his grace never leaving his ivory tower again.'

Clifford cleared his throat. 'Not meaning to speak out of turn, but if I might be so bold as to remind the present company that "It's still ruddy Christmas!" as Mrs Musgrave would put it?'

Eleanor shook her head, laughing. 'Clifford, you are incorrigible! Keep it up. I love it.'

He bowed, and then turned to Seldon, his eyes twinkling. 'Apologies, Chief Inspector, but I cannot disobey my mistress!'

The old gamekeeper's cottage couldn't have felt more festive. Nor smelt more mouth-watering, the scent of heavenly Christmas fare hanging in the air. All of Eleanor's favourite people in the world were there, chattering excitedly about her having won the competition. And all of them felt like family.

Her ladies beckoned her under an exquisite wide arch of spruce and silver-painted fir cones and mistletoe from the hallway into the sitting room, Seldon following behind. There, she was met with a stunningly decorated table laid for eight. Clifford's quiet delight at her genuine gratitude for their collective efforts was matched by the ladies' chorused, ''Tis our greatest pleasure, m'lady.'

'But just look at everything,' Eleanor said, with a sherry somehow already in her hand. A banner hanging from the central oak beam in the ceiling spelled out MERRY CHRIST-MAS! in red, white and green felt letters. The table was dressed in soft ivory linen, with a tasselled silver-lace edged runner. On it lay a yew garland of vibrant holly berries entwined with cinnamon sticks, clove-speckled dried crab apples and minia-ture gingerbread Father Christmases in cheeky poses, much to Eleanor's amusement. Each place setting was marked with a quilted red and green mat, edged in matching velvet ribbons and sporting a lovingly handmade Christmas cracker. The napkins were exquisitely embroidered with each of their names and had a little reindeer overlay, which the ribbon-bowed cutlery was tucked into. Every glass was ringed with a crocheted bow for the ladies, or tie for the men, all patterned with snowflakes, and sewn with a tiny silver bell at the centre. A quilted cushion awaited on each chair too. The captivating centrepiece, however, was three concentric rings of stiffened lace angels flying in glittering celestial contentment above a star arrangement of low burning candles.

She pressed her hands over her mouth, not trusting herself to speak.

'Ladies, Clifford, it's absolutely perfect, thank you,' Seldon said, speaking for both of them. 'But where are the terrible two?'

Clifford rolled his eyes good-naturedly. 'Waiting to show off more of their latest Christmas wear, I suspect.' He pushed open the kitchen door and unleashed a whirlwind of overexcited bulldog and tomcat, both sporting yellow and green elf hats with pom-poms and matching knitted jerkins.

'You soppy pair!' Eleanor laughed, dropping to her knees to delight in their eager kisses. As Seldon hunched down to join her, he looked up at Mrs Butters teasingly. 'Makes a change from knitted policemen's outfits, hmm?'

'Lawks, that was only the once, sir. To cheer up her ladyship,' Eleanor's housekeeper said over the other women's giggles.

'Oh, hopefully not. It was too hilarious not to be repeated,' he replied, chuckling.

'Maybe for next Christmas,' Eleanor whispered conspiratorially, 'you could knit an elf jumper for Clifford and Hugh. To pay them back for relentlessly teasing me together all year?'

'Beg pardon, m'lady, but we might've had summat of that thought already.' Mrs Butters reached behind the tree and held up a basket. 'A knitted elf hat for both the gentlemen. And us ladies, naturally. If as Mr Clifford gives permission, of course?'

He steepled his fingers over his nose as he shared a look with Seldon.

'Five against two,' they chorused, each holding out a hand for a hat.

'Food's ready!' Mrs Trotman called as they donned their festive headwear.

Eleanor clapped her hands and smiled impishly at Clifford as her stomach let out a loud gurgle. 'I could manage breakfast, brunch and lunch all at the same time.'

'And the unusual aspect therein, my lady?' he said wryly.

Danby popped an apologetic head into the room. 'Begging your pardon, but there was no answer to me knocking.'

'That's because we were all too busy laughing to hear you, Constable.' She hastened over to him. 'Please say you don't need to return to your village police room today? The table's already set for eight. And Clifford's holding to his promise to read *A Christmas Carol* to us all this evening.'

'I'll vouch it was on my orders if necessary, Danby,' Seldon said.

'If as you're sure.' He beamed, cheeks colouring as he glanced at Lizzie.

'A sherry, Constable. And your elf hat,' Clifford said, wearing his with remarkable aplomb. 'Welcome to Christmas, Lady Swift style!'

At the table, everyone applauded the centrepiece of the meal, Mrs Trotman's Yorkshire Christmas pie. Large enough to easily feed twelve, the tall oval pastry kingdom was topped with a golden-brown crust and filled with delectably tender game, melt-in-the-mouth carrots and celery, all steeped in sautéed onions, white wine, winter savory, thyme and parsley. It was surrounded by honey-glazed parsnips, roast potatoes and batter Yorkshire puddings. And as they ate, the platters of delicious accompaniments kept coming. As did the laughter.

Eleanor savoured another crisp herby sausage wrapped in bacon, delighting in the affectionate camaraderie between her staff. And how keenly they'd welcomed Danby into their midst. She caught Seldon watching the young officer.

'He did a fine job, didn't he, Hugh?' she whispered.

'Better than that,' he murmured back. 'That's why I took him aside just before we started eating. To tell him if he ever fancies venturing south to expand his experience, I'd find a place for him in my area like a shot.'

'Gracious! That must have meant the world coming from England's greatest detective, Chief Inspector.'

He smiled ruefully. 'Hmm? The one who seems to need a titled lady to help him solve a case more often than not? However, she looks too beautiful in her fun hat for talk of... well, you know what!'

Before she could reply, the sound of a motor car sliding to a stop outside the cottage caught her attention. After a moment or two, there was a loud knocking at the front door. Clifford rose to answer it.

Eleanor groaned. 'What now?' she muttered to her honey-roast parsnip. 'Will the romantic Christmas I'd planned never happen?'

50

A moment later Clifford returned and announced solemnly, 'His grace, the Duke of Auldwyke.'

'Lawks, his dukeness!' Mrs Trotman murmured as the duke's formidable frame entered the sitting room, Lofthouse just visible through the open door, standing outside by the duke's Rolls.

Eleanor leaped up, as did the others. 'Your Grace! What an unexpected and... and truly wonderful surprise. Could you bear to join us for lunch?'

In the doorway, the duke's bush of grey-white whiskers shook as he rapped his cane on the floor. 'I did not come to eat, Lady Swift. But to demand what the deuce you thought you were doing?'

She fought a frown. Even for a cantankerous old peer of the realm with a troubled past, he seemed to have lost all regard for how precious Christmas Day might be for others.

'Well?' He stepped forward. 'Why did you give away the shooting competition prize? You won it fair and square! Saw it myself through my field binoculars. Yet you sent that young woman who you beat, Miss Whitwell, up to me to request her favour instead.' He rapped his cane on the floor again. 'Explain yourself.'

She bit her tongue. 'I meant no disrespect to you, Your Grace. But Miss Whitwell genuinely deserves, and needs, a second chance in life. And I know you're the only man who could give it to her. As for myself.' She looked around the table. 'I have already been given a second chance. And I would never go back. So a favour from yourself, Your Grace, would have been wasted on me.'

For a moment, the duke said nothing, his eyes boring into hers. Then, to her amazement, he burst out laughing, which turned into a fit of coughing. Polly quickly filled a glass with water and offered it to him. He took it and, after a sip or too, regained his composure. Eleanor caught Clifford and Mrs Butter's look of pride as the young maid took the glass back and stepped away, Lizzie squeezing her arm.

The duke cleared his throat. 'It's as I suspected, Lady Swift. You are incorrigible. And truly the compassionate, fiery-spirited and remarkable young woman I took you for.' His gaze ran up to her festive headwear, then around the ring of the others, the corner of his eyes crinkling with amusement. 'And certainly, the most unconventional. Remind me next time I list your disgraces to the aristocracy to include partying with your staff!' He smiled as he cupped her hand in his. 'Thank you, Lady Swift.'

'Really, Your Grace, you shouldn't thank me,' she said genuinely. 'It was a team effort. Everyone at this table had something to do with helping bring the tragic events of the last few days to as happy a conclusion as they could.'

'So Lofthouse informed me.' The duke turned to Seldon. 'Thank you, Chief Inspector. And to your men there, too.' He nodded in Clifford and Danby's direction, then turned back to Eleanor. 'But I've more to thank you for than... than that business regarding the duchess we shall not mention. You saved my life. Not once. But twice.' As she went to reply, he raised his hand. 'The second time when you took away the guilt of the last ten years. And allowed me to live in peace with myself. And not locked away in my apartment any longer.' He nodded at her gasp. 'I am away to the chapel now for Reverend Yeadon's service for my wife. On whose grave I shall not weep for the first time, but instead smile, I hope, and remember the good times.'

'That's made Christmas more perfect than I can say, Your Grace,' she said, her eyes swimming.

She watched him leave the cottage and climb back in the Rolls, smiling as he forcibly refused Lofthouse's help. As if reasserting that he might have shown a softer side for a moment, but he was still the Duke of Auldwyke and those around him had better not forget it!

As the Rolls slid away, back down the road, she felt somewhat overwhelmed. Everyone else at the table seemed to feel the same.

After a moment, Clifford broke the silence. 'Ahem, pudding perchance, Mrs Trotman?' He rose and topped up Eleanor's wine. 'Though after that feast, I doubt if anyone except her ladyship has sufficient appetite left for pudding?'

'Eleanor?' Seldon muttered, reaching for her hand under the table. 'I can't wait for pudding.'

She laughed. 'You see? It's not just me!'

'No, I mean... you are impossible!' he murmured, rising to pull her chair out. 'Excuse us,' he said to the room in general. Linking his fingers in hers, he led her under the arch and out through the hallway to the front doorstep.

She smiled as he wrapped his jacket around her shoulders. 'What's this all about, Hugh? Not more roses? Or a Christmas present, surely? Because we all agreed to save those for when we get back home.'

He tutted gently. 'No. Nothing like that. It's about... us,

Eleanor.' He ran his thumb over her cheek tenderly. 'We never finished our conversation about the future.'

She winced. 'We got too caught up in everything going on.'

'Yes. But I don't care about that at the moment. I want to... to...'

'To what, Hugh?'

'To tell you that knowing Porritt could never marry the girl he loved. Nor Lord Grayson. And seeing his grace grieving for so long over his own lost love, it made me realise what a blinkered fool I've been to...' His eyes shone with emotion. 'To lose any more days not married to you, my love. Blast it, I wish I'd asked the captain of that ship I proposed to you on to marry us then and there! Rather than wait until I'd saved the money I felt I couldn't marry you without.'

Her heart skipped as he produced a large sprig of mistletoe from behind his back and held it above their heads before kissing her tenderly. Their lips still touching, he murmured, 'Lady Swift, will you do me the honour of walking down the aisle and into my arms as soon as humanly possible?'

'Yes!' she cried through a rush of happy tears. 'Only promise to look the other way when I trip over my wedding gown while racing down the aisle to shout, "I do!"'

A LETTER FROM VERITY

Dear reader,

I want to say a huge thank you for choosing to read *A Midwinter Murder*. If you did enjoy it, and want to keep up to date with all my latest releases, just sign up at the following link. Your email address will never be shared and you can unsubscribe at any time.

www.bookouture.com/verity-bright

I hope you loved *A Midwinter Murder* and if you did I would be very grateful if you could write a review. I'd love to hear what you think, and it makes such a difference helping new readers to discover one of my books for the first time.

I love hearing from my readers – you can get in touch on my Facebook page, through Twitter, Goodreads or my website.

Thanks,

Verity

www.veritybright.com

facebook.com/veritybrightauthor

x.com/BrightVerity

RECIPE FOR YORKSHIRE CHRISTMAS PIE

Mrs Trotman's version of this pie is based on the recipe in the famous cookery book by Hannah Glasse of which Eleanor's cook had a treasured copy. Published in 1747, *The Art of Cookery Made Plain and Easy* proved to be one of the most influential cookery books of its time, inspiring a range of people, including Fanny Cradock, many years later. It was so popular there were twenty plus editions published and it continued in print into the nineteenth century. One of its claims to fame is that it includes the first known recipe for curry written in English and the first use of the term 'Yorkshire Pudding'.

So, here is the original recipe. For a picture of what it should look like once it's made, go to 'YorkshireBylines.co.uk' and search 'Yorkshire Christmas Pie'.

Please note, the actual recipe is written in 'old' English where 'f' is often substituted for 's' and other anomalies (including irregular, or non-existent punctuation), so I have tried to render it in 'modern' English as best I could. Also, Hannah doesn't always seem to add her instructions in any kind of sequential order. Good luck! :)

How to make a Yorkshire Christmas Pie

First, make a good standing crust. Let the wall and bottom be very thick.

Bone a turkey, a goose, a fowl, a partridge, and pigeon. Season them all very well – take half an ounce of mace, half an ounce of nutmeg, a quarter of an ounce of cloves, and half an ounce of black pepper all beat fine together, two large spoonfuls of salt, and then mix them together.

Open the fowls all down the back, and bone them; first the pigeon, then the partridge, cover them; then the fowl, then the goose, and then the turkey, which must be large; season them all well first, and lay them in the crust, so as it will look only like a whole turkey.

Then have a hare ready cased (skinned), and wiped with a clean cloth. Cut it into pieces, that is jointed; season it, and lay it as close as you can on one side; on the other side, woodcocks, more game (possibly 'moor' game), and what sort of wild fowl you can get. Season them well – and lay them close. Put at least four pounds (!) of butter into the pie, then lay on your lid, which must be a very thick one, and let it be well baked. It must have a very hot oven, and will take at least four hours. This crust will take a bushel of flour. These pies are often sent to London in a box as presents, therefore the walls must be well built.

HISTORICAL NOTES

RURAL POLICING

Seldon recognises Constable Danby as a keen young policeman and even offers to help him get a position in the police station he's based in when not in London (Oxford). This might have seemed very attractive to Danby as working conditions for a rural bobby in Edwardian times were pretty stark. They were poorly paid and even more poorly trained. Their only means of protection was a wooden truncheon or a whistle to summon help (although in a small village like Danby's, he would have been the only policeman) and they walked dozens of miles a day using the only crime-fighting tools they had available – their eyes and ears. Mostly to spot drunks or petty thieves, so it wasn't surprising that Danby had little experience with serious crime like murder.

CLAY PIGEON SHOOTING

Originally live pigeons were used for a pigeon shoot. But eventually, the, er, 'mess', cost and organisation needed led to the development of clay pigeon shoots around the 1860s. Live pigeon shoots were actually banned in Britain in 1921. Strangely, the original substitutes for the live birds were actually glass, not clay, as used by the Duke of Auldwyke. These were often filled with powder, or even feathers, so a 'kill' or hit could be seen more easily. However, the clays left the shooting area covered in mounds of broken glass. A clay alternative was developed around the 1880s and soon most shoots had adopted these. Except, of course, the Duke of Auldwyke, who, as Eleanor would tell you, always did things his own way.

PRUSSIC ACID

Prussic acid is also known as hydrogen cyanide or, sometimes, hydrocyanic acid. Whether all three have exactly the same chemical make-up, I don't know. But prussic acid is basically hydrogen cyanide in water. And it is quite deadly. Even a concentration of 2000 ppm (parts per million) will kill a human in about one minute if inhaled, so Eleanor and Seldon really did need to act quickly to save not only the duke's life, but potentially theirs as well. Frighteningly, as per usual in Victorian and Edwardian times, people made merry with this deadly poison, using it in insecticides, rat poison, and even drinking it to alleviate hangovers!

INHERITANCE LAWS

Whether you like Willoughby Taylor or not, you have to feel for him. Through no fault of his own, he was burdened with the knowledge that if anyone discovered his parents' indiscretion, he could lose any inheritance he might have. Even a couple of years later, the 1926 Legitimacy Act excluded the passage of titles and estates related to illegitimate children, so he would still have been left hoping no one found out his (or rather his parents') secret. Unfortunately, Mr Taylor was murdered by Lord Grayson Auldwyke who, ironically, was born *in* wedlock but with little inheritance as he was the second son.

MINIATURE BOOKS

Miniature books have fascinated people since books were first made. One of the oldest is an ancient Greek manuscript written on papyrus around the third century. And it was recorded in 1586 that a complete, readable version of the Bible had been produced that could fit inside an ordinary chicken's egg. I'm not sure even Lord Grayson Auldwyke's reading glasses would have managed that! In 1904 Henry Frowde published a miniature version of *A Christmas Carol* and it may very well be this version that Seldon borrows from Clifford to test the eyesight of the suspects.

EDWARDIAN CHRISTMAS TREE

Introduced into Britain, it is said, in 1841 by Prince Albert, the Christmas tree soon became de rigueur at an Edwardian Christmas. However, normally they wouldn't be put up and decorated until Christmas Eve. (The Duke of Auldwyke has his staff erect his a few days earlier so it is there when the first guests arrive.) Like the ladies' tree at the old gamekeeper's cottage, most Edwardian Christmas trees were dressed with home-made decorations. Paper-chains, bows, ribbons and crystals were popular and reused each year, unless, that is, a naughty bulldog and his even naughtier companion stole them :)

ACKNOWLEDGEMENTS

Thanks to the wonderful team at Bookouture for their part in keeping us on the straight and narrow long enough so we could actually get *A Midwinter Murder* out in the world.

PUBLISHING TEAM

Turning a manuscript into a book requires the efforts of many people. The publishing team at Bookouture would like to acknowledge everyone who contributed to this publication.

Audio
Alba Proko
Melissa Tran
Sinead O'Connor

Commercial
Lauren Morrissette
Hannah Richmond
Imogen Allport

Cover design
Tash Webber

Data and analysis
Mark Alder
Mohamed Bussuri

Editorial
Kelsie Marsden
Nadia Michael